PIT BANK WENCH

Emma Price is only a pit bank wench, but she wins the love of Paul Felton. Colliery owner Carver Felton has no intention of seeing his brother throw away his future on such a humble girl and savagely rapes Emma, leaving her isolated and pregnant. It looks as though she is destined for the workhouse, but she is taken in by kindly Samuel Hollington and his wife, and gives birth to a son. Then when Carver Felton has ruthlessly achieved his business ambitions he needs an heir to the Felton fortune – and determines to track down Emma and her child...

PIT BANK WENCH

PIT BANK WENCH

by

Meg Hutchinson

Magna Large Print Books
Long Preston, North Yorkshire,
BD23 4ND, England.

British Library Cataloguing in Publication Data.

Hutchinson, Meg
   Pit bank wench.

   A catalogue record of this book is
   available from the British Library

   ISBN   0-7505-1714-X

First published in Great Britain 2000 by Hodder & Stoughton

Published in Large Print 2001 by arrangement with
Hodder & Stoughton Ltd.

Magna Large Print is an imprint of Library Magna Books Ltd.

Printed and bound in Great Britain by
T.J. (International) Ltd., Cornwall, PL28 8RW

For Judith Murdoch and Sue Fletcher, who both took a chance on an absolute beginner, and whose words of encouragement picked me up on the many times I stumbled.

Thank you both.

Chapter One

'Are you mad?'

Carver Felton stared at his brother.

'If you're thinking to marry that wench then you *are* mad. Stark, staring, raving, bloody mad!'

'No, Carver, I am not mad, but I am going to marry her.'

Steps long and easy, carrying his lithe frame with an almost feline grace, Carver crossed to one booklined wall of the octagonal-shaped library. Selecting a book he flipped it open, dark eyes following words that failed to register on his mind.

Seventeen years older than his brother, he had been appointed his guardian by their father's will, but that guardianship might well be ending sooner than Carver had anticipated. He had been given guardianship:

...until my son, Paul Beaufort Felton, reach the age of twenty-one years, at which time he shall enter into the inheritance I bequeath him. That being Beaufort House and estate together with co-ownership of all Felton works and businesses. In the event of the marriage of my son, Paul Beaufort Felton, taking place before his reaching the age of twenty-one years, the said inheritance is to become his on that wedding day...

The age of twenty-one years or that wedding day...
Carver continued to stare blindly at the book.

'So!' Snapping it shut he tossed it casually aside, glance lifting to his brother. 'You are going to marry this Price wench. By whose say so? I am your legal guardian for twelve months yet, you cannot marry without my consent and I am not about to give it.'

'But why?'

Paul frowned, bringing finely arched brows together over a well-shaped nose, his brown eyes questioning.

'Why? You ask why?' Carver met question with question, a tactic he'd used often before his brother. 'Can you really be so naïve? The wench is a nothing, a nobody. She lives along Doe Bank. That alone should tell you why I refuse to allow you to marry her.'

'She can't help where she was born!'

Carver's smile at this defence was harsh with contempt.

'Neither can I. But I can prevent her from thinking to better herself by marrying above her. She'll not be moving to Beaufort House and her bridegroom will not be you. She's not of your class, Paul. Take her to bed if you want to, ride her as often as the mood strikes you. But as for marrying her, forget it.'

A frown deepening across his brow, Paul Felton looked hard at his stepbrother. Born of different mothers, not only was their physical appearance different but their whole temperament too. Seventeen years was a wide enough gap to cause distance between two brothers; they had not

10

grown together as children, never seemed to form the bond of brotherhood, never developed similarities in thought and action that marked them as family. Carver was harsh in his dealings with other men, especially if those dealings threatened the business of which he had held sole charge for nine years. But he, Paul, was not just another man, he was Carver's brother. Though since when had that made any difference? To Carver he must always be a child, shown no indulgence to choose his own way. Well, in this he would.

'That is what you would do, is it, Carver?' His stare brown ice he held his brother's gaze. 'Take what you want from a woman then forget her!'

Carver's mouth was a cold contemptuous curve, one dark brow raised. 'You can always leave her a shilling for her services. You can be sure it is more than she will be paid by any man in Doe Bank or any place else in Wednesbury.'

'Those other men including yourself, no doubt?'

The smile remaining, Carver gave a half nod. 'Should I stoop so low as to acquaint myself with a woman from that end of the social scale then I would deem a shilling to be a high price to pay.'

'So social scale has a bearing on morality?' Paul asked, allowing his feelings to freeze his words.

'On mine, no.' Carver's smile widened. 'But on my immorality, then definitely yes. I take a little more care in the choosing of those with whom I share my bed.'

'Making no preference as to whether or not they be another man's wife.'

11

'You have been most observant, brother. It would have been churlish of me to refuse … but there, I must not name the lady.'

'Lady!' The word burst furiously from Paul as he watched his brother sink easily into a leather armchair. 'You call Cara Holgate a lady? I think a better term would be whore. The only difference between her and the lowest woman of the streets is the clothes she wears.'

Leaning back in his chair, Carver watched the anger play over his brother's face. Paul did not often cross verbal swords with him. That wench must have a stronger hold than he'd thought!

'That is a distinction I cannot make.' He crossed one leg over the other, the languorous deception of it hiding deep irritation. 'You see, I have not indulged myself with a woman of the streets. But it appears you have. How else could you make the comparison? I know the woman at the lower end of the scale but who I wonder was … is … the counter balance?'

'There is no counter balance!' Paul felt the blood drive furiously through his veins.

'No.' Carver ran a finger along the immaculate crease of his grey cashmere trousers. 'There is only Emma. The daughter of a coal miner. Tut-tut, dear brother, I hardly call that experience enough on which to base a judgement.'

'I don't need the experience of the likes of Cara Holgate to make my judgement or my choice.'

'Maybe not!' Carver's smile disappeared, his brows pulling together as his foot found the floor, 'and you don't need a slut of a miner's daughter for a wife. I have told you, forget Emma Price.'

12

'*You* have told me!'

Eyes burning, his whole body tense, Paul glared at the figure still seated in the comfortable chair.

'And that is supposed to be an end to it, is it? Master Paul must be a good boy, Master Paul must not ask for things his brother has said he cannot have. That is how it has been for nine years Carver, my whole life dictated by you, my very thoughts ruled by your decree. But not any more. You will not tell me what I can or cannot do. From now on I am my own man, Carver. I will make my own decisions and one of them is to marry Emma!'

Holding tight to the anger that strained the leash of patience, Carver chose instead to smile, the same infuriatingly mocking smile that proved such an efficient weapon against his brother whenever he tried to assert himself.

Looking at him now, eyes cold as black ice held none of the smile but all of the mockery. 'As always, Paul, you do not have things quite right. I only hope the next twelve months will see a change for the better, that by the time you take your place in the Felton business you will have learned to think things through more clearly. But...' Carver lifted his shoulders in an eloquent shrug. '... until that change takes place, I will just have to continue to set you straight. You are not yet a man, regardless of the antics you may have performed with your Wednesbury trollop. Until you are of legal age you will continue to do as I say, you will abide by my decisions, and it is my decision you have no more to do with that wench. You will not see her, speak to her, or in any way communicate with her.'

'You cannot forbid...'

'Oh, but I can.' Cutting quietly across Paul's furious interruption, Carver rose from his chair, the two inches of his superior height seeming more dominant as he moved towards the door. 'I can forbid it and I do. And you, dear brother, would be well advised to do exactly as I say.'

The door half open he turned, glance wandering over his brother's face. This time no smile touched his mouth.

'Remember, Paul, for the next year I am your legal guardian. Your life is mine to do with as I think best. And if I think it best ... for your own good, of course ... to have you confined to an institution, then that I will do. Think it over, brother, and this time think it through. All the way through!'

'Twelve months will pass, Carver. It will pass and then you will have no more jurisdiction over me. I will marry Emma, she will be mistress of Beaufort House. That you can do nothing about for the house is mine under Father's will.'

Carver watched his own fingers move dexterously over a grey silk cravat as he fastened it about his neck.

Paul had flung those words at him this morning after yet one more altercation over that damned wench.

The cravat fastened, he slipped into a matching figured silk waistcoat then reached for a deep plum-coloured jacket.

His brother had found himself more than a

14

trollop, he had found his own feet. From now on it would become increasingly more difficult to impose restrictions upon him. But it was no empty threat he himself had made a week since. Money could be made to do anything, including committing a sane man to an asylum; and Carver had money enough to pay for anything.

He glanced at himself in the long dressing mirror. Paul could marry, that was of no real concern to him, but marriage to the Price wench was out of the question. Even had she been the richest of the rich there would still have been no marriage.

Reaching for the calfskin gloves laid ready for him, Carver's mouth tightened as familiar thoughts pushed into his mind bringing the same old resentment.

He was the first-born. Felton's was rightfully his, in its entirely. Not a half, not a shared portion, but all of it. That was his birthright.

'A mess of pottage'. The quotation rang in his mind. The biblical Esau had been deprived of his heritage for a bowl of broth, but Carver Felton would not be so easily robbed. Their father had thought to divide not the business perhaps but certainly the running of it. He had thought that the terms of his will safe-guarded that intention. But their father had made a mistake, the mistake of appointing Carver his brother's keeper. He would share his authority with no man, and if that meant having his brother locked away, then so be it.

And the wench, the drudge his brother had hoped to make his wife? Carver smiled into the

15

mirror. He must be prepared to make some small concession. The girl would be taken care of.

'I tell you, Emma, nothing can come of this, nothing but heartache, ain't no coal master's son going to look for a wife among the like of us.'

Emma Price's lovely face creased into a smile lighting midsummer blue eyes.

'Paul has already asked me to be his wife, Mother, we will be married as soon as Father says I might.'

Turning from the pot in which she had been stirring broth for the evening meal, Mary Price stared at her eldest living child. Emma was so beautiful, with her hair the colour of wheat and a complexion like a lily fresh bathed with the dew of the morning, was it any wonder she had caught the eye of the Felton lad? But catch his eye or his fancy there would be no marriage made there. Want it he might, but what of his family? They would certainly harbour no Doe Bank wench.

'So he's asked you to be his wife.' The wooden spoon she had been using dripped gravy onto the floor but Mary had forgotten it. 'That be one question he's asked and one you seem agreed to; but what of the other?'

'Other?' Emma looked up from the pastry she was rolling. 'What other question?'

Mary felt a tug at her heart. Both of her daughters were pretty and she loved them both; but not equally. She had a feeling for Emma she had not had for the children who'd been taken from her, and one she did not feel for Carrie. Oh she loved

16

her younger girl, of course she did, but not with the depth of feeling she had for Emma. Now seeing the shadow that forever stalked women of their class looming close to her daughter she felt that strong, protective love burn hot in her veins.

'The question of you lying with him, of you being a wife to him afore the ring be on your finger.'

Mary saw the slow tide of colour rise in her daughter's cheeks and a sharp stab of anger and despair shot through her. Was it already too late, had Felton already taken what he was really after? Doubtless that was all it could be. To him, Emma would be no more than an entertainment, a pastime to be cast aside once he tired of it ... or when it became an embarrassment.

'Paul has not asked ... asked any such question.' The flush in her cheeks burned bright but Emma's eyes, as they rested on her mother's face, were cool and steady. 'He would never ask such a thing, he would not even think it.'

'All men think it.' Mary's glance turned inward, remembering. All men think it and many ask it, but how many stand by the consequence? Pushing back the ghosts of the past she looked again at Emma and this time her own faded blue eyes suddenly shone with an intense new burst of life. 'Tell me Emma, tell me true, has Felton laid with you?'

Her own love answering her mother's, Emma felt no resentment or shame at the question, only a strange turning of the heart, a deep wrenching inside as she looked at the thin lined face.

'No, Mother.' She answered softly. 'Paul has

not lain with me.'

Across the room Mary Price's eyes glowed with a passion they had not held for twenty years, and her words came with a low almost ferocious urgency.

'Then you must not! No man is a saint, they all gets the urge, some stronger than others. It be a sweet pain that drives and drives, a hunger that gnaws until they has to satisfy it. The promise of a wedding ring is many a man's route to paradise and many a woman's road to hell. Take heed of what I says Emma, take heed of your mother for I be treading that road still. Keep what you can give only once, keep it until the ring be on your finger and the sheet you soil be on the marriage bed. Be no man's whore no matter what the promises he makes. Give me your word, Emma, give me your word.'

Despair and sadness vivid colours that painted every word, Mary stared hard at her daughter but in her mind she saw a different, younger face; a face drawn with fear and washed with tears.

'Be no man's whore,' she whispered, 'for heart-break be the payment they give, sorrow and shame the coinage they use, and the woman has a lifetime in the spending of it.'

Her fingers suddenly trembling, Mary dropped the spoon bringing her hand to cover her face, long shuddering sobs shaking her thin body.

Ignoring the flour on her hands, Emma ran to her mother, flinging her arms about her, understanding for the first time the full rawness of the pain always present in her tired face, the sadness haunting her weary eyes. But what had

18

caused so much sadness and pain, what was it haunted her mother?

'You have my promise Mother,' she murmured, her fingers stroking the hair that had long lost its lustre. 'You have my promise.'

But Mary did not hear; she heard only the words followed by heartless laughter: *'What else can you expect? You play the whore, you get treated as a whore...'*

'But I was not a whore...'

Emma felt her nerves tighten as she caught her mother's whisper. 'I was not a whore. There was no man but him. I loved him, I loved Luke Carter, and he said he loved me, that we would marry in the summer. "Lie with me, Mary," was what he asked. "Show me the love you have for me," was what he said. But when the new life quickened within me he turned from me, he would not marry a whore...'

Sobs cutting off the words, Emma held her mother tight in her arms, the dreadful implication of what she had just said hitting her with the force of a blow.

Luke Carter, her mother had said. She had lain with a man named Luke Carter. But her husband was Caleb Price! Her mother had known two men. Emma felt a tremor in her knees. Which of the two was her father? Was she Caleb Price's daughter or Mary Price's bastard?

Her sobs quieting, Mary sank to a chair, her hands closing about Emma's as she dropped to her knees. 'I know what you be thinking, what everybody thought when they found I was pregnant and no man to take me...'

19

'No, Mother.' Her eyes glistening with tears that were more for her mother's pain than her own fear, Emma pressed her cheek to the thin hands. 'I am not thinking what others may have thought, you are my mother and I love you. What happened when you were younger makes no difference.'

'Oh, but it does, it will.' Mary looked at the head bent over her hands, at the shining pale gold hair so like her own had once been. 'The stigma is never allowed to die, it passes from woman to child, an unjust heritage; and that heritage will be used against you, used to keep you in misery should what I did so long ago ever be brought to light.'

A heritage of shame. The words branded themselves on Emma's brain. She was not the daughter of Caleb Price. She was another man's love child! But where was the love when that man had turned his back on her mother?

'It will not matter that you are not the fruit of my transgression, of my wrongdoing; that will not deter the hand that is raised against you, stop the tongue that speaks ill of you. Should it be known you are the daughter of a woman left in shame then that shame will become yours, such is the way of this world.' Releasing her hands, Mary cupped them about her daughter's face, reading the uncertainty in those lovely eyes, her own heart crying out afresh at the thought of how soon that must give way to condemnation, to disgust.

'You might not be thinking what others have thought.' She spoke softly but her eyes cried out to her daughter from the depths of her soul. 'But should the time come when you are tempted to think in such a way, then remember what I say to you now. Before God and before heaven I tell you, you are not the child folk may say you are. You are not my first-born, though you be the first I bore of Caleb Price. You are his true daughter though he has always fear of the truth of that. He took me knowing I had given birth to another man's son, a child that lived barely a month. In twenty years he has not forgiven. Once a whore, always a whore is Caleb Price's thinking.'

'But you were married!'

'Yes, we were married.' Mary gave a half smile that was as heartbreaking to see as her sobs had been to hear. 'But the condemnation never stopped, the judgement sentence never fully served. In the eyes of Caleb I could never be trusted. He could never be sure the babes I carried were his. His fears have cast a coldness over this house, one that can never be warmed. It killed what love I could have felt for him, killed it nigh on twenty years gone. You, Emma, were the only one of his children gotten in tenderness, a tenderness that died long before your carrying was done. Mistrust and bitterness was his marriage gift to me. I suppose I could expect no other in exchange for a dowry of shame.'

'But you have not...'

'No, not once in twenty years.' Mary smiled through a film of tears. 'I have looked in no direction but that of Caleb Price, but bitterness be a hard taskmaster and jealousy a cruel mistress. Your father danced at their bidding until

21

they became second nature to him. Had he even wanted to shake them off it soon became impossible and they have lodged in this house ever since, a grinding obsession of his he will not forsake until we are both carried out in a box.'

'But surely Father must know?' Emma stared up at her mother. 'He must know you would never be untrue to him.'

Mary touched her lips first to the soft gold of her daughter's hair, then dropped her hands to her lap. 'He knows. But the seeds of doubt are strong. They flourish in the driest of ground, and once sown can never be fully harvested. Caleb has his beliefs and I have my bitter harvest. But you, Emma, you must never go the way I trod, you must give yourself to none but the man who weds you, and then not until after the marriage lines be signed. Remember that when next a man smiles into your eyes and takes your hand in his.'

Half an hour later, her hands washed and a cup of tea made for her mother, Emma returned to her baking.

She would not forget what Mary had told her, but she need have no fear that the same pain would be hers. Paul was not of that breed. He would not ask her to give herself before marriage and certainly would not leave her should she expect his child. Paul Felton loved her, and tonight when they met he would tell her so again. It would shine in his eyes, ring in his voice as he asked her father's permission to marry her.

Rolling pastry on a floured board, Emma glanced at her mother, thin shoulders hunched as she stared into the fire. Caleb Price had married her knowing she had borne a child by another man, but what had motivated him to do so? Had it been pity for a young girl reviled by others? Was it charity?

Lining an enamelled dish with pastry, Emma filled it with chopped mutton and potato.

Watching her mother rise, steps slow as she walked into the scullery, Emma guessed it was neither of those things. Caleb Price had brought no happiness and precious little comfort to the girl he had married, his continued fault finding and demanding ways making her old before her time. No, he had not married to comfort her but to satisfy his own desires, the greatest of which was to be seen as a pious, godly man.

Placing a pastry lid over the dish, Emma crimped the edges with a vengeful thumb. The only one he cared for was himself, the only religion he followed was his own. Caleb Price was god in his own kingdom.

But her own marriage would not be like that. Paul Felton loved her. There would be no unhappiness for her, no stigma in the eyes of the world. Hers would be no dowry of shame.

Chapter Two

Emma picked up the empty basket with one hand, the other lifting her shawl over her head.

'It be a kindly thing you do, bringing me a pie every week.'

Jerusha Paget followed Emma to the door of the tiny back-to-back cottage, its rear joined to an identical house. They were two in a block of eight, each damper, colder and more rat-infested than its neighbour.

'I only wish it could be more,' Emma's answering smile was filled with sympathy.

'Nay, wench, your family has precious little as it is. We as serves the Feltons all be in the same boat. Work a man 'til he drops and then to buggery with him, that be their way. They have love for nobody 'cepting themselves.'

Emma felt the sting of those words but even so could not deny them. But Paul had told her of his plans to alter the living conditions of the miners' families; told her of all he intended to do once he reached his majority. Once he was twenty-one he would have a full say in the Felton business and that included how its workers were housed and treated. But until that time, he had said, she should say nothing to any of them.

But why? Emma tucked the corners of the shawl tighter beneath her small breasts. Was it because of his brother? She knew from odd snatches of conversation that Paul had a brother. He never discussed him, not even saying his name, but she knew it. Carver Felton. That name was all too familiar, she'd heard it often enough, spat out by the men of Doe Bank. But she had never seen him. What was he like, the brother of Paul's, and why had she not been taken to meet him?

'I will call again next week.' Emma glanced over the woman's shoulder to the iron-framed bed that occupied most of the poky room. 'I hope Mr Paget will be better by then.'

'That be a hope we will both be denied,' Jerusha answered quietly. 'But there be more will be denied you yet.' Drawing the plain gold band from the third finger of her left hand she held it towards Emma. 'This be all I have to give you, Emma Price, but had I riches a-plenty I could not give you anything that will be of more use to you in the days that lie afore you.'

'I don't want anything, Mrs Paget.'

'I knows that.' Jerusha nodded. 'What you have done for me and my man been offered from the kindness of your heart; you have shared what little you have and now I am doing the same.'

'No.' Embarrassed, Emma took a step away. 'I can't ... I won't. That is your wedding ring.'

'Arrh, that's what it be.' Jerusha stared down at the circle of gold held between thumb and forefinger. 'That be the ring Jacob Paget set on my finger forty years ago and one I vowed would not leave it until the day him and me were parted.'

'Then you must keep it.' Emma felt relieved.

She could not accept payment for a few pies, hard as it had been for her to stretch the housekeeping so as to give them.

'Until the day him and me were parted.' Jerusha's tired eyes lifted, and in the slant of the evening sun Emma could see the pain in their depths. 'That day be here. By the dawn Jacob will be with the Lord and I will have no further need of this.'

'Please, Mrs Paget, you must not think like that.' Emma pushed the ring away. 'Your husband will...'

'Be with the Lord.' Jerusha smiled, a brief sad smile that accepted life as it had been set out for her. 'I know what I know and that be part of it. But I also know that you will have need of this ring, and of the protection it can afford.'

Grabbing Emma's wrist, she pulled her hand free of the shawl. Pressing the ring into the girl's palm, she folded each finger firmly over it.

'Take it, Emma Price,' she murmured. 'Take my gift to you and remember Jerusha Paget when the time comes for you to wear it.'

Emma usually enjoyed the two-mile walk from Plovers Croft to Doe Bank even though it always meant hurrying to reach the house before her father got home from work. Caleb's pretended piety did not extend to the giving away of anything, he would not take kindly to her taking food to the Pagets.

But this evening she found no pleasure in the clover and the kingcups, their mauve and gold glinting among the greens of gorse and purple of ling; nor did her gaze appreciate the strange beauty of furnace stacks and colliery winding houses, their bony silhouettes etched in gold against the pearly colours of the evening sky.

She was aware only of the ring. Pushed deep into the pocket of her skirt, it seemed to weigh heavy against her leg. Why had Jerusha Paget insisted she take it? What had she meant when she'd said Emma would need the protection it could afford?

Hitching the basket higher on her arm, her skirts brushing the wild flowers that on any other evening she would have gathered, Emma could not rid herself of the fear those words had brought to her heart; a sudden cold touch that chilled it still.

But it was stupid to feel afraid, nothing could harm her. Lifting her face to the last rays of the sun she slipped the shawl from about her head, freeing her hair to the breeze. Soon she would be Paul's wife and would have a wedding ring of her own. What need could she possibly have of the one in her pocket?

Poor Jerusha. Emma felt a rush of pity for the woman her mother had often called upon for help in times of sickness, as did all the women of Doe Bank. There was no talk of payment then. It was accepted that a kindness was not done in hope of reward, one woman helped another in any way she could, it was the only way to survive in the coalfields. She would return it on her next visit. Yes, she would give the ring back to Jerusha when next they met.

A short distance ahead the coppice adjoining

the grounds of Felton Hall rose like a dark island from the heath. Emma hesitated, eyes lifting to the tops of the trees. They were so beautiful, cloaked in lush greens, their tips crowned by the sunset. Beautiful but forbidding somehow, their leafy branches forming a barrier in her path. It was almost as if they forbade her approach, the guardians of Felton Hall.

The thought bringing a shiver to her spine, Emma stood staring at the wood. This was the second time today she had felt the coldness of fear, the second time some unknown chill had touched her.

A sudden clatter among the branches sent a shower of leaves spinning to the floor and the blood racing in Emma's veins. One hand rising automatically to her throat she stood staring, then loosed a long sigh as a wood pigeon flew from the trees, its loud indignant cooing shattering the silence.

Relief warming away her fear, Emma smiled at her own foolishness. A dispute over nesting rights and for one moment she had been a young child again, imagining demons in the dark.

At the edge of the heath the sun allowed itself to be drawn down into the arms of night and the scarlet-tipped clouds faded to mourning grey.

She had not thought it to be so late. Emma glanced again at the densely packed grove of trees. She should not take that way home, so late in the evening, but to go around it would add to her journey; another hour's absence to explain to her father. Well versed in his anger, Emma's mind was made up. Drawing the shawl close about her shoulders, she walked in to the shadow of the trees.

Leaving his bedroom, Carver glanced across the wide landing towards the closed door of his brother's room. Paul had wanted to leave the Hall after that last row about the Price girl, to take up residence in Beaufort House, the home that would come to him at the age of twenty-one. But as his legal guardian, Carver's refusal had had to be accepted.

The age of twenty-one! Carver's face darkened. That phrase had haunted him for years, figured in his waking thoughts, taunted him in his dreams. Paul would have half of everything then: land, money...

But what was money? What was land? He could make one and buy the other. At the head of the wide staircase he halted, gaze taking in the tasteful sweep of the entrance hall below. Felton Hall was his, deeded to him by his father as Beaufort House had been to Paul. But would his brother be satisfied with taking just the house? Would he renounce responsibility for the running of the coal mines and iron works, taking half their market value, instead, selling his inheritance?

'A mess of pottage'. The quotation rang again in Carver's mind as he began to descend the stairs. He had no intention of becoming another Esau, but then ... would Paul?

'Will the staff wait up for you, sir?'

'No.' Carver refused the topcoat the man-servant held out for him. 'Let them go to bed, I probably won't be back until tomorrow. If I am,

I will see myself in.'

'What of Mr Paul, sir?'

'My brother will most likely not be home before the end of next week.' Carver let the answer drift over his shoulder as he walked toward the rear of the house. 'He is in Blaydon on the business of iron for a bridge they are constructing across the river there.'

'Blaydon, sir? I don't think I am familiar with a town of that name.'

Carver smiled as the butler held open the door that gave on to the half-moon courtyard around which the stables and carriage houses were grouped.

'I'm not surprised you are unfamiliar with the name. It's a small town in the North East. They want to bridge the River Tyne to link themselves with Scotswood, and my brother is there to tender for the supplying of the girders.'

'I hope he meets with success, sir.'

'So do I, Morton. So do I.'

Swinging into the saddle of the horse ready prepared for him, Carver glanced at the sky. The sun already hung low over the horizon, it would be after nine when he reached the Mounts, but he was in no hurry. Langton was a bore, but a bore who must be tolerated at least until the venture Carver had in mind was achieved.

Touching his heels to the animal's sides he set it to a steady canter. Paul had been reluctant to go to Blaydon, no doubt thinking of his Doe Bank wench. But Carver had insisted he must acquaint himself with the overall running of the business, told him to make himself as conversant with it as he could so he might slip more easily into his place as co-owner.

But that had been a lie, a stratagem to get his brother safely away from Wednesbury. And when he returned? When Paul returned there would have been changes made.

Reaching the tall stone pillars that held gates wrought from iron forged in Felton foundries, Carver reined in his horse. Before him the heath stretched like a green carpet to the distant town, only the steeples of the parish church and its RC fellow competing against the belching chimneys of iron works and the great winding wheels of coal mines. It was no paradise that town, but beneath its perpetual pall of black smoke it made the kind of money that could buy a man a share of paradise.

But Felton would share with no man. He touched his heels to the horse's sides, body moving in perfect unison with it as it cantered on. Wednesbury or paradise, it must be theirs alone. Money and land that and the power they brought would belong to none but them.

But what if Paul would not agree, would not relinquish the Doe Bank wench. Would he, Carver, truly confine him to a mental institution? Turning the horse towards the coppice he allowed himself a smile. The answer was yes the only question being, how soon? How could he broach the subject with his brother?

A short distance into the wood, Carver tightened his grip on the reins, knees pressing into the stallion's body as it reared. Startled by a covey of partridge breaking cover at their

31

approach it had gone up on its hind legs, a snort of fear clouding from its nostrils. Holding firm to the reins, keeping the stallion's head high, he rode out its shocked reaction, voice calm in the horse's pricked ears, soothing, bringing it gently down under his hands.

With the horse steady once more he sat contemplating the idea that had formed in his mind. A partridge shoot. What would make for a more perfect excuse to bring Langton and a few other coal owners together? And what better time to put his proposition than after a day's good shooting followed by a hearty dinner?

This notion a pleasant conclusion to a problem he had pondered for several days he made to urge his mount forward, but a sound from the trees stayed him. That had been no partridge breaking cover nor a fox either, that had been the sound of a twig snapping beneath a man's foot. Damned poachers! Carver's mouth set in a straight line, his fingers tightening about his whip. This one would be sorry he had chosen Felton land to poach from!

To back the horse further into the cover of the trees would cause at least a rustling of the coarse bracken, and if the animal should choose to snort or even take fright again it would be enough to warn the poacher. That Carver did not want. Tonight would prove a lesson for the men of this town, they would learn that it was wiser not to trespass on his land.

Holding the reins in one hand, the other clutching the whip loosely at his side, he listened to the intruder's approach. The man was either stupid or very inexperienced at what he was about. A cold smile touched the corners of Carver's mouth. A few minutes of the whip and the fellow would have the kind of lesson that should rectify at least the latter.

The trees were sparser here, forming a natural clearing. He glanced to each side of him. Should the fellow make a run for it, the horse could easily overtake him. The coppice was not so dense as to prevent that. A few yards ahead, following a faint track that led through the heart of the wood, a figure came into view.

Holding the animal's head firm, Carver stared. This was no man poaching his land. Overhead the risen moon filled the clearing with a cool pale light, its silver gliding blonde hair, touching a high-buttoned collar and spilling over dark skirts.

A woman! Carver sat motionless. A young and pretty woman if the moonlight had not deceived him.

'Good evening.'

A touch of his heels swinging the horse across her path, Carver touched the stock of his whip to one side of his brow. His sudden appearance had the desired effect. The woman gasped, one hand going to her throat while the other clutched a basket.

'Isn't it a little late to be gathering herbs?' He lowered the whip, a slow, deliberate movement meant to catch the eye. 'That *is* what you're in Felton Wood for ... or is it to carry away a poacher's ill-gotten gains?'

'I ... I was not gathering herbs.'

Emma felt the tightness at her throat and the

thumping of her heart against her rib-cage, but forced herself to answer calmly. This man was merely passing through the coppice, no doubt taking a shorter route home as she was.

'Oh, then it *is* a poacher's trophy you are here to collect!'

Emma lifted her head, the movement trapping moonbeams in her hair, turning her eyes to silver. Carver felt a quickening low in his stomach. The moonlight had not deceived him, the woman was pretty. Damned pretty. Pretty enough to delay him ... for a while. His glance quickly scanning each of her hands he noted the absence of a wedding ring. Pity, he thought, a husband could make a useful scapegoat. A pity but hardly a disaster!

'I'm not collecting from any poacher!' Indignation sharpened her voice as she answered. 'I am on my way home from visiting a friend. I left a little later than usual so decided to cut through the wood, it takes quite some distance off the journey.'

'I see.' Carver traced a glance over the length of her. A pretty face, a pleasant voice. And the body beneath those shabby clothes, would that be as appealing?

'And where might this friend live?' He directed his horse to the right and then to the left, matching Emma's steps as she tried to pass.

Indignation retreating before a fresh surge of fear, Emma clutched the basket to her. He had no right to question her but arguing would only serve to lengthen an encounter she wanted over and done with.

'She … they live across the heath, over towards the path that links Coppice Bridge to Lea Brook Bridge. Mr and Mrs Paget.'

He knew the place, a few vermin-ridden houses. They too figured in the project he intended putting to Langton.

'And you?' Carver leaned forward as the moonlight fell once again on the face turned up to his, and the quickening in his stomach became a jolt of desire. 'You said you were on your way home.'

Fear lodging like a solid barrier in her throat, Emma looked at the figure bent forward over his saddle but the moon at his back threw his face into shadow.

'I … I live at Doe Bank. My father is Caleb Price.'

Price! Carver straightened, the tension in his stomach slackening, the heat that had begun to build in his veins as he'd looked into that pretty face becoming cold and dead. The man he had paid to bring him information concerning the girl his brother thought to marry had said she was young and beautiful, with hair the colour of wheat washed in moonlight. Carver had laughed cynically at the man's over-poetic description but he did not laugh now. The man had been correct in his appraisal, the girl *was* beautiful and her hair *was* the colour of wheat washed in moonlight.

'It is Emma, is it not?' He once more countered her attempt to pass.

His voice had taken on a cold sound, but in her fear the words barely registered. Clutching her shawl protectively across her, fear drumming in her veins, she stammered, 'Please, let me pass!'

Sliding from the saddle, his back still to the pale light, Carver balanced the whip in both hands. 'Oh, I will, Miss Price – Emma – after I have properly introduced myself. I am Carver Felton, brother of Paul, the man you think to marry.'

'Paul … you are Paul's brother?' Emma felt her fear fall away. This man was Paul's brother, she had been silly to be so frightened. He would do her no harm. A smile wreathing her mouth, she looked into the shadowed face. 'Paul has talked of you.'

'And of you!' The whip still balanced in his hand, Carver took a step forward, his height throwing her slight figure into shadow.

'I was hoping to meet you.' Emma dropped a small curtsy.

'And now you have!' Bringing the whip down hard across the basket he sent it sliding from her arm, at the same time catching her wrist in a grip like steel. 'Before we part you will know me just as well as you know my brother. Maybe even a little better!'

Throwing the whip aside he wound his fingers into the neck of her blouse, wrenching the cheap cotton until it split to the waist.

'How well do you know my brother? As well as this?' Snatching her hard against him he pressed his mouth to hers, biting into the soft flesh of her mouth. Releasing her, he stared for a moment into her shocked face then, the palms of both hands coming down hard on her shoulders, sent her tumbling backward, the suddenness of her fall driving the breath from her body.

'As well as this, Miss Price?'

Staring down at her, mouth fixed into a cold smile, Carver loosed his clothing, his black eyes holding hers all the while in a hypnotic stare.

'No, don't!' Emma tried to twist away as he dropped down beside her. 'Please … let me go.'

'I have said I will.' Carver stroked one finger across her cheek, the touch of her pale skin reawakening the quickening in the base of his stomach. 'But *after* I have introduced myself properly – this being the proper way for a slut like you!'

Moving like quicksilver he threw her skirts up to her waist, ripping away her bloomers, knees forcing her legs apart as he lifted himself on to her.

'No, no … please!' Emma sobbed, trying to fling him from her, but another blow to the face sent her senses reeling.

'Did you say no to my brother, Miss Price?' he hissed in the darkness, cold and venomous as a snake. 'Did you pretend with him as you are pretending now? Was your long-lost virginity a bribe to lead him on? Did you offer him the dubious delights of your body in the hope of getting him to marry you? Was that the price he was to pay for *this*?'

The last word vicious as the pain that seemed to split her body he thrust into her, pushing and driving deeper and deeper until the agony of it enfolded her in a sheet of darkness.

How long it lasted Emma could not tell. She knew only the pressure of his body on hers, the relentless rhythm, then the relief that sobbed in her when at last he moved away.

Afraid to move, shock holding her limbs rigid, Emma lay with her eyes closed, praying silently. Let him go now. Please, God, let him go, let him leave!

Dressed once more, Carver looked down at the figure lying on the ground, moonlight gleaming on limbs naked as he had left them. Reaching for the whip where he had thrown it, he turned towards the horse quietly grazing the tender bark of a tree. Then, hesitating for a brief moment, he reached into the pocket of his silk waistcoat.

Moonlight sparking from the coin he twisted between thumb and forefinger, he glanced again at the girl he had raped, and laughed, a soft cynical sound that scraped the silence.

'Ask him now, Miss Price. Ask my brother to marry you now. And when you do, show him this and tell him I was right. It was too high a price to pay!'

Bending over her, he slotted the shilling between the lips of her vagina.

Chapter Three

Leaving the brougham in the care of a man who shuffled across the yard, one leg dragging painfully after the other, Carver ignored his deferential touch of a dust-blackened cloth cap, striding past him into the mine office.

'Never mind them!' He waved away the ledgers the startled accounts clerk reached for. 'Where's Barlow?'

Only half listening to the faltering reply, he ordered the overseer to be brought to him.

It had been a month since his brother had left for Blaydon. It had taken several strongly worded letters to keep him there but Paul had stayed. For how much longer? Not that it really mattered, a few more days and it would be of little consequence. Carver had put the case for the digging of an arm from the Birmingham Canal to link the Topaz mine and those belonging to Langton and other mine owners to the waterway. He had argued that constructing a basin at Plovers Croft would facilitate the transporting of their coal as well as his. Loading and docking facilities for the narrow boats would be of benefit to every coal master from Lea Brook to Ocker Hill and those who chose to use it could be charged accordingly. The venture would pay both ways, he had told them. Their own coal could be moved more quickly and in larger quantities. One narrow boat

39

could shift at least three dozen times the amount of a horse-drawn wagon. And there'd be the revenue from any other mine owners who used the new link. They had seen the practical sense of the idea and agreed that same night that work should start as soon as agreement was reached with the Birmingham Canal Navigation Company to breach their waterway.

Knocking down those houses at Plovers Croft would have caused Paul to object, he would have been against putting the families out; but what did that matter against the beauty of the plan? The place would be better off without them. Besides, Paul wasn't here to object. Carver had achieved a great deal in the past month. It was so much easier to get business done when his brother was not around to sermonise, continually throwing a spanner in the works every time a suggestion was made to improve the business.

Paul... Carver stared through the dust-grimed window to where young lads bent double and used their shoulders to push the coal-filled bogies from the pit head and link them to the donkey, the steel cable that hauled them to the loading bank. Paul set too much store by the workers, both in the coal mine and the iron foundries. They should have decent housing and proper schooling for their children, he said. Well, they were living in the 1880s, Carver argued in return. Men were no longer serfs but were free to leave his employ at any time it did not suit them!

But Paul was not the only one to throw a spanner in the works. Carver smiled inwardly. He had been shown a double portion of Lady Luck's favour that night a month ago. He had solved two problems, not only that of the canal venture but that of his brother's proposed marriage. He had taken the Price girl, and not because he wanted her. A shilling would buy him more interesting sport and a better playmate in any tavern in Wednesbury. She had been pretty enough, granted, but her looks had been of no interest to him. His only reason for taking her in that grove had been to prevent his brother from marrying her.

Carver turned from the window, the smile inside him cold and cynical. After all, even Paul, despite his high-flown ideas, would not want marriage with a woman who had sold herself to his brother. And that was what he would hear, regardless of anything the little slut might tell him. That he, Carver Felton, had lain with her and paid her for her services. She had taken the money he had left, of that there could be no doubt, and thus there'd be no marriage.

Glancing at the door as it opened, he concealed the smile. He had put an end to the business of the Price girl. There would be no Doe Bank wench marrying into the Felton family!

Waiting until the clerk withdrew, Carver turned again to the window and asked in a cold impersonal voice, 'Do we have anyone by the name of Price working here?'

Barlow's shoulders visibly relaxed and he loosed the breath anxiety had tight in his chest. Felton was out after some poor bugger, but thank the Lord it wasn't him! 'We 'ave the preacher man ... he be named Price.'

'Where does he live, do you know?'

Brow creasing as he searched his brain for the answer, Barlow looked at the man he worked for as he turned to face him. Hair black as a crow matched the clipped line of sideburns that outlined a strong jaw, its darkness relieved by two narrow swathes of silver that ran from above each glittering eye like silver horns. The trademark of evil, Barlow thought. The touch of the Devil who always marked his own.

'We 'ave several Prices working here, sir.'

Barlow winced as Carver released an exasperated breath. Whatever it was this man Price had done it had Felton wound tight as a spring.

'I can get the wages ledger, Mr Felton, the addresses will be there against the names.'

'Ledger!' Carver crashed his fist on to the table that served as a desk. 'I haven't come here to read a bloody book! You should have these things in your head, that's what I pay you for.'

'Price is a common name, Mr...'

Carver eyed him, slow and easy, threat in every line of his dark-suited figure, lips hardly moving, voice dangerously pleasant.

'I want no excuses Barlow. And I want no overseer who cannot do the job as I expect him to.'

Sweat gathering in the palms of his hands, the overseer almost felt the tin being shoved into them. Christ what did the man think he was, a bloody file ledger on legs!

Nervous tension squeezing his throat he coughed, but as those black eyes settled unblinkingly on his own, giving their unspoken

42

message he stammered, 'There ... there be a Joby Price working in the long tunnel, he lives up along Dudley Street; then there be Davy Price, he be in the winding house, lives in Potters Lane...'

Barlow coughed again as the toe of Carver's boot began a measured tapping against the table leg.

'...and then there be the preacher man, Caleb Price, he works the donkey engine. You know, Mr Felton, it winds the bogie trucks along the tracks ... to the loading bank...'

'I know what a bloody donkey engine is!' Carver's foot ceased its rhythm.

'Yes ... yes, o' course you do.' Barlow swallowed the acid blocking his throat. 'The preacher man he ... he lives up along of Doe Bank.'

'Doe Bank!'

The name was only breathed but it stopped Barlow and he waited, intuition telling this was the man that was sought.

'What do you know of him?'

'I ain't never had a deal to do with him, sir. I can't be doing with his spouting the Bible at every turn.'

Carver's eyes glittered with suppressed anger. Irritation was plain in his answer.

'That was not what I asked.'

'No, Mr Felton.' Sweat trickling over his palms and along his fingers the overseer glanced towards the window in an effort to avoid that piercing black stare, but he knew he must face it again. 'I know he has a wife and family, two wenches but no lads. The eldest must be around eighteen and the other ... sixteen or so.'

'Names?'

The curtness of the question brought Barlow's glance back to his employer.

'Like I says, sir, I ain't had a lot of dealings with the man so I can't say gospel like that these names be certain, but I remembers him mentioning two, Carrie and...' he paused '...Emma. Arrh, that be it, Emma, though I don't know as whether one or the other be the name of his wife.'

Emma. Carver felt satisfaction glow in his chest with the warmth of a good brandy. Emma Price of Doe Bank. The man Caleb was her father, he had the right one.

'Will I 'ave them fetched, sir?'

'No,' Carver answered coolly. 'That will not be necessary. The one who works the donkey engine, give him his tin tonight. He's finished at the Topaz mine.'

'Finished!' Surprise pulling his straggling brows together, the overseer stared. 'But why, Mr Felton? I mean, what shall I tell him? I 'ave to give a reason.'

Carver walked to the door then turned, one dark eyebrow raised. 'Why is because I say so, and that is reason enough. Tonight, Barlow. See that it's done!'

It had been a month ... a month since Carver Felton had raped her. Emma held the shawl close around her. And in all that time Paul had not come to see her once. But that was not surprising if he knew. His brother must have told him. Yet would he? What man would admit his rape of a brother's sweetheart? The girl who was to have been his sister-in-law?

But that would never happen now. Even supposing Paul still loved her, still wanted her for his wife, she could not marry him, could not live so close to Carver Felton, probably seeing on a daily basis the man who had treated her with such heartless contempt.

Drawing the shawl over her head she pulled it low over her brow and across her cheeks, trying to close out of her range of vision the trees forming the coppice where he had raped her.

A slut was what he had called her. She would know him as well as she knew his brother, the words implying she had lain with Paul. Then he had left that shilling, paying her as he would pay a whore, and to Carver Felton she was no different. Emma felt disgust and shame rip through her as they did day and night, memories she could not dispel tearing her apart.

He had stood looking down at her. Clamping one hand across her mouth, Emma stemmed the bile of revulsion that threatened to spill from her lips. He had looked at her, still naked to the waist, then bent over to place that coin in her vagina.

One shilling! One silver shilling! That was all it had taken to salve his conscience. But it was not enough to buy her forgiveness. Carver Felton would never have enough money to buy that or stave off her revenge.

She would return the amount with interest. Emma's hand tightened on the shawl as she thought of the coin hidden beneath the underwear in her drawer. She would never spend that shilling, never let it pass to another living soul, not until the day she could hand it back to Carver Felton.

She had carried it home clutched in the palm of her hand, still clutching it as her mother had hurried her up to the bedroom she and Carrie shared. Caleb had not yet returned from the mine, she'd said, they must get her washed and into bed before he did. Though her mother had been incensed at what had happened she had shown no real surprise. Emma visualised her mother's expression as she had gathered her in her arms. There had been no shock in those faded lacklustre eyes, only pity. It was almost as if she had expected what had happened.

'Men,' she had muttered, holding Emma tight in her thin arms. 'They be all the same, bad through and through, and his sort be the worst of all!'

It was later, after the tin bath had been emptied of coal-filmed water and Caleb given his evening meal, that her mother had come to sit beside Emma's bed. It was then, between stifled sobs, that the whole story came out. Mary had listened without interruption until Emma had reached beneath her pillow, bringing out the small silver coin.

Taking it into her own hand she had stared at it, glinting in the light of the candle. 'One paltry shilling!' she had murmured almost to herself. 'That is the price of a woman's virtue, the payment for shattering her life. One single shilling and the man goes scot free!' Folding her fingers over the coin she had tilted her head back, eyes tight closed, just a shadow of movement about her lips as she spoke. 'May the Good Lord call him to book for what has been done this night. May the hosts of heaven pay him back!'

Now, her head bent, Emma hurried on. Carver Felton would be made to pay. With or without the help of heaven, he would pay!

That was her solemn vow.

'You say your fear be that you may be carrying the seed of rape?'

Jerusha Paget sat, hands folded in her lap, eyes on the drawn face of the young girl sitting opposite, the firelight dancing in her pale hair as she nodded.

'That be the first time a man has lain with you? There has been no other?'

'No!' Emma's head lifted sharply, denial in her eyes. 'He must have thought I had, he implied that his brother and I...'

'That his brother had taken the privilege of a husband?'

'Yes. But he had not ... *I* would not. That man called me a slut, treated me as a whore, but I have never been that, not even for...' Dropping her gaze to her fingers moving restlessly against her skirts, Emma left the rest unsaid.

'You have given no name to the man who forced himself upon you, though it lies in your heart in letters cut deep.' Jerusha shifted her gaze to the fire, its glow seeming somehow to spread itself about her, wrapping her in the veil of its light, touching her worn features with new life, smoothing and renewing, setting a circle of soft

47

radiance about the faded hair.

The strange, almost frightening beauty of the scene caught at Emma's throat and when Jerusha began to speak she felt the nerves in her spine tingle, for the usual softness of the woman's voice had changed, becoming dull and flat.

'Those letters lie hidden deep and your tongue has spoken them to none, but this night will see the loosing of your tongue. Yet will you carry that name with you as you will carry the desire for revenge, but one will not still the pain of the other. The mark of rape goes too deep ever to be wiped away completely. It will come to you at night cloaked in darkness, it will break in upon your thoughts in the light of day, tormenting you with its evil. Time ... time can be your only healer and love, one man's true love, your only physician. Deep lie the letters, but not so deep Jerusha Paget cannot read them, nor the reason you have come to Plovers Croft. You have not yet asked for the potion you want, that which will carry away the seed of Carver Felton...'

Emma caught her breath, the sound loud in the shadowed room, but Jerusha seemed not to hear.

'...but that potion I am forbidden to give – ask not by whose hand I am stayed. There is a child within you, a child that will be born into the world, one that will carry the name of its father.'

'No!' Emma's cry was as keen as the grief within her. 'Why? Why should I carry a child I do not want, a child I did not ask for?' Dropping her head into her hands she sobbed. 'Why has this happened to me ... what have I done to deserve this?'

48

A half-buried coal settled low in the grate swamping the flames, the glow that had settled about Jerusha dying with it.

'You have done nothing, wench.' Her voice held it customary gentleness as her gaze returned to Emma. 'The wrong that has been owes nothing to you...'

'Then help me, Jerusha!' Emma thrust forward her whole body, pleading. 'Help me as my mother said you would. As you have helped other women.'

'Mary Price spoke truly.' Jerusha's head moved with a slow bobbing motion. 'I have helped other women in the way you came to ask. I have given the potion that flushed away the seed they did not want, that which they could not afford to keep, and I would help you too...'

'Then do it, Jerusha!' Emma pushed herself from the chair, going down on her knees before the older woman. 'Give me the potion ... please!'

Bringing her hand to the head now lying in her lap, Jerusha's face lapsed into the old careworn creases, her eyes reflecting the pity they had held so often for women who came to her asking for herbal cures, for their men or themselves or their sick children when the money to pay a doctor could not be found; that pity, deep and rending, when she knew her skills would not be such as to bring a cure and more rarely when, as now, she had been forbidden to try.

It had been a silent voice in her mind, a vision visible only to her inner gaze, only a feeling. But a feeling so strong it could not be denied. It had been this way from girlhood. An inner sense so

49

powerful it filled her whole being, lifting her, holding her, closing off the world until it seemed she floated within its silence, the peace of it absolute, and from that peace came the knowledge, from that silence the direction she must follow.

'That is not the help I must give you.' Jerusha stroked the silken hair. 'That is not to be the way of things.'

'But you *can*, Jerusha!' Emma lifted her tear-stained face. 'You said yourself I was not to blame so why won't you do what I ask? I will pay...'

'No, Emma.' Jerusha dropped her hand. 'I would take no payment from you or any other soul I could bring help to. It is true you are not to blame as it is true the cure you seek you will not find; not in Plovers Croft nor any place else. As for blame and the carrying of it, that will be yours for years yet to come. You are bound, as I am, by cords that cannot be seen, the cords of fate. They bind us all in one way or another and will not be broken, not 'til that which has been set be at an end. The child will stay within you until the time of its birthing even though now you think to turn to some other for the shifting of it.'

Emma dropped her eyes. The thought had risen in her mind, the thought of looking for someone else skilled in the use of herbs. But how could Jerusha have guessed ... and how had she guessed the name of Carver Felton?

Cupping Emma's face, Jerusha tipped it gently upward. 'Save yourself the pain, Emma wench,' she said softly. 'There will be enough of that when the months of carrying be over.'

Despite the thoughts that must have shown in her glance, Emma looked up. 'But how do you know? How can you be so sure, so certain it cannot be taken away?'

Jerusha closed her eyes, and in that brief moment it seemed once more she was in that silent golden place, enfolded in a peace that knew no end; and when she opened them again that same certainty glowed in their faded depths.

She smiled and in her eyes there was a sadness that seemed to Emma as she watched to be a sadness outside of that the woman might feel for her, a sadness that was Jerusha's alone. 'I know what I know, child. I ask no question as to how, I only take that which is given to me. That I speak and no more. This also I know. What is given to Jerusha Paget by the voice of silence, that is what will be. Trust me, child. That I'll tell you and no more.'

Emma rose to her feet. Her mother had been so certain Jerusha would give her that which would leave her clean of Carver Felton's vile act, take away the seed growing within her. None but the three of them would ever know. But now! Emma turned to the door. The whole of Doe Bank would soon know Emma Price was carrying a child but had no husband. Her mother had understood, she had believed her. But what of her father? Emma felt the world reel about her. Her father would never accept the truth, he would never believe she had been taken against her will. To Caleb she would be as guilty as

Carver Felton. How would she live with her father's condemnation? A condemnation she knew he would hold to for the rest of his life.

Tears gathering in her throat, she drew her shawl across her shoulders and as she turned again to the older woman, caught the sorrow that showed in her face as she stared at the empty bed. Jerusha Paget had her own unhappiness with the loss of her husband, Emma would not be the cause of more.

Swallowing her tears, she placed her arms about her friend. 'Thank you for believing me,' she said softly. 'You would not turn me away without cause. You would have helped if you could, I know that.'

For a moment Jerusha stood silent, feeling the tremors that shook Emma's body. The child had suffered a great hurt and there were more yet to come; but the man who had wronged her would feel the hand of heaven against him. The torment this girl was feeling now he too would feel and only she would have the power to end it.

'I wish I could comfort you more, wench.' Holding Emma at arm's length Jerusha looked deep into her swamped eyes. 'But it was not to be. The fates have their reasons though they do not always choose to show them to me. But this I can tell you: a few years will see the changing of your life. Many times it will seem to you that you have not the strength to bear the burdens that will be a part of those years, but the strength will be given you. Have faith, wench, remember my words, and when the time comes remember too the ring that hangs from a bootlace about your

52

neck; it will bring you the comfort no word can give.'

'*The comfort no word can give.*' Walking home across the heath those words returned to her. The only words she had wanted to hear would never be spoken now. Paul would not ask her to be his wife. Carver must have told him, why else had he not come?

Words! Emma felt bitterness, dry and harsh in her throat. They could bring so much happiness, so much despair! Jerusha had talked of her life being changed. Those words at least carried truth.

A bastard child. That would change her life in Doe Bank. From now on Emma Price would be an outcast among her own.

Chapter Four

'But I've been away for over a month. You cannot possibly expect me to leave again so soon?'

Paul Felton got up from the table, his face stormy. Home less that twenty-four hours and already his brother wanted him to make another business trip.

'How else can you meet with clients?' Carver watched him steadily. 'They cannot all visit Felton Hall. You have to learn, Paul, business is as much diplomacy as it is commerce. You have to know when to give as well as when to take; that includes your time. We all have other things we would prefer to spend our time doing, but that is a luxury we cannot afford to indulge.'

'Meeting new clients is all very well, but does it have to be so damned quick? I didn't get back from Blaydon until last night!'

Drawing a slow affected breath, Carver placed his linen napkin beside his plate. 'If Felton's are not there when coal and iron is required then some other firm will be. We are not the only iron masters in Wednesbury, brother, nor is the Topaz the only coal mine. Trade will not always come to our door, so if we wish to keep it then we must be prepared to pander to our clients a little. Trade has its whims, rather like a woman. You want the favour, you pay the price.'

'The price should be shared, Carver!' Paul

rounded on him sharply. 'Surely this time you should be the one to go?'

'If that is what you wish.' Carver's reply showed none of the anger beginning to build in him. Argument was something he did not tolerate lightly, especially when it might affect plans he had so carefully laid. 'But bear in mind the fact that I learned the art of meeting prospective business associates, of doing business with them, long before you were out of the school room. I know what it is all about. But you, Paul, what do you know? How many buyers have you come up against ... how many rivals outbidding you on every deal? Where did you learn to match cunning with cunning, to recognise which hand to shake and which held a knife? The answer is, you have not learned, and you never will so long as you are not prepared to go out and do so. I do not need that education Paul, you do. My meeting those clients will not provide you with it. I am afraid that the putting aside of personal preferences is all part of running a business and if you intend taking your place as a co-director then that is a fact to which you must get used.'

'So how long will this proposed trip take?'

The expression on Carver's face remained the same but inside he smiled. It had never taken him long to impose his will on Paul. His brother would leave Felton Hall tomorrow, and this time for much longer than a month.

Helping himself to another cup of coffee from an elegant Spode china pot, Carver added cream and sugar. 'That will very much depend upon you. Your personality is one way of putting it. You must sell yourself if you wish to sell iron. Be pleasant and agreeable, show an interest in all the customer has to say, visit with him if that is what he wants. A quick, "How do you do, sir? I am leaving" will fill no order books.'

Displeasure still drawing his brows together, Paul answered, 'You sound as though you expect it to take some time?'

Carver stirred his coffee, his eyes on the creamy swirls. 'I expect you to do what is best for the business.'

'The business!' Paul kicked the leg of a dining chair. 'Why always the bloody business?'

'For God's sake, Paul, grow up!' Giving way to his anger, Carver threw the spoon he was holding across the table. 'It is that "bloody business" that has kept you all those years. It is the business that put food in your stomach and fancy clothes on your back. What paid for your schooling? What keeps Felton Hall and Beaufort House if not the business? That is what you have lived on in the past and it is what will keep you in the future. But it did not build itself. Father left the foundry and the coal mine but it is me that made them what they are today. *My* time … *my* sweat … it was *my* preferences that were put aside time and time again. And I tell you, brother, it is time you played your part. If you wish to go on living in the style to which you are accustomed then you will shoulder some responsibility for providing for it. You will go to Birkenhead and you will stay there for however long it takes!'

The spark of defiance dying in his brown eyes, the frown of annoyance turning to dull resignation, Paul glanced at his brother. 'When?' he asked dully. 'When do you want me to leave?'

'Tomorrow. There's a train in the afternoon. It will leave the Great Western station at Wednesbury at two. I'll take you there in the brougham.'

'So soon?' Paul's glance lifted automatically to the mantel of the carved fireplace, looking for a clock. Finding none he drew a gold hunter from the pocket of his waistcoat.

'I did request you go a week from now,' Carver lied with consummate ease. 'But Aston insisted it be tomorrow, and as I said a moment since...'

'I know, I know!' Paul's answer was resigned. 'Putting aside personal preferences is all part of business.' Flicking open the front of the watch, he glanced at the dial before snapping it shut. 'Can the business spare me for a few hours this afternoon or is that too much to ask?'

'Of course. You may take the rest of the day to do with as you wish. If you would care to use the carriage, I'll...'

'No.' Paul returned the watch to his pocket. 'I will take my horse. The afternoon is mild, it will prove a pleasant ride to Doe Bank.'

Carver's lips tightened imperceptibly. Doe Bank meant only one thing: the Price girl. She was the reason Paul was reluctant to go on business trips and the month away had made no difference to the feeling his brother had for her. Well, maybe it hadn't. But the fact that she had lain with Carver and taken payment for doing so should put paid to any feeling of Paul's ... infatuation or otherwise!

'You're going to see...' He paused, giving the

57

impression he could not recall the name that had risen so easily to his mind.

'Emma.' Paul strode to the door. 'Her name is Emma, and yes, I am going to Doe Bank to see her. I am going to ask her to become my wife.'

'It is as well she has a year to prepare for the wedding.'

Carver took a sip from his cup and when he replaced it in the saucer the glance he lifted to his brother was one of icy cynicism. 'She will need every moment of that time to earn enough to buy a decent nightgown much less a trousseau. Pit bank wenches make very little money picking over the colliery waste heaps. But then, there are always the taverns and beer houses.' He raised one eyebrow, the movement at once disparaging and supercilious. 'She can no doubt earn a shilling or two in those. There are always men not too fussy about where they buy a woman for the night, or as to how many times she has been bought before.'

'Damn you, Carver!' Paul whipped about, fists clenched. 'I'll push every one of those words down your bloody throat!'

His movements unhurried, Carver rose to his feet. 'Before you get yourself hurt, little brother, I suggest you go see the wench. Ask your question then if you must. But remember to tell her there'll be no marriage for a year. You'll be given no consent by me.'

The slam of the door reverberating around the dining room, Carver smiled as he picked up his cup again.

Yes, a great deal could happen in a year.

Emma heard the hoof beats before the horse breasted the small rise in the ground that was Doe Bank.

Carver! The pain that had twisted her stomach for several hours lanced her again, sharp and griping, snatching the breath from her lungs. Only the Feltons rode in these parts and Paul had gone away, left a month ago with no word. It could only be that he had thought better of wanting to marry her; he must have realised he was not in love with her after all. But to leave without a word...

Then had come that terrible night, the night Carver Felton had raped her. He had done it quite deliberately. It had not been an act of passion or even of lust. It had been a cold, calculating move designed to bar any hope she might have had of becoming his brother's wife.

And now he was here at Doe Bank! But for what reason? He had done his evil. Repeating it would serve no purpose, hold no logic.

Pain striking her again, Emma clutched at her abdomen, breath coming out in a short hard gasp.

Were purpose and logic part of Carver Felton's make-up? She gasped again. She had only met him once but that meeting had shown her that they were. Logic and purpose were very much a part of the man ... was his purpose in coming here to rape her again?

Emma glanced about her. The small group of houses stood silent, their occupants at work earning their living; except for the old who sat close to their fires, or the sick like her mother laid up in their beds.

Was that why he had chosen this time of day to pay his visit? Knowing that even the children of the village would be away with their mothers; all but the very youngest hands must work to live. Had he called at the pit bank and learned she had taken the half-hour break to run home to see to her mother, then followed her here?

Forcing herself to stand upright, Emma turned to face the rider breasting the hill. Thank God she had not allowed Carrie to come home in her place.

'Emma!' The rider swung himself to the ground, sunlight glinting on his rich brown hair.

'Emma, it's so good to see you.'

Another wave of pain twisting through her, Emma stared at the man approaching her with long easy strides. Paul ... it was Paul Felton come to Doe Bank, not his brother.

'Emma, I've missed you so.' Catching both her hands in his, he smiled down into her face.

'Why haven't you been to see me? It has been almost a month.' The question came out abruptly. If Paul had been missing her so much then why had he stayed away so long?

'I have been away on business. Carver insisted I go, left me no time to come and see you first to tell you I would be gone for such a length of time.'

Carver had insisted? Emma felt her senses whirl. Had theirs been an accidental meeting that evening? Perhaps, but his rape of her must have been the outcome of long consideration. *'Ask my*

60

brother to marry you now!' Those were the words he had spoken. His violation of her had not only been deliberate, it had been planned. With his brother out of the way, Carver Felton could carry out his scheme at any time, their meeting had merely played into his hands.

And now Paul was back and here at Doe Bank. How much did he know of his brother's attack on her? Had Carver told him or said nothing at all?

'Did my brother send no word?' Paul caught the shadowed expression in her eyes. 'Did he not spare a moment to come and see you, to tell you the reason for my absence?'

Emma dropped her glance. It was obvious not only from Paul's happy smile but also from his question: Carver had said nothing of what he had done. But there could be no doubt he would, should Paul introduce her as his future bride. That would be the obstacle he would raise and it would be insurmountable. How could Paul marry her, knowing what he would then?

Even should the fear she had carried since that night prove unfounded, should her monthly flow still come, even then she could not marry Paul. That terrible truth would always be there between them. Carver's sentence upon her had taken only minutes to execute, but the serving of it would last a lifetime. Her lifetime! Never would she be free of the memory of it, never free of the shame.

'Your brother sent no word,' she said quietly, but could not bring herself to add that he had indeed seen her.

'Damn him!' Paul's smile faded. 'Too wrapped

up in the business to think of anything or anyone else. Emma, I'm sorry you were not told, but this time you will know…'

'This time?' She looked up sharply.

'Yes. It's a bind, I know, but there is nothing I can do. Carver insists I go to Birkenhead to-morrow. He says that to have a proper understanding of the business I need to meet people on their home ground, and until I reach twenty-one I have to do whatever he decides.'

Whatever he decides… It was almost a malediction, a curse pronounced by Carver Felton on all who might dare to question him; a power he would wield over his brother as he had wielded it against her. But Paul would eventually be free from Carver's hold, whereas she never would.

'But once I am of age…' Raising her hands to his lips Paul kissed each in turn '…we will be married, and then I will never have to leave you again. We will be together always.'

Together always. Emma felt coldness seep into her veins. Or until Carver should decide other-wise?

Tense with the pain in her stomach and the coldness in her veins, Emma struggled to keep her voice steady.

'Paul, thank you for coming to explain. It was kind of you to take the time when you must have so many preparations to make before tomor-row…'

'I had to come, Emma.' He drew her close, his arms going about her. 'I had to see you to tell you that I love you and want you for my wife. A year

62

seems an eternity to wait before that dream can come true. But it will, my dear, it will.'

Letting herself rest against him, her head against his shoulder, Emma gave herself up to the one moment of joy left to her, the last time she would be in Paul's arms. This was all she would have of the bright promise of a few weeks ago, all that was left of the dream Carver Felton had destroyed.

Pain rising like a tide, Emma watched him ride away. Carver Felton had imposed his will upon them both. Paul would not be allowed to marry a girl from Doe Bank, and his coming of age would have no bearing on that.

'Eh, Emma! What have you done?' Carrie stared at her elder sister, who was clutching her abdomen, her already pale face turning chalk white.

'Only what ... what had to be done,' she gasped. She would not have believed it would give her so much pain. She had gone from Jerusha Paget's house to another of which she had heard women on the waste heaps talk. A woman who for a shilling would give a potion that would rid another of an unwanted child, clear it from the womb without hurt. The house had been dark, but not dark enough to hide the dust and dirt within from Emma's shrinking gaze.

'How long?' the woman had asked, already knowing in her mind the reason for Emma's visit. 'How long 'ave you gone?'

'I'm not sure,' Emma remembered the look the

woman had squinted at her, a look that spoke the silent question: Have there been that many times … so many men?

'How long since you've seen … how long since you last had a show of blood?'

The question was sharp, irate; the woman obviously thought her an idiot. 'A little over a month,' Emma answered, once more suffering the squinted appraisal.

'How little?'

'Two or three days.'

'Tcha!' The woman stood with her hands on her hips. 'That don't be long enough for you to be certain. Could be you be throwing your money away.'

'Perhaps,' Emma had answered quietly. 'It could be that my monthly flow is late in coming, I know there can be many causes of that happening.'

'But there be one cause you don't be prepared to risk?'

Waiting for Emma's nod, the woman had gone into her scullery, returning with an enamel mug.

'Drink.' She had shoved the chipped mug into Emma's hand. 'Get that down you, it will put an end to what be worrying you. There'll be nowt for you to fret over by this time tomorrow. Not 'til the next time anyway.'

She had laughed as she added the last, a horrid cackling laugh that had set Emma's nerves on edge.

'Go on, wench, drink it. It will do no good you staring at it.'

In the shadowed gloom of the house, Emma

could not see the colour of the liquid in the cup but the smell as she lifted it to her lips caused her to heave. She had drunk it. Drunk whatever it was the woman had given her, then paid her shilling.

'You weren't sure,' Carrie protested, helping her to the bed they shared in the tiny back bedroom. 'You could have waited a few more days.'

'And if it didn't come then how many more days should I wait? How many before it becomes too late?' Emma whimpered as pain seized her again. 'I couldn't wait, Carrie. I can't risk being pregnant, Father would never forgive me.'

'Father!' Carrie suddenly trembled. 'Why does he do such things? Why, despite all his preaching and sermonising, does he ... does he fon... Mother is with child so often it's a wonder she is not dead. Oh, I know very well why she is sick now. Another baby to be got rid of, another bout of suffering while he struts about spouting the Bible and being all holier than thou!'

'Carrie!' Emma's eyes widened.

'It's true!' her sister returned, almost to herself. 'He knows what he does is wrong, it cannot be as he says it is – that it is the duty of every woman to satisfy the man, let him...'

'Carrie, stop!' Emma looked at her sister, usually so timid and quiet, hardly ever speaking of their father, going up to the bedroom as soon as he came home.

'Carrie, you should not talk like that. How do we know whether or not Mother is...' Emma broke off, embarrassed by the turn the conversation had taken.

'How?' Carrie rose to her feet, her eyes brimming with tears. 'For the simple reason she makes so many visits to Jerusha Paget. You know what she goes for, I know what she goes for. It is the same thing *you* went to ask for, the potion that ends a pregnancy; the potion that will kill her if she goes on taking it. And it will be *his* fault!'

What Carrie said was true. Emma folded her arms across her stomach, trying to ease away the pain. Their mother did go to Jerusha, two or sometimes three times in a year, afterwards suffering the same agony she herself was presently sharing. But better that, she had told Emma, better to suffer the pain of the body than the pain of the heart trying to raise a houseful of children on the wage their father earned, raise them in the squalor of Doe Bank, and so each time she visited Jerusha.

'It's so unfair, Emma. Why should women suffer so much? Why can a man take pleasure where he pleases when we feel only pain and heartbreak?'

'It might not be like that for every woman.' Emma watched her sister through eyes dulled with pain.

'You think not?' Carrie turned away, her face hidden from her sister. 'I have not known a single woman in Doe Bank give birth without suffering torture. I'm afraid, Emma. I don't want to go through that...'

'What do you not want to go through, Carrie?'

Both girls looked sharply towards the door of the bedroom where their mother stood watching them.

66

'I asked you a question, child. What is it you do not want to go through?'

A hint of colour touched Carrie's cheeks and her eyes lowered. 'The pain of childbirth. I ... I'm afraid of...'

Mary Price's faded eyes melted with love as she crossed to where her youngest child stood trembling. 'You need not be afraid, my love.' She looked across the girl's bent head to Emma and her eyes asked forgiveness. 'There is nothing to be feared of. You have been listening to the gossip and dirty talk of the pit bank.'

Held against her mother's breast, Carrie shuddered. 'It is no lie what they say, is it, Mother? I have only to look at Emma and at you to see that. Both of you drinking that ... that brew, while Father and whoever...' She lifted her head, her eyes at once apologetic. 'Emma, I didn't mean...'

'Go downstairs, Carrie.' Mary spoke to one daughter but her eyes stayed fixed on the other. 'Your father will be home soon, go see the meal is not spoiling.'

'No!' Carrie's fingers tightened on her mother's hand. 'I want ... I'm afraid...'

'Afraid?' Mary kissed the soft hair. 'Afraid of the dark? Not my girl! The lamp is lit and your father will be home in a few minutes. He'll let nothing frighten you, he will let no harm come to you.'

Carrie walked slowly from the room, the words echoing in her heart. No harm, Father ... no harm.

'Don't scold Carrie for listening to those

women. She is very young yet, Mother.'

'Arr, she be young and every bit as foolish.' Mary sat beside her daughter. 'But time will put the first right, and with God's help and the love of a good man she will lose her girlish fears. But you, Emma, I never thought you to be so foolish … as to walk through those woods alone.'

Clutching her stomach as breath closed her throat against the hot lash of pain, Emma turned her face to her mother. 'I did not lie willingly with … with the man, Mother. Let heaven be my witness, I did not!'

'You don't have to tell me that, I know you would never do such a thing.' Taking her daughter in her arms, Mary touched her lips to the pale shining hair. Emma was beautiful, far too beautiful for the life Doe Bank would give her, and some man had seen that beauty, used that slender body then thrown her aside. But who was the man? Why had Emma given him no name despite a mother's asking?

'I meant you were foolish in going elsewhere than to Jerusha Paget,' she said, gathering her daughter in her arms.

Pressed close against her, Emma felt the tears squeeze from beneath her closed eyes. 'Jerusha would not give me what she gave to…'

'To me,' Mary finished the sentence quietly.

'I … I had to go to that other house.' She sobbed. 'Jerusha would not help so I had to find someone who would. I had to, Mother. I could not take the risk of carrying Ca – a child. The woman said it would be all over by this time, that there would be no pain…'

'But she was wrong, wrong on both counts. You have seen no blood, have you, Emma?'

Feeling her tremble, Mary's arm tightened. If that man's seed had taken root then there would be no flow of blood despite the potion Emma had drunk. The child would grow and it would be born ... and her daughter would know the shame of it.

'Mother.' Emma lifted a face stained with tears. 'Supposing I am with child? Supposing what that woman gave me does not work, what will happen? Father will not believe I was ... was raped.'

No, Caleb would not believe that. Mary rested her head against her daughter's. Caleb ... the preacher man ... would see only a temptress, a Jezebel, for in his eyes it would be Emma who was to blame.

'We can only wait and see,' she murmured. 'We can only hope.'

Chapter Five

Emma watched her mother leave the bedroom, her wasted body seeming to wince with every step. Carrie had been right, their mother did suffer too many pregnancies, each more painful to end than the last. Surely their father knew why his wife always looked so tired? Why she was regularly confined to her bed with gripe of the stomach? Yes, Caleb Price knew, but it seemed his rantings against the sins of the flesh applied only to women.

If he should discover *her* sin... Emma felt her blood turn cold. There would be no pity in him, no forgiveness.

But perhaps he need never know? The pain of the last few hours had seemed to tear her apart. Surely the potion must have done its work?

Even though she was alone in the room, Emma crossed to the corner farthest from the door. Keeping her back discreetly towards the bed, instinctively seeking the only privacy the room afforded whenever her sister was present, she took the folded cloth from between her legs.

It was unmarked! Emma felt despair sweep over her. There was no stain upon it, no trace of blood. Whatever the mixture she had drunk, it had had no effect other than to put fire in her belly.

She stared at the rag. So much pain, so much fear. And all for nothing! If Carver Felton had left her with child, then the child was still inside her.

'*There is a child within you...*'

Emma heard the words in her mind, the words Jerusha Paget had spoken.

'*...a child that will be born into the world...*'

That then was how it would be! A sense of acceptance wrapping about her like a cloak, Emma took a piece of paper from the chest of drawers she shared with Carrie. Wrapping the cloth, she pushed it into the pocket of her skirt. Carver Felton's child would be born into the world but the Feltons would never know.

Downstairs she took the paper-wrapped cloth, thrusting it deep into the fire. Behind her Mary Price's face twisted with sympathy. Her daughter was condemned to a life of sorrow. She would bear her burden alone, with every hand but her mother's and her sister's turned against her, with no hope of a father for the child other than the man who had...

Mary turned away, the bitterness of the rest of that thought stinging her heart like acid. But who was that man? Why would Emma not say his name? Had it been someone she knew, someone who knew her? Suddenly Mary felt a new coldness. Was it a man who already had a wife and children ... a man from Doe Bank?

'Serve the meal.'

Mary glanced up as Caleb strode into the house. Usually he washed away the dirt of the mine before taking his food.

'Serve the meal!' Caleb's narrow features were drawn together with the anger that rang in his voice. 'Serve the meal and then gather your

71

belongings. We be leaving this house afore morning.'

'Leaving?' Mary's startled glance changed to a frown that creased her brow. 'Caleb, I don't understand.'

'Neither do I.' He crossed to the fireplace, staring into the crimson flames. 'He gave no reason, said no cause.'

'Who, Caleb?'

'Who? John Barlow. He be manager of the Topaz. Who else but him tells a man he be finished?'

Who else! Emma felt the blood surge along her veins. The Topaz coal mine belonged to the Feltons. Was this the work of Carver Felton? Not satisfied with raping her, had he raised his hand against her family?

'Finished?' The plates she had taken from the dresser clattering in her shaking hands, Mary stared at her husband. 'You mean, you've been given your tin?'

Turning slowly, Caleb thrust a hand into the pocket of his jacket drawing out a slim rectangular tin box. The coins inside rattled as he threw it down on to the table.

'That be the last we'll get from the Topaz.'

'But what will we do?'

Emma took the plates from her mother's trembling hands, eyes going to Carrie, warning her not to interrupt.

'We will do as the Lord ordains.' Caleb crossed his forehead and chest. 'If it be His will we leave this house, then His will be done.'

It was not the Lord's will. Emma's fingers

tightened on the plates. He had not ordained that her father be robbed of his livelihood. That was Carver Felton's doing.

'But why?' Mary sank down on a chair, eyes riveted to the box. 'You've done your work as well as the next man, so why should John Barlow sack you?'

'I asked him the same,' Caleb answered, 'but he would say naught but that I was finished.'

'Is the Topaz mine to be closed, Father?' Having warned Carrie not to speak, Emma knew she should do the same but the surging in her veins drove the question from her.

Caleb swung his head slowly from side to side. 'Not that I be knowing.'

'Then why lay off the men?' Mary's bewildered question followed her daughter's.

Drawing a long heavy breath, Caleb lowered himself into the only comfortable chair the room boasted, his dust-laden sleeve on the cream cotton arm rest his wife had crocheted. 'There be no laying off,' he said dully, 'I be the only one.'

Her father was the only man being laid off. Emma set each plate in its place on the table, her movements slow and ponderous. The mine was not to be closed, nor was any other miner to lose his job. There could be no other reason: Carver Felton wanted them out of Doe Bank, gone before his brother could return. He would know that the few shillings the women could earn picking coal from the waste heaps would not be enough to keep them. By sacking her father, Carver had rid himself of her in the most effective way. By driving her family from the village.

'I was told at the end of the shift,' Caleb continued to explain. 'Told John Barlow wanted to see me at the mine office. He had my tin ready made up when I got there. Said as I was finished at the Topaz and that I must be gone from this house by the morning. He would say no more, answer no question.'

He did not need to. Emma watched her sister lay knife and spoon beside each plate. It did not take John Barlow to tell the whole of Doe Bank who was behind his action, nor did she need to be told that every man and woman in the village would be asking why – why should Felton's sack just one man? Nor would speculation be limited to that. Once her father was over the shock, once the bewilderment had faded, he would put two and two together. Then he would know without being told. Know she carried Felton's child.

'Gone from this house?' Mary's faded eyes lifted to Emma's. 'Gone before morning. But to where ... and with what?'

Almost as if her words were a challenge, Caleb rose to his feet. The fingers of one hand curling about the lapels of his jacket as they did about the black tail coat he wore to Sunday chapel, he took the stance he always adopted when lay preaching.

'We will follow the Lord's guidance.' He lifted his hand towards the ceiling. 'He will provide.'

'The Lord will provide?'

Mary pushed herself to her feet, taking the pot of potatoes from the bracket above the fire, her tired eyes suddenly blazing like the coals at its centre.

'Like He has provided for us up until now? Will

74

He give us another hovel to live in, another plate of boiled potatoes for a meal!'

'Speak not against the Lord lest He lift His hand against thee!' Caleb's face darkened, anger turning his voice to thunder.

'No, speak not against the Lord. Nor against any man. A woman can say nothing against one of them, not a husband nor a father ... nor one who lies with a woman he has not wed!'

The silence that fell over the room was like a living thing, touching each of them with numbing fingers, creeping into ears and mouths, holding them in its own embrace.

Beside the table Emma felt the world stop turning.

'What gives you reason to speak such filth?' Caleb's stony glance settled on his wife.

'No reason. I ... I mean...'

'Be careful to speak the truth.' He lowered his hand. 'What prompted you to speak of a man lying with a woman he has not wed?'

'I ... I was angry.' Mary dropped the pot on to the hob, a flush rising to her cheeks.

Caleb's eyes glittered with the promise of righteous anger. 'That can be no cause for uttering filth, there is more to your words than anger. Speak, woman, for I will know. And remember, the Lord will not be mocked with lies.'

'I speak no lie!' Mary's head came up, all the bitterness of her hard-lived years burning in her eyes. 'A woman has no say against a man. Her life belongs to one or other of them from the moment she is born. She must ask his permission for this and for that, she is not allowed a mind or

75

a voice of her own. But a man need ask no permission of her. Not to take the money she might earn, not to do that which places a child in her body...'

'Enough!' Caleb raised his hands to his ears, his eyes closing. 'To speak such evil is to know such evil.' Opening his eyes again with dramatic slowness he glared at Mary. 'These thoughts are placed in your mind by Satan, his are the ways of wickedness. You have given yourself to his murmurings. To think such evil is to flout the teaching of the Lord, to go against His commandment...'

'No!' Her voice was sharp in denial. 'The teaching of the Lord does not state that a woman exists simply for a man's use!'

'"From Adam did God take a rib and from it fashion a woman whom he gave to Adam..."'

'As a helpmeet, not as a chattel! You take His words and twist them until they become not His will but yours.'

'And you are using words to take my mind from those that fell from your tongue a moment ago. Words that spoke of a man lying with a woman he has not wed. What woman, Mary Price? Who is the woman you spoke of?'

'There ... there is no such woman.'

'Satan holds your tongue.' He stared at her with a cold, almost calculating stare. 'Do not give him access to your soul, speak no more lies for they will carry you into everlasting damnation. Is that woman you, Mary Price?'

'Me!' Mary's astounded whisper reached into the room.

'"Thou shalt not commit adultery!"' Caleb intoned the words, his eyes relaying an almost fanatical relish with the speaking of each one.

'No. No, a woman must not indulge in fornication.' Mary continued to stare at the man who had ruled every minute of most of her years. 'Though a man, it seems, may practise that very thing as often as he wishes. Sowing his wild oats – is that not what it is called? And he may sow them in any girl he fancies for he does not have the reckoning. *"Thou shalt not covet thy neighbour's goods, neither his ox nor his ass"*.' She laughed, a short cynical sound. 'You must know the quotation, Caleb, you throw them about often enough. But it does not apply to a neighbour's daughter. Man is made in god's image, all things are subject to him. Especially women!'

'You are condemned out of your own mouth.' His hands dropped to his sides. 'A neighbour's daughter can only mean yourself. You are a child of iniquity, a tool of the devil who has tempted some man and caused him to fall.'

'Oh, how predictable!' Mary avoided Emma's restraining hand. 'How very predictable! The man was tempted … there can be no blame upon him, it was the fault of the woman. All *her* fault.'

'Stand away, Emma!' Brushing the air with one hand as if to push her aside, Caleb glared at his wife. 'Stand away from her, do not contaminate your hand by touching that which is evil.'

'Mother isn't evil!' The awfulness of what had been said had held Emma speechless, but as her father lifted his hand the fear that he would strike her mother released her tongue. 'She has done no wrong.'

'Done no wrong?' His glittering eyes were fixed on Emma. 'You call lying with a man who is not her husband doing no wrong?'

'Mother has lain with no man.' Emma took her mother's hand, weaving the fingers into her own.

'It is not she who is the wrongdoer in this house.' Her lips trembling, Carrie stepped forward. 'Her only wrong is in answering you as she has. You do not care to be questioned, do you, Father?'

'"*Honour thy father and thy mother*",' Caleb uttered one of the Biblical quotations that were balm to his soul. 'Carrie, do not disregard the Lord's word, do not speak so to me, keep a silent tongue lest you...'

'She did not mean it,' Emma answered quickly, fearing his anger would turn to Carrie. Things were going to get worse without her sister adding to them.

'She did not mean it, neither did your mother?' Caleb's eyes took on a meaner glint. 'Then why speak as she has, why speak of lying with a man if she has no knowledge of such? Your mother is a fallen woman, she will pay the price of that.' His glance swung slowly to Emma. 'I will have no fornicator under my roof ... she will leave this house!'

'We are all leaving,' Mary said at last. 'You are no longer a tenant of this house, Caleb. When I leave then so do you.'

Full of righteous indignation he had temporarily forgotten that fact. Now with his wife's reminder he cast around for words, but for once

78

his store of Biblical quotations failed him.

'Yes ... yes.' He stumbled over the words. 'We all have to leave, but you will not travel with us. From this day on I have no wife and my daughters have no mother.'

'Then you will have no family at all,' Emma said at her mother's strangled gasp. 'If Mother does not go with you then neither do I. And neither will Carrie.'

'What?' Caleb moved a step forward, his heavy clogs making no sound on the rug his wife and daughters had pegged from clippings cut from worn out clothes. 'You will do as I say, Emma, you and your sister, and I say you will turn your back upon that ... that follower of Satan. Step away from her, do not soil your hand...'

'As the Sadducee and the Pharisee stepped away?' Emma smiled scornfully. 'I see you take my meaning, Father. You are like them. You quote the Scriptures to suit your own ends, but when it comes to charity you are no Good Samaritan.'

'I will not tolerate evil.'

'Nor would you have to, not with Carrie, nor with Mother.' Emma slid an arm about her mother's shoulders as Mary cried out. 'It has to be said so it is as well I say it now. You see, Father, it is as I told you. Mother has not lain with a man ... I have.'

Eyes hard as stone, lips working soundlessly, Caleb slumped forward, his hands palm down on the table, head hanging low between his shoulders.

'It is the truth, Father,' Emma went on quietly. 'Mother is not guilty of that.'

'You!' he whispered. 'I would not have thought that of you.'

'There was no willingness on my part. I was attacked by … by someone while coming home.'

'Attacked?' Caleb glanced at her though he did not straighten up. 'By whom?'

'I … I don't know.' Emma felt the pang of guilt that accompanied the lie. 'It was dark, I could not see his face.'

'Then where?' Caleb's eyes glanced with passionate anger. 'Where did this … attack … take place?'

'In the coppice that borders the Hall.' Emma saw despair flood her mother's face but there was no going back. Her mother must not suffer for what had been done to her.

'Did the man speak?'

What did another lie matter? Telling the truth now would not alter her father's thinking. Emma shook her head.

'Did you scream … run away?'

'I tried but he rode me down.'

'Rode?' Caleb straightened up in the same slow deliberate manner in which he had raised his eyelids. 'The man was on horseback and riding in the coppice of Felton Hall?'

Emma realised her mistake. She had spoken without thinking and Caleb had pounced on her words like a diving hawk.

'There are none ride in these parts except the Feltons, and no visitor to that house would leave by that path, no rider or carriage. Now I see the reason for my being finished at the Topaz. I heard talk of the younger Felton paying you some attention but I dismissed it as tittle-tattle. It seems I was wrong. He has paid you a great deal of attention and now he is feared of being found out. That is why I have been given my tin. Get them all out of Doe Bank, that way none will know of his doings!'

'It wasn't Paul...'

'Not Paul you say?' Caleb caught the lapel of his jacket. The role of inquisitor he enjoyed even more than preaching. 'But you told me you could not identify this man who is supposed to have attacked you? You did not see his face, it was in shadow. You did not hear his voice for he did not speak. How then do you know it was *not* Paul Felton?'

'It wasn't Paul.' Emma's nerves were stretched tight as bow string. 'He would not attack me.'

Caleb's thin mouth seemed to turn in on itself, lips folding away to nothing. 'Why not? Could it be because he did not have to? He did not need to take by force that which was willingly given ... given and enjoyed.'

'No ... no, that isn't true!'

Ignoring Emma's cry, Caleb turned on his wife, seeing her faded eyes widen with fear. 'Did you know of this?'

Fingers twitching at the apron that cover her black skirts, Mary nodded.

'How long?' It rapped the silence like a cane.

'It was...'

'Not you ... neither of you!' Caleb's hand shot up. 'The question was asked of your mother, the answer will be given by her.'

'Mother isn't well.'

Brows drawing together Caleb's eyes alone moved, slithering sideways until they held Emma in their sight. 'I said, your mother will answer. You will not speak until I say.'

'But...'

'Silence!' The hand he had raised in the air shot out his fingers curling before striking Emma a blow across the mouth.

'Stop!' The blow galvanising her into action, Mary was on her feet her own body shielding Emma as she stumbled backward.

'Leave her be, Caleb.' Her voice quite steady now, Mary faced her husband. 'Raise your hand to her no more for if you do, I swear I will kill you.'

'You would be wise to listen, Father. Should Mother lack the courage, I do not. Put so much as one finger on Emma and you will feel this in your heart.' Carrie stepped forward, a large kitchen knife gripped in her hand. But it was the hatred in her eyes that stopped Emma's heart.

'Carrie, don't! Don't make things worse.' Blood pouring from her split lip, Emma tried to take the knife but Carrie pushed her away.

'It would have come to this anyway,' she whispered, eyes fixed on Caleb. 'It would have come to this very soon. You know why, don't you, Father?'

Caleb's hand dropped and his face became suddenly closed his eyes becoming wary. 'Do not break your word. Vows made before the Lord must be kept.'

'Don't bother quoting the Lord to me!' Carrie hissed. 'And don't think to hide behind heaven's shield any longer. It is finished, Father, over. You will never again force yourself on me...'

Standing beside Emma, Mary Price gasped, all the colour draining from her thin face. 'Caleb, no! Tell me, Caleb ... what Carrie has said. It ... it's not true?'

The light of the oil lamp glinting on its blade, Carrie raised the knife higher, holding it like a dagger. 'Tell her, Father!' she said through clenched teeth. 'Tell her. You can say it. You can tell that lie as you have told so many others. As you told me it was God's will a daughter should do as a father asked, that it was her duty to heaven she should please him. Duty...'

She laughed softly and in it Emma heard all the pain and misery of a frightened child. What was it placed so much hate in her sister's eyes, so much loathing in her voice?

'*"Brother will betray brother, and the father his child".*' Carrie laughed again, the sound bubbling harshly from between set lips. 'You see, Father, I too can quote the Scriptures. I know them as well as you do. I learned them while waiting for you in Chapel, learned them in the room you took me to after the congregation had left. I listened and I did as I was told because I believed what you said, but the words you spoke did not come from God, did they Father? They were your words, spoken to hide the evil you did...'

'Carrie ... Carrie, child! There was no wrong...'

'No wrong?' Her voice rising, Carrie slashed at the hand that reached out to her. '*"Thou shalt not commit adultery"*. You told my mother that, but

83

what of yourself, Father? What of your own adultery? Isn't that what it is ... or is there some other term for lying with your own child?'

'Carrie.' His wounded hand dripping blood on to the pegged rug, Caleb's eyes swung wildly from one horror-stricken face to the other. 'She ... she doesn't know what she is saying. Mary – Mary, my dear, the girl is ill, sick in the mind.'

'Not me.' Carrie stepped clear as Emma tried to hold her. 'I'm not the one who's sick, you are. Caleb Price, the preacher man! Spouting the Bible while he rapes his own daughter. Quoting the word of God while he walks with the Devil.'

'That is an evil thing to say, girl.' Caleb drew himself up, eyes piercing, brows downdrawn, his good hand still holding his lapel in his most formidable sermonising attitude. 'Remember the teaching of your Sunday school. *"The man who curses his father or his mother must suffer death!"*'

In the lamplight Carrie's face was sickly pale, only her eyes as they stared at Caleb held any life.

'So be it, Father,' she whispered. 'I curse you. May you be given no peace in this life nor find rest in the next. May the God you preach reject you, may you suffer the torture of the hell you damned me to!'

Bringing the knife streaking downward, Carrie plunged it into her own breast.

Chapter Six

'Carrie ... Carrie, my baby, my little girl.'

Mary's stunned whisper was drowned by Emma's scream as she ran to her sister lying slumped on the floor.

The pain in her mouth not even a memory, she took Carrie in her arms. Her heart racing with fear she looked at the small pale face, the closed lids showing a delicate tracery of carmine veins, the lips very slightly parted; then at the knife, its heavy bone handle rising grotesquely from the ruffles of a white cotton blouse turning rapidly scarlet as blood seeped into it. The knife! Emma stared at it. It should be removed, pulled out, but would doing so harm Carrie even more? It might ... it might kill her!

Her face white, showing all the fear of her whirling thoughts Emma looked to her father. One hand dripping slow drops on to the rug, the other still clinging to his lapel, Caleb stood transfixed, eyes glued to the slight form in Emma's arms.

'Father!' Emma called. 'Father, we must get help.'

But Caleb did not stir, only his lips moved, jerking spasmodically.

'Carrie...' Emma's hand hovered about the knife, the thought of touching it bringing waves of sickness to her throat. 'Carrie, can you hear me, can you speak?'

'Don't bother her now, Emma.' Walking as if in a dream, Mary crossed the room and dropped to her knees beside her daughters. 'Don't wake her, let her sleep … it be better for her to sleep.'

Gently, as if holding a newly born child, Mary took the still form, gathering it close, the blood oozing from the base of the knife seeping into her own blouse.

'Mother, Carrie needs help, we have to get a doctor.'

Cradling her daughter, lifting a hand to stroke the light brown hair then touch the bloodless cheek, Mary answered quietly, 'There be no doctor in Doe Bank.'

'But she has to have help … we must … Father, please!'

The half-crazed scream breaking in on him, Caleb lowered his hand, at the same time taking a step towards them. But as he moved Mary flung up her head. Eyes blazing with a loathing kept hidden for so long, lips drawn back in a snarl over clenched teeth, she glared up at him like a wild animal.

'Don't touch her, preacher man. Don't come near my baby! You won't touch her, you won't touch her ever again with your dirty, sickening hands…'

'Mother, please, we have to think of Carrie. She must have help quickly.'

'She be all right.' Mary rested her lips against the pale forehead. 'She be safe now, she's with her mother. She will always be safe, he won't touch her again.'

86

'Mother, I have to get someone before...' Emma hesitated, fear of what the words held in her mouth meant. 'I ... I'll go and get Mrs Butler.'

'No,' Mary answered, lips brushing her daughter's brow. 'Polly Butler will be no help, nor any other in Doe Bank. Go and fetch Jerusha, she be the one will know what to do.'

'But she lives a mile off, maybe more!'

'And the parish doctor lives more like three miles off. It will take that much longer to bring him, even supposing he would come. Go for her, child.' Mary lifted her head and the look she gave Emma was almost serene. The bitterness and hatred of moments ago were gone and in their place a gentle smile curved her mouth, tenderness lending a soft glow to her eyes. 'Go and fetch Jerusha Paget, she will know what to do. Go, Emma. Now, child.'

Grabbing her shawl from behind the door, Emma glanced once more at her mother still cradling Carrie in her arms; her sister's small face looking even smaller, colourless lids closed over soft brown eyes. A sob breaking from her lips, Emma flung the shawl about her shoulders and ran out under the darkening sky.

'She be dead, Caleb.' Mary's face lifted to her husband's as the door closed behind Emma. 'My girl is dead!'

It seemed that in that fraction of a moment Caleb's fears dropped away, the hunted look leaving his narrow eyes. One hand finding its favourite position about the lapel of his jacket, the other lifted a little higher in the air, he let his head move several times in a slow condemning swing.

'It was her hand plunged in the knife.' He stretched his head back on his neck, eyes lifting to the ceiling. 'But it was the Lord God who guided it there! He will not be mocked nor have His word gainsaid. Whosoever follows not the way of the Lord...'

'Is this the way of the Lord?' Mary hissed, hatred filling her eyes. 'Was it His will you use your own child like a whore!'

His head lowering quickly, Caleb stared at the kneeling woman and when he spoke his voice was icy with warning. 'Think carefully how you speak. *"Judge not so you be not judged".*'

'You hypocrite!' Mary's laughter, a low tormented sound, followed her half-crazed denunciation. 'You bloody hypocrite! Do you think your Bible punching will relieve you of the blame for this? It was your fault, Caleb, your fault my child is dead.'

'Carrie was sick in her mind.' His hand was lowered to his side but his eyes remained narrowed. 'Just as her mother is ill of the same sickness. One that could lead to the madhouse.'

'I hear your threat, Caleb.' Mary stared up at him. 'But it does not frighten me for all of Doe Bank will hear of your treatment of Carrie before I am taken. They will look to their own children, ask themselves how often they were told to stay behind after the service was over. They will talk, Caleb, and word will spread...'

'They will not believe...'

'Oh, they will believe, Caleb. They will believe!'

Pushed out on a long slow breath the words undulated into the quiet lamp-lit room.

His back turned to his wife, Caleb stared into the fire then closed his eyes as the crimson of its flames became the crimson streaks of spreading blood. 'You are sick, Mary, you have been so for some long while.'

'Yes, I have been sick,' she whispered, 'but the sickness I had was not of the mind, it was of the eyes. I made myself blind, Caleb, refused to see what I knew was happening. You and the women you bedded. You see, I know them, I know them all by name. The ones from Doe Bank who think I do not hear their sniggering behind my back. The ones from Lea Brook who came to buy their coal from me in order to stare at the wife of the preacher man. I didn't see your carryings on because I didn't want to see, I was only too glad of your leaving me be, of the rest I got from your pushing and heaving, the relief it gave me from having to suffer the touch of your body on mine. But I did not think … I did not dream you would practise your vile lust on a child!'

Turning slowly, Caleb faced his wife still cradling the girl's body, his cynical smile matching the tone of his voice. 'A child with a sickness of the mind stabs herself and naturally her mother is overwrought. It is understandable she should grab at any excuse for a cause, blame anyone, even the most innocent.'

'Like the preacher man!' Mary spat. 'But there are those who know he is far from innocent, those who know the preacher man for what he truly is. Will they see what I say as an excuse or will they place the blame where it lies?'

'You will say nothing!' The smile fading from his mouth, Caleb took a step forward. 'You will say nothing ... do you hear me?'

Gently, as if lowering a sleeping babe, Mary laid her daughter's body on the ground then rose to her feet. 'I hear you, Caleb, but...'

'There will be no buts!' His eyes blazed. '"*The husband shall be the head of the wife*".'

'No more, Caleb.' Mary swung her head slowly, gaze fixed on his. 'No more of your quoting the book to me, no more of your preaching. You killed my daughter as surely as if you had driven the knife with your own hand and I will make sure every soul you meet from this day on knows of it. No more will you stand and preach the Gospels from the horseblock at Springhead for you will be given no peace in Wednesbury. You will find no rest in Tipton nor in Darlaston nor any place you go. For I will follow you, Caleb, follow all the days of your life, and wherever you pause to speak to any human being my voice will rise above yours. "*Judgement is mine, I will repay...*" This time I quote the Lord's word, but only to deny it. I take your judgement unto myself, Caleb, and I will be the one to repay.'

'Mary.' Allowing his voice to soften, Caleb reached out towards his wife. 'Mary, my dear, you do not mean what you are saying. To speak such words would ruin our lives...'

'Ruin *our* lives?' Mary's laugh was hoarse and empty. 'You mean *your* life, Caleb. *Mine* is already ruined. You want me to keep silent, let you go on with your filthy ways as if nothing had happened. But it has happened, Caleb. My child is dead and the only way you can keep your sordid life is to take mine as you took hers, to kill me as you have her. Only by ending my life can you hold on to yours.'

His hands hanging loosely at his sides Caleb stared at the woman threatening to take from him all that he valued. How could he face the people of Doe Bank if she were heard? How could he attend Chapel or speak the Lord's word in the streets? Turning away, he walked slowly into the tiny scullery, returning just as slowly, a coil of heavy rope held in his fingers.

'I cannot listen to your words, Mary.' He lifted the rope waist-high. 'I cannot listen to you defile my name.'

She did not even glance at the rope but kept her eyes on his face, cold condemning eyes that held no trace of forgiveness. 'You could defile our daughter, but I must not defile your name in the telling of it. Well, I will tell of it, Caleb, in every place you go.'

'No, Mary, I cannot allow that.' He uncurled a length of the rope, holding it stretched between his hands.

Her eyes steady on his, Mary showed no fear. Her voice soft, she answered, 'Then you know what you must do.'

'It will be on your head.' Caleb uncoiled the rest of the rope. 'You will answer at the Day of Judgement.'

'Be that day brought by God or man, I will be ready.'

His movements silenced by the clipped rug

91

beneath his feet, Caleb took a chair from beside the table. Throwing one end of the rope over a large meat hook set in a beam above the chair he tied both ends into a loop.

'This will be your own doing, Mary,' he said as he lifted the noose toward her.

Unflinching, she mouthed softly, 'My own doing, Caleb.'

The quiet ticking of the clock the only sound, he glanced at the chair. 'I ask you one more time, Mary. Do not speak of what the child said.'

'The Devil take you, Caleb,' she murmured. 'The Devil take you into Hell!'

A cold smile re-curving his thin lips Caleb stepped on to the chair, his eyes as he looked down at her demanding she apologise, beg him to stand down. Slowly he slipped the noose over his head.

'Welcome to judgement, Caleb!' Stepping forward, Mary kicked the chair away.

The pain in her side making her gasp, Emma stumbled on toward Plovers Croft. Jerusha might not be at her cottage, it could be she was somewhere tending a sick child, people often came to ask the old woman for her help, but would her herbs and remedies aid Carrie? And supposing she were not at home? Emma's glance lifted in the direction of the town beyond Plovers Croft, the stacks of its foundries and the winding wheels of its coal mines rising black beneath the fiery light that flooded the bowl of the sky as furnace doors were opened. If Jerusha were not home then she must go on to Wednesbury. She must find the parish doctor and bring him to her sister.

'Don't let Carrie die. Please, God, don't let Carrie die.' The words repeating themselves over and over, Emma ran on in the darkness.

The throbbing in her side increasing with every step, her chest tight from dragging in every breath, Emma sobbed as she came within sight of the Croft and saw the pale gleam of a lamp at Jerusha's window.

Inside the house Jerusha Paget listened for the girl she knew this night would bring. She had been told what would take place, the words whispered silently into her mind. Told of the death of Mary Price's younger child and of the evil that had caused it. Jerusha drew her shawl closer about her shoulders as she stared at pictures in the fire. Pictures of a preacher man, his hand raised, mouth opening in endless screams as the flames of everlasting torment licked his flesh. Yes, she had been told Emma would come and she would return with her to Doe Bank, but in the silence that had closed off the world, the silence in which only its own words were heard she had been told. There would be no such relief for Emma Price. Only sorrow awaited her at Doe Bank, and yet more beyond it. But the face Jerusha turned to Emma as she stumbled in through the door showed none of what she knew.

'Jerusha!' Emma clutched at the throbbing pain in her side. 'Jerusha, come ... come quickly, Carrie is...'

'Be still, child, catch your breath.'

'No, there is no time,' Emma gasped. 'Mother said to ... to fetch you. It's ... it's Carrie.'

'Jerusha Paget knows what it is brings you here. I know what it is has happened to your sister and that your mother sent you to bring me.'

She reached for the basket she kept ever packed with a mixture of the herbs she picked from the heath. She could have added that she knew also that Carrie was beyond human help as Caleb now was, but she kept her silence, saying only that Emma must rest for a few minutes.

'Bide you still, child,' she said when Emma protested again. 'Where be the good if you go collapsing from fatigue when we be halfway to Doe Bank? What's to be done will be done. You running yourself into the ground will serve no purpose.'

Pouring milk into a cup, she handed it to Emma then placed the small linen cover back over the jug, her fingers pausing a moment to touch the green glass beads. It was a long walk to the house of Mary Price, and the journey would be fruitless, but she would make it just the same. And when it was done? Jerusha looked about the room, the fire barely warming it, the lamp only a focus for the shadows. She had spent the greater part of her life in this house, it was from this room they had carried her husband Jacob. She whispered the name in her heart. They had loved each other for so long and now he was gone, laid to rest in the churchyard of St John's at the lower end of Wednesbury. His journey of life was finished and she would have stepped across that threshold into eternity with him; but not yet, the silence had told her, there was work yet for her to do before the reward of joining Jacob again.

Laying the basket across her arm as Emma finished her drink, Jerusha turned towards the door. She would not return to this house, that too the silent voice had told her, but it held no sorrow for her. Glancing around at the cheap figurines beside the clock on the mantel, at the neatly made bed, the lamp burning at the window, she smiled softly. She would take nothing of those, all she wanted of Plovers Croft she carried in her heart. She stepped out into the blackness of the night but her soul was filled with light, the light of Jacob's smile.

'Welcome to Judgement, Caleb!' Mary watched the figure swing slowly at the end of the rope. He had kicked and jerked for fully a minute before the gurgling in his throat had finally stopped, fully a minute in which her heart had laughed. 'What of your sermon now, preacher man? Spout your quotations before the Judgement Seat and may you receive all you deserve!'

Going into the scullery she returned with an enamel basin and a candle stood in a chipped saucer. Setting them beside the body of her daughter, she fetched the kettle from the hob and filled the bowl with hot water. Lighting the candle with a spill from the jar inside the brass fender, she reached upward pulling a cloth from the line strung above the fireplace, her body brushing against that hanging from the beam, setting it swinging a little faster.

'Dance, Caleb,' she laughed, reaching up again

95

for a nightgown set to air on the line. 'Dance now with Him you have walked with all these years. Dance, Caleb, dance with the Devil!'

The creak of the rope her only answer, Mary knelt beside the body of her daughter. All emotion gone from her she grasped the knife, feeling no horror as she drew it from Carrie's chest. Then, struggling with the stiffening limbs she stripped the clothing from her.

'You shall go clean into your reckoning, my darling,' she murmured as she washed the cooling body. 'There will be no mark upon you as you stand before the face of the Lord, no stain of the filth of Caleb Price.'

Drawing the white cotton nightgown over the still head, adjusting the sleeves over each arm, the length of it over the feet, Mary fastened each linen-covered button, closing away the hole where the knife had entered the smooth flesh.

'Don't be frightened, my baby ... my little girl.' She stroked the soft hair, smiling as she saw the light from the candle flame flicker over its curls.

The smile still about her mouth she carried the basin back to the scullery, emptying the contents and rinsing the bowl with fresh water from a lidded bucket set beneath a window. Once more in the tiny living room she folded the cloth and set it back on the line, then taking the paraffin lamp she tipped the oil over the clipped rug, splashing some over the swinging body and spreading the last of it over herself.

'Don't be afraid, Carrie...'

Squatting beside her daughter, she gathered the body into her arms.

'…you won't be alone, my darling. Mother will be with you. Mother will hold you…'

Taking up the lighted candle Mary threw it on to the oil-soaked rug.

'…yes, Mother will be with you.'

Pressing her lips to her daughter's head she stared at the body of Caleb already half engulfed in rising flames.

'Welcome to Judgement, Caleb,' she murmured as the fire closed about her too. 'Welcome to Judgement!'

Emma could not hurry the old woman, darkness on the heath was treacherous; well as you might think you knew it, danger always awaited the careless or unwary. Emma held the basket she had taken from Jerusha, her other hand supporting the woman's elbow. Should she trip it could well mean broken bones. Yet every fibre of Emma cried out for her to run, to go on ahead of Jerusha. Every vessel in her blood screaming that Carrie was lying injured … that Carrie might die.

Walking beneath the great star-strewn canopy of night, Jerusha sensed the turmoil within the girl at her side. But even though she knew the strongest of legs and the fleetest of feet could not get them to Doe Bank in time to save the girl's family it would be heaping cruelty upon cruelty to tell her so.

Beneath the wrapping of her shawl Jerusha sighed. There was so much evil in the world, so much unhappiness, and the girl who walked beside her would have more than her share of it.

'I didn't see what she held.' Emma spoke suddenly, as if words trapped within her had at last found a way of escape. 'Not until it was in her hand. And then...' She swallowed a sob. 'Carrie was always so quiet, so timid, but tonight... It was when Father raised his hand. She must have thought he was about to strike Mother. I never saw such a look on Carrie's face before, it was so full of...'

'Hush, child.' Jerusha drew her shawl more firmly about her head. 'Keep your mind on where Jerusha be placing her feet, old eyes are no match for darkness.'

Jerusha spoke out of sympathy. She would save the girl the pain of speaking, at least for tonight, for there was torment lying ahead across the heath. Old eyes were no match for the night but Jerusha Paget did not need the light of day to see what was happening at Doe Bank.

'Mother will be so frightened,' Emma went on, despite Jerusha's words. 'So worried for Carrie. She was so pale and there was so much blood. Oh, Jerusha, will ... will she be all right? It would kill Mother if...'

'Do you trust me, child?' The question was simple, rising quietly out of the darkness.

'Trust you... Jerusha, you must know that everyone at Doe Bank trusts you. Mother would have no one else to look at Carrie...'

'I did not ask if everyone at Doe Bank gave me their trust, I asked you, Emma Price. Do you trust me?'

The potion! The potion that other woman had given her, Jerusha must know of it. But how? Beneath the cover of darkness Emma felt the flush of colour rise to her face. But Jerusha did not always need to see nor yet to be told to know of a happening, every woman on the pit bank said so, said that Jerusha Paget had the sight, that she could see that which was forbidden from others; and hadn't she, Emma, already had proof of that when she'd asked Jerusha for a potion? She had not spoken Carver Felton's name, but the old woman had known it, and now she was questioning Emma's trust in her.

'Yes,' Emma replied, surprised at the relief that one word engendered in her. 'Yes, I trust you.'

The heath receded from beneath her feet, all around the night sounds faded into silence, one that engulfed Jerusha, lifting her into herself, a vast light-filled silence of which she was the heart.

Coming to a halt she stood with her head slightly tilted and in the moonlight her face seemed to lose all signs of age, all marks of a life of hardship and worry, a look of such serene peace taking its place, such quiet beauty, that looking at her, Emma caught her breath.

'Mary Price feels no fear.' Jerusha's lips barely moved, her words no more than a breath on the wind. 'She knows no anguish. She is with her daughter, the child of her body, they are together. There is no pain. The sting of the knife is gone...'

The breath in Emma's throat hardened like a stone. She had not spoken of the knife.

'...the mother holds the child in her arms and they are comforted. But the eyes of Mary Price turn to the daughter who stands now on the heath, a daughter who will go on alone. She stretches out a hand to that child, a hand that will be felt whenever sorrow seems too heavy to bear. She will always be close, and though your eyes may not see, your heart will hear.'

Overhead a bank of cloud swallowed the moon and in its shadow Jerusha lowered her head. Ignoring the past moment she began to walk on. Emma, still lost in what she had said, had to skip to catch up.

Jerusha's words on that other night had proved true. She *had* gone to someone else to seek a potion that would rid her of the child Carver Felton may have left within her, but it had not worked; there had been a great deal of pain but nothing else. The child was still there, just as Jerusha had predicted.

Emma walked on, forcing her steps to keep pace with Jerusha's.

All had gone as she had said, so why should the words she'd spoken a moment ago be any less true? Carrie and her mother were comforted, Carrie was in no pain, everything would be all right. In the near distance the crimson glow of an opened furnace outlined the rise of Doe Bank. A few minutes more and she would be with her mother. Cresting the last of the rise Emma stood stock still.

Then, her mouth opening in an agonised scream, she ran towards her burning home.

Chapter Seven

Carver Felton adjusted the pearl-coloured silk cravat. His brother had gone to Birkenhead as he had been ordered. His little brother! Carver smiled at his own reflection. Trust Paul to do as he was told, he always did. He was in Birkenhead, and from there would be sent somewhere else, and from there to the next place, until he had got the Price girl out of his system. Not that his brother could be entirely blamed should that take some time. Carver thrust a gold tie pin into the silk. From what he could remember of that face swathed in shadow she was quite a pretty little thing, and the hair... His fingers fondled the silk. The hair had been the silver of moonlight. Had she been of their class, with the same breeding, she would have made an acceptable wife. Supposing, of course, she brought money. But she had neither of those things. All she had was her beauty. Slipping his arms into his coat, Carver smoothed it over his hips. But, by God, she had that, and for many a man it would have been enough. But it was not enough, not enough for her to become a Felton.

Turning from the mirror he glanced towards the door of his dressing room.

'Excuse me, Mr Felton, sir, but Barlow is downstairs asking to see you. Will I tell him to call back tomorrow?'

Coming into the large well-furnished bedroom Carver drew his gold hunter from his waistcoat pocket, glancing at the time before replacing the watch.

'I have a few minutes yet, I am not due at Miss Holgate's until nine-thirty. Show him into the study and say I will be with him directly.'

'Very good, sir.'

Carver continued to stare at the door as his manservant withdrew. Barlow. That meant the job was done, or at least it had better be if the manager wanted to hold on to his own.

'Good evening, Mr Felton.'

John Barlow shuffled his feet nervously as Carver entered the room.

'Is it done?' He ignored the greeting.

'I did as you instructed, sir.'

'And?' Carver demanded.

'And … and nothing, Mr Felton,' Barlow stammered, uncomfortable at being in Felton Hall, and wary of the man who stood glaring at him with eyes black as the coal his miners ripped from the earth. 'What else could there be?'

'The man Price, did he say anything?' Carver grabbed a pen from the desk, twisting it irritably between his fingers. 'Did he ask why?'

Barlow touched the palm of one hand to the edge of his jacket with a quick nervous movement. Why had he been told to report here to the house? Why didn't Felton wait until his next visit to the mine … in fact, why ask for a report at all? He had given men their tins before and never asked how they reacted, so why this time? What was so special about Price?

102

'Arr Mr Felton, he asked, but like I told him, the owner don't 'ave to give no reason. You said as 'e was finished at the Topaz and that was all the reason necessary. I 'ope I did right, sir?'

'Of course you did right!' Carver threw the pen on to the desk, watching it roll the width before dropping off the edge. He gave no man a reason for his actions, explained himself to nobody. Yet the feeling of guilt that had resolved itself into anger persisted as he asked, 'The man ... this Price ... you are sure he was the right one?'

John Barlow swallowed, the Adam's apple of his throat moving visibly. A man needed to take care in his dealings with the like of Carver Felton. One wrong word was all it would take, just one wrong word, and he would be in the same boat as Price was in now and the bugger would sink just as fast.

'You said as the one I was to finish was the one living up along Doe Bank.' Barlow hesitated, then when Carver made no answer went on, 'Well, the preacher man lived there...'

'Preacher man?' Carver looked up from watching the pen.

'That be the name folk have given him, though 'e were baptised Caleb ... Caleb Price.'

'So why the title? Is the man a priest?'

'Caleb Price ain't never been ordained, he be no true priest.'

Carver's brows drew together and beneath the branched gasolier the twin streaks of silver shone among the darkness of his hair.

'So where did the name come from?'

His throat still working, John Barlow studied the face of his employer. So many questions about a man he had never mentioned until yesterday, questions that did not come from an easy mind. But why the preacher man? What was it about him that so disturbed Carver Felton?

'Caleb Price fancies himself as something of a lay preacher. He sometimes takes a service down at the Chapel and teaches a bit of Sunday school for the young 'uns, though I've not heard him myself, being a Church of England man. But I 'ave heard him spouting off to the men at the mine. A real Bible thumper is Price, I reckon he quotes the Scriptures more often than did any of the Disciples.'

'The preacher man.' Carver mulled over the name. 'Interesting. Did he preach you a sermon when you gave him his tin?'

Barlow shook his head, though his glance as it rested on Carver was keen as before. 'Not as such, sir, though 'e did say as how no man acted of his own accord. That all was done according to the will of God.'

The will of God. Carver smiled as the mine manager left. Or the will of Carver Felton.

'I thought at first it was a furnace being opened.' Emma sat in a neighbour's house. It had taken two men to drag her there, to prevent her from racing into the burning house, and all the time she had screamed her mother's name.

'It looked so beautiful, the crest of the hill black against the red glow ... how could I?' She sobbed into her hands. 'How could I have thought it beautiful when it was my own home that was burning?'

104

'You were not to know, wench.' Polly Butler spoke soothingly as she brewed a third pot of tea. Tea and sympathy, that was all anybody could offer at a time like this. Emma had come flying over the heath, hair and skirts spread on the wind, her screams like those of the damned; it had only been the quick action of Sam Davis that stopped her racing into the flames. Now he stood guard at the door lest she try to run back. But there was nothing to run back to except a smouldering ruin.

'Come on, try to drink a drop of tea.' Polly placed a cup before Emma. 'It'll help you feel better.'

Nothing could do that. Emma closed her fingers over her face, wanting to hide herself away, to hide from the awful reality, to shut out the scene that seemed to be painted on her eyes. She would never feel better, never forget the events of this night.

Getting up from the stool Polly Butler had drawn to the fire, Jerusha drew back the cloth cover she had placed over her basket. Taking out a small dark blue glass bottle she sprinkled a few drops of clear liquid into the cup, a faint shake of her head warding off the other woman's enquiry.

'Drink this down, Emma.'

Jerusha's tone was firmer than that of Polly, she was used to handling the sorrow of those who had lost loved ones; only her own sorrow, that of parting with Jacob, only that did she find hard to deal with. But deal she must until her time came.

With the obedience of a small child Emma took the cup. 'How could it have happened?' She looked into Jerusha's face. 'What could have caused it?'

Jerusha could answer each of those questions but now was not the time. That moment would come, Jerusha felt such pity for the girl, but when it did it must be in a moment of comfort. To speak the truth now would only add to the burden of sorrow that was crushing the girl's heart. For now that terrible truth must remain locked inside Jerusha's own, she would tell no one what the silence had revealed to her.

Taking the cup as Emma finished her drink, Polly glanced at Jerusha. 'The wench best stay with us, my lads can bed down in the scullery...'

'But I can't take your sons' room!' Emma was almost on her feet as she spoke.

'Well, you can't go back to...' Polly checked herself, a faint blush rising fast to her cheeks. 'You can't go back to Jerusha's place again to-night, it be overfar for her to walk.'

Catching Polly's eye Jerusha nodded, approving the quickness of the woman's recovery.

'And you certainly ain't going to sleep under no hedge. It be best you both bed down here in this house. Unless, of course, you would rather go to another in Doe Bank? Every door be open to you.'

Jerusha placed her empty cup on the table, nodding as Polly held up the tea pot offering a second cup. 'That we be aware of and both of us be grateful. Thank you for your kindness, Polly Butler, we will bide the night beneath this roof.'

'But your sons...' Emma felt suddenly weary, her protest fading as tiredness swept over her.

106

'My lads will take no harm from bedding in the scullery or here on the hearth afore the fire. 'Tain't nothing they haven't done many a night gone. Now you just sit you there a minute longer while I puts clean sheets on the bed and then we'll have you tucked up.'

Taking her cup, Jerusha sipped the tea, eyes following Polly as she drew two spotless white sheets from one of the long drawers set beneath a tall cupboard built into an alcove alongside the black-leaded fireplace. Still folded as the day they were bought, she knew they had never yet seen use for these were the burying sheets. Kept by every family, even if the buying of them meant going without food; they were the sheets that would cover bed and body whenever death struck the family. Using them now was a measure of the woman's pity for the young girl, for it meant the sheets could no longer be kept for the purpose they were intended. Pennies would be scratched and scraped together, set aside in some secret place until there were enough to buy another pair that would be laid away for 'the burying'.

'I should have been with her. With both of them.' Tears rose fresh and hot and Emma brushed them with her fingers. 'Mother must have been so terrified. If only I had been there … I should have been there … I should not have left them. It's my fault … oh, God! It's all my fault.'

'No fault lies with you, child.' Jerusha moved close, arms going about the sobbing girl. 'It was not meant for you to be in that house.'

'But I could have helped them, helped Father

107

get Mother and Carrie away from...'

'No, child.' Jerusha laid a hand on Emma's head, holding it against her. 'Believe me, you could not have helped your father. Nor either of them.'

Sobs choking her throat, Emma drew away to look into the face of the woman who held her. 'But how do you know? How can you be so sure?'

'How? That I can only answer vaguely, child. I can only say it is given to me to know, and I am sure because never once have I been given that which proved other than true.'

'Then who is it gives you this knowledge ... where does it come from?'

Above Emma's head, Jerusha stared into the fire. Flames tinged with blue and gold suddenly shot high, losing themselves in the black void of the chimney.

'I ask no questions as to who or where. I ask none for myself and will ask it for no other. The truth guides Jerusha Paget, that is all I need to know.'

'But...'

'No, child. Ask nothing more tonight.' Jerusha directed her glance to Polly as she came into the room. 'Go with Polly now and try to sleep. The days ahead will have time enough in them to ask your questions.'

Time enough to ask her questions. Jerusha watched the two women, one with a helping arm about the waist of the other, leave the room, then turned her eyes once more to the fire. But for all their length they would not hold time enough for her to find the answers. Emma Price would carry the mark of this night ever in her heart. Forgive and forget. How often had that been preached? Time! Jerusha stared at the dancing flames. Time would bring about the first, but all eternity would not achieve the second.

Emma Price would forgive, but she would not forget!

'Are they really going to put money into that scheme of yours?'

Cara Holgate raised one skilfully plucked eyebrow, her fingers toying provocatively with the ribbons of a silk velvet bed coat.

'Do you doubt it?'

The man lying with arms folded beneath his dark head, his naked limbs gleaming against the deep peach of the bed cover, smiled at her, confidence visible in every line of him.

'No.' Cara pulled a silk ribbon, a slow enticing movement that was not lost on her companion. 'I don't doubt it, knowing you as I do. I do not doubt you could achieve anything ... once your mind was set on it.'

His smile curving the corners of his well-shaped mouth, he watched the long slender fingers toy with a second ribbon. 'You always did show sense as well as taste, Cara.'

'Thank you.' She drew the tie long and slow, holding it outstretched, green-gold eyes regarding him from beneath a sweep of dark lashes. 'But you forgot to add influence. I have a great deal of that ... to use in any way I please.'

'And which way pleases you?'

Every movement sensuous, Cara let the tie

drop from her fingers then reached up to pull the
diamanté comb from her hair, the fall of it
covering her shoulders in black silk.

'That depends very much upon you.'

'On me, Cara?'

Shrugging the bed coat from her, letting it slide
down her arms, she stepped away, leaving it a
heap of pale rose on the floor.

'Yes.' She smiled, showing perfect teeth. 'I have
a lot of friends, some of whom are your business
associates.'

'And some of whom are very much subject to
your ... influence!'

'Very much, my dear.' Every line of her
caressed by the expert cut of a matching silk
nightgown, Cara crossed to her dressing table
carelessly throwing the comb down on it. 'It
would be very easy to persuade them that a
certain project was too risky for them to commit
their money.'

Stretched out on the bed the man watched her
every move, his smile hiding the cold anger
beginning to gather in his stomach.

'But a little of my money would persuade you
in a different direction, is that it? You are a
woman of many talents, Cara. Is extortion yet
another of them?'

'Proportion.' The smile played easily about her
painted mouth but Cara Holgate's eyes narrowed
like a hunting cat's. 'I think that is a much better
word. I use my influence to ensure you get what
you want, and you give me what I want – and that
is a proportion of the enterprise.'

'And what is your idea of a proportion of the

enterprise?' Lifting himself on one elbow, the soft light of candles caught the twin streaks of silver receding from his brow, and now Carver Felton did not smile.

'What if I tell you your little proposal has come too late, Cara? That the business is agreed.'

Coming closer to the bed, the light displaying the body beneath the almost transparent silk, she smiled down at him. 'Then I would have to tell you you were a fool, but I do not think you are. You know the men you are dealing with, Carver, you know they would not think twice about breaking an agreement not with you or any other man should it suit them.'

'But the agreements they make with you are not broken, I take it?'

'No, Carver.' She shook her head, familiar with the effect of candlelight on her sable hair. 'Not if they wish their pleasures to go undisturbed. You see, my dear, it is not just men who can be influenced. A word in a wife's ear ... you follow, I am sure?'

His black eyes sweeping the length of her, Carver allowed the smile to return, but the anger was still there. 'Would that not achieve a negative result?'

Slender fingers going to her throat, Cara slipped the tiny mother of pearl buttons through each buttonhole, pausing at one set into the fitted waist. 'If you mean, would I lose the friendship of the men I ... influence, then the answer is no. They take their pleasure much too seriously for that. A present of – shall we say, considerable value would help me change my mind.'

'And *my* present, what is the considerable value of that to be?'

Fingers toying with the last button; green-gold eyes glinted. 'Twenty per cent.' She said it softly. 'A twenty per cent share in your canal project.'

Carver lay back on the bed, his arms going back behind his head. 'That *is* a present of considerable value. Do you think your talents worthy of so much?'

She laughed, a sound as smooth as the silk gown. 'Do you?'

'We could find out,' he answered. 'Or is that button the only thing you're going to play with tonight?'

Slipping the last button Cara parted the gown, revealing taut white breasts. 'Not the only thing, Carver.' She let the gown slide, her eyes fixed on his. 'Not the only thing.'

Kneeling beside him on the bed, she traced a long slow finger from his throat down across his chest and stomach, a smile of satisfaction curving her lips at the jerking of his flesh. Her hand continuing its downward path, she bent over him, brushing his chest with her breasts, mouth following the movement of her finger. Her tongue touching the base of his erect penis, she murmured, 'Isn't this worth twenty per cent Carver?'

'Let's seal the bargain.' His body curving in one swift agile movement, he caught her shoulders, drawing her upright and at the same time rolling her on to her back.

The silken laugh rolling in her throat, she lifted her arms, spreading her legs. 'The candle,' she whispered, 'shall we leave it burning?'

Raising himself on his hands, Carver stared into her green-gold eyes. 'No.' He blew at the flame burning at the bedside. 'I don't need a candle to find my way into you.'

Driving deep into her, he smiled in the darkness. Neither would he need one to find a way of destroying her!

Riding home across the heath, Carver let his mind wander over the preceding few hours. Cara Holgate had satisfied his appetites many times, but tonight... He glanced at the coppice rising tall and black against the skyline ... tonight there had been none of the pleasure he normally took in her soft white flesh, that hair smelling of pomade and French perfume. Tonight there had been only lust. The woman beneath him had been Cara Holgate; the body he thrust into, supple and willing, was Cara's; the cries soft against his ear, her cries. But in his mind he had lain with another, very different woman. The perfume in her hair had been that of the flowers of the heath; the flesh of her body, though soft and white, had been taut as a bowstring as she fought against him; there had been no willingness in that union and her cries had not been those of pleasure. Yet it was her, that Doe Bank wench, who filled his brain, memories of the feel of her beneath him, not the body of his mistress, had brought tonight's fulfilment. And the thought of her had dominated his nights with Cara for almost a month.

Why was that? Why had Cara's face become *her*

face as she clambered on to the bed beside him? Why had raven hair softened to pale gold and the eyes that smiled down at him become the blue of wild hyacinths?

Guilt? Carver glanced again at the thicket. Was he feeling guilty for raping that girl? The thought brought a cold smile to his mouth. The very idea was ridiculous. Why should he feel guilty, why should he feel anything at all? The girl was nothing, nothing but a pit bank wench!

But it was the pit bank wench who regularly found her way into his thoughts. Irritated by the admission, he touched his heels to the animal's flanks, adjusting easily to its quickened step.

He had taken her not for pleasure nor from lust. He had used her to serve his own purpose, as from tonight he would Cara.

In the shadowed dawn the smile faded, his face becoming hard as tempered steel.

Cara had taken one step too many. She had allowed her own lust, that for money, to override her judgement. She had thought to sink her greedy fingers into his business.

'A mistake, Cara,' he whispered, 'and one that could prove fatal.'

Carver glanced upward. Sliding from behind a patch of cloud the moon spread a silver canopy over the heath. Carver smiled.

One step too many!

Chapter Eight

'Will you be taking the girl to live with you in your house?'

Her two boys settled to sleep in the scullery, Polly Butler brewed yet another pot of tea.

Jerusha watched tea follow milk into the cheap heavy cups; none of the fine china of the moneyed classes would be found in Doe Bank, here it was thick platter plates and cups, all that mining families could afford, and some of them could not even afford those. She thought of the many times she had seen jam jars used as drinking cups when she had visited those without a penny to buy tea to put in them; the jars themselves taken from the rear of a grocer's shop when he was not looking.

'Will you be letting her make a home with you?' Polly looked up from pouring tea.

'I have no home.' Jerusha took her cup. 'Emma Price isn't the only one whose home this night has taken.'

Polly set the large enamel teapot heavily on the hob then turned back to the woman beside her table. 'No home! What do that mean? I don't understand.'

'It takes no understanding.' Jerusha sipped the hot liquid, holding it against her tongue. 'Mary Price's house was taken by fire, as mine is taken by a landlord. Hers is a smoking ruin this night.

115

The next will see mine tumbled to the ground.'

Polly stared at a face time had dealt with as cruelly as her own. 'You turned out! When was you told of this? Did the bailiff call at the other houses in Plovers Croft or be you the only one?'

'No bailiff came.'

Polly held her own thick pottery cup between both hands. She knew enough of Jerusha Paget not to ask how, if no bailiff had ordered her from her home, she knew it was to be so. And how she knew it would be demolished so soon afterwards. If Jerusha said it would happen then happen it would.

'And I won't be the only one put from house and home. Before three days be gone by Plovers Croft will be nothing but stones in the dust.'

'But what will you do?' Polly's voice rang with concern. 'Where will you go, do you have family anywhere?'

Her lips against the rim of the cup, Jerusha shook her head. 'I have no family, there was only Jacob and he be gone now.'

'Then you and the girl must both bide here. There will be a place on the Bank for you both.'

'I can speak only for myself.' Jerusha stared at the fire, her eyes seemingly drawn to its glowing depths. 'For the girl I cannot answer, that she must do for herself, but I fear Doe Bank will never be home to her again.'

'Then where?' Polly was genuinely concerned. 'It ain't right for her to go wandering off alone, not every place be as 'ospitable or as safe for a young wench as Doe Bank.'

Safe! Jerusha kept her glance at the crimson

116

coals. She could tell Polly Butler just how safe this village had been for its young girls, but that danger was gone and no good could come of raking over the ashes.

'Emma Price be able to suit herself, Polly. She be without parents to say what she must do and there be no guardian set over her. That leaves her free to follow what she will. But I reckon a lot of sense to that girl. She may find life hard but she will do nothing foolish. Nothing Mary Price would take exception to, God rest her soul.'

'Amen to that.' Polly crossed herself piously. 'Poor Mary, not to leave out the other two, that young daughter and Caleb. Lord, what an end! What away to go! Burned to death in your very own house. What do you reckon to be the cause of that fire?'

Jerusha sipped again at the hot sweet tea. She'd known the question would come and had known the answer she gave would be a lie.

The silence had come in the late afternoon wrapping about her like a cocoon, closing off the world about her, lifting her into its own heart, into a floating endless space of golden light. Then the soundless voice had come, speaking formless silent words; words that nevertheless rang in her mind with the clarity of a bell. She would leave this house, it had told her, leave it for the last time for soon after it would be demolished. Then it had spoken of the deaths of three people, of a fire set by a woman to take from the earth all mark of the evil done by a man. One who had abused his own child and those of the people to whom he preached.

The preacher man! The words had been said over again and then the light had faded and with it the silence.

Mary must have found him out. That was her reason for watching him hang himself. She could not live with the knowledge of what he had done, not live with Carrie's pain or her own, so she had sent Emma far enough away so she would not witness that to which Mary set her hand.

'Who knows what set that house to burning?' Jerusha answered Polly. 'A red hot glede dropping from the grate on to the rug, a fallen candle, there be many things could be the cause.'

Arr, many things. Polly kept a still tongue. But with three waking people in the house, a red hot cinder or a fallen candle would have small chance of burning it to the ground. And then there was Emma, what was that business of her running to fetch Jerusha Paget at night? There had been no sickness in Mary's house or it would have been spoken of, and Mary Price had said not a word.

'It were a blessing Emma weren't in that house.' Polly lifted her cup. Jerusha Paget could be close-mouthed when it suited her, a direct asking would bring no reply.

'A blessing,' Jerusha nodded.

Seeing both cups empty, Polly reached once more for the teapot. There was nothing better for loosening a neighbour's tongue than a cup of tea.

'Still, to cross the heath to Plovers Croft in the dark, and by herself! Something must have been worrying Mary to let her wench do that.'

Accepting the tea, Jerusha nodded and met the other woman's glance. Polly Butler was a kindly soul but one who liked to know the top and bottom of everybody's business. Tell her something one day and the next it would be all over Doe Bank and on its way to Wednesbury.

'Arrh, I reckon you be right in your thinking, Polly.' Jerusha allowed a little of the truth to escape, enough to satisfy the other's curiosity. 'But what they were worrying about we will never know now. All that girl sleeping upstairs could tell me was that her mother asked I should come.'

'Arrh, it be the wench we must feel sorry for.' Polly emptied the dregs of the teapot on to the fire, sending a cloud of acrid-smelling steam sizzling into the chimney, then banked the fire for the night and collected the cups. 'They all be out of the misery of this world; young Carrie, her mother and her father. But that one, Emma, she has to live with the memory of this night.'

Cups in hand, she bustled into the scullery, stepping over the sleeping boys to rinse the cups in water taken from the bucket. Returning she glanced at the older woman still hunched in her chair. Jerusha Paget could shed a great deal more light on the happenings of the past hours should she choose, but that light would never shine. 'Yes, I feel for the wench. There be many an hour of crying afore the memory fades.'

'That be the way of it,' Jerusha agreed. 'But it be the way to healing. Tears help wash away the pain.'

The words were easily said. Bidding Polly good night, Jerusha climbed the narrow stairs to the room she would share with Emma.

The saying was easy, it was the living that was hard.

Emma stood before the charred bricks and blackened timbers that were all that remained of her home. Wisps of smoke curled up from the smouldering ruins and the morning air was heavy with the smell of burning.

They had been inside, her mother and sister, her father. They had died there. Had Carrie known of the fire, felt the agony of its touch, the choking of its breath as her parents must have?

How had it happened? Why had it happened? And why had Emma herself been spared? Unable to look any longer at the burned out shell, she covered her face with her shawl, her body shaking with grief.

'Why?' she sobbed. 'Why leave me? Oh, God, why be so cruel? I can't live without them, I can't … I can't!'

From the doorway of Polly's house, Jerusha Paget watched the slight figure drop to its knees. Although she had not heard her words she knew why Emma cried. She knew the pain, the heartache of losing a loved one, the emptiness of being alone. As the girl was doing now she too had questioned the Lord, she too had asked Him why. But unlike the weeping girl she had been given an answer, an answer spoken in silence, an answer that had chilled her to the bone.

Drawing her shawl about her, black skirts brushing dew from the ground, Jerusha walked slowly over to the figure huddled in its shawl.

'They be gone, child.' She bent over Emma,

one arm about the heaving shoulders. 'Let them rest.'

'I want it to be me...' Beneath the shawl Emma's cries were pitiful. 'Oh, God, why could it not have been me!'

'Come.' Urging Emma to her feet then folding her in her arms, Jerusha held her while sob after sob wrenched free from her shaking body. 'Cry it out,' she said softly. 'Cry it out. There be none save Jerusha to hear.'

Holding Emma half slumped against her, Jerusha guided her a little away from houses, huddled together close as frightened children, then waited until the sobs quieted.

'You knew, didn't you, Jerusha?' Lowering the shawl Emma turned tear-washed eyes to the woman standing staring out across the heath. 'You knew about the fire?'

The old woman nodded. 'I knew, child.'

'And the reason for my coming to Plovers Croft?'

Eyes fixed on the circles of pit wheels outlined against the sky, Jerusha waited. Perhaps the moment she'd thought to be a long way off was already here. Perhaps the time for truth was now. Emma knew one answer, and with hindsight would eventually guess the other. But guessing was not knowing. Only knowledge would salve the hurt, heal the wound.

'Did you know that too, Jerusha? Did you know that Carrie...'

'Did I know your sister plunged a knife into her own breast?' Jerusha drew a long breath. 'Yes, child, I knew that too. As I know her life ended before the flame was lit, she felt none of its sting.'

'I ... I didn't know she had a knife, I didn't see her take it. Then she said my father...'

'He has gone to a judgement more forgiving than any he would have received from the hands of men, and Carrie is at peace now, that is what you must remember.'

'But why did they have to die, Carrie and my mother? They never did harm to anybody. Why didn't God take me? Mine is the sin!'

'Question not the Lord or His ways, child, trust only His love.'

'His love?' Bitterness and pain throbbed in Emma's voice. 'Trust His love as Carrie trusted our father? Where was the love in what he did to her ... is that what trust brings? So much torment that a young girl must take her own life. Is that love, Jerusha. Is that *love*?'

As the storm of tears broke afresh, Jerusha held the trembling girl. What Caleb Price had done, the sin he had committed against his own child and those of other folk, could never be described as love.

'And what of the love my mother had for him, the trust she placed in him? The preacher man!' Emma choked on the laugh that warred against her sobs. 'If only they knew ... if only they knew!'

'Would that make you feel better, Emma?'

Jerusha's words, quiet as they were, penetrated the storm of grief and anger and Emma was still.

'Will telling the people of Doe Bank what their preacher man really was, of his hypocrisy and wickedness, bring you peace? Will your sorrow and torment be relieved by bringing the same to

122

them? I think not, child, I think not.'

'You knew that too, Jerusha! You knew what he did to Carrie?'

Her glance again fixed on the distance Jerusha thought of that light-filled silence, one that had spoken of so much pain.

'Yes, I knew,' she answered an astonished Emma. 'Though heaven be my witness, I knew nothing of Caleb Price's acts until yesterday. Only then was I told and by that time it was too late for me to face him with it. But now there is an end to his wrongdoing.'

'Too late!' Emma echoed the desolation inside her. 'As it is too late for my mother. Oh, if only I had not left her, I could have saved her.'

'I asked you not long since if you set store by my word. I ask you that same thing now – do you trust me, Emma Price?'

Feeling her nod, Jerusha went on.

'Then listen to the truth. A truth that comes not of me but by me. Mary Price could not stand to live knowing what she did: the suffering of her child, the betrayal of her husband. Death was her only salvation, but it was a salvation she could not let you share. That was her reason for sending you to Plovers Croft. She knew Carrie was beyond my help, it was the only way to get you clear of that house before she cleansed it with fire. Yes, Emma.' She paused, feeling the girl's slight figure stiffen. 'Your mother's hand set the fire that took your home.'

Emma lifted her head, bemusement stark in her wide eyes. 'But surely my father would not have allowed ... surely he would have prevented her?'

'Your father was beyond preventing.' Jerusha answered gently. 'He too could not face the years that would follow, he chose to go where his daughter had led. Like her he did not feel the sting of fire.'

He had followed where Carrie had led? Stepping from Jerusha's arms, Emma turned to stare at the remnants of her home. Her father had taken his own life.

'It was hard for you to hear, child,' Jerusha went on quietly. 'But only by hearing will you know any respite. Caleb Price will answer to his maker for his sin. Let it rest there. Though in your heart you may not forgive, give him his peace.'

Give him his peace? Emma stared at the curls of smoke spiralling into the sky. Give the preacher man his peace. But who would give *her* peace?

'Has it been done as I ordered?'

Carver Felton stood in the yard of the Topaz mine. Beside him John Barlow touched one hand to his badly swollen face.

'I sent half a dozen men with pick axes over there at first light. Them folk will be out and the houses half down by this time.' Barlow winced from the pain of moving his split lip.

Carver watched as a young boy pushed against a bogie loaded with coal then struggled to hitch it to the steel rope of the donkey engine that would haul it the rest of the way to the loading bank. The houses at Plovers Croft were being demolished to make way for the canal that would carry his coal and his steel. The fact that families would be put out on the road caused him not a moment's concern.

'I want no hitch,' he snapped, watching the boy run back towards the shaft head where yet another loaded wagon waited to be pushed to the donkey line. 'See that it is finished before dark. I want nobody slipping back there.'

Pain registering the move of sore limbs, Barlow touched a finger to his brow as Carver turned away. 'There'll be nowhere for them to slip into, Mr Felton. Rest assured, Plovers Croft will be nowt but a pile of broken bricks afore nightfall.'

Swinging himself easily into the saddle, Carver touched a heel to his grey stallion. It would be as Barlow said, but nevertheless it would do no harm to see for himself.

It could be he had razed those houses for no purpose. He considered the possibility, allowing the horse to set its own pace. He had the agreement of Langton and Payne, they had seen the extra profit a speedier means of getting their wares to their respective markets would bring. But to do that, to connect a waterway to the existing canal, meant getting the consent of the owner and the aristocracy were not noted for their concessions to what they called tradesmen. But there were means and there were ways. Carver smiled. He knew them all. The master of Aston Grange might be a lord, but he was also a man, one whose appetite for pleasure went far beyond the bedroom door. There would be no problem meeting the price of Anslow Lacy. And that other problem ... how would he meet the price set by Cara Holgate?

Beautiful, greedy Cara. Satisfaction in his smile, Carver glanced towards the distant town. He already had the answer to that.

But did he have the answer to his other problem? The one that had haunted him day and night since raping that girl. What in hell had driven him so far?

Paul was his only brother, it had been done for him, to save him from himself; the young fool couldn't possibly know what he was doing, marrying a pit bank wench. Talking to him would have done no good, his brother could be obstinate ... too obstinate. No, it had to be done that way. Only by his turning the girl into a whore would Paul be made to see sense; and he had to see it. Keeping his place in society made that a must, and to keep that place meant marrying well; if Paul could not see that for himself then Carver must look to it for him. Losing the wench might sting Paul's feelings for a while but he would get over that. He would see the name of Felton had to come first, that it was for his own good...

And the girl's good, what of that?

'*A present of considerable value...*'

Cara Holgate's words returned to his mind. She had asked for twenty per cent of his canal venture for the use of her body while he had taken the pit bank wench for a shilling.

A shilling for her virginity!

The thought a guilt-tipped spear in his mind, he touched heels to the horse.

There could be nothing of greater value, nothing more precious for any woman to give to a

126

husband, and he had robbed that girl of hers.

But he had done it for Paul ... done it to prevent his brother from making a mistake, the mistake of marrying beneath himself, of tarnishing the family name.

That was what he told himself each time that lovely frightened face stared at him behind his closed eyes, each time he tried to sleep.

He had done it for Paul!

But had he? Carver's fingers tightened on the rein.

A man could lie to anyone except himself.

Cresting a small hillock he stared across a flat expanse of heathland. This was where his canal would cut through. Felton Canal. He liked the sound of it. He had chosen an ideal spot; this land would need no levelling to take warehouses or a wharf.

'Why did you order our houses flattened?'

Immersed in his thoughts Carver paid no attention to the people straggling across the heath. Now he looked down into the face of a young man, an old one holding to him for support.

'Are you questioning me?' His reply as cold as his stare, Carver tightened his grip on the reins.

'Yes, I'm questioning you. Why have you had Plovers Croft flattened?'

There had been no touch to the forehead, no begging his pardon or calling him sir, none of the respect a labourer commonly showed when speaking to his superior. The open lack of it annoyed him more than the question and his reply was curt.

'You were given the reason!'

'Oh, arr.' The young man's eyes flashed. 'That arsehole creeper you call a manager gave the reason and laughed at the giving, but he weren't laughing when he left.'

So that was what had happened to Barlow! Carver continued to stare at the younger man. The manager had been beaten, and not lightly judging by this man's physique.

'Plovers Croft was home to us Mr Felton, sir.' The old man lifted a finger to his brow. 'Begging your pardon, but what do we do? We 'ave no place else to go.'

'He's not interested in whether or not we have a place to live, Grandfather, all he's interested in is profit. Who he steps on to make it is of no consequence to him.'

'Correct.' Carver's mouth hardened. 'You have a sharp tongue as well as a hard fist. Take care you don't find them both cut away!'

'And you have a high seat.' The young man stepped forward. 'Take care you don't find yourself tumbled from it!'

'No, Seth!' The old man caught at his grandson's arm. 'There has been enough brawling. More will bring nothing but hurt to the body and a sure sending down the line for you. Leave it be, we'll find a place.'

'Where?' Furious eyes glared up at Carver. 'Where will we find a place ... can you tell him?'

The stallion moved restlessly, sensitive to the anger in Seth's voice.

'I can tell him where he will *not* find a place, and neither will you!' Carver answered. 'That

128

being anywhere on Felton land. Nor will you find employment in any mine or foundry owned by me. Now, get out of my way!'

'Why, you...'

Shrugging away the hand that had rested on his arm, Seth reached up to Carver, catching his breath as the whip slashed across his face. Whistling as it cut the air, the snake-like strip of plaited leather rose and fell, slicing into his flesh with every stroke. Only when the younger man's knees buckled and he slumped to the ground did Carver stop.

'Get him off my land!' he breathed. 'And if you don't know where to go, I believe the workhouse is in that direction!'

Setting his heels to the animal's flanks, Carver put it to a gallop. One man had learned today it was not a good idea to cross Carver Felton. Others remained to be taught.

'But what of the burying?'

Polly Butler frowned deeply as she looked at the girl who had spent the night beneath her roof.

'Surely you will stay for the burying?'

'There's nothing to bury.' Emma suffered agony at each word. The fire had taken every trace, her family was gone.

Polly felt the warmth of colour in her cheeks beneath the film of coal dust that clung to her. She had spoken without thinking. Emma was right. The men had searched the burnt wreckage of that house but had found no remains. Even so, there had to be a service of sorts, it would not be right not to have one.

'Eh, but Emma wench, you'll stay for the funeral?'

She'd known she would be asked that. Jerusha had told her so before they parted. It would be easier on her to go in some other direction than toward Wednesbury, her friend had said. By doing so she would avoid the stares of the women picking coal from the pit bank. But Emma could not leave without thanking Polly. Now as the woman lifted the corner of a rough black apron, wiping it across her face, Emma shook her head. How could there be a funeral when...

'No,' she murmured, tears thick in her throat.

Polly dropped her apron, one hand smoothing it over her long skirts, her glance quelling the disapproving murmurs of the listening women.

'Look, Emma. I know this is a terrible time for you, that all you be wanting is to hide yourself away, but the dead must be given their due. They must be laid to rest in the proper manner.'

Eyes brimming, every word a fresh lance of pain, Emma cried out: 'How? How can I lay the dead to rest ... where do I find them ... where? Tell me!'

Pity rising in her, Polly touched one hand to Emma's. 'There can be no coffin, that we know. But still we must ask the Lord to take the souls of those you loved, and we respected, into His keeping.'

'Amen.' The watching women each crossed her breast as she spoke the one word.

'We can't not hold a service for the man who was always ready to do service for the folk of Doe

130

Bank. We can do none other than give him the respect he deserves. You see that, don't you, wench?'

Respect. Emma felt a sudden desire to laugh. They must show their respect for her father, for the preacher man? Show respect for the things he had done for them. And what of those other things, the vile things he had done to Carrie and maybe others besides? What if she told these women about that, where would their respect be then?

'I understand.' Emma drew her hand away. 'And I thank you for the respect you wish to show to my family. But I will not attend any service. Ask the Lord what you will, I'll never set foot inside that Chapel again.'

Undeterred by Polly's scolding glance, withering rebukes followed on her heels as Emma turned away.

Respect and love? She needed no church in which to show them. She would carry them in her heart for as long as she lived. They would both have respect and love forever, her mother and her sister. But what of her father, the preacher man, what would she carry for him?

One hand pressed to her mouth, holding back the sobs, Emma walked away across the heath.

Chapter Nine

'Carver, how pleasant. I had not thought to see you here.' Cara Holgate stretched out a hand.

'I have business in Wednesbury.' He lifted the gloved hand a little short of his lips. 'But I had not thought it to bring me the pleasure of seeing you.'

Head bent over her hand, his eyes glinted with suppressed amusement. There was no pleasure for Cara in this meeting, that had showed in the strained look of her painted face and the quick glance she had darted at her companion.

Tight-lipped, she half turned to the woman standing beside her. 'Lissa, may I present Carver Felton. Mr Felton, my cousin, Miss Melissa Gilbert.'

Carver had not missed the lack of enthusiasm in the introduction, and as he acknowledged the younger woman he wondered at it. Would Cara prefer they had not met? Did she not wish to introduce him to her cousin?

Releasing her hand he gave his most charming smile. Hair the colour of ripe chestnuts and drawn deliberately severely back beneath a pale blue bonnet gave added intensity to the grey eyes smiling back at him from an oval face. The woman, just a little into her twenties, he guessed, was pretty, yet there was something about her that belied the softness of her mouth. The look in those pale eyes held little but calculation.

132

Alike in more than looks, Cara and her pretty cousin. Carver's smile deepened. But why had this one not been seen before? Was her delightful chaperone afraid she might meet with undesirable influences, or was the devious Cara protecting her own interests?

If the latter then he must discover just what those interests were.

'Wednesbury is doubly fortunate.' He looked deep into the obvious invitation of those grey eyes. 'Two very beautiful women is one asset this town will be happy to possess. You must stay with us a long time, Miss Gilbert.'

'Melissa will shortly be returning home, her visit is to be a brief one!'

Carver saw the hand go protectively to her cousin's elbow and the tightness about Cara's lips.

'A pity,' he returned. 'But not *so* soon, I hope? Perhaps Miss Gilbert will accompany you to dinner at Felton Hall this evening? You did consent to grace my table with your presence, Cara. Allow us also the privilege of your cousin's beauty.'

Cara's glance spit a coldness that would challenge an iceberg. 'Melissa is still convalescing from a recent illness, she must not be overtired.'

'Oh, but I am quite well now, Cara.' Grey eyes smiled directly into Carver's. 'I would be delighted to visit Felton Hall. I look forward to it, Mr Felton.'

'Not as much as I.' Carver took her hand, pressing it lightly against his mouth. 'Until this evening.'

Lifting his silver-topped cane in farewell, the smile he gave Cara was triumphant. He turned in the direction of the Golden Cross Hotel. Cara Holgate most definitely did not want him within miles of her attractive cousin. Dear Cara. His smile faded. We cannot always have what we want.

The sound of horses' hooves and the rumble of carriage wheels roused Emma. It was dark. She glanced towards the distant road that cut across the empty heath, watching the carriage lanterns bob away into the blackness. She must have fallen asleep. She had talked to Polly then... She blinked, trying to clear her brain of the shadows of sleep. Then she had walked, but how far? She had been so tired, so utterly weary, that she must have drifted into sleep almost the moment she had sat down in the shelter of a rock.

Which way should she go now? She had crossed the heath many times, but tonight in the darkness it looked so different, so terribly empty. In the distance a fox barked and was immediately answered by another. Emma drew her shawl more closely about her shoulders. There was nothing to be afraid of, it was only foxes. Yet still she shivered as they barked again.

She glanced again in the direction the carriage had gone. That was the road that led between Wednesbury and Dudley. If she followed it in either direction she must come eventually to a place where she could ask shelter for the night.

It was as she reached the road that the heavens suddenly turned a rich fiery red, the glow of

134

furnace openings lighting the whole bowl of the sky, outlining the tall stacks of iron foundries and the winding wheels of several coal mines. But it was the church spires, two sharp pointed fingers of stone rising black against the glowing skyline, two spires set close together on a rise of ground, that took her attention.

Wednesbury! Emma felt relief seep into her as she recognised the sight. The parish church of St Bartholomew and the Catholic church of St Mary. If she made towards them she would pass close by Plovers Croft, the people there would give her shelter. Maybe she would find Jerusha had changed her mind and returned to her own home there.

Gaining the road as the red glow flared across the night sky, Emma hurried on the way she had chosen. Why had Jerusha decided not to come with her earlier today? They could have walked back to Plovers Croft together. But she had turned away when Emma had made the suggestion. There was no home for her there any longer, she had said. But why ... why turn her back on the house where she had lived so many years, the home she had shared with Jacob? It seemed as if with his passing Jerusha wanted no more of life. The same way it seemed her mother had wanted no more of life!

...she could not live with the knowledge...

The words Jerusha had spoken returned with vivid clarity to her mind. The hurt and the pain that had been her mother's, Emma could understand as too much to bear. But Jerusha! The death of her husband was a vicious blow but it was one the woman had known must one day come. It could not be that which had caused Jerusha to make the decision she had, so what was it?

Cresting the gentle slope, Emma stared across the heath. There was the answer to her question. In the last of the fading light she stared at the heaps of rubble that once had been Plovers Croft.

Jerusha had known her home was to be destroyed, the same as she had known those other things. But her neighbours, people now without homes, had they known? The Croft was built on Felton land. Emma walked on. Only one man could have ordered it pulled down: Carver Felton. No need to ask why of that man, he needed no reason to do anything. 'But one day,' she murmured, 'one day he will meet his reckoning.'

Rain that had slept in the sky most of the day began to fall in large heavy drops. Emma pulled her shawl more tightly about her, though the worn cloth offered little protection. There were hollows in the outcrops of rock where as children they had played at being pirates, but they were over on the other side of the heath and it was madness to cross it in the darkness. Besides which, she reasoned, she would be as wet when she reached them as she would be when she reached the town. Six and two threes! Holding her shawl firmly, she walked on.

'You be another of 'em?'

A narrow-faced woman looked over the shoulder of the man who had opened the door to

136

Emma's knock. Water dripping from her skirts, she had seen the gleam of a lamp and made for it, coming to a small farmhouse flanked by a low building she guessed might be a barn. It would be dry in there, it might even be warm. They would not turn her away. Almost too exhausted to lift her hand, she had knocked at the door.

'You be from the Croft, don't you?' The question held no note of sympathy. 'They've been passing through 'ere much of the day, the last of 'em I saw off some hours since. If you be of their number how come you be passing at this time of night? Be you crippled?'

'No.' Emma brushed raindrops from her face. 'I am not crippled.'

'Then why so late?' In the light of the lamp the man held high, the waspish features tightened. 'Did you find business on the road? Is it that has kept you so long behind the rest?'

Raindrops beating a monotonous rhythm on her head, Emma shivered as they soaked through the wet shawl to trickle down her neck. 'Business?' She shivered again. 'I don't understand. I … I had no business.'

'She don't understand.' The woman laughed, a harsh mocking sound. 'You hear, Eli, she don't understand!' Pushing the man aside, she stood with hands on hips glaring at Emma.

'Like bloody hell you don't understand! Don't you try coming that with me! I know your sort. You makes your money where you can, be it in a bed or under a hedge. You ain't choosy so long as the man has a shilling to pay you. Well, there be no place under this roof for the likes of you. I'll give no shelter to a prostitute!'

'I am no prostitute!' Emma's head shot up. 'I am later than the others because ... but why should I give you the reason? It is obvious you give no assistance to any of the folk who knock at your door, and it is obvious your intention is the same now. Forgive me for having disturbed you.'

'Wait!' The man spoke as Emma turned away. 'My wife was being no more than cautious, we have all sorts pass by on their way to the town. But we know our Christian charity. There be a place to sleep in the barn. It be dry and the hay be soft. You be welcome to bed down in there.'

'I ... I have no money to pay.'

'Like I said, we know our Christian charity.' The man waved the lamp. 'There be the barn over there, the door be on the latch. Take it or leave it.'

'Thank you.' Emma bobbed her head. 'Thank you both.'

Inside the barn Emma waited for her eyes to adjust to the deeper darkness. Smarting from the woman's accusation, she felt the tears well. What was happening to her world? Raped by Carver Felton, then the death of her whole family and the loss of her home ... what was she to do?

'Oh, God!' Covering her face with her hands, she cried into them, 'Oh, God! Please ... I can't take any more!'

Shaking from head to foot, her cries echoing eerily in the darkness, she let the agony of it all flow from her. Sobs still breaking from her throat, she stripped off her wet clothing.

Accustomed now to the gloom she draped her skirts and underwear over a hay manger, her blouse and bloomers over a low door that closed off a stable in which a horse whinnied softly. Settling into the sweet-smelling hay, her hands came together. Many years with her father had made prayer an automatic process, one often carried out while her mind dwelt on other things. But tonight every ounce of her concentration went into her silent words, all the fervour of her heart in her prayer.

'Forgive them, Lord,' she whispered. 'My mother did not know ... she did not know what Carrie was suffering, and my sister ... so much pain ... so much heartbreak. Do not blame them, Lord, but take them into your loving care.' Crossing her breast, Emma lowered her hands. She could offer no prayer for her father.

Deep in sleep she did not hear the creak of the barn door as it opened, not did the pallid gleam of the lantern disturb her as it played first on her face then slowly over her naked body.

Passing a tongue over his parted lips, the man who had answered her knock at the farmhouse door placed the lantern on a nail hammered into a thick wooden post. He had long waited for an opportunity such as this and it would not be wasted. Slipping out of his trousers – he had not waited to don any other clothing – he kicked them aside then dropped to his knees beside the sleeping girl.

Beautiful. He played a glance over the small breasts, the stomach flat and the colour of ivory in the lantern light, the patch of shadow at its base. His already hardened flesh was throbbing as he eased himself across her, settling his knees between legs parted in sleep.

Folded back on each side of her head, Emma's arms moved and instantly he grabbed her wrists, fitting them into one large hand while the other groped at her breast.

'Be no call for you to cry out.' He leered down into her face as her eyes widened. 'You knowed I would come. That be why you said you had no money to pay, 'cos you intended to pay in other ways – ways that please a man.'

'No!' The mists of sleep dissolving before this new horror, she tried to struggle free. 'Get away from me ... get away!'

'Come now.' The hand left her breast to clamp across her mouth. 'Not too loud in your pretending, we don't want the wife to hear. Gets a bit jealous does the wife.'

Eyes blazing with fear and anger, Emma tried to twist from under him but his weight was too much.

'You be as eager as I am, do you?' he laughed as he raised himself, displaying the hard flesh jerking between his legs. 'You be wanting to make your payment real bad. But let's not hurry things, take our time. That way there be more enjoyment.'

Emma trembled with revulsion as he lowered himself on to her, nausea thick in her throat as she felt that throbbing flesh, hot and hard, leap against her stomach.

Not again. Oh, God, not again! This couldn't be happening again! But by the sting of her lips

140

pressing against her teeth as his mouth replaced his hand she knew that it was.

'I was telling the truth,' she gasped as his mouth lifted fractionally. 'I have no money, and I never intended to make payment this way. I am no prostitute.'

The hand fondling her breast squeezed hard, and the kick of stiffened flesh against her stomach increased. 'Money or no money,' he slurred against her lips, 'intended or otherwise, this be the way you be going to pay!'

'No, please...'

'Quiet!' Releasing her wrists, he raised himself to his knees, bringing his hand down hard across her mouth. 'If you want to walk from here in the morning you'll keep this closed, but closed or open I'll have what I want. And what I want be this.'

Slowly, knees biting painfully into her flesh, he forced her legs wide apart. Then, touching the end of his bloated penis, to the base of her stomach, he rocked slowly back and forth, his flesh stroking hers.

'Don't,' Emma sobbed. 'Please don't do this ... please!'

Her mind flew to that other time. He had left her a shilling. Carver Felton had raped her and left her with the shilling sewn into the lining of her skirts.

'Wait!' She raised her hands to his shoulders in an effort to hold him back. 'I ... I do have a shilling. That is all I have but take it, take it, please, and go...'

'I'll take your shilling and gladly.' He struck her

hands away. 'But first I'll take you!'

Thrusting his body forward he groaned and dropped heavily on to her.

'Serves you right, you filthy swine! I hope you're dead ... I hope you are dead!'

Heaving the still form off her, Emma rolled sideways into the hay.

'It serves you right, you *deserve* to die!'

Her senses reeling Emma looked at where her attacker lay, face down and unmoving, on the bed of hay. Standing over him was the thin figure of a young girl, the piece of wood with which she had struck him on the head still raised in her hand.

'He got what was coming to him,' the girl said softly, eyes never leaving the still figure. 'I vowed I would kill him. Folk like him don't deserve to live.'

'No!' Emma raised a hand as the girl lifted the weapon. 'You must not strike him again.'

'Why not?' She turned towards Emma, her thin face blank and expressionless in the pale light of the lantern. 'Why not hit him again? Why not make sure he won't do to another what he has done to me – what he was set to do to you? Killing him would do every woman a good turn.'

'No.' Scrambling to her feet, Emma grabbed for her clothes, alarming the horse who whickered. 'No, it is wrong to kill.'

'It isn't wrong when you kill a pig, and that's what he is. A dirty pig!'

Damp clothing sticking to her skin, Emma pulled it on. 'I don't doubt the truth of that, but we mustn't kill him. That way we become as bad as he is.'

142

'I don't reckon that!' The girl still held the piece of wood at a threatening angle. 'He be no better than vermin, the whole world would be better off without him! Why leave him whole, to rape some other woman? Why let him get away with that?'

'No!' Emma lunged forward, grabbing the girl's wrist as she swung the wood.

'I thought as how I would find you in here, Eli Coombs. I guessed where you would be, bare arse upward in the hay and that trollop underneath you!'

Her hand still on the girl, Emma looked towards the door. A candle in her hand, the narrow-faced woman stood staring down at the figure lying in the hay.

'I knowed what her game was, coming here that time of the night, same as I knowed yours... Christian charity, hah! The only thing you've ever been charitable with is that which swings between your legs, and any woman can have that for nothing. But the one you be covering now won't find the next man so easy to lead astray. No, by God she won't. Not once I be finished with her!'

The candle flickering as she lifted it above her head, the woman advanced further into the barn and Emma felt the young girl beside her tremble.

'Get up. Do you hear me, Eli Coombs? You get off that dirty trollop afore you gets this candle up your arse!'

'He won't be getting up, not yet he won't.' Her voice shaking, the girl broke free of Emma.

Standing now in the pale circle of light thrown by the lantern, the woman's face showed disgust.

'Not you as well? He ain't playing with two at a time? No wonder he's having a job getting to his feet.'

'It isn't what *he* has done is keeping him from standing up, it is what *I* have done, and if it were not for the one you called a trollop he might never have stood on his feet again!'

'Why? What have you done to him? If you have harmed him...' The woman's anger swung rapidly from her husband to the girl.

'Harmed him?' The girl laughed, a lost hopeless sound. 'I should have killed him!'

'Eli.' Placing the candle on the ground, the woman knelt beside her husband. 'Eli, be you all right?'

'This be your fault.' She glared up at Emma.

'He ... he came to the barn. I had no idea...'

'No idea?' Emma's protest was lost on the woman. 'You had every idea, and each one of them along the same lines. And that being to get my man out here.'

'I thought no such thing!' Emma was aghast. 'I was asleep when your husband came here, I woke to find him forcing himself upon me.'

'Forcing, was it? So how much did he pay to "force himself" on you?'

'He gave me no money. I tell you, he...'

'And I tell you, what you have done to my husband is going to cost you dear. You'll get ten years for this, ten years' hard labour. There won't be many men will want your services after that, not the way you'll look. That pretty face won't look so good any more. Ten years, that's what you'll get for this...'

144

'She didn't do it, she didn't hit him, I did.' The quaver in her voice testifying to her fear, the girl lifted the piece of wood still gripped in one hand. 'It was me, I clouted him with this.'

Beside her the still figure groaned but the woman's attention was on the girl. 'You!' She glared. 'You hit him? Why, you ungrateful little toe rag!'

'He deserved it.' The girl's voice rose as the woman scrambled to her feet. 'It's right what she says, he did come in here and force it on her, same as he forced it on me more than once. I seen him. I been in here all the time so I seen him do it.'

At her feet Eli groaned again, rolling on to his back.

'Here.' Grabbing his discarded trousers, his wife threw them at him. 'Get yourself dressed, you've got the bobbies to fetch.'

The police? Emma felt her stomach turn over. She had never even seen a policeman in Doe Bank. The thought of possibly being arrested and taken to prison filled her with horror.

Still dazed from the blow the girl had struck to the back of his head, Eli groaned afresh, pulling on his trousers as his wife screeched at him again to go for the police.

'There'll be no bobbies brought here!' He rubbed his head, wincing as he touched the place where the blow had fallen.

'But this wench and this … this trollop knocked you down, they like to have killed you!'

'He didn't need no knocking down, he was already near enough on his face when I hit him.'

145

'You hear that? You hear what this little toe rag be saying? It was her hit you, swiped you with that piece of wood. She could have knocked your brains clean out, 'cept you don't have any. Now you get that horse out of the stable and ride into Wednesbury. I want them bobbies bringing in and these two carted off to jail where they belong.'

Getting to his feet, Eli swayed. 'I said, no bobbies!'

'Best you listen to him.' A tremor still marked in her voice it was the girl who answered. 'It might be I'll get ten years but it will be worth every minute to tell the whole of the town what it is Eli Coombs does with the girls he gets from Meeting Street. What it is *you* turn a blind eye to!'

Even in the faint illumination of candle and lantern, Eli's face visibly paled.

'Get out!' he hissed. 'Get you gone before I decides to take a pitchfork to you!'

Picking up the candle as Emma grabbed the girl's arm, pulling her towards the door, the woman turned to the stable.

'If you won't fetch the bobbies, then I will!'

One hand holding his half-buttoned trousers Eli struck out with the other, sending the lighted candle flying into the dry hay.

Chapter Ten

'You look very charming, Cara. And you, my dear Miss Gilbert, look positively enchanting.'

'A flatterer as always.' Acid beneath the smile she returned, Cara Holgate swept into the drawing room of Felton Hall.

'There is no need for flattery when the truth is adequate. But adequate as that is, my words do not do either of you justice. What do you say, Payne? Do you agree with me?'

'Indeed.' Arthur Payne smiled at the two women. 'It would take the Poet Laureate to do justice to such beauty.'

'Enough!' Cara waved her fan. 'Melissa, my dear, don't listen to them.'

'Why not when I quite like that they say?' Rouged lips showing white even teeth, Melissa Gilbert gave a dazzling smile. 'I confess, Mr Payne, I rather enjoy being flattered.'

'Then I shall devote the whole evening to doing what you enjoy.'

'Then our evening together will be a short one. *I* have no liking for twaddle, listening to you playing the Lothario will bore me to tears.' Cara flipped open her delicate lace fan then snapped it closed, movements sharp and irritated.

Keeping his smile hidden Carver Felton handed sherry to each of his guests. Cara had no liking for twaddle! Except when that twaddle was directed at her alone.

Seating himself in a brocaded Hepplewhite armchair, he glanced at the younger woman. 'I hope your recovery from your illness is continuing, Miss Gilbert?' He directed the conversation with consummate ease.

Giving another of her dazzling smiles, Melissa switched her glance from Payne. 'Oh, yes. I feel better with each day. I must say, my cousin takes such excellent care of me I am becoming thoroughly spoiled. I fear I shall not want to return home.'

'Oh, but that time must be far away yet.' Recovered from Cara's acerbic snub, Arthur Payne added his entreaty to Carver's. 'You must press her to stay, Cara.'

'I would very much like Melissa to stay, I would like her to make her home with me, but she insists upon returning to Rugeley though there is no one to share that huge house with her except a few staff.

'Really, cousin, what would Bessant do if I left her all alone?'

Cara pulled a wry face. 'Bessant is Lissa's nanny and should have been pensioned off to a cottage years ago...'

A tap on the door cutting off further explanation, Cara glanced up as Carver's manservant entered to announce the arrival of more guests.

'Carver ... I'm so sorry we're late, do forgive us.' Harriet Langton, maroon taffeta gown swathed in ribbons and bows and topped by feathers and diamanté clips in her elaborately coiffed hair, sailed into the room.

'I would only not forgive you if you did not come at all.' Rising to his feet Carver took the podgy hand half covered in a fingerless black lace mitten, touching it to his lips.

'Carver, you're so sweet. Isn't he sweet, Cara?'

'Isn't he!' Her glance meeting that of her host, Cara made no attempt to conceal her cynicism.

'Blasted carriage horse cast a shoe and we had to come halfway at a walk.' Rafe Langton followed his wife into the room. 'Sorry, my dears, didn't see you there. Language not suitable in front of ladies.'

'If I've told him once I've told him a thousand times about his language!' Harriet's simpering smile faded. 'The trouble is he never listens. I told him, I said one day he would forget himself, and then were would we be!'

'Exactly where you are now.' Melissa's smiled passed from the embarrassed Harriet to her husband. 'Among friends. Please, Mrs Langton, do not scold. A slip of the tongue is something we all make, myself most of all. I am certain no one takes offence.'

'True, my dear, true!' Rafe's smile spread across an expansive face whose sidewhiskers and beard were a perfect replica of those worn by the Prince of Wales. 'A slip of the tongue, anybody can make one. But my apologies just the same.'

Settling the portly Harriet in another of the graceful chairs, Carver caught the eye of the attentive servant waiting at the doorway.

'Mr Langton will be needing the loan of a carriage horse later this evening. See to it, Morton.'

'Yes, sir. I will have his horse taken to the farrier tomorrow. Will I then have it returned to Mr Langton or would he wish to collect it himself?'

'Send it over to Portway House.' Rafe dropped heavily on to a matching couch, the weight of him jolting the seated Cara. 'That be a good man you have there, Felton.' He accepted the glass held out to him. 'If ever you be going to give him the sack, you let me know. I could find a place for him over at my house.'

'You must wait in line, Rafe, I have staked a prior claim. And you know the saying: women and children first.'

Swallowing half of his drink in one mouthful he pressed his lips together, savouring the after taste. 'I don't know as to children,' he laughed, 'but as for ladies, I'd never deny them anything. Especially when they are as pretty as you, Cara. You too, Miss Gilbert.'

'Prettily said, Rafe.' Cara returned her untouched drink to a small table set at the arm of the couch. 'You are every bit as much of a flatterer as Arthur.'

Somewhat peeved at the attention being paid to the younger women, Harriet took the arm Carver held out to her as dinner was announced. Seated at the table she took control of the conversation. 'Tell me, Carver, how is that young brother of yours? Rafe tells me he is away somewhere.'

'Rafe is correct,' Carver answered, aware the question had caught the ear of everyone seated in his dining room, including that of Arthur Payne who had been paying intensive court to the delicious Melissa.

'I am disappointed,' Harriet continued though Carver's short answer had implied he preferred not to. 'I was hoping to see him, such a charming boy. When can we expect him back?'

Waiting until the first course was served, Carver answered, 'That depends upon how quickly he can conclude his business.'

'Business?' Rafe looked up from the plate he had filled liberally from the serving dishes offered him. 'What business might that be?'

Having no intention of satisfying the other man's curiosity, Carver smiled across the beautifully appointed table. 'I think we may leave that discussion until some other time, Rafe, we should not talk shop when ladies are present.'

It was enough to deter the iron founder but his wife was not so easily put off. Her husband returning concentration to his roast beef she pressed her point. 'When he does return you must bring him to Portland House, it has been much too long since he was there. I hope that happens before you leave us, Melissa.' She smiled at the girl. 'I know you would enjoy meeting Paul, he is such a pleasant young man.'

Pale grey eyes sweeping to Carver's, holding them for a moment before lowing, Melissa answered softly, 'I look forward to meeting him if he is anything like as charming as his brother.'

An expert dissimulation! Carver smiled to see it. A man might be forgiven for believing this girl to be shy. But if Cara Holgate was anything to judge by, shyness was not a character trait of the family.

And that, he thought with an inward smile, would be to his advantage.

Her fingers tight about the wrist of the girl who had saved her, Emma ran from the barn as Eli Coombs shouted and his wife screamed. The rain had stopped but the sodden grass brushing against her skirts soaked a line almost to her knees but she gave no heed, her only thought being to get as far away from that barn as she could.

'Hold on ... hold on!' Gasping for breath, the other girl at last pulled her wrist free. 'I've got the stitch!'

Leaning against one of the low outcrops of limestone that dotted the heath like pale ghosts, she pressed one hand to her side as she gulped in air.

'I'm sorry.' Equally breathless, Emma stood panting beside her. 'I ... I just wanted to get away from that man.'

'You and me both.' The girl had bent almost double, keeping her hand pressed to her side.

'Are you all right?'

'I will be in a minute.' She straightened up slowly. 'I always get the stitch when I run too far, but it'll pass, it always does.'

'I didn't think.' Emma was contrite.

'You thought quick enough a couple of minutes since.' In the wash of moonlight the girl's smile was visible. 'You got us away from that swine Coombs, and I reckon he won't be following after us tonight, not with that to see to!'

Following the line of the girl's nod, Emma caught her breath.

Across the heath flames shot upward, splitting the night sky.

'That's Coombs's barn and I hope to God the filthy swine be in it!'

The girl's mouth was twisted, eyes brilliant with hatred.

'That's what they do with pigs.' The girl's voice fell to a whisper as she stared at the leaping flames. 'They roast them. *He* should have roasted long ago and *her* along with him!'

In the lee of the rock the ground had been sheltered from the driving rain. Taking hold of the girl, Emma drew her down, sitting beside her as she sank to the ground.

'I vowed one day I'd kill him.' Knees drawn up to her chin, the girl seemed to speak to herself. 'That I would make him pay for what he did to that child...'

Feeling her tremble, Emma put her arms about her, holding her close. 'Don't talk about it now.'

'That were what *he* said.' A long sob cracked the quiet voice. 'He said not to talk about it or I'd go the same way. She were only a child when he fetched her from Meeting Street, no more than nine years old. Pretty she were with yellow curls and eyes blue as a summer's morn. To help in the house, that was what he told the Board. Not that they cared what work she was to do so long as she was off their hands, one less mouth for the parish to feed. But within a month of coming to the Coombses' farm she were like a scraggy shadow, whimpering every time he came in sight. One night I heard her sobbing. Eli had come downstairs and was taking Lily ... that were her name ... almost dragging her across to the barn. And I knew what for. He was doing to her what he once

153

did to me. Not satisfied with what his wife was giving him, he'd forced himself on me not three days after getting me from the parish workhouse. It became a regular thing and I was too frightened to do anything to stop it for he swore he would kill me if I said a word. Then, when he took Lily from the workhouse, it stopped and I thought it was over, that maybe he had been found out. But that night it began again, only the agony was not mine, it was hers.'

'Don't!' Emma tightened her arms about the trembling body. 'Don't go on, try to rest.'

But in between the racking sobs, the quiet almost soulless voice went on.

'I followed them to the barn. I saw him snatch the frock from her, take her clothes off one by one, run his great hands over her nakedness, slap her hard when she tried to pull away. I thought...' almost choking the girl looked into Emma's face '...I thought that would be all he would do, that he wouldn't ... that she was too little. But then, when he began to undo his trousers, I knew that he would, even with a child like Lily! So I crept out of the barn and made a noise, calling his name as though I were Liza come to look for him. He scuttled off pretty quick then and I went into the barn to comfort Lily. She told me what Coombs had been doing to her though I needed no telling. I held her for hours, held her while she cried for her dead mother, but in the end I fell asleep and when I woke Lily was gone. She were found that morning floating in the canal. The child had killed herself because of Eli Coombs and from that moment I vowed someday to kill him!'

'You must not think such a thing,' Emma said softly. 'Believe me, I know what you are feeling but you must not think of killing. You must leave the punishing to God.'

'God!' The girl threw up her head. 'There is no God. If there were he would not permit a man such as Eli Coombs to live!'

A man such as Eli Coombs. Emma stared towards the dull red glow. Nor one such as Caleb Price.

And what of Carver Felton?

'You must leave the punishing to God.'

That was what she had told the girl sobbing in her arms. But was she prepared to do the same?

Langton had not asked again about the business that had taken Paul from home.

Carver untied his silk cravat, drawing it slowly through his fingers.

It had gone as he'd known it would, the liberal supply of wine washing all thoughts of business from Rafe Langton's mind, leaving only those centring around the pretty Melissa.

Laying aside the cravat Carver continued to undress, concentrating hard on the events of the evening to keep his mind from returning to that night some weeks ago when he had encountered the girl. No, he would not think of it now. Kicking free of his trousers he walked into his bathroom and plunged his face into cold water. She had been a pit bank wench, nothing for him to dwell on.

But Melissa Gilbert was no pit bank wench.

Drying his face, he returned to the bedroom.

Harriet had continued to ask about Paul. Why had he been sent to Birkenhead? When did Carver think he might return? Her questions had been relentless and he had answered them, but all the while his attention had been on her husband. He had watched Rafe's face. Not once had the man's eyes left Cara's cousin, and rarely had Cara's own eyes left Rafe. Jealousy! Even from his seat next to Harriet he had seen it burn in those green-gold eyes. Jealousy! He smiled slowly. It was a useful tool. One that he would use when he was ready.

It had been while they were seating themselves in the elegant drawing room – Carver grateful once again that his mother's taste in furnishings had not followed the heavy Victorian styles – that Harriet at last arrived at her intended goal.

Did Paul have a special friend? Was there perhaps a fiancée somewhere? The smile died from Carver's mouth, leaving a tight line. Harriet Langton was an inquisitive bitch but her ferreting this evening had produced no rabbit. Paul was nearing his majority, she had announced, calling to Melissa to listen. Soon he would no longer be his brother's ward. Then he would be wanting a wife, someone to share his life and his home. She had beamed at Melissa Gilbert, a world of meaning in her eyes, and Carver had caught the open annoyance in Cara Holgate's face. His brother was a catch for any woman. Money, property, a half share in a business that dominated the area and gave much of the town its living. Yes, Paul Felton was a prize worth the winning but he was not on Cara Holgate's carousel. Or was her cousin not the prize on offer?

Her reply to Harriet's ill veiled innuendo had been razor sharp, her voice hard as steel. Melissa was currently recuperating from an illness, certainly not husband hunting.

Carver walked over to the bed.

Cara had insisted that her cousin was too young yet to think of marriage, to tie herself to husband and family. She should travel, see a little of the world before settling down.

The shadows at the edges of the room remained untouched by the flickering light shed by the oil lamp he preferred to gaslight. Carver saw in them the shadows that had crept into Cara's eyes, that had touched her mouth as her cousin had replied that, yes, she would like to see the other parts of the world, but would enjoy them more with a husband at her side.

Cara had laughed then, but Carver saw the shadows remain. When that time came, she had said, Melissa would not make her choice from among mine owners and iron founders, she would not make her home along the smoking chimneys of the Black Country. Why, even the Queen had ordered the curtains of her carriage closed when she had travelled through it by train.

That might be true or it might not, Harriet had retorted, her pride in what she saw as her own high social standing locally stung. But black or not it was the heart of this country. The coal and the iron taken from it and the graft of its colliers and iron workers had done more to secure wealth for England than any backside that had sat on the throne or any of them that called themselves lords.

Carver smiled now as he had then. Harriet, for all her injured pride, was right. The towns were the heart of England, they were its treasure, its black pearl. One Cara wished to own but was reluctant to wear. Or, it seemed, to permit her cousin to wear.

Reaching for the night wear he had ordered specially tailored, and continued to have made since rejecting odious flannel nightshirts, he slipped his arms into a blue silk jacket, feeling the coolness of it against his skin.

Just what had Cara in mind for her cousin? He slipped buttons one by one through hand-stitched buttonholes. If not a husband from among her wealthy acquaintances, then what? Was it her intention the pretty Melissa should follow her example, not take a husband at all but an assortment of lovers, receiving no wedding ring in return for her favours but just about everything else?

Perhaps it was not such a bad return. He fastened the last button. Certainly for him anyway. He could avail himself whenever he wished for the price of a bauble, and without sharing a marriage bed. Yes, that suited him, or at least it had until Cara had turned her beautiful greedy eyes on Felton industries.

Blue silk trousers clutched forgotten in his hand, Carver stared hard into the lingering shadows. Paul would soon be twenty-one, he would be entitled to his share of Felton industries. That he could have; wealth, property, land, a part in the running of the business! All of that he could have. The experience he was gaining and had gained would serve the purpose it was meant to, to separate him from that girl; for marriage to her he could not allow his brother. A wife Paul may take, but she would not be the child of a Doe Bank collier!

Slipping his legs into the cool silk, drawing it over his hips his mind returned the picture of a young girl with hair the colour of harvest moonlight. A girl with a basket over her arm and a shawl about her shoulders.

Throwing back the covers he dropped into bed at the same time turning off the lamp. Lying back on the pillows darkness rushed in on him but the shadows that filled his eyes gained no entry to his mind. The face imprinted upon it stared back at him, that soft mouth trembling with fear, lovely eyes wide with accusation.

'Bloody wench!' Carver swore softly. 'It's as well I sacked her father. Now we are rid of them Paul will soon forget he ever knew the girl!'

But would he, Carver, forget? Could he forget when at every instant his guard slipped that lovely face returned to haunt him? He had wronged her but it had been for Paul, for his sake. He had wanted only to protect his brother.

But had it been just for Paul? Carver stared into the shadows. How much of the truth would he allow even himself to know?

Memory sweeping him back to that night in the coppice he saw again the beautiful startled face upturned to his, the wisps of moon-kissed hair floating in the breeze.

A wife Paul may take, but she would not be the child of a Doe Bank collier...

Remembering his own words Carver lay still beneath the realisation of the truth.

Jealousy. It was a useful tool...

Thoughts he had smiled over earlier in the evening returned to him but he was not smiling now.

Sometimes tools could be turned against their user.

Chapter Eleven

Her joints aching after spending the rest of the night in the lee of the rock, Emma pushed herself wearily to her feet. In the distance grey smoke curled into the soft pearly light of the morning sky. The barn had been consumed by flames, just as her own home had been.

Pain, hot and fierce as ever, flooded through her. All of her family gone! Her mother, her sister and her father, all taken from her by that terrible fire.

And that other fire, the one from which spirals of smoke still drifted, had that too taken life? Had Eli Coombs and his wife, guilty as they might be of abusing the girl still sleeping on the ground, also been taken by the flames? 'No,' she whispered from white lips. 'Please, God, no!'

'What?' Rubbing sleep from her eyes, the girl looked up at Emma. 'What did you say?'

'Nothing,' she parried the question, not wanting to talk of what had happened at Doe Bank, nor ready to share the horror.

'Where will you be going?'

Emma glanced at the horizon, the tendrils of smoke returning memories that curled icy tremors along her spine. Clenching her teeth she tried to force back the past horror, tried to face the new fear forming in her mind. Where *could* she go? How would she earn her living. She would not be welcome on the waste heaps of any other coal mine; pit bank women had a hard time scraping together the coal chippings they sold for a few pence. It was difficult enough for them to earn their keep locally. They would not share it with her, she would not be tolerated on their territory.

Scrambling to her feet, still rubbing at her eyes, the girl Emma had pulled from Coombses' barn looked at her as she put the question again.

'Where are you going?'

That was a question Emma had asked herself, only one of the many hiding in her heart.

'I don't know,' she answered honestly.

'Where were you bound for last night when you came to the farm?'

Emma brushed stalks of grass from skirts still damp from the night's rain.

'I was not bound for anywhere in particular.'

The girl's thin face clouded and her lips trembled as she turned away.

'You don't have to worry that I'll tag on to you. I just thought we might walk a ways together, that's all.' Her voice shook. 'But you go wherever it is you were headed last night and … and I'll go somewheres else. I don't want to be a burden, not to nobody.'

Seeing the hurt in the girl's eyes as she turned away, Emma felt its echo inside herself. The girl did not want to be a nuisance, she would hold her own pain locked inside herself, just as Carrie had done.

'I didn't mean that having you with me would be a burden,' Emma said quickly. 'It is simply that the place I'd meant to go, where I'd hoped to

162

stay, isn't there any more.'

'I see.' The girl's voice was dull and flat with disbelief. 'It just disappeared, like in a fairy story!'

If only it *had* been a fairy story. If only she could have woken to find that Carver Felton's rape of her, that the deaths of her parents and sister, had been a story she had read the night before and the horror of it would disappear with the morning mist. But it would not. Emma felt the sharp ache of it anew. It would not disappear, would never leave her.

'It has gone,' she said gently. 'But not by any stroke of a fairy wand. Plovers Croft was knocked down, flattened on the orders of its owner.'

'I heard tell of that.' The girl twisted round to face her. 'The folk that passed through told of it, about losing their homes and having to leave behind what they couldn't carry. Many of the women were in tears and the men close to it. But though they hadn't had so much as a cup of tea since early morning, they got nothing from Liza but sharp words. That woman never knew the meaning of the word charity! But why did the owner have the houses pulled down? Nobody seemed to know when they were asked.'

'Owners don't give reasons.' Emma remembered her father's summary dismissal from the Topaz coal mine.

'No, they just chuck people out on to the street. Lor', I wish the same thing would happen to a few of them. Let *them* feel what it's like to be without a home and with nowhere to go. They wouldn't be so quick to give folk their marching orders if they'd had a dose of their own medicine!

So what has become of the folk you hoped to lodge with? Have they gone on the road?'

Drawing the shawl from her shoulders Emma gave it a brisk shake, dislodging blades of grass and stalks of heather. 'Jerusha lived alone. She was a friend of my family's and I had thought to stay at her house at least overnight. But when I reached the Croft the house was gone.'

The girl's hurt giving way to curiosity, she asked, 'Jerusha? Would that be Jerusha Paget who knows the use of herbs and such? I've heard Liza speak of her, but can't say I remember a woman of that name pass by the farm yesterday.'

'She didn't go by way of the farm.' Emma replaced her shawl, fastening the corners beneath her breasts. 'She's gone to live at Doe Bank.'

'She's a friend of your family, you said? So how come you aren't travelling with your folk?'

'I think it's time we moved on.' Emma's mouth set firmly. The girl's enquiry was only natural. Why would Emma not be with her family? But she was not prepared to answer.

Emma's reaction telling her to press no further, the girl brushed at her own ragged skirts. 'Is it all right then? For me to walk alongside you, I mean? It will only be until we get to Wednesbury, then … then I'll be off.'

Where would she be off to? Emma glanced at the stick-like figure walking beside her. The Coombses had taken her from the workhouse was that the place she planned to return to … was it the only place Emma herself would find? The workhouse! The very name evoked dread. People chose to die on the road sooner than be taken into such institutions. But could she make that choice? She was almost certainly carrying a child. Had she the right to kill it too? But then, hadn't she tried once already.

'My name is Daisy ... Daisy Tully.'

Emma smiled into the girl's haggard little face, realising her silence had been taken for rebuke and this was the girl's overture of friendship. 'Mine's Emma,' she said, 'Emma Price.'

'Emma ... that's a pretty name. I like it.'

'Daisy's a pretty name too.'

'My mother used to say it was her favourite, that it was the name *her* mother had. My mother was pretty...' The girl choked on a sob. 'If it hadn't been for me she would still be alive. She worked herself to death so as to keep me!'

Coming to a halt, Emma drew the girl to her. 'Then she must have loved you very much, Daisy.'

'Yes.' The girl sniffed. 'I know she did, but I wish she had put me in the workhouse from being born. She could have left me there and run off, same as the man who ran off and left her pregnant. I wish to God she had then she would still be alive today.'

'We can't know that, Daisy,' Emma soothed. 'But supposing she had left you. Ask yourself, loving you as she did, what kind of life would it have been for her after giving you up? What happiness would she have known then? Be grateful for what you had together, the love you shared. Nothing can take the place of that.'

'I know, but I'm so lonely, Emma, and so afraid of being used by another man such as Eli Coombs.'

Emma's grip on the girl tightened. She was beginning to know what that loneliness was like: to be without the ones you loved, entirely alone in the world. And she had already met with the like of Coombs.

'There can be no substitute for your mother,' she told the weeping girl. 'But we might both be a little less lonely if we stayed together.'

'You mean it?' The girl's eyes lit up. 'You truly mean it, Emma? I can stay with you?'

'For as long as you wish.' She smiled.

Wiping away tears with the back of her hand, Daisy beamed up at her. 'That will be forever, Emma. I will never leave you.'

Emma looked over to the chimneys rising tall and black from the ironworks and coal mines that dominated the town.

I will never leave you, Emma.' Paul Felton had used those very words to her.

But he had left her!

He had been sent away by his brother. And then Carver Felton had deliberately raped her.

'Daisy, I'm sorry but we have to do it, we have to go to the workhouse.'

'No, Emma, we can try...'

'We've tried everywhere.' Emma sank tiredly to the ground. 'There's no one in Wednesbury will give us work or a place to sleep, and we can't go on sleeping under hedges.'

'But, Emma, you don't know what it's like to be in that place. It doesn't just break your heart it destroys your soul. I spent five years in there and, I tell you, I would rather die than go back.'

'That's easy to say.' Emma stared blankly towards the still busy High Street. 'But what of the winter? We can't sleep out in the open in the ice and snow. It has to be the workhouse, Daisy, or we'll both die.'

'It isn't winter yet!' Daisy's mouth set in a defiant line. 'Besides we have pie for supper.'

'Pie?' Emma looked up questioningly.

A smile breaking out on her thin little face, Daisy brought a small crudely wrapped package from her pocket.

Watching her peel back the wax paper Emma felt her stomach cramp with hunger. It was the first food she had seen since that slice of bread and cheese Liza Coombs had grudgingly pushed at her. Two days without food, her only drink being water from the horse trough in the centre of the town or from the brook that bordered the heath.

'There.' Daisy broke the pie into two pieces, holding out half to Emma.

'Where did you get this?' Reaching for the food she paused, eyes widening with horror. 'Daisy, your hands!'

'They don't hurt!' Daisy's mutinous look was back but as Emma made to touch her hands she drew them quickly away.

'Daisy, they *must* hurt, they're red raw. What on earth have you been doing?'

Squatting beside Emma, the girl pushed the pie towards her. 'I been cleaning, that's all, just cleaning. The woman that keeps the pie shop in Union Street said she would give me a couple of mutton pies in return for scrubbing out the shop. I scrubbed all day yesterday while you was looking for work. Then when it came time for her to close up she said there was nothing left, not a crumb, so I was to go there today for what was owed me. Then when I went this morning she said she would pay me what was settled on together with a shilling if I scrubbed the rest of the house. I agreed. Well, I had to, a shilling isn't to be sneezed at, only when time came to settle...'

'She didn't break her word again?'

'No, but that don't mean she didn't try.' Above the mutinous set of her mouth the girl's eyes twinkled. 'Said there was nothing left, just like afore, so I told her I would take the eightpence two pies sold for along with a shilling for the cleaning. Well, that wiped the smirk off her face, but I could see she was thinking of a way to get out of giving me the money, so I told her if I wasn't paid what we'd agreed then come the morning there would not be a whole pane of glass in her windows.'

'Daisy!' Emma tried not to smile. 'You didn't?'

'I bloody well did!' Daisy bit into her share of the pie, chewing with noisy satisfaction. 'That old bag weren't going to cheat me again. I said I was happy to leave it at that if she were; that it would cost more than a shilling and eightpence to get her windows put back in. She threatened to call for the bobbies but I gave her a small reminder that changed her tune.'

'A reminder?' Emma stared at the girl who suddenly seemed so much older than herself.

'Arrh.' Her mouth full of pie, Daisy nodded. 'I reminded her there be some things that even a bobby has to turn his back to and while his back is turned... Anyway she could tell I were taking no more of her fancy dealings so she paid up.'

'But you still got only one pie?'

'That be true.' Daisy smiled. 'This time there were only one left. It were the one she'd laid aside for her own supper!'

Emma took the pie the girl still held towards her, mouth watering with hunger.

'Then the woman did cheat you?'

Picking each separate crumb from her skirts and popping it in her mouth, Daisy licked each red finger with a slow appreciative tongue.

'She'd have to be smarter than she is to do that, Emma. I only got one pie, true enough, but I got the fourpence in place of the other one. Mind, it would have been worth taking a penny less to see the look on her face. Eh! If looks could kill, the preacher man would be saying his words over me right now.'

The preacher man! Emma's hand dropped from her mouth, food forgotten, as the horror of that night flooded back in stark reality. The preacher man. That was what the whole of Doe Bank had called him. The man who'd helped sort out problems, who'd preached in the Chapel. The man who'd quoted the Bible while abusing his own child.

'Emma, be you all right?'

Daisy's anxious voice brought her back from the edge of the darkness that beckoned. ''Twould be better if you ate that pie rather than nursed it. Lack of food has made you feel faint.' Anxiety sharpening her voice, Daisy fumbled once more into her pocket drawing out a small bottle she had filled with water.

'Jackson's chemist's shop,' she explained, pulling out the cork. 'He weren't looking so I borrowed a bottle. We'll give it back when we're finished.'

The water helped clear the awful shadows from her mind. Emma handed back the bottle.

'I ... I must be more hungry than I'd thought.' The explanation failed to bring the smile she had intended. 'But I'll be fine once I have eaten.'

'Then stop talking and get that pie inside of you. Then we'll talk about that workhouse!'

'He is very handsome.' Melissa Gilbert studied her own reflection in the triple mirrors of her dressing table. 'Those silver streaks in his dark hair lend him quite a devilish look.'

'And you like that?' Cara watched her cousin pull a brush through long chestnut hair that gleamed in the gaslight.

'It helps make a man more interesting, and Carver Felton is certainly that.'

'Carver ... or Carver's money!'

Melissa smiled into the mirror. 'I find both more than a little interesting.'

'Forget Carver Felton!' Cara snapped. 'He would do you no good.'

'Laying the brush aside, wide swathes of soft shining hair falling over her shoulders, covering shapely breasts hidden beneath soft white silk, Melissa twisted about on her small gilt chair. 'Maybe he would not, Cara, but his money most certainly would.'

A snatch of breath marking her irritation, Cara

Holgate's handsome face darkened. She had not expected this. She had not thought Melissa and Carver Felton would meet.

'You can do better for yourself than him. There are plenty of men with money enough to make him look like a pauper.'

Melissa smiled in the way she knew would heighten her cousin's annoyance. She had always been able to get under Cara's skin. Ever since they were children she had played this game, and she had always won.

'But do they have his looks?' she asked softly, grey eyes following every nuance, every shade of emotion that flickered across the other woman's face. 'I prefer a man I am considering as a husband to have both those qualities: money and a handsome face.'

A husband? Cara felt her nerves quicken. If Melissa and Carver were to wed, where would that leave her?

'Carver Felton your husband!' She laughed lightly. 'My dear girl, how can you even think it? He's a womaniser. He has made love to at least a dozen women I can put a name to, and probably as many again that I cannot!'

'Including yourself, Cara?'

A smile painting her mouth like rouge, Melissa waited for the reply, inwardly congratulating herself. The question had obviously taken Cara off guard.

'I...' she stuttered. 'I ... that has nothing to do with it!'

'I agree.' Turning back to the mirror Melissa took up the brush once more, drawing it through the rich thickness of her hair. 'The number of women Carver Felton has had or who they are is of no importance. I want only his name, his money and the position that goes with them. The other things that go with marriage can be found elsewhere. By Carver and myself.'

'So, you are thinking of Felton for a husband?' Cara stared back at the smiling grey eyes while inside her jealousy tumbled like rushing waters.

'Only thinking of it, Cara.' Brush held in mid-air, Melissa watched the effect of her answer on the older woman. 'At the moment.'

Aware of the iron will beneath her cousin's smile, Cara turned away, walking to the other side of the room before answering. 'I would have thought that had you to choose a husband from among iron masters and colliery owners you would have chosen someone younger. Someone like Arthur Payne, for instance.'

'Arthur Payne?' Touching the back of her brush to her mouth, Melissa adopted a pensive look. 'He's younger, of course, and is handsome in a pretty boy sort of way. But then, I do not care for men when they are quite so young. They're so ... so gauche, don't you think Cara.'

'No, I do not,' she snapped. 'What I do think is that you would be a fool even to consider Felton. He would only take what he wanted then drop you. And think how *that* would go down in the drawing rooms of Wednesbury, not to mention Rugeley.'

'It would cause a stir. But then a woman has merely to change her gown to set this town talking.'

172

'I am glad you see that. So unless you wish to be the centre of attention you will cease throwing yourself at Carver Felton!'

Turning once again so her gaze was on the mirror, Melissa shrugged her silk-clad shoulders. 'If being the centre of their attention means I have all of Carver's, then so be it. I suppose a woman must be prepared to suffer a little censure to get what she wants.'

'Or a great deal of pain getting what she deserves!' Cara's eyes blazed angrily. 'Play your games if you must, Melissa – and, God help us we both know you must – but don't play them with Carver Felton. He is not for you!'

Setting the brush on the dressing table, Melissa watched the older woman's reflection, saw the fingers curl and uncurl at her sides, the full mouth tight as a drawstring. This was far enough for now. Annoy Cara further and she might just send her packing back to Rugeley, where it was doubtful Felton would follow. He was only just sniffing at the bait; he had to swallow it before he could be reeled in.

'You're probably right, Cara, maybe he's not for me. But you must agree he would make an excellent catch for somebody?'

That he would. Cara watched her cousin rise from the small gilt chair, shapely body moving sinuously beneath its silken sheath, the wealth of chestnut hair gleaming against skin that might be mistaken for alabaster. Melissa was beautiful but that beauty would not be wasted on Carver Felton. Melissa would never become his wife.

'I was being silly.' Her pretty mouth drooping,

Melissa held out her hands to her cousin. 'You shouldn't let me tease you so, Cara. You have always been like a sister to me, letting me say and do the most hurtful things and never once reprimanding me. I feel dreadfully ashamed. I know you and Carver have an understanding, that you are to marry in the future. I have behaved stupidly. Forgive me, Cara, please?'

Anger melting from her, she took the hand stretched towards her. 'Let us forget all about it. I think we should both say goodnight and go to bed.'

Grey eyes glistening beneath half-closed lids Melissa's voice was husky, her mouth softly penitent.

'I'll say goodnight, Cara, but not until you say you forgive me. Really forgive me.'

Releasing one hand, Cara touched the tumbling chestnut curls.

'I forgive you, Lissa,' she murmured, kissing the girl's pale cheek. 'Of course I forgive you.'

Chapter Twelve

'That were good!' Daisy brushed the flecks of pastry from her skirt. 'That woman has a face like a fourpenny hock but she makes a good pie.'

'Is she really so long-faced?' Emma smiled as she too shook away the last remnants of supper.

'Long-faced?' Daisy laughed. 'I tell you, Emma, were she to lie down it could be mistaken for the Holyhead Road.'

Listening to the girl's laughter ring across the heath, Emma's own smile faded. Sometimes when they had been alone her sister had laughed like that. Carrie! Emma glanced away towards the twin spires of the churches on the distant hill and the pain of that night came sweeping over her again. If only she had known, if only Carrie had told her, she could have helped ... done something. But what? Would she have had any more courage than her sister had had? Could she have faced their father, openly accused him? And if she had, what then? In the quiet that followed Daisy's laughter she seemed to hear the voice she had heard so often. *'Brother will turn against brother, the child against the father....'* Caleb Price, the preacher man, would have wielded the words of the Bible like a weapon, leaving Carrie and herself to suffer the barbs of guilt.

'Eh, don't go to sleep yet.' Mistaking silence for sleepiness Daisy touched Emma's shoulder. 'We are not sleeping on the heath tonight.'

Keeping her eyes lowered so the girl would not see the torture she hid, Emma reached for the hand extended to her, feeling the wince of pain as her fingers closed over it.

'It's nothing,' Daisy said as Emma cried an apology. 'It's just soda causes the soreness. It bites away the skin, and old long face at the pie shop likes plenty of it in the bucket when you be cleaning, same as they do in the workhouse.'

Emma released the girl's hand. 'Daisy, I know how you feel about going back there but we have to. We can't go on sleeping in the open, depending on charity for food.'

'No, Emma!' Daisy burst out. 'You *don't* know what it's like 'cos you've never been put there! You've never been ordered to keep a still tongue from morning 'til night save for one hour. To scrub floors and stairs 'til the blood runs from your hands. To stand with head bent whenever a wardress passes. To fetch and carry for them like a dog only to be kicked like one and then have to stand and thank heaven for its mercy and the parish for its beneficence. No, Emma, you *don't* know what it's like or how it feels!

'You speak of depending on charity for food. Don't be fooled. You get no charity from the parish. Every crumb is slaved for, every slice of bread paid for in a sweat. The parish workhouse!' Daisy laughed, a low cynical sound. 'The only charity they give is the charity of death. That's the only relief to be found inside those walls!'

The shadows beginning to creep over the sky matched those in the girl's eyes, and the ones that darkened Emma's heart. Daisy and Carrie, two girls not much more than children, what they both had suffered! Drawing the girl against her, feeling the shiver than ran through her thin body, Emma felt the same desperation. Not to go to the parish might mean death from cold and hunger, while to knock on its door would certainly result in heartbreak.

'It's all right, Daisy,' she murmured. 'We'll ask for no charity, and we'll find somewhere to sleep.'

'We'll ask none for a night or two anyway.' Daisy brightened. 'We have a shilling and fourpence. That will buy a bed at Joe Baker's and a breakfast of bread and dripping. We ain't starving just yet, Emma.'

Daisy would spend the money she had worked two days to earn on buying them a bed in a lodging house, while she ... Emma felt a warm flush suffuse her cheeks ... while she kept the shilling Carver Felton had left her.

'Two shillings and fourpence,' she said softly. 'I have a shilling also.'

'Is that the money you offered Coombs to leave you alone?' Then, when Emma nodded, 'If it took rape to get you to part with that shilling then I reckon you'd better keep it, least until we be desperate. And we ain't that, not yet. Come on, I know a place we might spend the night. It won't cost the price Joe Baker asks, and there won't be so many fleas neither.'

Matching the brisk pace set by Daisy, Emma followed her along Lower High Street, pausing to let the occupants of a hansom pass into the Turk's Head Hotel.

Grabbing her arm, Daisy hauled her on. 'Step lively, Emma. The Shambles will be picked clean afore we get there.'

Almost running the remaining distance she turned left into a narrow street. The pungent smell of meat and offal hung heavy in the air. Along one side wooden trestles strung with unlit candle jars lay empty; only one stall still boasted a feeble light.

'Good!' Daisy released her hold on Emma, running ahead to where a man in a long apron and straw boater was packing knives into a large wicker basket.

'Evening, Mr Hollington.' Emma watched as Daisy bobbed him a polite curtsy. 'Am I too late? Oh, I hope not, my mother said not to buy sausages from any other butcher. She said not to bring any but the best and that could only be got from Samuel Hollington.'

'Did her now?' His busy side whiskers bristling as he smiled, the man looked at Daisy. 'Told you to watch your manners too so it seems. Well now, I reckon I can find a couple of sausages.'

Reaching deep into the basket, knife clinking against knife, he drew out a string of plump sausages. Counting off a dozen he grinned at Daisy. 'So, me little wench, do you reckon that be good enough for your mother?'

Delight showing in her answering smile, Daisy nodded, delving into her pocket for the coins she had earned earlier.

'How much is that, please?'

Wrapping the sausages in a sheet of paper retrieved from the basket, the man smiled anew.

'That'll be tuppence.' He passed the parcel to her. 'But the price be halved by that smile of yours. Now you go back to that sister waiting along of you on the corner and both of you be off home.'

Bobbing another curtsy as she smiled good-night, Daisy ran back to Emma, pulling her out of earshot before she spoke.

'I reckoned on Hollington still being there, he's always the very last to leave the market.'

'But how did you know?' Emma questioned when Daisy paused for breath.

'You get to know a lot when you work for Liza Coombs. I had to come to the Shambles every Saturday night and wait 'til Hollington were near enough sold out. Come ten and eleven o'clock at night he would be near enough giving stuff away, 'specially to them he could see hadn't hardly a halfpenny to bless themselves with. Good-natured don't describe Butcher Hollington and grasping don't describe Liza! She would send me with sixpence full knowing I would get a pig's head and near enough a loin of chops or an aitchbone of beef that would feed them for a week and still get threepence change. But even so she was never satisfied. Greedy old cow! But forget Liza, let's go and cook these sausages.'

'We need a pan and a kitchen fire to do that,' Emma said as Daisy set off at a trot. 'And we don't have either.'

'Watch and learn, Emma.' Daisy's laughter floated behind her. 'Watch and learn!'

After Cara had left for her own bedroom, Melissa

179

dropped the penitent pose. Her cousin intended to have Carver Felton for herself, but what Cara wanted and what she was allowed to have were two entirely different things! But Melissa would play the pliant young girl ... until it suited her to change the game.

Returning to the mirror she stared at her reflection. Drawing the silk nightgown close about her body, she studied the slender curves of waist and rounded hips then with one swift movement pulled the nightgown over her head, throwing it from her with a soft exultant laugh.

This was what would buy her all that she wanted. Placing a hand on each hip she stroked the soft flesh. *This* was all it would take to make her mistress of a fine house.

Grey eyes gleaming, lips parted, she continued to stare at her own nakedness, watch her own hand caress her stomach then slide slowly into the curving hollow of her waist and upward to cup the burgeoning mounds of her breasts.

This would buy her any man's name, and the man she wanted was Carver Felton.

And he wanted her. That much had been plain from the looks and little attentions he had directed towards her at dinner. Much to the chagrin of Arthur Payne, not to mention Cara.

Oh, he may think that like her cousin Melissa Gilbert would be willing to become his mistress, and maybe she would. For a time. Smiling at herself, Melissa squeezed her nipples gently between thumb and finger. But only so long as it suited her. She would let him taste the wine but it would take a wedding ring to purchase the whole bottle. And once she was the wife of Felton of Felton Hall, cousin Cara could go to hell!

Ignoring the silk lying like a tiny heap of newly fallen snow on the pale jade carpet, Melissa turned off the gasolier, leaving only a night light to combat the shadows, and slid naked beneath the sheets.

It would only take a few nights. Or maybe she would grant him just one. Once having held her body in his arms, sampled the delights of her soft flesh, he would not be able to resist. But she would. She smiled in the darkness. Melissa Gilbert would not be such easy prey or so willing a partner as her cousin. Poor Cara! Spreading her arms wide, Melissa pressed herself into the soft caress of fine linen sheets. Cara thought to see Carver Felton at the altar, and so she would. But the bride he would be taking would be her cousin.

'Daisy, just where are we going?' Emma caught up with the figure trotting before her. She had followed her friend through a maze of narrow streets and alleyways, each darker and more forbidding than the one before, the close-packed houses showing no more within them than the flicker of a candle.

'We're almost there.' Daisy slowed to a walk.

'But where is that?' Emma panted.

'The Monway.' Daisy pointed over to where a large building loomed in the darkness. 'That be the Monway iron foundry. The watchman there will let us cook the sausages over his brazier, and if we share them with him he might let us sleep the night in his hut.'

'We ... we couldn't do that.'

'I bloody well could!' Daisy expostulated. 'It beats lying out on the heath all night. It'll be warm and dry and it won't take any of our money.'

'But I have a shilling, that will buy us a bed...'

'No!' Daisy retorted sharply. 'I don't want to know how you came by that money, but I do know it must have been a way you won't forget in a hurry seeing as what you have gone through without the spending of it. So you leave it lie where it is. We'll get by, Emma, we ain't beat yet.'

Slipping her hand into Emma's, she smiled. 'That watchman won't be able to say no to Hollington's sausages.'

The soft growl of a dog warning them not to come any nearer, Emma held back from the welcoming heat of the glowing brazier.

'What you be about?' A man with shoulders stooped by age stepped out of a nearby hut. 'Don't you come no nearer.' He peered into the shadows. 'Not lessen you want to feel General Kitchener's teeth in your arse!'

'We only wanted to stand a minute at your fire,' Daisy called.

'A wench, be it?' the man answered. 'Well, step you up. But I warns you, the General's bite be a lot worse than his bark. One wrong move and he'll have you!'

Her hand still in Emma's, Daisy stepped into the circle of firelight. 'We don't mean any harm, mister. Me and my friend want only to warm ourselves. The heath gets cold at night.'

The old man dropped his hand to the dog's head and it sank to its belly, though its eyes, glowing redly, stayed fixed on the two women. 'It does that, but how come the pair of you be on the heath at this time of night?'

'It makes a bed when you got no other,' Daisy answered while Emma stood groping for words.

'Oh!' The voice, gravelly with age, took on a note of apprehension that was immediately picked up by the dog whose throat rumbled another warning. 'How come you have no bed? Be the bobbies after you?'

'If they are I'd let them catch me.' Daisy grinned. 'At least then I'd have a place to sleep. In the cells. It has to be better than sleeping under a hedge.'

'You don't know what you be saying, little wench.' The watchman coughed in the back of his throat. 'A few nights in one of them gaols and you'd soon sing a different tune, you'd pray to be out on the heath. I know, I've seen men and women after they've served a term along the line and I tell you they ain't been pretty to look at. No, by God they ain't. Well step up and warm yourselves. That's what you came for, ain't it?'

Drawing the package from beneath her shawl, Daisy held it out. 'We came to warm ourselves and … and to ask could we cook these over your fire? We're willing to share them with you, and there'd be one for the General too.'

His interest caught, the old man took another step forward. 'What you got there?'

'Sausages fresh from butcher Hollington in the Shambles.'

'The General be partial to a sausage.' The old man coughed again. 'You wait there. I've a pan in the hut. And remember his teeth – he ain't choosy who he sinks 'em into!'

Droplets of fat jumping from the pan sizzled on the glowing coals, arousing the attention of the dog who raised his short muzzle to sniff the air appreciatively.

'You make a good job of cooking.' The old man eyed Emma in almost the same way. 'Same as you make a good job of not answering my question.'

She glanced up from prodding the sausages with a fork the watchman had produced along with a tin plate. 'What question, Mr...'

'Birks,' the man supplied. 'My name is Enoch Birks.'

Politeness an instinct with Emma she bobbed him a small curtsy. 'Good evening, Mr Birks. May I present my friend, Daisy Tully, and myself, Emma Price.'

In the light of the brazier the old man's eyes twinkled and he grinned beneath the generous moustache.

'Well, if that don't be the prettiest introduction I've ever been given! You be fair well-mannered, the two of you. Makes a change to be addressed civil in this day and age, you be more like to be ignored by young folk today; they think 'cos a body has a few years they be bound to be senile or stupid. No manners.' He shook his head. 'That be what's wrong with folk today, no manners and no respect. But you two have been brought up to

184

know better, that be plain.'

Smiling her thanks, Emma returned her attention to the frying pan, turning each sausage while trying to avoid the darts of hot fat that sprayed with each move.

'But I ain't senile,' Enoch resumed. 'Old I be, but I ain't stupid. That were a pretty speech you made, wench, but it still didn't tell me where you be from nor how come it is you have no bed?'

Glancing quickly at Daisy, Emma caught the faint movement of her head. Daisy was warning her to say nothing. But the old man had been kind to them, he had not turned them away. He could so easily have set the dog on them but he had let them stay. Such an action deserved an answer that contained, if not all the truth, at least an element of it.

'I come from Doe Bank.' Her voice just audible above the splutter of the pan she kept her eyes lowered, hiding the pain that immediately leapt to them. 'My home was ... was accidentally burned and my family died in the fire. I was visiting a friend who lived at Plovers Croft at the time. That's how come I too did not die.'

'Plovers Croft?' Touching the dog's ears Enoch soothed its rising enthusiasm at the smell of cooking. 'That place were flattened days since. Several of the folk stopped by here on their way into the town.'

'Yes,' Emma answered quietly. 'When my own home was destroyed, I'd hoped to stay at Jerusha Paget's house...'

'Jerusha Paget?' Enoch broke in quickly. 'Be that the woman that physics folk?'

'She uses herbal medicines.'

'Arrh, that be the one. She helped my Mary many a time. She dead?'

'No. Jerusha decided she was too old to go on the road so she stayed in Doe Bank, but I ... I could not face staying there.'

Staring into the brazier, Enoch moved his head slowly from side to side. 'The road be a hard place at any age, but there be more danger there for two young wenches. No respect, you see, no respect for women!'

Forking the sausages on to the plate, Emma took the thick wedges of bread that were to have been the watchman's meagre supper and dipped each one into the sizzling fat. Adding several sausages to each, she handed them to Enoch.

'Share and share alike.' Breaking each sandwich in half he handed a portion to each of the girls, laying another on the ground for the eager General Kitchener.

Biting into the still too hot food he danced his jaw up and down jiggling the sausage on his tongue as he grabbed quick shallow breaths to cool his tongue.

Hiding her smile, Emma laid the smoking pan on a nearby pile of bricks, sitting herself beside it.

'So what you two be going to do?' More wary this time, Enoch blew on his sausage before taking a second bite. 'I doubt you'll be taken on anywhere in this town. Folk with money have all the help they need, and them without...' he shrugged '...them without have a hard time feeding themselves. You'll find there be precious few have anything to spare. So I reckon you two will have to settle for the parish. I hear several from Plovers Croft have already gone into the workhouse, God pity them, and you for having to follow.'

'No!' Squatting beside the brazier Daisy's eyes flashed bright as the sparks shooting from the coals. 'We're going into no workhouse! This time I do know what I am saying, Mr Birks. I spent years in that hell and I'll die before I go back there. Nothing can be worse than that place ... nothing!'

In the ensuing silence Emma heard Daisy's stifled sobs and moved closer, taking the younger girl in her arms. Beside the old man the dog nudged its nose into his palm.

'Seems General Kitchener agrees with me,' Enoch said at last. 'He reckons you should spend the night in the hut. That be if you two young ladies can trust an old soldier?'

'Implicitly, Mr Birks.'

Smiling at Emma's answer, the old man rose to place a kettle of water in the heart of the brazier.

'Then get you inside while I brew a mash of tea. A warm drink and you can settle to sleep. And you need have no fear of being disturbed, not with old Kitchener on guard. Don't even a beetle get past him.'

Helping Daisy to her feet, Emma paused beside the old man then shyly kissed his cheek. 'Thank you, Mr Birks,' she whispered. 'Thank you very much.'

'I told you!' Daisy smiled broadly, every trace of her sobs vanished as they entered the small brick hut. 'I told you we'd get shelter here for the night, and I was right. Give the watchman a share of the sausage and he gives us a place to sleep.'

'Yes, you were right, but it can only be for one night.'

'But why?' Daisy grinned, settling herself into a corner. 'Share and share alike, the old man said so. We share our supper, he shares his hut. There's nothing wrong with that. It can go on just as long as we have money to buy supper.'

'No, Daisy, it cannot. Mr Birks is an old man, he needs his rest more than we do. He can't be put out of his hut night after night, he has to sleep.'

Daisy sat up, tucking her skirts over her feet. 'But he's a night watchman. He's supposed to keep watch, not sleep.'

'We both know that. But he's old, Daisy. Too old for this job but it's probably the only way he can earn enough to keep him from the workhouse. It's the dog that does the watching, you must see that.'

Her grin dissolving in a shame-faced expression, Daisy nodded. 'I guess I knew that all along, but the thought of that workhouse keeps everything else away. I'm sorry, Emma. We'll share the tea with him and then we'll go.'

'Go where?' Balancing a tin cup and two jam jars filled with tea on a broken slate, Enoch stood in the doorway.

Emma turned. 'We were thinking, Mr Birks. We shouldn't deprive you of your hut. We'll share your tea and gladly, but then we'll leave.'

Holding out the slate first to Emma and then to

Daisy, the old man took his cup and sipped his tea.

'So you would leave!' Grey head lifting, he stared deep into Emma's eyes. 'You would share your meal with an old man then refuse the only hospitality he has to offer in return?'

The heat of the tea burning her through the glass jar, Emma set it down on the upturned tea chest that served as a table.

'You were welcome to a share of our food, Mr Birks, but Daisy and I both feel we must not deprive you of your hut.'

Dropping into the lone chair, Enoch placed his cup beside Emma's jar. 'I was welcome to what you had to give.' He spoke quietly, one hand falling to the head of the dog that padded in after him. 'But my hospitality is not welcome to you. This hut holds little comfort, but then I thought you would have known that afore you accepted. Seems I were wrong, that you expected more.'

'No, we didn't. We expected nothing more.' Emma glanced unhappily at Daisy sitting huddled in the corner, the jar of tea untouched on the floor beside her.

'Truth is, Mr Birks, it were my idea, all of it. I told Emma you'd likely let us spend the night in your hut in return for a few sausages.'

'Which I did.'

'Yes, Mr Birks, which you did,' Emma answered. 'And very kindly. But we feel we cannot put you out of your hut. You cannot spend the night outside.'

'Share and share alike!'

Recognising in his tone a mixture of hurt pride

and dignity, Emma blushed for shame. Glancing again at Daisy she saw contrition on the girl's face. Returning her glance to the old man, Emma smiled.

'Then share with us, Mr Birks. Share the hut.'

Old eyes displaying his appreciation of the trust placed in him, Enoch fondled the dog's ears. 'The General and me appreciates that, wench. We both hopes you find the sort of life you deserves.'

The sort of life she deserved? Lying beside a sleeping Daisy, Emma's mind refused the opium of sleep. What did she deserve, a girl who never saw the torment that drove her sister and her mother to suicide? Never recognised the evil that lay behind her father's preaching. She deserved only what she had: a life on the road and a bastard child in her womb.

Chapter Thirteen

'So you see, Langton, we bring a canal through here and getting our products to market can be accomplished in less than half the time.'

From the carriage's stopping place on the road, Carver Felton pointed out over the expanse of empty heathland.

'A canal is only part of it, Felton.' Rafe Langton ran one hand over his bushy side whiskers. 'There be other things to be taken in consideration. Things like wharves and loading sheds and like as not a basin barges can pull into while they wait for cargo. It all takes money.'

'He's right, it does take money, and I for one am not certain I wish to invest in such a scheme. We're getting our steel away quite comfortably using the present carrier. I don't see any real necessity for change.'

Arthur Payne couldn't see a brick wall at five paces! Carver glanced at the young man. Show him an Italian leather boot or a fancy jacket and he'd see every stitch. But business? It was a pity old man Payne had no son but this to leave his steel works to; but the son of Carver Felton would be different; he like his father, would see the chances in life. He would continue where his father had left off, build Felton's into a commercial empire.

But for the moment it would prove beneficial to

carry these men with him into the venture. Their money would help to make the prospect a reality, and then...

'It takes money to make money.' Carver kept his voice level. 'Your father was a man who saw that.'

'My father is no longer head of Payne Steel.'

Carver's black eyes glinted and his mouth held a touch of mockery as he looked at the man leaning back languidly against the carriage's blue upholstery. 'That is an obstacle one can only pray Payne Steel will surmount!' he rejoined.

'Look here.' Rafe Langton took a watch from his waistcoat pocket, checked the time then returned it. 'You two pups can snap and snarl all day but I have a good lunch waiting and I don't intend to see it wasted. We came out here to decide once and for all what we mean to do regarding this canal. Now either we do that or I'm off!'

Shrugging his shoulders, Arthur Payne flicked a gloved finger over the hat resting on his knee.

'What about labour, Felton?' Langton went on without pausing. 'That will add considerably to the final investment.'

'Not so much, the way I plan it,' Carver replied, glancing back to the heath. 'I propose to bring in my own labour force, one that will work for half the amount we would normally expect to pay.'

'Eh!' His interest freshly kindled, Rafe Langton edged forward in his seat. 'Half the amount, you say, and just how do you propose doing that?'

'There is a threatened famine in Ireland. Their potato harvest has all but failed yet again, so I am reliably informed. When men are starving they will work for pennies. I intend to bring some of them over here to dig out this canal.'

'But will that not give rise to further expenditure?' Arthur Payne smiled triumphantly. 'There are men hereabouts who have need of work, you would not need to pay to have them brought in.'

'That is very observant of you, Payne.' Carver nodded indulgently. 'But once more you seem to have missed the point. A man from Ireland will not only work more cheaply, he will work twice as hard for fear of losing the job that will keep his whole family from starvation. He will also bear in mind the fact that if that job is lost, so are his chances of earning the fare to return to them. So, you see, we can only benefit from bringing them here and will recoup the cost of their transportation in a matter of days.'

'And the cost of housing these men?' Arthur retaliated. 'Have you considered that in your book keeping?'

'Housing?' Carver turned his head, the sunlight flashing silver from the twin streaks sweeping back from his brow. 'We undertake to give a man a job, we do not offer a house to go with it!'

'But they will need a place to sleep. Surely, Felton, even you can't expect them to live without shelter?'

The derisory smile once more touching his mouth, Carver climbed back into the carriage. 'Even you, Payne, must have heard of tents? We provide tents. If they want more than that, they provide it for themselves.'

'My God, Felton, you've thought this business through.' Rafe Langton's fat jowls wobbled as he nodded his approval. 'I must say, I'm impressed. How about you, Payne?'

Eyes the colour of burnt toffee were fixed on Carver, the message they contained very different from the words Arthur Payne spoke. 'Oh, I'm impressed! But then, Carver never fails to impress.'

'So, can we say we're agreed? Are you definitely in?'

Toffee-coloured eyes never wavering, Arthur Payne inclined his well-groomed head. Felton made money whatever he touched, and like the fellow or not, the chance to share in his profit could not be overlooked. Especially when some other fellow did the donkey work.

'You have my word upon it. Shall we say tomorrow at eleven to sign the necessary contracts?'

'We need no contracts.' Rafe Langton's heavy body swayed as the carriage lurched forward. 'A man's word is as good as his signature any day.'

'Agreed.' Arthur's brown eyes met Carver's black stare. 'But a man's word cannot be locked in a safe.'

Young Payne might be a bit of a fop but beneath it all there lay a brain. If only his father had forced him to turn it to the steel works instead of letting him fritter away his time in gambling houses and whores' beds.

Carver ran a glance over the rack of shirts hanging in his dressing room.

They had signed contracts that morning, each

194

taking a copy as proof of his one-third share in the canal venture. Carver had not counted on that happening.

Selecting a shirt of ivory silk, he slipped it on, fastening each tiny mother-of-pearl button with dextrous fingers.

Contracts had a way of binding a man to his word. But contracts could be bought or given away!

Settling on an amber silk cravat, he slipped it about his neck, fashioning it into a graceful knot at his throat.

It was fortunate Payne liked the ladies; even more fortunate that one of those ladies was Melissa Gilbert. It had been obvious that night at dinner. Arthur Payne would like to know that particular lady a little more intimately. Carver gazed into the mirror. But there was the problem of the over-attentive Cara. The woman was possessive where the pretty Lissa was concerned. One would almost think she was the girl's mother! Though even mothers could be persuaded.

Shrugging into the dove grey cashmere jacket set out for him, Carver brushed his finger over its velvet collar, a speculative expression on his face.

Cara too could be persuaded, if it was to her final benefit. A contract in exchange for a rich husband for her beloved cousin, the exchange of a contract for a hefty sum for Cara Holgate. Taking gloves and handkerchief from a mahogany tallboy, Carver smiled. The contract would not lie long in Arthur Payne's safe!

Dismissing the smile but not the thought as his

carriage stopped at Cara Holgate's house, he walked inside.

'There's no need for introductions.' Cara gestured gracefully to a chair as he was shown into the drawing room. 'You know everyone here, Carver, we're all friends.'

'Indeed we are.' He acknowledged each with a nod but coming to Melissa Gilbert, raised her hand to his lips, saying, 'But with some we would have that friendship become ... deeper.'

'We were just discussing a shopping expedition.' Cara moved quickly to stand beside her cousin's chair. 'Melissa is very fond of enamels. She was enchanted by the brooch you gave me for Christmas. I thought we might visit Birmingham, they have a larger selection of shops than we have here.'

'They have shops it is true.' Carver smiled at Cara's cousin. 'But we can do better than any shop. A visit to an enameller's workshop, to commission a trinket of your very own design. You would not find such in a Birmingham store.'

'Oh, come now, Carver.' Harriet Langton admonished him. 'You cannot possibly mean to propose a visit to such a place? The dirt and the smells ... oh, my dear Melissa, you have no idea what those places are like!'

'They are dirty, just like an iron foundry is dirty.' Carver continued to look into Melissa Gilbert's cool grey eyes. 'They smell of chemicals and smoke as do the factories of this town, but the skills of the Bilston enamellers are worthy of a visit. Their work is the finest in the world, even Her Majesty has said so.'

'But Melissa can see their products just as well in a shop.' Harriet waved one hand dismissively. 'Tell him so, Cara, tell him you will not allow her to go swanning around filthy workshops...'

'My cousin does not order me,' Melissa broke in before Harriet could say more or Cara could answer. 'She advises, Mrs Langton.'

'Then listen to her advice, child!' Harriet flapped her ornately painted fan. 'Men sometimes forget there are places where it is not seemly for a woman to be seen.'

'Harriet is speaking sensibly, my dear.' Cara watched Carver settle into an elegant Sheraton chair. 'The workshops at Bilston are not a suitable place for you. You will do far better to visit the shops at Birmingham.

'Have you ever visited the enamel workshops, Cara?'

Eyes widening innocently, Melissa twisted around to look into her cousin's face.'

Taken aback by the question Cara breathed a relieved sigh as dinner was announced.

'You did not answer me,' Melissa reproved as they took their seats at table. 'I asked, have you paid a visit to these Bilston enamellers?'

Damn Carver Felton! Cara spread a perfectly laundered napkin across her lap. She knew what lay behind this talk of a Bilston visit. Carver would have Lissa to himself, maybe for longer than it took to view some pretty bits and pieces. He was not interested in where the girl chose her trinket. So just what was it that interested him?

Her smile not reaching her eyes, Cara lifted a crystal glass, taking a sip before replying. 'Yes, I have. Carver took me there a year or so ago.'

'Then that settles it! If it is a place my cousin can visit then I am sure, Mrs Langton, you will agree it is not unseemly for me to do the same. And since you have been once already, Cara, I will not ask you repeat the disagreeable experience. I shall ask Mr Felton to take me. I am certain you will have no objection to that, Cara?' Melissa turned her face to Carver. 'You will take me to Bilston, will you not, Carver?'

'Providing your cousin has no objection to your being alone with me, then I would deem it an honour.'

Bastard! Lids veiling her green-gold eyes, Cara hid the animosity that rose high in her. He knew an answer such as he had given left no room for refusal without downright rudeness. Not that she and rudeness were strangers, but for now she would observe the proprieties.

But soon, very soon now, Carver Felton would be brought to heel. Once they were married the situation would be very different indeed.

'Wait for me at the top end of Union Street.' Those had been Daisy's words before they had parted early that morning. They had both agreed it might be easier for them to find work singly rather than together. Emma drew her shawl more tightly about her. For herself it had been another day that brought no reward, the answer the same wherever she asked. No help wanted.

Things could not go on this way. Sick with hunger, she leaned against a shop wall. They had talked of their situation for a long time last night, sheltering behind the sheds at the railway sidings. Emma had told Daisy that there was no alternative, they must go to the workhouse. But she had not told the girl of the child she carried. Maybe Daisy would have been more understanding had she done so; as it was she had made no answer, merely lowered her face into her shawl. And now she was not where she had promised they would meet!

Pushing herself away from the wall at the approach of quick footsteps, Emma caught her breath as a woman turned the corner and collided heavily with her, knocking Emma off her feet.

'Why don't you shift yourself out of the way!' the woman snapped angrily. 'You'd do a bloody sight better were you to find yourself work instead of hangin' about the streets getting under the feet of honest working folk! I don't know what things be coming to, I really don't – standing begging in the streets, living off the backs of others afore you'll do a day's work!'

'I apologise if I was in your way.' Emma steadied herself as the woman hitched a basket higher on her arm. 'But I am not begging, I am...'

'If you ain't begging then what do you be doing standing on the street and it almost ten o'clock at night?' the woman replied tartly. 'Waiting for some man who'll part with a shilling for a feel beneath your skirts? Well, we'll see what the bobbies have to say about that!'

Muttering beneath her breath, she swept on her way.

That woman had thought she was a beggar. In the darkness Emma's cheeks flamed, then just as quickly her blood turned to ice. It was worse than that. The woman had thought she was a whore! Behind her the shop door rattled loudly as it was flung wide and a tall man, made taller by the top hat he wore, came out.

Peering at Emma threateningly, he raised the stick he held to shoulder height.

'What be you up to?' he shouted and stepped closer, the stick lifting several inches. 'I seen you bump that woman, trying to knock the basket from her arm!'

Nervously Emma stepped backward, feeling the brick wall hard against her back. 'I … I beg your pardon? I think you have made a mistake.'

'I made no mistake.' The stick danced in the air. 'I seen you, through my shop window. You deliberately pushed that woman!'

Both hands clutching the shawl across her breasts, Emma stared at him with frightened eyes and when she answered her voice shook. 'I … I told you, sir, you have made a mistake.'

'And so have you!' he snarled. 'If you think you can rob folk outside my shop then it be *you* have made the mistake.'

'Rob?' Nerves taut as a pulled thread Emma stared in disbelief at the shopkeeper, the stick now held above his top hat. She had tried to rob no one. That woman had bumped into her, had almost knocked her down, he must have seen that.

'Your sort need a few strokes of the cat.' The stick cut through the darkness and Emma screamed as it bit through the thin shawl and slashed her shoulders. 'A swish or two of that one's tail and you won't be so quick to rob the next woman.'

'I didn't rob her, I didn't...' Her words fell away as the stick whistled once more, striking her arms heavily as she curled her head protectively into them.

'Gaol be where you belong.' The stick struck again, tumbling Emma to the ground. 'Ten years' hard labour be the lesson needed to teach you to keep your thieving fingers to yourself!'

At the sound of footsteps coming towards them the man took a step away from Emma's crouching figure and the stick dropped to his side. Glancing quickly sideways as two women rounded the corner, he said loudly. 'It's as well I caught you, woman, or who knows how many more you would have robbed tonight?'

'Robbed!' One of the passersby gasped, drawing back as though a leper's bell had rung.

'Your sort are a disgrace to this town and a danger to honest folk.' He affected not to have seen or heard the two women. 'You walk the streets, waiting your chance to rob...'

'No!' Emma pushed herself to her feet. 'I have robbed no one. I had no intention...'

'Oh, I know of your intention, I *seen* your intention, now the magistrate will hear what you were up to.'

'What has this woman done?' A little braver than her companion, a woman in a feathered bonnet stepped up to the shopkeeper.

Pretending surprise, he raised his top hat.

Standing aside for the woman to pass, he shook his head sorrowfully. 'I regret you had to come face to face with such a woman, ladies, really I do. I would not have had you witness such a distressing scene.'

'I asked what it was she has done?' The feathered bonnet bobbed irately.

'Perhaps you would care to take shelter in my shop?' The tall figure bowed obsequiously.

'Take shelter?... Take shelter, pah! Is the woman about to attack all three of us, and you so brave as to take a stick to her?' The woman turned to Emma. 'You, girl, what is it you did to deserve a beating and an appearance before the magistrate?'

'I have done nothing, ma'am.' Emma looked the woman in the eye, her glance open and unwavering. 'I was waiting for my friend when a lady bumped into me and I fell against this shop window. I did not rob her, I would never do such a thing.'

'I seen...'

'No.' The woman spoke quietly, her own glance on Emma. 'No, I do not believe you did rob anyone. Now get you home before any other mischance occurs.'

'But I saw her!' the shopkeeper protested, seeing his moment of glory fading before it got started.

'You believe what you *think* you saw.' Turning her cool stare on the shopkeeper, feathered bonnet bobbing in the pale light from his window, the woman answered firmly. 'But we cannot allow what we think to influence us unduly. Has that person returned … whoever it was who claimed to have been robbed?' She glanced again at Emma. 'The light here is not too good and mistakes are easily made. Now do as I say and go to your home.'

Sobbing her thanks, Emma gathered her skirts, and as the women turned away she began to run.

'Bloody interfering do-gooders!' Muttering beneath his breath, the shopkeeper watched the two women disappear into the shadows. 'No wonder there be thieves on the streets when there be folk like that to stick up for 'em!'

Turning towards the shop he halted. There on the ground, right where the lady with the feathered bonnet had stood, lay a small dark object, only just visible in the weak gaslight from his shop.

A smile on his mean mouth, he picked up a small leather purse.

'Bloody do-gooders,' he chuckled, slipping it into his pocket. 'They done a bit of good after all!'

Her lungs bursting for breath, Emma came to a stop, shrinking back as a handcart rumbled past. Daisy wasn't coming. She must have thought that without her Emma would go into the workhouse. Fright and hunger too strong for her to contain, Emma sobbed aloud. Daisy had been such a loyal friend, she could have left before spending the money she had earned by scrubbing 'til her hands bled. It would have lasted longer with only one mouth to feed. Then there had been the nights in the lodging house;

they had cost money too but Daisy had made no complaint. She had paid the cost but if she had been alone she would not have taken lodgings. She had only done it for Emma's sake – and all the time she had positively refused to allow the spending of Carver Felton's shilling.

Carver Felton! Emma pressed one corner of her shawl to her mouth, holding back the sobs. Did he ever think of what he had done to her, ever feel remorse? No, Carver Felton would feel nothing. To him she had been a woman of no account, someone to use and then forget, just another of the things he had abandoned.

And Paul, did he think of her? He had promised that on his return they would be married.

'Ask my brother to marry you now!'

The words mocked her from the darkness as they had mocked her then. Carver Felton had deliberately raped her to prevent such a marriage.

'Paul,' Emma whispered. But there was no answer. There never would be. Paul was lost to her. She would never be his wife. And the child she carried? Jerusha had said it would bear its father's name. But Carver Felton would never own to the bastard child of a Doe Bank wench.

'Leave me be!'

The cry was that of a woman, one as frightened as herself. Unsure whether it had come from her own fearful mind, Emma listened.

'Let me go! Leave me be!'

Daisy! Emma's head jerked up, her own fear fading instantly. That was Daisy's voice. Hearing the harsh laughter that followed it, Emma sprinted towards the sound. From the alley beside the Turk's Head Hotel the noise of a scuffle and the throaty cursing of a man caught her ear.

'Daisy!' she shouted and rushed into the alley. Almost hidden in the shadows she saw the figure of a man, his back to her. 'Daisy!' she called again, then hurled herself at the struggling shape.

'Leave her alone, you beast!' Emma screamed as she pulled at the man attacking Daisy. 'Leave her…'

The rest was lost as she felt herself knocked backward, the breath forced from her as she was slammed against a wall.

'Well now, if there ain't another of 'em!'

Beer-sodden breath fanned her face. 'Now ain't that a bit of luck? Here's old Charlie a-waiting of his turn with the young 'un, but there be no need of waiting now. I'll take you instead.'

'No!' Emma screamed again as he pressed against her, one hand restraining her shoulders, the other drawing her skirts up over her hips.

'You can take your time with that 'un, Tom…'

Emma's stomach turned as fumes of beer and sour breath touched her face.

'…old Charlie Bates has one of his own.'

'Old Charlie Bates best leave that woman alone unless he wants to leave this alley in a bed cart!'

An oath falling from his lips, the man turned away but his hold on Emma stayed firm.

'You go find your own whore, you bloody…'

'I said, leave that woman. Do it now or I'll lay this about you.'

'You hear that, Tom?' The man laughed again. 'This here bloke threatens to hoss whip Charlie Bates. What say we do him first then turn our attention to the women? They'll be the more enjoyable for the wait.'

Growling his assent the one called Tom joined his companion, leaving Daisy free to run to Emma.

Staring past them to the man who had just challenged them, Emma caught her breath. Holding a candle jar in one hand and a short-handled whip in the other, butcher Hollington stood his ground.

'You're going to be sorry you stuck your nose where it had no business,' Charlie Bates sneered.

Hollington made no move as the two men stepped towards him.

'Arr, bloody sorry,' Tom added. 'I don't take kindly to being interrupted when I be with a woman.'

'Even if that woman does not welcome your dubious attentions!'

'They be a couple of trollops,' Charlie sneered. 'What other reason to hang round this alley? 'Sides, they don't belong to no man, they wears no wedding ring. In my book that makes 'em fair game!'

'Not in mine.' Hollington raised the whip.

'What you standing there chuntering for!' Tom pushed past his mate. 'The more you talk, the longer I have to wait. And this between my legs won't last all night.'

Lunging forward, he recoiled as the whip sang past his ears.

'Why, you bastard!'

Defying the threat of the lash the man rushed forward, shielding his face with one arm. His hand grabbing the wrist that wielded the whip, he yanked at it but the butcher held on tight.

'Mr Hollington ... is that you in there?'

Emma could not hold back a cry of relief as a voice called from the street.

'It is that.' The butcher wrenched his hand free. 'And I'd welcome your help.' He lifted the jar and light from it illuminated the men's faces. 'We have men in Wednesbury who will give you pair the beating you deserve,' he declared, 'and that without the sovereign I am willing to pay them. We don't take kindly to our women being threatened in the street, and give short shrift to a man who dares attack one of them.'

'That what these two been up to?' The brawn of them filling the narrow alley, four men came up behind the butcher. 'Then you can keep your sovereign, Mr Hollington, we'll see to this scum for the pure pleasure of it. You get on home. And you women do the same.'

Clinging to each other, Daisy and Emma squeezed past the men who had attacked them, the hands of the others passing them safely out onto the street.

'Oh, Daisy!' In the light that spilled from the bow windows of the hotel, Emma's face glistened with tears. 'Daisy, we can't go on like this ... we can't!'

Her own face wet with tears, Daisy nodded. 'You're right, Emma we can't go on like this. We'll go to the workhouse tonight.'

Chapter Fourteen

'They came out of the Turk's Head just as I was passing.' Daisy still held tight to Emma's hand. 'They grabbed me before I could do anything and dragged me into that alley. I was so scared, Emma.'

'I know, I know.' She felt her heart twist in sympathy. Carrie must have felt like this when their father ... so scared... But Carrie had not screamed or struggled. She had probably thought at first that what was happening to her was a normal thing, the act of any loving father.

Loving father! The words were like dry dust in her soul. Caleb Price had loved only himself. Even his love for the Lord must have been only a pretence, a show put on for the benefit of others, while he... Emma swallowed the bile in her throat. While he abused his own daughter.

'They said ... they said they were going to...'

'Shhh.' Squeezing the hand held in hers, Emma tried to still the girl's fears. 'It's over, Daisy, they won't hurt you now. Try to forget it.'

Feeling the tremor run down the girl's arm, Emma realised the futility of her last words. Had Carrie been able to forget? Had she herself been able to forget what Carver Felton had done to her? Could any woman ever truly forget the man who raped her?

Her own father, Carver Felton, Eli Coombs ...

how many such men were there in the world, men who saw women as inferior to themselves, objects fit only for their amusement?

Even as the thought rose within her Emma knew it was unfair. She had never received so much as an unkind word from the men of Doe Bank, and though some of the jaggers who had bought the coal she picked from the waste heaps of the Topaz had been rough, they had never made an untoward remark. And then there had been Paul. He had shown her nothing but gentleness. Had said he loved her, said they would marry. But his brother had damned that hope, destroyed that dream forever. Paul Felton would return but she would be gone.

'I tried, Emma, I wanted to keep you from going into the workhouse ... I'm sorry.'

Emma glanced at the building looming out of the shadows, the steep angles of its roof cutting into the night sky, a low-slung lantern throwing a dim light over pilasters and moulded architraves that lent an air of false grandeur to the heavy door, the small windows that flanked it closed and blank, like blind eyes turned on a pitless world.

The workhouse.

The uneven cobbles before its entrance biting through the thin soles of her boots, Emma felt the misery of this place drift out to meet her, touching her like a living thing, and shivered.

'Oh, Emma, I'm so sorry!' Daisy turned to her, taking her shiver for fear.

The shelter of shadow hiding her true feelings, Emma tried to keep despair from her voice. 'It's not your fault, Daisy,' she murmured. 'If it weren't for you we would have been here a week ago. Don't worry, they may find us work somewhere.'

'So long as it isn't with another Eli Coombs.'

How would they be able to tell? Until it was too late. Grasping the other girl's fingers firmly in her own, Emma walked towards the door of the workhouse.

'Be you positive that is the place you seek?' His handcart rumbling on the cobbles, Samuel Hollington came up behind them. 'That there be naught but a stopping off place for the cemetery. I pity the poor souls who find themselves in there.'

'It's the only place left to us, Mr Hollington.' It was Emma answered him. 'We have both tried to find work but without success.'

'Arrh, times be hard.' Samuel ran one hand over the bushy whiskers that framed a face ruddied by long hours spent in the open. 'But the workhouse be harder.'

'Beggars do not have the luxury of choice,' Emma answered quietly.

'If each man were given his choice then the world would hold naught but kings. Then who would tend a farm, or labour at a steel furnace, or even sell meat in the Shambles?' The butcher chuckled. 'King Samuel! Don't sound right somehow, but butcher Hollington ... yes, that be more like it. I guess I would still be a butcher.' Resting the handcart on the ground, he pushed his straw boater back on his head, peering at Emma.

'I've seen you two afore that shemozzle in the alley.'

Daisy stepped forward. 'I've been to your stall every night for a week. I bought a pound of sausages each time.'

'Yes, you did.' He chuckled again. 'I got to look forward to them visits, to your smile and chatter. It were so polite but bright and breezy at the same time.'

'I enjoyed it too, Mr Hollington.' Daisy smiled despite her dread of the building that stood, bleak and stark, behind her. 'I don't suppose I will have that pleasure again so I thank you for your kindness now.'

'Well said, my little wench.' Samuel Hollington beamed.

'I offer my thanks too.' Emma smiled. 'Especially for your help tonight. Those men...'

'Arrh, them!' Samuel's voice hardened. 'I don't reckon they come from these parts. I haven't seen them afore and I know most of the men in Wednesbury. They're likely travellers, out on the road seeking work, or a way they can have themselves a good living without it. But you rest assured, wench, you won't meet with them again, not in this town you won't, not after the handling they'll get tonight! Men who go around raping women aren't dealt with lightly hereabouts.'

Her smile fading as she glanced up again at the dark building, Emma murmured goodnight.

'Hold up!' Samuel raised a hand as if to hold her back. 'You don't have to go to that place.'

'I am afraid we do.' Emma shook her head. 'We cannot spend another night under a hedge.'

Touching the back of his boater, the butcher slid it to the front of his head. 'You slept under a hedge … you mean, every night for a week?'

'Usually,' Daisy volunteered. 'One night we swapped a share of our sausages for a place in the watchman's hut along of the Monway. I thought it were fair trade but Emma wouldn't have we do it again. She said the man were old and needed his sleep.'

'But a watchman isn't supposed to sleep.' Samuel smiled.

'I told her that an' all,' Daisy answered ruefully. 'But she still refused. I reckon he would have been glad to trade, seeing what short work he made of our sausages.'

'And I reckon you'd have been right in that assumption.' Samuel chuckled again. 'You be a bright little wench who understand trading for a profit, even if that profit be no more than a place to sleep on the floor.'

Her face clouding over, Daisy turned away. 'A place on any floor is preferable to a bed in this.'

'Then don't go in, least not tonight. Look, I'm not saying as Mrs Hollington will say yes to a permanent place but she will find a corner for you both for tonight, that I am sure of. It would be one night less in that hell hole, but I leave the choice to you.'

Daisy swung around. 'Eh, Mr Hollington! Do you really mean it?'

'I mean it, little wench.' His smile answering hers, the butcher lifted the handles of his cart. 'And I'll throw in a sausage or two for your supper.'

'They belong to no man...'

Washing her face and hands in the wash house at the back of the Hollington house, Emma remembered the words of one of the men who had attacked Daisy and herself.

'*... ain't neither of 'em wears a wedding ring...*'

Had the fact that she and Daisy were unwed made them fair game for such men, and would it again?

And what of Sarah Hollington's comment last night when her husband had produced two girls in need of a night's shelter.

'A woman settled with a husband be one thing, a girl still not married be another. They be more nuisance than they be worth, what with lads coming a-calling every evening. I don't want that, no ... I don't want that nuisance!'

Where had her answering lies sprung from? Emma's face coloured rapidly. She had never been given to lying before yet they had slipped from her lips.

'But I *am* married, Mrs Hollington.'

Even now, after thinking about them all night, her own words surprised her. 'I was married in the Chapel at Doe Bank three months ago. My husband is with the Army in India.'

'In India, you say?'

Emma's stomach tightened now as it had when the question had been asked.

'Yes.' She had forced her eyes to meet those of the woman studying her keenly. 'He was to be stationed in a place called Myapore.'

'Was?'

213

It had been asked abruptly and Emma had answered without blinking an eye though the breath was tight in her lungs.

'William ... my husband ... wrote that his regiment was moving there from Calcutta. That was six weeks ago. I have heard no word since then to say they have arrived.'

'And when did your husband leave England?'

Sarah Hollington's glance had dropped to the hand holding the shawl across her breasts and Emma realised why. A wedding ring! Sarah Hollington was looking to where a wedding ring would be.

'Two days after we were married.'

Reaching for the piece of rough huckaback that served for a towel, Emma pressed her face into it, holding it over cheeks that had coloured hotly at the memory of her own deceit.

'I cannot show you my marriage lines for they were destroyed in the fire that took my home and everything I had in the world, including my family. Everything except for this...'

She had taken Jerusha's ring from the string about her neck.

'...my wedding ring. This is all that is left to me. I took it off for fear of being robbed on the road. It ... it is very precious to me.'

Slipping the towel over a rope strung inside the wash house, she carried the bowl of water out into the yard, emptying it into the channel that ran between the cobbles.

She ought not to have lied. Emma looked at the gold band glinting in the morning light. Lies did no one any good, her mother always used to say.

Why? Why had she said those things? To gain one more night away from the workhouse? The bowl in her hands, Emma turned back to the wash house. Or had the reason run deeper than that, deeper even than she had realised? Had all those lies been a cover, made to hide the truth, to conceal the fact that the child she carried was a bastard?

'Mrs Hollington says there is breakfast in the kitchen.' Daisy's bright smile welcomed her back to the wash house.

Replacing the bowl beside the shallow sink, Emma turned slowly. 'Daisy, I … I don't think I should stay.'

'What!' Her bright smile fading, Daisy stared. 'You mean, leave without breakfast? Why? It might be the only meal we'll have today.'

'The Hollingtons have been kind,' Emma went on. 'Too kind to be repaid by lies. I'd rather take the workhouse than lie any more. Besides, I will have to go soon. But you, Daisy, you have told them no lie. You stay.'

'Not without you!' she interrupted quickly. 'If you go, I go.'

'But there's no need. Mrs Hollington as good as said...'

'I don't care what she said.' Mouth set in a firm line, Daisy stared back. 'Nor do I care whether I lied or not. But I do care about you. I want to be with you, Emma, no matter where. We've neither of us got no family but while we be together...' A sob shaking her voice, Daisy covered her face with her hands. 'Just let me be with you, Emma, please let me be with you.'

215

Taking Daisy in her arms, holding her as she had often held Carrie, Emma stared into the sunlight that streamed through the small window.

'*Whither thou goest I will go, thy people shall be my people…*'

The quotation ringing in her mind, she stroked the girl's auburn hair. Daisy held the same love for her as the Biblical Ruth had held for Naomi. Pray God she would find the same reward.

'How very sweet of Carver.'

Cara Holgate looked at the beautifully enamelled casket her cousin held in her hand.

'Yes, wasn't it?' Melissa Gilbert's pretty mouth curved in a smile. 'He also ordered me a brooch painted to my own design. The man said it would be ready by next week. Isn't that clever, Cara? Though how they manage to work in those poky little rooms, so hot and full of fumes… It was all I could manage simply to breathe. I was so relieved when Carver took me away.'

'I can imagine.'

'We found the most delightful little inn. I had no idea there could be such a charming place beside a canal. But then, Carver seems to know so much, I doubt there's anything he could not do.'

So does Carver! The thought bitter in her mind, Cara turned away. But if he thought to take Melissa as a wife then Carver Felton had met his match. It would take more than an enamelled casket and a meal in a pretty inn, and a damn' sight more than a share in his business. Maybe Carver was having second thoughts about

216

marriage to herself? If that proved to be so then Cara Holgate could have second thoughts, very expensive second thoughts.

'I am pleased you enjoyed your day.' Cara moved restlessly from chair to window, the elegant sitting room seeming suddenly to stifle her. 'Though quite why it took so long...'

Watching her, Melissa smiled inwardly. Cara *was* jealous. She wanted no other woman to take Carver Felton's attention, no rival to vie for his affection ... or his money! But she must play her hand carefully. It was too soon yet to be banished home to Rugeley.

'That was my fault I'm afraid, Cara.' She pulled a tiny frown, allowing her clear grey eyes to cloud. 'Carver said we should return, that you would be anxious, but I was so enjoying the scenery. I have not seen narrow boats before. They are so quaint, painted all over with flowers and greenery. Why, even their kettles and buckets were decorated, and with the most delightful designs. Really, you would not think such ... such people capable of painting so well. I was quite enchanted.'

And Carver, was he enchanted? Cara swept back to the chair, resting her hands on its carved back, her thoughts souring her mind like vinegar. Was he enchanted! Was he taken in by your act as you think I am?

'Well you are home now.' The reply sharper than she would have shown, Cara followed it quickly with a smile. 'Though I shall have words to say to Carver Felton when next we meet. I cannot risk having my cousin made ill again because of his failing to curtail an outing when he knew very well that he should. He put your health at risk simply to prolong his own pleasure!'

'Carver is really not to blame,' Melissa said as Cara faced her from behind the chair. 'We got to talking of his brother. I believe you know him quite well?'

'Fairly well.' Cara nodded slightly.

'He is much younger than Carver, so I'm told.' Cara nodded again.

'Carver said he would be taking his place in the business very shortly, that he would reach his majority in a few months. He said his brother was becoming quite adept at dealing with customers.'

Irritation fluttering through her, Cara kept a grip on the emotion riding high. Carver said ... Carver did ... the girl seemed obsessed with him!

'He told me that Paul ... his brother...' Melissa's mouth curved into a coy smile as if she really should not speak the man's name and Cara's irritation increased.

'...that he owned his own house. It was left to him by their father. I was most interested...'

I bet you were! Green-gold eyes fixed on her cousin's pretty face, Cara's thoughts were acid.

'I said how much I would like to meet Paul and to see his house. Oh, I know I should not have said it ... well, not in quite that way, perhaps. It seemed so ... so...' She shrugged her shoulders expressively. 'Well, Carver was so very sweet, he could see I was embarrassed at making such an awful faux pas. He said that while he could not introduce me to his brother for a short while yet, he was certain Paul would want him to show me the house himself. I tried to decline, of course, I did not want to appear inquisitive, but Carver insisted.' She paused, a mischievous smile replacing that coy look. 'And I really did wish to see it. Beaufort House ... it sounded so impressive.'

'And were you impressed?'

Stroking one finger over the enamelled casket Melissa hesitated, her face suddenly thoughtful. 'It was a delightful house, but...'

Her lips so stiff they barely moved, Cara echoed the word. 'But?'

Lifting her eyes to her cousin's, Melissa gave the answer she knew would cause Cara the most concern, though that knowledge was hidden behind her honeyed smile.

'But it is not on quite the same scale as Felton Hall. Paul sounded quite interesting, a good prospect as a husband, but then not such a good one as his brother. Given the choice a girl would be a fool not to take Carver.'

Her fingers curling on the chair back, Cara felt her nerves tense as a drawstring. She had always known Melissa was a calculating little thing, yet she had always...

'And is that your intention?' she asked through set lips. 'To take the larger portion?'

The razor-sharp tone telling her she had achieved her intent, that her cousin was more than a little perturbed over her outing with Carver Felton, Melissa smiled inwardly. Then, chestnut curls tumbling about her shoulders, her soft mouth slightly parted, grey eyes wide and filled with tearful contrition, she dropped the casket on to the couch beside her as she stared up at the older woman. Lips trembling, she murmured, 'Cara … Cara… are you cross with me? You sound so angry.' Tears silvering her lashes, she lifted one hand to her face. 'Oh, Cara, I couldn't bear it if you were cross with me. I'm sorry if my staying out so long has made you angry … dearest Cara, I'm so sorry!'

For a brief moment Cara stared at the figure sat now with hands covering her face contritely. Melissa had always been good at play acting, and she was acting now. That at least was certain. But then, Cara had always been a fool where Melissa was concerned!

The bitterness of a moment ago melting like butter in the sun, she came to sit beside the younger woman. Gathering her into her arms, she touched her lips to the cloud of shining curls.

'I am not angry,' she murmured, rocking the weeping Melissa as she would a child. 'I was merely anxious for you. The workshops of Bilston are not the safest of places.'

Against her cousin's chest Melissa smiled, though when she answered she was careful to do so with a sob. 'But … but I was with Carver.'

Her lips still touching the girl's hair, Cara stared at the fire glowing in the hearth. Yes, Melissa had been with Carver, and that was another cause for anxiety!

'We will forget about the brooch.' Melissa sniffed. 'I will not go to that place again, I will not have you anxious on my account.'

'You shall have your brooch, my dear.' Cara's

eyes lingered on the dancing flames. 'But we will ask Carver to bring it here to this house. Now I think you should go upstairs and rest. I'll have dinner put back.'

Releasing her, Cara watched as Melissa stood up, her perfect figure swathed in stiff moiré taffeta, the delicate turquoise colour setting off the chestnut hair to perfection. Melissa was pretty enough to turn any man's head, pretty enough to make him forget many things.

At the door Melissa turned, her smile appealing, her eyes gleaming. 'Cara.' She held out her hand. 'Would you come up with me? Talk to me for a little while.'

Pushing herself up from the couch, Cara crossed the room to catch the outstretched hand in hers.

'Yes.' She smiled into those appealing grey eyes. 'Yes, I will come up with you.'

There had been no contrition in her cousin's apology, and those tears were simply crocodile tears. Cara accompanied the trim figure up the broad, well-polished staircase. Melissa had not fooled her, nor had the fact that nothing of consequence had been forthcoming about the day she had spent with Carver Felton. But then, he would have said nothing of consequence, nothing that might be relayed to her. Carver was too smart for that. Yet what had they talked about for so many hours? Had they all been spent in talking?

Taffeta falling in a turquoise pool at her feet, silken petticoats and fine linen chemise following, Melissa stood like a beautiful alabaster statue; high firm breasts touched by chestnut curls, a tiny waist that would fit into a man's hands, a flat stomach revealed as silken bloomers fell to the floor. Her eyes dark and smiling, she looked at her cousin asking softly, 'Would you pass my robe, Cara?'

Catching up the robe, Cara felt a red hot wave of envy surge into her every vein.

Melissa had youth and beauty.

Youth! Cara drew a deep breath. And a beauty Carver would weigh against her own.

Chapter Fifteen

'Thank you for your kindness in finding us shelter for the night, and for the offer of breakfast, but we will leave now.'

Hands and face glowing from the sting of cold water, Emma stood in the kitchen of butcher Hollington's trim little house.

'What be the hurry?' Samuel looked up from a plate liberally piled with bacon, sausages and eggs, their yolks golden as tiny suns.

'We thought by being down at the market place early we might stand a chance of finding work.'

Samuel's eyes flicked to Daisy as she answered.

'You will do a better job of a day's work after getting a good meal inside of you.' He stabbed a sausage with his fork and lifted it to his mouth.

'If you be going to bite into that sausage, Samuel Hollington, then you say no more 'til it be ate. I won't have you talking with a full mouth.' Sarah Hollington patted the gleaming white apron stretched across her dark skirts, then glanced again at the two young women stood already dressed in shawls ready for outdoors. 'But what my Samuel has said makes sense. A good breakfast will set you up for the day's work, so both of you sit you down at the table.'

Beside her Emma felt Daisy half step forward and for a brief moment she herself felt the urge to forget that earlier resolve and take her place at the table. Then the urge was gone and eyes wide she lifted her own glance to the woman watching her. 'No, thank you, Mrs Hollington. We'd best stick to what we have decided and get to the market place early, before the day's hiring is over.'

''Tain't started yet nor will be for another hour or more.' Sarah Hollington glanced at the tin clock set on the mantel above the fireplace, the fingers pointing to five o'clock. Bushy whiskers moving up and down in solemn unison as he chewed his sausage, Samuel's bright button eyes stared fixed on Emma's face. The girl had pride. Despite the poor light that illuminated his stall in the Shambles he had seen that pride as she had stood with her friend buying sausages, and it had printed itself on his mind. Work she might want, and badly, but it was not want of just that had this girl refusing Sarah's breakfast. Whatever it was went far deeper than that.

'Emma be right, Mrs Hollington.' Daisy stepped into the breach of silence when Emma failed to answer. 'First there stands the best chance of a day's hire, so thank you kindly for your 'ospitality but we'll be going now.'

Watching them turn towards the kitchen door, Sarah Hollington glanced at her husband. Whiskers still moving as he chewed Samuel's brows lifted, crawling up his ruddy forehead like white hairy caterpillars.

Slapping one hand against her apron, Sarah turned her glance back to the girls who were now opening the kitchen door. Samuel had spoken no word, his mouth being full, but his eyes had twinkled. He knew full well what it was she

224

wanted to say, just as he knew full well he must not say so.

"'Tain't the hope of a day's hiring has you refusing my breakfast.' Sarah's voice was sharp but not unkind. 'Ain't that has you haring off as though the Devil be twitching your skirts. So why not be honest and say what it is you wants to say but can't bring yourself to? Taking it with you will bring you no ease, and the telling of it to me and my Samuel will bring no condemnation.' Her voice softening, Sarah went on, 'I know there be something troubling you, wench. I seen it in your eyes last night when you spoke of your husband.'

Her hand on the door knob Emma froze. The woman had seen it in her eyes, seen that all was not as Emma would have had her believe, yet still she had let them stay.

Closing the door, Emma turned back slowly. And though her cheeks were stained pink with the thought of all her lies of the previous night, Emma's eyes shone now with the light of truth.

'No, it is not the hope of a day's work has me refusing the food you offer.' The words came slowly, the pain of embarrassment holding Emma's lips stiff. 'It's the thought of what I said to you last night. I lied to you. After all you had both done for me, I lied to you. That's beyond forgiveness and I ask none. But Daisy told no lie. She did not betray a kindness. Therefore I ask no forgiveness for her but I do ask you if you can find it in your heart to give her work and a place to stay?'

'No!' Daisy caught at Emma's arm, her eyes bright with consternation. 'I won't stay anywhere

225

without you. You promised, Emma! You promised we would stick together.' Her voice cracking on the threat of tears, she glanced wildly at the butcher's wife. 'It ain't that I'm not grateful, Mrs Hollington, I am. But I want to be with Emma, no matter where that might be. She's the only real friend I've ever had. Weren't ... weren't no friends in the workhouse...' Her fingers tightening on Emma's arm, Daisy choked, 'Don't turn your back on me, Emma, don't leave me ... please don't turn from me!'

In the warmth of the kitchen lit by the glow of oil lamps mingling with the light of dancing flames leaping into the dark chimney, Emma placed her arm about the girl's shoulders as sobs shuddered in her throat. She had wanted only security for Daisy, but what was security when balanced against a young girl's breaking heart? If leaving here meant going to the workhouse or even taking to the road again then at least they would do it together.

'Daisy didn't mean...'

'I know the wench's meaning.' Sarah nodded. 'Same as I knows there was no rudeness in it. She loves you, that be the all of it. No need to say more.'

Her arm still about Daisy, Emma smiled but in an instant it was gone, sadness taking a little of the light from her lovely eyes.

'Maybe not for Daisy, but for myself there is every need. I lied to you last night, to you and Mr Hollington. I told you I was married when it is not true. This ring...' she lifted her left hand slightly then let it fall back to her side '...was not

226

about my neck through fear of its being stolen. It is a wedding ring, yes, but it was not given to me by a man.'

Her sharp intake of breath audible over the gentle hiss of the lamps on the dresser and beneath the window, Sarah's glance went to her husband.

'I should explain. This ring belonged to a very good friend of my family's. Jerusha wore it over three-quarters of her lifetime but when her husband died she said she had no further use for it and gave it to me. I still remember what she said to me at the time: "It will bring you a comfort no words can give". I think now I understand what she meant. Wearing her wedding ring will give me a measure of protection from men such as those your husband saved us from last night.'

'And a measure of protection for the child you carry!'

It was Emma's turn to gasp, an exclamation from Daisy quickly following.

'You don't have to affirm what I say.' Sarah's hand once more smoothed an already crease-free apron.

Drawing a deep breath, Emma looked first at Samuel and then his wife. 'Nor will I deny it,' she said quietly. 'I am carrying a child...'

'Emma!' Breaking free from her grasp, Daisy made to pull her to the door. 'There be no need for you to say more. Ain't nobody's business 'cept your own. Come away, we'll find something...'

'You be right, Daisy. It be none of our business, the child your friend be carrying.' His mouth though not yet empty Samuel spoke out, ignoring the reprimand he would surely receive later. 'And my wife isn't prying, she is merely...'

'I am merely trying to say that a girl who is expecting should not be on the road!' Sarah interrupted, her tartness hiding a genuine concern. 'And the workhouse be a poor place for a child to enter into the world.'

'A poor place, yes.' Emma's mouth drooped. 'But a safer one than beneath a hedge, and that is all that matters.'

'Yes, that matters,' Sarah agreed, 'but it is not *all* that matters. A child needs love as much as anything, maybe *more* than anything. What sort of love will it get in that place?'

'It will get all I can give,' Emma whispered, her lashes drooping over eyes clouded with misery. If what she had heard of workhouse procedure was true she would be given precious little time to spend with her child, and should she be boarded out to work she would not get to see it at all, for who would take on a woman hampered by a newborn infant?

'I'll love the baby, Emma, I'll help take care of it.' Daisy squeezed the hand that hung at Emma's side.

'And who will have the keeping of you while you do that?'

Lost for a reply, Daisy stared helplessly at the woman who the night before had as good as said she would take her on to help in this house.

Reaching a large boldly striped teapot from the hob, Sarah filled the cups set at three places then refilled Samuel's large pottery mug. Replacing the pot, she pointed to the empty chairs. 'Both of you start showing a bit of common sense and sit down. A bite of breakfast will help things seem all the clearer. Come on now, I won't have no refusing!'

Hearing the sympathy beneath the covering tartness, feeling the slight tug of the hand fastened about her own, Emma felt the impossibility of refusing both Daisy and Sarah Hollington, but still pride held her back.

'I ... I will accept your kindness only if you will listen...'

'We want to hear nothing of what has gone before.' Samuel smiled understandingly. 'Explanations ain't a prerequisite of a meal in this house. But if it be what you truly want then we will listen ... after you have eaten!'

Pushing the milk jug, a gaudy match to the teapot, towards Emma, Sarah smiled. 'My Samuel speaks for both of us, wench. Speak only if the need drives you. We respect the fact that you have already admitted to not telling the truth last night. We did not ask it of you...'

'Which only makes what I did the harder to bear. You gave us shelter in your home and I...'

'Say no more,' Sarah interrupted, spooning sugar into her own cup.

Careful this time to swallow the food from his mouth, Samuel glanced at the girls sitting at his table, shawls spread neatly over the back of their chairs. 'My Sarah and me got to thinking last night. For some time now we have both realised we could do with taking on some help, she with the house and me with the stall in the market ...

well, what I be saying is this. If the two of you feel it be the work you wants then the jobs be yours.'

A cup halfway to her lips, Emma held it steady while tears spilled down her cheeks. After what she had told them, knowing her to be nothing short of a liar, these people were offering her employment!

'Come on now, Emma wench!' Samuel's voice was gruff, a manly reaction to tears. 'That tea don't want no weakening. Like I tell Sarah, there be enough water in it already to sail a boat on.'

Placing her cup on the table, Emma brushed her fingers across her cheeks. 'I ... I'm sorry. It's just that I never expected...'

'Neither did I.' Daisy beamed, slicing into a sausage. 'But the answer be yes, Mr Hollington, we wants them jobs, both of us, though Emma can't tell you as much 'til her be finished blartin'.'

'A cry never hurt a woman.' Sarah's tartness disappeared in her ready defence of Emma. 'It be far better out than in. A bellyful of tears is a weight a body be all the better for not carrying.'

Pushing back his chair, Samuel drew out his pocket watch, checking it with the time showing on the tin clock. Taking her cue, Sarah stood up.

'I put you a bite of dinner in the basket along of Samuel's.' She smiled at Emma. 'Just in case you accepted his offer.' Then, as Emma made to move, added, 'There be a few minutes yet afore he has the cart loaded, time enough for you to finish your breakfast.'

But as she followed her husband from the kitchen Emma thrust her plate away, already full with the emotion that surged in her. Yes, she

230

would take the employment offered and she would work hard. And in some way ... some way she did not yet know she would find the means to repay the kindness this couple had shown her.

'Did you have the man dismissed?'

Standing in the beautiful octagonal drawing room, Paul Felton confronted his brother.

Seated beside the fire, Carver turned a page of his newspaper with slow deliberation.

'I asked you, Carver, did you have the man dismissed?'

The anger behind the question quite obvious, Carver kept his eyes fixed on the newspaper. Paul had returned unexpectedly early from his last assignment and his first act had been to ride over to Doe Bank.

Flicking over a page, Carver answered non-committally. 'His work was not up to my expectations.'

'Wasn't it!' Paul's voice, harsh with anger, rang around the lovely room. 'Or was it the man's daughter who was not up to your expectations? That's it, isn't it, Carver? Emma didn't match up to your requirements, she was not a suitable candidate for marriage into the Felton family. Isn't that nearer the truth?'

He turned another page, his eye travelling slowly over it before he answered. 'Since you already know my opinion on the matter, why bother to ask the question?'

'So you trumped up some excuse about her father's work at the Topaz, just so you could get rid of him!'

Lowering the newspaper, Carver lifted his glance, coal black eyes cold and indifferent to the fury obvious in those of his brother.

'I need no excuse to give a man his tin and certainly need give you none for my actions. I am in control of the Topaz mine and of you, brother. Both are subject to my decisions.'

'And it was your decision to evict the Price family,' Paul answered scathingly. 'To turn a whole family on to the road just to make sure you got your own way. Well, no doubt you have heard and taken joy in the fact that Caleb Price, his wife and his daughter, died that same night. Died in the flames that reduced the house to ashes.'

He had been told. Carver returned his glance to the paper in his hands though it remained unread. He had been told of the fire and of the daughter who had not been home at the time. The elder daughter. His fingers tightened on the paper. Emma had been away on some errand, so Barlow had reported to him, returning when the blaze was at its height. Others from the village had been forced to hold her, to stop her from racing into the heart of the flames. And the next day she had left Doe Bank.

He had not asked where she had gone. For a moment he saw again in his mind the vision that came so often to haunt him in the night: a vision of a lovely young face wreathed in silver-gilt hair, eyes wide and terrified as they stared back at him. No, he had not asked where the girl had gone, nor had he admitted the reason why. Acknowledged his fear he might be forced to follow after her.

'But Emma didn't die.' Paul laughed scathingly.

232

'So you see, Carver, all your underhand conniving was for nothing. Emma's alive and I intend to bring her home. She will be my wife, the mistress of Beaufort House, and there isn't a thing you can do about it!'

Blinking away the vision that filled his eyes, Carver kept them averted as he replied, 'Have you forgotten, I am your legal guardian?'

His breath hissing between clenched teeth, Paul swung away to the window overlooking a garden heavy with the blooms of late summer but the anger inside him blinded him to its beauty.

'Not for much longer, Carver,' he grated. 'A few months more and I will be my own man, responsible only to myself. In a few months I will become a co-owner of Felton's and be in a position to marry whomsoever I please. And that woman will be Emma Price.'

Flicking the paper again Carver deliberately took his time before answering. 'As you say, brother, in a few months. But these months have yet to pass and until they have you are under my jurisdiction and will do as I say.'

Anger blazing from him, Paul swung round to face the brother for whom all his childhood love was fast fading. 'Damn you, Carver!' he hissed. 'Where is she? Where has she gone? Don't tell me you don't know – you know everything that goes on in Lea Brook, you make it your business to know! I realise you would not follow after her, would not bring her back to Doe Bank, but nevertheless you would know where she went.'

'You would not follow after her!'

The words seemed to ring in Carver's ears.

How many times had he been on the brink of doing just that, of searching for the girl who gave him no peace? Only to save himself by the reminder she was nothing but a Doe Bank girl, the daughter of a coal miner.

'How right you are.' His reply held no trace of the feelings of a moment ago, of the lurch of his heart as he'd stared into those lovely phantom eyes. 'I would follow after no woman, still less one of her station, but you are wrong to say I know where she is for I do not. The whereabouts of that girl bothers me not at all.'

Covering the room in swift strides, Paul swiped a downward blow at the newspaper, tearing it from his brother's grasp. 'Dammit, Carver!' he breathed. 'For once in your life tell me the truth. Where's Emma?'

Bending forward to retrieve the fallen paper, Carver made an elaborate show of first smoothing then folding the crumpled sheets. Then, calmly looking into the furious young face, he slowly shook his head.

'Tut-tut! Still very much the child, I see. Perhaps Father should have named me your guardian for several more years, give you more time to grow up.'

'There was no need, Carver!' His brown eyes gleaming, Paul stared at the man sitting before him. 'I have done a deal of growing up these last weeks, enough to realise many things. Such as your reluctance to allow me any say in the way things are run here. But that will end soon, you will have no legal hold over me. And as for any other kind – don't try, Carver. Don't even try!'

Chapter Sixteen

Jerusha Paget drew the worn woollen shawl about her shoulders. The evening sun on her face showed every line and wrinkle but her eyes were clear and bright with a common sense that never faded despite her years.

'Emma Price said naught to me of where she might be headed, nor to any in Doe Bank so far as I know.'

'But you were with her that night?' Paul Felton gazed into her time-worn face.

'True.' Jerusha nodded, settling herself on the stool it had become her habit to carry outside and sit on in the warm evenings. 'I was with Emma, and it is true I spoke to her the morning after, but all she said was that she could no longer bide in Doe Bank.'

'But why?'

Eyes squinting against the setting sun, Jerusha looked into his drawn face. She needed no golden silence, no silent voice to tell her of the pain this young man was suffering, nor the cause of it. He loved Emma Price but that love had been forbidden him and the price of its taking away had been the death of Emma's family.

'You can ask that,' she answered quietly. 'You can ask why, after all you have heard? Could you stay in a place where those you held most dear in life had burned to death?'

'No.' He shook his head, lowering it so as not to see the reproach in the old woman's eyes. 'No, of course, I understand. But not why she didn't say where she intended going!'

Behind his tall figure Jerusha watched a spider scuttle over a web, its strands glinting pale gold in the last rays of the sun. Pale gold ... pale and silken as Emma's hair. She too had disappeared as the spider had now disappeared. But they might meet again, she and Emma. The silence would tell her if that time came. Until then she could say nothing.

'I understand my brother caused Mr Price to be dismissed from his job at the mine. I am very sorry for that.' Paul looked up, meeting eyes that held no blame. 'I wish I could tell Emma so.'

'There be no need to give any apology to me.' Jerusha gave him a rare smile. 'Though it be good to hear you speak those words. They be ones I know that brother of yours would never utter.'

No, Paul thought grimly. They were words Carver would never say. Doe Bank people were too far beneath him even to warrant an explanation, much less apology.

'Then you cannot tell me where I might look to find Emma?'

She could ask. Jerusha lifted her face, eyes closing in appreciation of the sun's last gift of warmth. She could ask that silent voice, ask to be enfolded in that wonderful golden peace, to be told what this man wanted to know. She could ask, but she would not. She would not cast aside the practice of a lifetime. The voice would come at its own appointed time. If she were to know any more of Emma Price it would tell her then. Until that time she must wait.

'I could suggest many places.' She opened her eyes. 'But there be no telling whether or not you would find her in any one of them. Search if you must and the Lord guide your steps. Jerusha Paget cannot.'

Looking into his face she knew she could say much more. She could tell this tall young man with tumbling brown hair and eyes turned to brazen copper by the light of the dying sun to be wary of his brother. She could tell him to guard against a woman's greed for power that would stop at nothing. But her lips clamped together and Jerusha let her tongue lie silent. She would not come between family, set brother against brother, though in her heart she felt there was already a gulf between the sons of Edward Felton. It was not for her to interfere. The fates would set the path both these men must tread, just as the fates would determine their fate.

Glancing once more, his eyes relaying the thanks his mouth could not smile, Paul swung himself into the saddle of the horse he had tethered to a nearby gorse bush. Holding the animal tight to the rein as it pranced, eager to be away, he looked again to Jerusha.

'If Emma should return, or should you hear of her whereabouts, would you be kind enough to send me word, Mrs Paget?'

'Arr, lad.' Jerusha nodded, her answer holding none of the deference the villagers of Doe Bank habitually used when replying to one of the Feltons. 'I'll send you word, though whether that word will reach your ears be summat else again.'

A nod his only answer Paul turned the horse towards Felton Hall. He knew what lay beneath the woman's final words, the intimation that word of Emma might be prevented from reaching him. He touched his heel to the glossy flanks, setting the animal to the gallop. This time he would take the necessary precautions. This time Carver would not find it so easy to dupe his brother.

Reaching the stables of the Hall, he jumped from the saddle as the under-groom, a man a few years older than himself, ran out to take the horse.

'You eat in the servants' hall?'

His brow creasing, the groom took the bridle in one hand, the other fondling the muzzle of the sweating animal. 'Arr, Mr Paul. I takes my meals along of the others.'

Paul nodded. 'Then you hear of all that goes on in the house?'

Concern deepening in his eyes the man felt for an answer. He needed to be cautious, there was no telling what lay behind this question. 'I wouldn't say all, Mr Paul.'

'But there's little that does not find its way to the servants' hall?'

'I ... I suppose not, sir.'

'Then you would no doubt learn if a messenger came to the Hall, asking to see my brother. You need have no fear for your place here,' Paul added, seeing the look that flashed across the other man's face. 'I'm not questioning you on his account. Nothing that passes between us will be relayed to Carver. Not by me, that is.'

'Nor by me, sir, you have my word on that.'

'That is the strongest bond a man can offer.' Paul's glance followed as the horse tossed its head pulling the man's arm upward. 'And the one I value the most. That being so, I would ask you do me a service, but should you not wish to do so then no more will be said.'

'If I can do anything for you, Mr Paul, you may consider it done. You have always been both fair and polite with me, ever since you was a little 'un, and anything I can do to show my respect ... well, like I say, you just consider it done.'

'Will you get word to me of any message my brother might receive that has any bearing, any at all, on the village of Doe Bank? That is all I ask.'

Shortening the bridle as the horse tossed its head yet again, the under-groom smiled. 'You just let me know where to send word, Mr Paul, and I vow to get it to you.'

'Thank you.' Paul's answering smile shone briefly. 'There is one more thing,' he said quietly. 'In a few months' time I shall be moving into my own home, Beaufort House. I will be needing a head groom there. Would you consider taking the post?'

'Ain't no need for you to go rewarding me with any promotion.' The man's reply was dignified. 'I holds a respect for you that don't go necessitating that. I will do what is asked of me for that reason and need no other.'

'I beg your pardon, the offer was crudely put.' Paul felt a sharp surge of regret. It had been seen as a bribe and the man's feelings had been slighted. 'But it was meant sincerely. I will need a head groom and I want the best. You are that man. I have seen the way you handle the horses, the feeling you show for them and their welfare. That is the care I will want taken in my stables. I ask again, will you consider the position? Whether or not you send me word of what I asked first has no bearing on my offer.'

'Then I accept, Mr Paul, and rest assured your horses will have no finer care than what I'll give them.'

Satisfied, he turned towards the house. Tomorrow he would begin his search for Emma.

'I was on my way home to Doe Bank.'

Emma stared into the fire, its dancing flames teasing the shadows festooning the walls of the Hollington kitchen. Sat in chairs each side of it the butcher and his wife watched in silence as the girl they had befriended spoke quietly, telling the story she'd insisted they hear.

'I had called on Jerusha Paget with a pie my mother had baked. I should have gone home the usual way but it was getting dark so I decided to take a short cut through...'

She paused, unwilling even to say the name, to give any clue as to the identity of the man who had raped her. Beside her Daisy reached for her hand, giving it a gentle squeeze.

Swallowing hard as the memory of that night brought a surge of bile to her throat, Emma went on.

'...I took the shorter way through the woods. It was there I was accosted by a man. He seemed polite enough at first...' she drew a long breath threaded with dry sobs '...then he attacked me.'

'Did you know this man?'

Emma shook her head in reply to Sarah's question, and in a way told the truth for until that night she had only heard of Carver Felton, had never met him.

'Would you be able to point him out, should you see him again?'

''Twould do little good should her do so.' Samuel ran a finger over his bushy whiskers. ''Twould be her word against his. Besides the fact it was already nightfall, her couldn't have seen the blackguard all that clear.'

'It was later...' Emma forced herself to go on, fearing this couple's questions might lead her into disclosing the identity of the father of the child in her womb. 'It was later I feared I might be pregnant. My mother knew what had happened though my father did not.'

'He wouldn't have believed you were attacked!' Sarah said, head moving from side to side in sympathy.

'No, he would not have believed it. That was why I went back to Jerusha. I asked her for a potion that would take away any ... any child I might be carrying.'

'Oh, you poor girl!' Fingers catching the corners of her snowy apron, Sarah pressed it against her mouth.

In the silence that followed Emma stared into the fire, watching the pictures that seemed to form in its brilliant heart. Jerusha, her old, lined face transformed as the silence took her; her mother's face, almost as lined by the hardness of her life, but eyes melting with love and sympathy as she reached out her arms; then it was the face of Carrie, so young, so very afraid. Closing her eyes tightly, Emma shut away the pictures. Shut them away before they could show her the face of her father.

'Jerusha refused,' she continued, speaking on as Sarah's relieved sigh sounded noisily in the small room. 'She told me the child inside me would be born even though I would seek a potion from another woman.'

'Oh, Emma, you shouldn't ought to 'ave done that!' Daisy glanced at her with anxious eyes. 'You could 'ave done yourself a lot of hurt.'

'Did this other woman give you anything?' Sarah waited for an answer, swinging her head sorrowfully as Emma nodded.

'She gave me something to drink, she did not say what it was.'

Daisy's fingers tightened again on Emma's. 'Oh Emma, that was a daft thing to do.'

Dry sobs rattling up from her chest Emma concentrated once more on the glowing bed of the fire. What use would it be to tell Daisy and the others of her father, of the things he would have accused her of doing while he himself performed the same on his own daughter? Caleb Price, the preacher man! The man who preached the Lord and served the Devil.

'I did not want to bring a fatherless child into the world.' Her lips tightened. 'A child who would face the finger of scorn all its life. No one has the right to do that, no one should cause another such pain!'

'Just as no man should force himself on a woman. Any that does should be given a hundred strokes of the cat!'

'Hmmph!' Sarah's disgusted snort overrode Samuel's comment. 'The lash be too good for a man of that sort. You wouldn't catch me letting him off so light. Were I magistrate on the bench I would order they cut...'

'Sarah!'

Samuel's exclamation halting her outburst, Sarah fiddled with her apron then defiantly continued, 'I would order him castrated. That way he would leave no other woman to raise his seed or abandon it at the door of the workhouse!'

'I ... I don't think I could do that.'

'No more you'll have to. My Samuel and me will see to that, don't you go having any worry to the contrary. I just hope the good Lord visits some suitable punishment on the vile creature who did this to you.'

'Leave the Lord to work in His own way, Sarah.' Samuel pulled at his whisker. 'I'm sure He needs no advice from us.'

'Did you pay this other woman for the potion you drank?' Daisy piped up, voice high with derision.

Emma nodded. 'A shilling.'

Her answering snort every bit as disgusted as that of Sarah had been Daisy snapped. 'Well, it ain't worked, has it? You and me will go and see the old fraud come Sunday. I'll get your shilling back if I 'ave to stomp all over the old witch!'

'No, Daisy.' Emma returned the pressure of

fingers still twined in her own. 'I got what I asked for...'

'Including a deal of stomach pain for the taking of it, I've no doubt!' Sarah said, tartness again masking her true feelings.

Agreement reflecting in eyes the firelight tinged to blue midnight Emma continued, the pain of that night forgotten as the pain of what still remained to tell pressed into her heart.

'My mother came into the room I shared with Carrie, my younger sister, she saw the pain the potion caused. I think she guessed it would serve no purpose. Later, when my father was told, he was very angry and ... and somehow there was an accident and Carrie was hurt.' Emma paused, knowing she was only skimming the surface of the truth, but she could not tell the full horror of what had really happened, not the terrible cause of her sister's taking her own life. The dancing flames shooting into the blackness of the chimney suddenly became those of a burning house, leaping high into the night sky, and her breath caught on an agonised sob.

Leaning towards her Sarah was restrained by Samuel's hand, a brief shake of his head telling her soundlessly that it was best for Emma to continue, to break open some of the bonds that clasped her heart.

'Mother sent me to fetch Jerusha, said she would know what to do. But when we returned the house was in flames and my parents and Carrie...'

'Don't say any more, child!' Shrugging off her husband's hand, Sarah was on her feet, her arms

244

about Emma. 'Don't say any more. The Lord will give them rest.'

Held against Sarah's ample bosom, Emma felt a dull throb of pain. *'The Lord will give them rest!'* Tears squeezing out beneath her lashes, she curled the fingers of both hands tight into her palms. But who would give *her* rest?

'How do you do?'

Melissa Gilbert's long dark lashes dropped demurely as she dipped a slow curtsy. 'I was so longing to meet you. Your brother told me of you.'

The lashes lifted, revealing grey eyes their smoky depths displaying a message that was more than one of mere welcome. 'But his description was less than adequate.'

'I hope the reality does not destroy the illusion.' Paul touched her perfumed hand to his lips before releasing it.

'Not destroy.' Melissa's smile was devastating. 'It re-shapes it. Though from now on I need be under no illusion.'

'Then you can't be fooled by it.' Handsome in deep burgundy, the cashmere cloth expertly tailored to his muscular figure, black hair highlighted by silver streaks brushed back from his forehead, Carver Felton stepped forward to take the hand his brother had relinquished.

'Nor by you, Carver!'

Having watched the scene being played out in her sitting room, Cara Holgate's mouth twisted into a caricature of a smile.

Lowering Melissa's hand, Carver looked up

245

into her smoky eyes, his own relaying nothing of the amusement that lurked within him. He knew the game she was playing and he knew she would not win. Melissa Gilbert was not for his brother, any more than that Doe Bank girl.

'Fooled by me!' He turned to Cara. Hair raven dark as his own and piled high on her head lent height to her figure which tonight was expensively gowned in deep red Shantung covered in pale gold lace, the silk clinging to every curve. 'Since when have I ever tried to fool anyone?'

Green-gold eyes holding his, smile unwavering on her full sensuous mouth, Cara batted her eyelashes at him.

'Since the first moment you drew breath. But even given your years of practice, you are still not proficient enough to dupe me.'

'Then I shall not bother to try.' Flicking back his coat tails, Carver lowered himself into a nearby chair. Why would he bother to fool Cara? She could manage that infinitely well for herself, especially if she were looking to take a percentage of Felton money.

Accepting the brandy she now held out to him, he ignored the lingering touch of her fingers, directing his attention to her cousin instead.

'Have you told my brother how much you enjoyed your visit to his house, Melissa?'

Paul looked up as he too accepted a glass from Cara, his brows drawing together quizzically.

'You have visited Beaufort House?'

Her mouth holding just the right amount of self reproval, grey eyes widening like a child caught at the sweet jar, Melissa touched her fan to her nose.

'It was dreadful of me, I know,' she murmured, letting her lashes droop once more. 'I should have waited until you were home to make a proper call, but I was so intrigued.'

'Intrigued?' Paul's frown deepened. 'By Beaufort House?'

Dropping the fan to rest in her lap, Melissa kept her lashes lowered, adding a touch of embarrassment to her voice as she answered, 'Not by the house, more its owner.'

'That, I confess, is down to me.' Carver laughed lightly as Paul's quizzical glance switched to him. 'I took Melissa to view the enamels at Bilston in order to choose some trinkets. On the way home we fell to talking of you and of the home our father left to you. Melissa expressed a wish to see it and since you were not there to satisfy that wish, I took it upon myself to play host.'

Lashes lifting, to reveal a devastated look Melissa's voice dropped to a whisper. 'I ... I hope you do not mind? I am so very impetuous, as my cousin will tell you. I never could wait for anything on which I set my heart.'

Carver's amused glance shifted to Cara. He saw the intensity of the stare she directed towards the younger woman. Who was it said jealousy had green eyes?

'We were there only a very short while and I took only the tiniest peep.' Her magnificent eyes filling with liquid appeal, mouth adopting an apologetic droop, she added, 'Do say you forgive me, please, Paul?'

'There is nothing to forgive.' Paul smiled. 'But

247

Beaufort House deserves more than the tiniest peek. You must allow me the privilege of showing it to you myself, at a more leisurely pace.'

'Oh, how lovely!' Her embarrassment giving way to a dazzling smile, Melissa hid her triumph. 'Do make it soon... But, oh! There I go again with my impetuous demands.'

'Why not make it tomorrow?' Carver withdrew his glance from Cara, but not before he saw the tightening of her mouth. 'Paul will have no other opportunity for some weeks as he will be away on business. No doubt by the time he is finished you will have returned to your home in Rugeley.'

'That would be perfect.' Melissa clapped her gloves hands then looked at her cousin. 'You had not made any plans for tomorrow, had you, my dear?'

'No!' Her glance razor sharp, full mouth drawn to a thin line, Cara turned away. 'I had made no plans for tomorrow.'

'Then that is settled.' Carver drove home the final nail. 'And you, my delicious little bundle, must wear this when my brother comes to pick you up.'

Taking a blue vellum-covered box from his pocket he handed it to Melissa, but as she exclaimed over the beautifully enamelled brooch his eyes were on Cara.

Picking up a crystal goblet he smiled into its glinting depths. His giving Melissa the brooch had annoyed the beautiful Cara, but it was not the sole cause of her annoyance nor was it the root of her jealousy. There was more than that biting away behind that beautiful face and clawing at her greedy heart.

Lifting his glass, Carver watched the myriad facets of coloured light dance from its intricate surface.

Cara Holgate was indeed jealous of her pretty cousin. And Carver knew why.

Chapter Seventeen

'We've done well today, my little wench.'

Samuel's smile spread as wide as his bushy whiskers as he wiped his hands on the apron that reached to his feet.

'I could have sold half as much again. It be that pretty face of yours has drawn the customers.'

'More likely their curiosity. They came to see who it was serving meat at butcher Hollington's stall.'

'Mebbe, mebbe!' Samuel gathered his knives, placing them in the large wicker basket. 'But if they be just as curious tomorrow then I'll have no complaining. Ain't nothing left but the chops I laid aside for you and Daisy.'

He broke off as a woman came hurrying to the stall.

'I'll take a pound of sausages – good thick ones, mind. I can't 'ave no thin ones that don't 'ave a good bite in the length of 'em!'

'All my sausages are good and they be packed with the finest pork...'

'Arr, I knows that!' The woman fumbled beneath the shawl that draped her head and covered the whole of her upper body. Bringing out a tattered black purse she drew a coin that shone silver in the light of the candle jars that lit the stall. 'That be why I be here and why I always buys my sausages from you. Now wrap me a pound so I can be getting 'ome before the old man gets in.'

'I would and gladly.' Samuel dropped the last of the knives into the basket. ''Cept I don't have a pound. In fact, I don't have a single sausage left, the whole lot be gone.'

The woman's head lifted sharply and in the flickering anaemic yellow glow of the stall's candle jars it showed pale and lined, a face worn by worry and long hours of labour. A face so like her mother's had been that Emma caught her breath.

'Sold out?' Glinting in the dim light the woman's eyes darted from one face to the other. 'But I always comes at this time and I always takes a pound of your sausages, my 'usband won't eat anybody else's.'

'I'm sorry, missis, but tonight you come too late. I sold the last few sausages more than an hour gone.'

'But you 'ave to 'ave a few!' The woman's voice was stricken and her eyes held a frightened look. 'He said special I was to get sausages for his supper. If I don't bring 'em he'll make my 'ead ring like the bells in St Bart's steeple.'

Hand resting on the handle of his large basket, Samuel shook his head. 'If I had any at all I'd give them to you and gladly, but like I says, the last of them be gone more than an hour since.'

Her hand closing over the coin, the woman clasped the shawl tight beneath her chin as if already shielding herself against a blow. 'What am I to do?' She glanced at Emma but her eyes held only fear. Then as she walked away she murmured again, 'What am I to do?'

Catching Emma's glance, Samuel lifted both his hands in a gesture of helplessness. Halfway along the Shambles by now, the woman's steps were slow. Watching the huddled figure Emma could almost feel the fear held in that small frame.

Deaf to Samuel's warning for her to heed the razor sharp blades, Emma plunged her hand into the basket. The package of chops gripped tight, she ran after the woman.

The short run adding to the tightness sight of that tired face had set in her throat, Emma gasped as she caught up to her.

'Please, take these. Your husband might enjoy a pork chop as much as he would a sausage.'

Glancing at the package in Emma's hand, the woman shook her head.

'He be partial to a nice pork chop, 'specially if it 'as a slice of kidney in it, but I can't take them. The money I 'ave don't run to the buying of pork chops on a Thursday.'

'Mr Hollington sent them,' Emma lied quickly. 'He said, would you take them with his apologies and there would be no charge.'

'I don't 'ave to pay for 'em?'

Emma smiled into the tired face and shook her head.

'A pork chop with a kidney, a pound of Jersey 'tatoes and a few green beans...' The woman's face brightened. 'He'll like that. And the money I don't 'ave to spend on these chops will buy him a quart of Old Best. That'll put a smile on his face.'

And hopefully keep his hands in his pockets, Emma thought as the woman thanked her.

'Well, now, that were a right daft thing to do! Them chops were intended as supper for Daisy and yourself,' Samuel reprimanded as she returned.

'They'll do that woman more good, especially if they save her a beating.' Emma blew into a jam jar, extinguishing the candle inside it. 'And I'm sure Daisy won't mind when I explain.'

'Don't go taking any bets.' Samuel smiled. 'That young wench likes her supper.'

So did she. Emma blew out the remaining candles. But it was worth going without to help that woman who'd looked as if one more beating would be enough to kill her.

'Don't go leaving them candles in the jars.' Samuel looked back from placing the wicker basket on the hand cart. 'We've given one present tonight. No call to go leaving them for the first light-fingered Johnny who passes by. Eh!' He took up the handles of the cart. 'Fancy giving your supper away!'

Dropping into step beside him, Emma pulled her shawl over her head. 'You said *you* would have given the woman sausages and been glad to.' She smiled in the darkness. 'Why shouldn't I do the same?'

'Arr wench, why shouldn't you? It was an act of Christian charity, and like the Lord told us, there be no greater act. Be sure He's seen it and will repay in His own way.'

I will repay, saith the Lord. Emma shivered as her father's preaching suddenly echoed in her mind.

Had he been repaid … had the Lord given his deserts to the preacher man?

Pulling the shawl closer about her face, Emma hid the spilling tears.

'It's a lovely house, Emma, I never seen anything as pretty. Mrs Hollington her let me touch vases and them little statues that stand on the parlour mantel. Oh, I forgot, you haven't seen the parlour. Eh, Emma, it be so clean! And the lamps they have these long pieces of glass dangling down, just like long blue fingers. Oh, wait 'til you see!'

Her back aching from long hours spent standing in the market followed by the walk back to the Hollingtons' house, Emma wanted only to sit down and close her eyes.

'…and the garden, it has flowers and trees. Mrs Hollington says there be apples and pears and damsons. She said we could pick some come a couple more weeks…' Excited by her own day, Daisy prattled on.

Emma had often been weary after a day spent scrabbling for coal chippings on the pit bank but her mother had always been there with a word of comfort, and Carrie… She closed her eyes against the wave of emotion that left her shivering… Carrie and her mother had always been there, a part of her life. Their love had been the threads that held that life together and now those threads were broken as was her life, destroyed by two men, her father and Carver Felton.

'…but the best of all be this. Come and see,

Emma. Come and see what Mrs Hollington has given to us.'

Grabbing her hand, Daisy pulled her across a cobbled yard that ran behind the house, the whole enclosed by a high garden wall.

Too full of memories of Doe Bank to protest, Emma allowed herself to be led towards a small brick building set a little apart.

'It be all right, Emma.' Daisy gave a little laugh as Emma hesitated at the door. 'We ain't going where we shouldn't. Mrs Hollington says we can stay here, can have this place as our home. Look!' She threw open the door, pulling Emma inside. 'Look at it, ain't it lovely?'

Blinking in the light as Daisy turned up the oil lamp, Emma looked around the small room. Pretty curtains sprigged with honeysuckle hung at the single window beneath which a brown-stone sink gleamed. Set against one wall stood a bed covered with a patterned quilt, while the centre of the room held a scrubbed table and two straight-backed wooden chairs.

'Didn't I say it was lovely?' Daisy jigged up and down, her face radiant. 'Oh, Emma, we'll be so happy here.'

Looking at her friend's grinning face, Emma felt her own tiredness and misery fade. 'Yes, Daisy.' She smiled. 'We will be happy here.'

A sound at the open door catching their ears, the two girls turned.

'My Samuel told me about the pork chops.' Sarah Hollington stepped inside, an enamelled pot in her hands. 'I'll not say as it weren't a daft thing to do, to go giving away your own supper,

255

but it were a kind one.'

Putting the pot on the cast iron stove, she faced the girls. 'This don't be much of a place, being only the old brew house, but it be dry and the stove will keep it warm and cook a meal.'

'It's very nice, Mrs Hollington.' Emma's eyes reflected her gratitude. 'We are both very grateful for your kindness and we will work hard for you.'

Her fingers going to her apron, Sarah fiddled with its corners. 'Samuel and me don't hold no fears on that score. Now you get that broth inside of you and then get yourselves to bed. 'Specially you, Emma. You needs to take care of yourself with a child coming.'

'Mrs Hollington?' Emma began as Daisy lifted the lid from the pot, sniffing appreciatively at its contents. 'How did you know I was pregnant?'

Her mouth quivering, Sarah Hollington glanced at her fingers still twiddling the corners of her apron, and when she spoke tears trembled in every word.

'When a woman has carried three times then she recognises the symptoms in another.'

'I didn't know you had children, Mrs Hollington? You never said.' Daisy returned the lid with a clatter.

'That's because I don't have any.' Sarah's face was clouded. 'I said I'd carried children but I never birthed not one. Seven months they stayed in my womb, for seven months they were a part of me, and then they were gone. I could never carry full-term, that was what the doctor told me, and his words were true. Samuel and me, we never did have a child.'

256

Emma felt her heart swell with pity. What was it that caused people like the Hollingtons to be afflicted by such sorrow while those like Caleb Price and Carver Felton were spared it? Was this God's will? Her veins turning cold as once more Carrie's frightened face showed in the mirror of her mind she shivered, the next question filling her brain. Or was it that there was no God?

'Mrs Hollington, I am so very sorry.' The words inched out as the woman drew a long breath.

'Arr, wench, so were we. But it be long past, and what the Lord denies with one hand He makes up for with the other. Me and Samuel have one another and life hasn't been a bad one.'

They had one another! Emma watched the door close behind Sarah. Her own family had been denied her and what had she been given in return? A bastard child. What God would allow such things to happen?

'It won't work this time, Carver, I won't go.'

Lips white with temper, Paul Felton faced his elder brother.

'You deliberately withheld telling me until we were at Cara Holgate's house. You thought that way there would be no refusal, no opposition. Well, you were right. But we are not at Cara's now and I am telling you: if you want business done anywhere at all before I have found Emma, then you can do it yourself!'

'You still intend searching for her?'

'Yes!' Paul snapped. 'And I'll go on searching until I find her, no matter how long it takes.'

Returning the pen he held to the crystal ink

stand, Carver studied his brother now glaring at him from the other side of the heavy walnut desk. Hands resting lightly on its polished surface, he said quietly, 'I must warn you yet again, Paul, time may be all you have in the future.'

'Don't give me any more of your warnings!' Paul's own hand slammed down hard beside Carver's as he leaned across the desk. 'That is all I have heard from you since Father died. Well, they don't frighten me any more. There is nothing you can do. I am going to look for Emma and you can't stop me!'

'Oh, but I can!' Eyes like black ice looked deep into Paul's. 'You know very well what I can do. I will brook no argument. Believe me, brother, either you agree to do as I say or you will be under lock and key before nightfall. Should you decide to run after that slut you will greatly facilitate my actions. A runaway minor is always more easily committed to an institution than an obedient one. Think about it, Paul. You have until lunchtime to make up your mind.'

Straightening up, his hands dropping to his sides, Paul stared at the man sitting at the desk where once his father had sat.

'What has happened to you, Carver?' he asked. 'I don't know you any more.'

Sunlight from the window catching the silver streaks in his hair, Carver leaned back in his chair, his mouth barely moving as he answered.

'Don't worry, you'll learn to!'

'Yes.' Paul turned away. Opening the study door he glanced back. 'Yes, I'm sure I will.'

What the hell did his brother see in that girl?

Carver pushed himself angrily away from the desk and crossed to the window. A common, no-account wench, scratching a living from the waste heaps of the Topaz. A girl with no more than the rags on her back. Was it her looks? True she was pretty enough judging from what he remembered, but there were other girls with pretty faces and breeding to go with it.

So what was it had Paul ready to risk everything to go haring off after her? Carver stared sightlessly out over the garden. The question plagued his every off guard moment, but it did not worry him so much as the one he would not answer. Why was he deliberately preventing his brother marrying Emma Price?

'Your pardon, sir. You asked to be informed when your visitor arrived.'

Turning from the window, Carver nodded briefly. Grateful for the interruption he walked from the study, but knew that was all it was, an interruption. The question of the Doe Bank girl, together with the vision of that frightened face, would return to haunt his sleep.

'Sir Anslow has considered your request.'

Carver tensed as the man withdrew a sheaf of papers from a black Gladstone bag but his mouth and eyes betrayed none of his anxiety. He had already sunk a lot of capital into this canal project. If it should be turned down...

'He has had his own engineers study the plans you sent to him.'

The man paused, clearing his throat. Damn you, say what you have to say! Carver forced himself to remain silent though the words were shouted in his mind.

The man went on importantly, 'They ... the engineers ... reported to Sir Anslow...'

Reported! Carver felt tension turn to irritation. Why could not this ferret of a man just give him the decision?

'...the plan was quite sound provided...'

'Provided?' His temper mounting, the word snapped from Carver's mouth.

Adam's apple bobbing up and down in his throat, the man held out the sheaf of papers, his glance dancing nervously over Carver's tight features.

'Provided you had a good engineer of your own to oversee the work. Sir Anslow seemed to think Mr Telford...'

Carver released his breath he had not realised was dammed in his throat. 'You may assure Sir Anslow that none other than Mr Telford will supervise the work.'

'Sir Anslow was certain you would agree.' Closing the Gladstone bag, the man edged towards the door. 'You will find his signature on the papers. Good day to you, Mr Felton.'

He had agreed. Sir Anslow Lacy had agreed! Carver swept up the papers, carrying them to the study where he spread them on the desk. He could cut a link into the Birmingham Navigation Canal and thereby triple Felton business in a year. That was how it would be once he had those damned contracts from Payne and Langton in his safekeeping. Signing those was obviously Arthur Payne's idea. So far as Carver knew Rafe Langton had never signed a contract in his life.

260

He was of the old school where a man's word was still his bond.

Gathering the papers together, Carver stared at them. At present he had two partners in the venture, two other people to reap its profits. But he had a plan in hand to ensure control of them came to him. Would he could do the same with regard to Paul.

Paul! His fingers whitened as they gripped the sheaf of papers. What would he do about his brother?

He could not go on sending him on errands about the country. In a few months Paul would indeed be his own man and have full say in the running of Felton's...

There is a way. Carver almost heard the words. There is a way to make sure he will not meddle too much. Help him find Emma Price! He would be so occupied he would want no part of directing business for a while. Marriage to the Doe Bank girl...

Marriage to the Doe Bank girl! His nostrils dilating, lips thinning, Carver's head whipped upward. Crushing the thought as if it were a weed between his fingers he strode from the room.

Chapter Eighteen

'Eh, Emma, don't this be wonderful!'

Running a few steps ahead Daisy jumped into the air, both arms stretched wide.

Yes, it was wonderful. Emma gazed over the heath. The first tints of autumn gave it a blush of amber and mauve. This had always been Carrie's favourite time. She'd said the colours were quiet after the brightness of the scarlet poppies and vivid yellow dog daisies, the brilliant blue of violet and cornflower that threw a riot of colour over the summer heath.

Bending she picked a stalk of ling, touching a finger to the soft mauve head. Carrie had loved the tiny plant; loved to take off her shoes and stockings and run barefoot through what seemed to them as children an ocean of purple silk.

'What are you thinking?'

Eyes blue as the cornflowers she had been re-membering, Emma smiled. 'I was thinking of when we ... I ... was a child.'

'You said we!' Daisy's ears, alert as ever, caught the slip. Coming to stand beside Emma, she glanced at the sprig of heather held between her fingers. 'You meant Carrie, didn't you? You was remembering her.'

'Yes,' Emma said huskily. 'I was remembering Carrie.'

Sitting down, legs outstretched in front of her,

Daisy plucked another stem of ling. 'I ain't never had a sister. Not as I know anyway. It must have been great, the two of you walking on the heath, doing everything together.'

Not everything! Emma's fingers stilled on the flower head. There were some things…

'Would you tell me, Emma, about your sister? Then I can pretend she was my sister as well.'

Daisy's words had driven away the terrible thoughts and Emma smiled gratefully. 'Yes, I will tell you about Carrie. And were she here, I know she would want to be your sister too.'

Sitting herself beside Daisy, she spread her skirts in an arc over the sweet-smelling heather.

'What are you smiling at?' Daisy caught the smile hovering about Emma's mouth.

'I was remembering Gertie Bowen's umbrella. Gertie was our neighbour at Doe Bank. She was a kindly soul who always had a smile for us children, except if one of us touched her beloved umbrella. No one quite knew where it had come from but it was her most treasured possession, coming out only on high days and holidays. Not that the folk of Doe Bank really had holidays.'

'What colour was it?' Daisy lay back, folding her arms beneath her head. 'Gertie's umbrella, what colour was it?'

Smiling at the flower between her fingers Emma seemed to look back over the years, across the barrier that divided childhood from the present.

'Black.' She smiled. 'It was black and several of its spokes were broken, but that made no difference to Gertie. She loved it as a king loves his crown. It was Easter Sunday when last I saw her carrying it. Carrie was about eight years old. We were there with our mother on the way to Chapel. Father had gone on ahead to prepare for taking the service....' Emma broke off, mention of her father bringing a coldness to her spine.

'Go on!' Daisy urged. 'What happened then?'

'Well,' she resumed, 'March was living up to its reputation, the day being chilly and quite blustery. Halfway to Chapel it came on to rain, not heavily but enough to give Gertie the chance to show off her treasured umbrella. It was such a comical sight! Gertie, her spine stiff as a ramrod, holding up an umbrella that hung lop-sided and flapped in the breeze. I remember Mother reprimanding Carrie and me for giggling, but when I looked up she too had a smile on her face.'

'Then what?' Daisy closed her eyes conjuring the scene.

'We only had a few yards to go to reach the Chapel when a huge gust of wind turned the umbrella inside out and snatched it from Gertie's hand, blowing it half across the field. Poor Gertie! I remember the cry she gave as she watched it go. Then a couple of the boys set off in pursuit.'

'Did they bring it back?'

'Not them.' Emma's smile returned. 'They turned back on seeing the bull. It had seen the umbrella sail across its field and then the boys following after. But the bull was having none of that. Head down, it chased them away.'

'Poor Gertie! Losing her umbrella to a bull!"

'She didn't lose it. Gertie wouldn't give up that easily. Watched by the rest of us, she hitched up her skirts and climbed the stile into the field.'

Daisy's eyes bulged. 'You mean, she went into that field? With a bull!'

Emma laughed. A laugh lightened by memory. 'She most certainly did. No bull was having her umbrella.'

'Lor'!' Daisy breathed. 'She had more courage than I've got. I wouldn't tackle no bull, not for a gold sovereign.'

'Ah, but you are no Gertie Bowen, and next to her umbrella a sovereign meant nothing. Spine straight as ever, she set off across the field, skirts flapping like crow's wings in the wind. The bull stood still. The steam from its nostrils was filmy white and I swear its eyes were red. Carrie hid her face in Mother's skirts as it began to paw the ground. Gertie was halfway to where her umbrella had landed when the bull let out an enormous bellow. I heard several women scream as it began to trot towards her but by this time my face too was pressed to Mother's side.'

Her tone laced with disappointment, Daisy shut her eyes again. 'You mean, you missed it? You didn't see what happened after that?'

Tempted to keep the remainder of the story to herself to tease Daisy, Emma at last relented.

'Not exactly. I heard the men's shouts and I just had to look. Several of them had jumped into the field and were waving their jackets to distract the bull's attention. Marching like a guardsman, Gertie went on regardless. Two of the braver lads caught up with her as she reached her goal, and even from the hedge we could see the look of horror that crossed her face. Spread in a black arc at her feet her beloved umbrella lay trampled ... across several mushy cow pats!'

Daisy's laughter rang across the heath, sending a pair of startled peewits winging upward, black and white plumage stark against the blue sky.

'You mean, Gertie's umbrella was covered with...'

'Cowpats!' Emma's eyes twinkled.

'Eh, poor soul.' Daisy wiped the back of her hand across her eyes. 'After all that she *still* didn't get her umbrella.'

'I told you, Gertie didn't give up easily. She picked up the umbrella and with the tips of her fingers folded it right way out. Then, with all the dignity of a queen, she closed it and marched back across the field. Then, as if nothing had happened, she sailed on to Chapel.'

'She took that umbrella into Chapel, cowpats and all?'

Emma nodded. 'She did. If the umbrella didn't go to Chapel then neither did Gertie. We were all even more relieved than usual when that service ended!'

'What happened to Gertie's gamp?'

'She cleaned it and treasured it every bit as much as before. It became something of a byword in the village. If someone had something a little out of the ordinary it was described as being "precious as Bowen's brolly".'

'Eh, Emma!' Daisy sighed. 'You and Carrie must have had such fun together.'

Emma's gaze travelled over the silent heath. Yes,

266

they had had fun, but they had also had sorrow.

'Sure, and didn't I think it were the little people I heard laughing?'

Startled, Emma scrambled to her feet as Daisy sat up.

'But then, isn't it the little people I be looking at, for you ladies be much too pretty to be mortal.'

'We ... we didn't hear you coming.' Emma brushed away the pieces of dry bracken clinging to her skirts.

'Now that's not surprising, the heather here be wondrous thick.'

'Ling,' Emma corrected. 'The plant is called ling.'

'Is it now?' The man smiled, the warmth of it reaching his eyes. 'Aren't I the ignorant one? My mother always told me lack of learning did a man no good, and isn't she proved right for here I am not knowing the name of a plant.'

'I think that can be forgiven.' Emma felt the infection of his grin and she too smiled.

'But not my startling you. That was thoughtless. But as my mother would tell you, rest her soul, Liam Brogan was never a great one for the thinking.'

'That style of speech, it ain't from Wednesbury?' Daisy was on her feet.

'No.' The man smiled again, the blue of his eyes deep as a sapphire. 'I am from Ireland, a village in the north. I have come here to work on the new navigation.'

Curiosity bright as her smile, Daisy regarded the man. Thick brown hair the colour of the cinnamon sticks in Sarah Hollington's pantry waved thickly back from an open, weather-bronzed face, its strong chin marred by a small Z-shaped white scar.

'Ireland? That be foreign parts, don't it?'

'You could say that.' He grinned. 'Seeing as there be a sea that divides it from this country, though the English landlords who profess to own much of the land would deny it.'

'You say you came here to work.'

'That I did, along of others.' He swung his glance to Emma. 'We were brought over by Mr Felton, to dig out his new canal.'

Brought over by Mr Felton? She felt the world sway beneath her feet. Was that where Paul had been since last she saw him? And would he come looking for her now as he had once before?

''Twill be a fine waterway when it be finished.' Liam Brogan shaded his eyes as he looked towards the town. 'Managed well it will bring work to Wednesbury and fortune to the builder. But then, Carver Felton be a man who knows that well enough.'

Carver Felton! Emma's senses reeled. It was not Paul he spoke of but his brother.

'Where are these new navigations to be built?' She swallowed the fear building in her throat.

His eyes still squinting in the direction of the two church spires set on the hill above the town, Liam Brogan answered, 'The link will join the main waterway to a basin that is being con-structed at a place they call Plovers Croft...'

Then it was true. The rest of what he said was lost on Emma. Jerusha Paget's home and those of

268

all the others living in the village had been sacrificed just so Carver Felton could build his canal. The man who had raped her and robbed her of her home, had razed an entire community in order to further his own ends. Just how many more people would he hurt?

Drawing her shawl about her, Emma managed a smile. 'It's time Daisy and I were going, Mr Brogan.'

'Daisy.' The name rolled off his tongue. 'To be sure that's a pretty name an' all. And what be your own? For 'tis sure I am that it will be just as pretty.'

'Emma.' This time the name clung to his mouth as if he were reluctant to let it go. 'No, 'tis not a pretty name, it be a beautiful one. A name such as heaven might give.'

'We have to be going, Mr Brogan.' Emma blushed and Daisy giggled. 'Good afternoon to you.'

'It is an afternoon such as you say for haven't I met the pair of you,' he called, the breeze carrying his voice across the heath.

'He was nice. I hope we meet him again.' Walking beside her, Daisy chattered on but Emma did not hear. Her mind was on Plovers Croft. Carver Felton had wiped it from the earth. And what of Doe Bank, had that too been sacrificed on the altar of his ambitions?

Her fingers clenched beneath the shawl she walked on. Were the houses of her own village still standing? Did Jerusha have a roof over her head? Some day, God willing, she might find out!

Arthur Payne glanced at the girl sitting beside him in the carriage. Pretty as a picture in ice blue velvet, a beribboned bonnet setting off her heart-shaped face, Melissa Gilbert returned his glance, her own eyes dark with invitation.

He had been a regular caller at Cara's house ever since Carver Felton had introduced them. Melissa settled her hands deeper inside her ruched muff. It had been so easy to hook him and now she would reel him in like a fish on a line.

'It is so kind of you to give me your time, Arthur.' Her lips, faintly rouged, parted showing small even teeth. 'You must have so many other things you should be doing.'

'Nothing so important as giving you pleasure, my dear. To be truthful, being alone with you is a joy I thought never to experience, Cara is so protective of you.'

Melissa gave a short tinkling laugh. 'That is precisely what Carver said only a week ago.'

'Carver?' Arthur Payne's mouth tightened within the frame of his well-clipped beard. 'Carver Felton called on you?'

'Why, yes. He is a regular caller, and such a dear. He escorted me to the theatre at Wolverhampton on Wednesday evening. What a wonderful time we had. Carver is so attentive.'

I bet he is! His thoughts acid sharp, Arthur flipped the reins, setting the pair of beautifully matched greys to the canter.

'He so often suggests outings for just the two of us, I think it makes my cousin a tiny bit jealous. But then, Carver is so terribly handsome I can quite understand her feelings.'

'So can I.'

Melissa's eyes adopted a look of concern, but the smile inside her was wide with satisfaction. She had fed Arthur Payne titbits concerning Carver's relationship with her; maybe those titbits contained more than a liberal amount of non truth, but Arthur Payne was not to know that.

Using a little girl tone she turned towards him. 'Arthur, you ... you are not cross with me, are you?'

'Not you, Melissa, but that Felton...'

Satisfaction mounting, she breathed audibly, 'Oh, Arthur, it is so selfish of me but I am so glad it is not me with whom you are annoyed.'

Guiding the carriage into Dudley Street, he released one hand from the reins, touching it gently to her arm.

'How could I be annoyed with you, Melissa? You are the sweetest, most thoughtful of women. You could never annoy me, my dear, for I...'

A cart laden with grain sacks turning in the road ahead and demanding his attention, he broke off.

Damn! Melissa swore silently to herself. She had spent almost an entire afternoon with this fool fawning all over her and just when he came up to scratch, he was stopped by a wagon!

Waiting until they'd cleared the obstacle and still using the little girl tone, she returned to the topic.

'I would never willingly annoy you, Arthur. I value your friendship too highly.' Withdrawing one hand from her muff she pressed it to his. 'Say you will always be my friend?'

He brought the carriage to a sudden halt on the heath that edged the road. 'I will say that if it is all you will allow me to say.' His voice thickening, he caught her hand, clasping it between both of his.

Triumph in every beat of her heart, Melissa dropped her lashes. 'I ... I don't know what you mean, Arthur,' she murmured. 'What more could you wish to say?'

'That I want to be more than a friend to you, my dear. I want to be your husband. I love you, Melissa, and I want to marry you.' Lifting her hand to his lips, he pressed them against her palm. 'Say you will, Melissa? Say you will be my wife?'

'Oh, Arthur!' Withdrawing her hand she lowered her lashes again, as if too shy to look longer into his pleading eyes. 'I ... I don't know.'

'I know you could not possibly be in love with me.' He kissed her palms again. 'But I will be a good husband to you, and in time perhaps...'

Keeping her voice as shy and demure as the look she now lifted to him she touched a hand to his face. 'I do not need time, Arthur. I ... I do love you, but...'

'But what?' Grabbing the hand that touched his face he smothered it with kisses.

'I ... I had always promised myself I would try my hand at business. Oh, I know what you will say, the same as my cousin does: a woman has no place in business. But I know if I do not try it will be a source of regret to me all my life.'

272

'There must be no regret in your life, my dearest. Of course you must try if that is what you wish, and my wedding gift to you will be a business.'

'Arthur,' she simpered. 'Arthur, what are you saying?'

'I will do more than say – I will *show* you your wedding gift.'

Taking up the reins he set the greys to a fast trot towards Lea Brook.

Pretended alarm, as much a part of the make up on her mouth as the rouge that coloured it, Melissa clung to his arm. 'Arthur, where are you taking me?'

Minutes later he brought the horses to a stand-still then pointed across the heath.

'There's where I am taking you. There is my wedding gift to you, my darling. A one-third share in the new Wednesbury Canal.'

'Oh, Arthur, I can't … I couldn't … I could not take on a venture of that sort. What if I should fail?'

'You will take it on, my love, and you will *not* fail. But should you tire of being in business then you can always hand it back to your husband. Provided, of course, you will marry me. You have not yet given me your answer?'

Letting her lashes droop again, Melissa concealed the triumph gleaming in her eyes. 'I … I do love you, Arthur, but I am afraid.'

'Afraid!' He caught her to him. 'Afraid of what? Of Cara?'

Her laughter soft against his chest, she whispered, 'No, not of Cara, but of accepting

273

your wedding gift. I fear you will think I accept your offer of marriage simply in return for that.'

Gently lifting her face, he touched his lips to her brow. 'I know that is something you would never do, Melissa.'

'Then I will marry you, Arthur.'

Exultation washing through her in a warm tide she gave herself to his embrace, then leaning back against the soft upholstery smiled up at him. 'Cara will never believe this, our becoming engaged and ... and your gift to me. Arthur dear, are you sure?'

'Never more sure of anything, my love. And neither will your cousin be when I bring you the contract I signed with Carver Felton, reassigned to you.'

Driving back, Melissa smiled that deep hidden smile of victory. One fly was in the web, the second would soon be joining him. Tonight she and Cara would celebrate.

Taking the brush she had bought for a penny from the bric-a-brac stall in the market, Emma pulled it through her hair.

'Wash yourself all over and brush your hair every night.' She smiled into the mirror, remembering her mother's words so often used to Carrie and herself.

'And say your prayers, remember always to say your prayers. A clean body and a clean soul find favour with God and man.'

She and Carrie, had they not always followed their mother's maxim, had they not prayed together each night before climbing into bed, prayed even after an evening of the long drawn out sermons their father was fond of preaching to his family?

The preacher man! Emma stared into the speckled mirror Mrs Hollington had given them. How could he preach the word of God, sermonise on the evils of waywardness and following after the Devil, when all the time...

'You have such lovely hair, it shines like wheat when the moon be on it. I wish I had hair like yours.'

'You have lovely hair too.' Emma turned to Daisy, sitting up in bed with her knees drawn up to her chin.

'You just be saying that. My hair be an awful colour, it ain't a proper brown, it be ... well, I don't know what the colour be but I know I wish it were the same as yours.'

'The colour is auburn, Daisy, a deep rich auburn, and it gleams like the last rays of a setting sun.'

'Oh, go on!' Daisy blushed but her eyes glowed with pleasure. 'You just be fooling me.'

'I am not.' Laying the brush aside Emma proceeded to plait her own hair. 'Yours is the colour my sister most admired, she always had a yearning for hair of that very shade.'

She had not quoted Carrie's words exactly, but Emma knew her sister would not have minded.

'Was your sister very pretty, Emma? Was she as pretty as you?'

Suddenly she was back with her mother and father and a six-year-old Carrie on a sun-gilded evening beside the stream that powered Fincher's flour mill. Carrie had found a tiny pool cut off from the stream and had knelt beside it, looking into its still water.

'*I can see a water nymph.*' The laughter that had broken from her drifted on the waves of memory and Emma's hands became still as she listened. '*Shall I ask her name?*'

'*Yes.*' Emma had knelt beside her. '*But I think I know it already.*'

Carrie's large brown eyes stared out of the mists of time, tugging at Emma's heart. '*Do you, Emma, do you? Tell me what it is?*'

'*Well!*' Emma had sat back on her heels. '*Her name is Caroline and she is not just an ordinary water nymph. She is the most beautiful of all the sea princesses and has swum upstream on an adventure.*'

'*How exciting!*' Carrie had clapped her hands. '*What sort of adventure?*'

'*The adventurous sort, of course,*' Emma had teased. '*But now, thanks to the wicked witch of the sea, she is trapped in this tiny pool.*'

Carrie's mouth had dropped. '*That's awful. Can't we do something to help?*'

'*We could try, but only if she agrees. Will I ask her?*'

Carrie had nodded so hard the ribbon had slipped from one of her plaits, landing in the tiny pool so the image was distorted.

'*Wait!*' Emma had answered her cry of disappointment. '*When the water is still maybe she will come back.*'

Almost afraid to breathe, Carrie had bent over the patch of water. '*Come back, sea princess,*' she had called softly. '*Please come back, we want to help you. We want to free you from the trap the sea witch set for you.'*

Gradually the ripples had died and Carrie's face was reflected once more on its quiet surface. *'She's come back.'* Carrie's smile had broken out again, lighting her small face. *'Ask her now, Emma, ask her before she disappears again!'*

'Very well, but don't call out or you may frighten her. Sea Princesses are very gentle as well as very beautiful.'

Carrie had smiled in that special way a child has of knowing when something is not true but being said to please them. Then, bending over the pool, she listened to Emma's whisper.

'Sea Princess Caroline, I know you are trapped by a wicked witch. Will I set you free?'

'Oh, yes!' Lost in the fantasy, Carrie had replied in a voice as hushed as her own. *'Oh, yes, please.'*

They had each found a stick then and scraped a shallow channel in the soft earth then stood watching the patch of water run back into the stream.

'Goodbye, sea princess.' Carrie had waved her small hand. *'Goodbye.'*

Carrie had been their princess and like the mythical one had found herself trapped, not by any sea witch but by her own father. Emma held the long plait of her hair, self-recrimination dulling her eyes. She should have known something was wrong. Carrie changed so much as she grew older, that wonderful smile so rarely lighting her face. Had Emma bothered to find out why she could have ended it, freed the real Caroline. But she had not!

In her mind's eye she watched the soft brown

eyes stare sadly at her, the gentle mouth whisper goodbye.

'Emma? Oh, Emma, I didn't mean to make you cry!' Daisy scrambled from the bed as a sob broke from Emma. 'I'm such a fool, I never think before I speak.'

'You did not make me cry, Daisy.' She sniffed. 'I ... I was just remembering.'

That was all she would ever have now. Memories of her mother and Carrie ... and of her father, Caleb Price, the preacher man.

Chapter Nineteen

A pottery jug held beneath her shawl Emma made her way along the Shambles. There was usually a lull at this time as women hurried home to prepare the midday meal. Samuel chose this time every day to eat his dinner and chat to fellow traders and she had got used to fetching him a pint of beer from the tavern.

He used to take his daily pint from the Turk's Head but would not have her go there. Fearing what had happened in the alley that ran alongside the Turk's, he chose instead to send her to the Grapes Inn which stood in Upper High Street.

Emma enjoyed this short daily walk, it gave her a break from handing out packages of meat to women mostly in too much of a hurry to do more than check their change.

But Jesse Newman always had a cheery word for her, and so did his wife. As one served her at the outdoor, the dark narrow corridor where ale to be taken off the premises was served through a small window, the other would come and pass the time of day.

Turning the corner at the end of the Shambles she walked to the crossroads, hesitating as a carriage swept past. Watching it stop at the George Hotel she felt her hands tremble.

Following behind a shorter, plumper man, a

tall straight figure stepped easily down to the pavement. A figure with raven hair, sunlight glinting on the twin silver streaks that swept back from his forehead.

Carver Felton!

He was here in Wednesbury, just a few yards from her.

Emma's senses swam, sickness rose in her throat and her legs began to tremble.

'Eh, up!' Dropping a package on to the wagon he was loading, a carter caught her as she swayed. 'You all right, missis?'

''Course her ain't all right.' A woman bustled out of a nearby shop. 'A wench don't go fainting off her feet if her be all right!'

Taking Emma by the wrist she led her into the shop, sitting her on a chair beside the counter. Fetching a glass of water she held it out.

'Get yourself a sip of that, wench. It ain't brandy but it will help just the same. I reckon that babby you be carrying has turned. It be frightening first time but after you've had six like I have, you get used to it.'

Taking the water Emma forced a little of it down, feeling her stomach churn, resenting the intrusion.

'Yes,' the woman breezed on as she took the glass back. 'Six of 'em I've had and like to have had six more if my old man hadn't up and left. Enough be as good as a feast, I told him, I was keeping my halfpenny well covered in future. So he buggered off, but between you and me I ain't missed him, not once in ten years, and I reckon I won't in the next ten.'

'Thank you.' Emma got to her feet. 'I'm all right now.'

'Arr, you might be.' The woman's yellowed teeth showed in an uneven line. 'But that jug won't be lessen you holds it tight.'

The carriage was gone. Emma forced her legs to carry her over the crossing, pulling her shawl well down over her face as she passed the hotel. Would he recognise her if he came out now, would he recognise the girl he had raped? If so would he drive her from Wednesbury as he had driven her from Doe Bank? Every nerve tingling, every inch of her body trembling, she hurried past the hotel, only breathing when she reached the inn.

Carver Felton had not seen her. He must never see her again.

'I must say you got a move on. Last I heard Sir Anslow Lacy was still considering the scheme. Now here you are with Irish workmen already digging out the channel. Like I said, that be quick work even for Carver Felton. How on earth did you manage it?'

'Forethought.' Carver studied the gilt-embossed menu card a waiter presented with a deferential bow of his pomaded head. 'My father taught me always to be one step ahead of the next man.'

'Your father were a wily old fox.' Rafe Langton laughed, his several chins moving concertina fashion beneath long sideburns.

'But a wise one. His teaching proved sound.'

'In more ways than just making money, eh, Felton!'

After ordering roast duck, Carver handed back the menu as Rafe nodded his agreement and called for a bumper of claret.

'His teaching has proved useful in many ways.'

'But especially so with women.' Rafe waved an impatient hand as the wine waiter poured a little of the claret for his approval. 'Fill it up, man, what do you expect a man to make of a toothful!'

Carver took half a glass.

'I wish I had a little of your expertise. What wouldn't I give for a night or two with a woman like Cara Holgate!'

'I have plenty of notions as to what you would not, but what exactly *would* you be prepared to give?'

Swallowing a mouthful of wine, Carver watched the other man over the rim of the glass.

'For a night with a woman like Cara?'

'No.' His movements slow and deliberate, Carver set the glass on the table but his eyes, black and calculating, stayed fixed on the other's plump face. 'For a night *with* Cara.'

Across the table Rafe Langton's brow furrowed and his eyes receded into their sockets. 'Ain't no chance of that. I've tried afore but she ain't interested in trinkets. No, Felton, I could never get Cara Holgate to play my game.'

Waiting as the meal was served, Carver shook open the brilliant white linen napkin, placing it across his knee.

'Perhaps you did not offer the right sort of trinket?'

His mouth half full of duck, Rafe spluttered indignantly. 'Not the bloody right sort! You don't

282

get no better sort than diamonds.'

Touching the napkin to his mouth, Carver reached for his glass, smiling into its ruby depths. 'Maybe no better, but a trinket more ... shall we say ... to Cara's taste.'

His mood deepening to truculence, Rafe stabbed his fork at his food. 'If diamonds don't be to her taste then what is? What do you give her to make her say yes?'

He might never have a better chance. Carver kept his glance fixed nonchalantly on his wine glass. Rafe Langton liked his mistresses, but he also liked a gamble.

'We're not discussing my method of payment, we are discussing yours. So, Rafe, what *are* you prepared to give?'

'Pah!' Rafe grabbed his glass, draining the claret at a single gulp. 'Ain't no use talking about it. I've tried, and I tell you that woman turned her pretty nose up every time. Necklaces ... bracelets ... she refused the lot. And you don't offer money, not to a woman of her class.'

In fact, there was no better inducement to offer Cara Holgate. Carver kept his smile beneath the surface.

'Not in sovereigns, perhaps.'

'Eh!' Gravy trickling down his chin, Langton swallowed noisily. 'What other way is there to offer it?'

Pushing his plate aside, Carver refilled the other man's glass; he would sow the seed, the wine would water it!

'Cara likes to take chances, but the stakes have to be high before they interest her.'

283

'Go on!' Rafe took his glass.

'Cara is not like most women. She prefers to be independent, that takes money...'

'But...'

Carver raised a hand. 'Hear me out. Cara Holgate likes her independence but in order to maintain it she must make money, and not the sort that comes from selling off her trinkets. Offer her that sort of money and she will warm your bed, not to mention your blood.'

Draining his glass and rubbing at the gravy on his chin as he watched it refilled. Rafe's expression was confused.

'How?' He shook his head, jowls wobbling. 'You said yourself she don't take sovereigns, and I've tried jewellery, what else is a man to try?'

'Paper,' Carver answered flatly.

'Paper?' The word exploded scattering a myriad drops of claret over plate and table cloth. 'Stop arsing around, Felton. I ain't in the market for jokes!'

'And I am not peddling them.' Black eyes glinting, Carver fixed them on the plump wine-splattered face opposite him.

'But ... you said...'

'I know what I said, and it is what I meant, and if you desire the woman enough you will pay her price.' Waving away dessert, he went on, 'Cara must have a more regular income than can be depended upon by accepting trinkets if she is to maintain her lifestyle. I ask you again, Langton, how high are you prepared to pay for the lady's favours?'

At a vision of Cara slowly releasing the

buttons of her gown, superb green-gold eyes smiling into his, he murmured hoarsely, 'As high as she likes.'

'As high as your share in the canal venture?'

'Eh?' The glazed look leaving his eyes, Rafe Langton stared. 'That be a high price to pay ... for any woman!'

'For any woman, agreed.' Carver picked up his glass and before putting it to his lips allowed the smile he had stifled to play secretly about his mouth. 'But, believe me, Langton, Cara Holgate is not just *any* woman.'

Fixing his gaze coolly on the other man's face, watching the rush of heat rise to those fat cheeks, Carver sipped again from his glass. Before the month was out Rafe Langton would have a new mistress, and Cara Holgate would be a new shareholder in the Wednesbury Canal.

Rolling the wine around his tongue Carver sat back in his chair. A new shareholder. But the game was far from over.

Taking off her apron, one of three Mrs Hollington had given to Daisy, Emma folded it neatly before setting it in the drawer of the rickety dresser Samuel had helped carry in soon after their arrival.

'That's enough for today.' Hands on hips, she stretched her back.

'I told you the same thing two hours since!' Daisy tossed the last of the potatoes she had peeled into the pot then set it on the stove. 'But did you listen ... no, you did not! You simply went on polishing that old dresser. I swear the furniture along of Buckingham Palace gets no more polishing than that thing, though I bet it be a deal grander and firmer on its feet.

Turning, Emma caught the girl's grin and responded immediately. 'And who is it gives it another polish whenever my back is turned and thinks I don't know it?'

'Well, a girl has to have something to occupy her time.' Daisy laughed again, taking up the bowl of potato peelings.

'Perhaps I should tell Mrs Hollington that?' Emma called as Daisy carried out the bowl to empty on the garden waste heap.

Rinsing the bowl beneath the pump stood in the centre of the cobbled yard, Daisy carried it back into the tiny room she and Emma had turned into a home.

'I told her meself.' The bowl beneath the sink, Daisy rubbed her hands on the scrap of towel she had scrubbed and boiled until it gleamed white. 'I said I could do more in the house but she said I do more than my share already.'

Reaching down the salt from the dresser, Daisy measured an amount into the palm of her hand. Tipping it into the pot, she wiped the residue off on her apron.

'If only the rest of the folk round here were like her then there'd be a lot more smiling faces in Wednesbury.'

And not only in Wednesbury. Emma turned away, afraid her thoughts might show on her face. There would be happier ones in Doe Bank and Plovers Croft then too.

'I say we leave the potatoes for later. Sunday

afternoon's much too nice for giving over to cooking.'

'I say that makes sense.' Daisy whipped off her apron, shoving it hastily into the drawer with Emma's.

'I'm glad we came this way,' Daisy said later. 'I prefer walking on the heath to following the road. That ain't never still, not even on a Sunday. Carts rattle up and down like they don't have a minute to spare. Sunday's supposed to be a day of rest, ain't that right?'

There had never been much rest to be had in her father's house. Meals were the only time spent sitting down, and even then his continual preaching precluded conversation. That was all Sundays had seemed to consist of. Three hours of Chapel in the morning, two hours of Sunday school in the afternoon and an hour in the evening. But the rest of the time had brought no respite from her father's everlasting sermonising on the evils of life and the eternal damnation that awaited those who fell by the wayside. But it had not been so bad for her as it had for Carrie. From the time her sister had been about eight years old, their father had excused Emma from Sunday school. Now she knew why.

She stared ahead across the mauve-dressed heath. The evils of life! Her sister had not fallen into them, she had been pushed, and by the very man who'd preached against them.

'Emma, ain't that the man who spoke to us on the heath last Sunday?'

Glad of anything that would chase away the

287

shadow of the past, Emma looked in the direction Daisy indicated. Cinnamon hair ruffled by the faint breeze glinted in the mellow autumn light as Liam Brogan's tall lithe figure strode easily towards them.

'Sure and wasn't I hoping to see the two of you today?' His Irish accent adding a lilt to his voice, his smile echoed deep within his eyes, Liam raised a hand in greeting.

'Good afternoon, Mr Brogan,' Emma returned his greeting. 'We decided to take a walk on the heath before the remainder of the day is over.'

'And a fine decision it was.'

'Is that what you was doing, Mr Brogan, taking a walk?' Daisy asked breezily.

Falling into step beside them, trimming his long strides to match theirs, he nodded. 'Now then couldn't you say that. I've been paying a visit to the timber yard in Camp Hill Lane. The owner there is willing to exchange logs for labour.'

'But didn't you say you were employed digging out a canal?'

'I did so.' He glanced at Daisy. 'And it was the truth I told. And now you're going to ask how it is I can work at the timber yard?'

'I am not.' Daisy's face turned a bright pink.

'Then that would have me asking why you didn't!' He laughed, the pleasant sound of it echoing over the empty heath.

Seeing embarrassment flood Daisy's face, Emma said quickly, 'We do not need to ask, Mr Brogan. We both understand the need for wood. Brushwood from the heath burns out quickly, it's not as useful for cooking over as logs.'

Laughter settling to a quiet smile that hovered around his mouth, Liam Brogan looked at the older girl, the beauty in her face catching at the breath in his lungs, a beauty that had played in his mind every moment since their first meeting.

Forcing his glance away he stared ahead. 'There you have it,' he said quietly, 'we need wood for the cooking.'

'Emma's a good cook.' Irrepressible as ever, Daisy grinned. 'I cook too but mine's never as tasty as Emma's. You should taste her pies, you would never want no other.'

Returning his glance to Emma, eyes holding hers, Liam Brogan's voice became husky. 'That I can believe,' he murmured, 'no sane man would ever want any other.'

Her hands wrapped inside her shawl, Emma pulled it closer about her as the heat of her own embarrassment began to climb her cheeks. Searching for a way to detract from it, she said sharply, 'We should turn back here. It was pleasant meeting you again, Mr Brogan.'

'Eh, Emma!' Daisy's face fell. 'We don't have to go back just yet. It'll be a week afore we can walk out here again – longer than that if it be raining! Can't we go on a while more?'

'Really, Daisy, I think we ought...'

The huskiness gone from his voice, Liam broke in. 'Seeing as you were headed that way and that you're three parts there already, I was thinking to show you the new navigation. That is, if you would allow me, Miss Price?'

The new navigation. The canal Carver Felton

was having cut, the one for which he had destroyed Plovers Croft. Why should she want to see that, what good would it do? Emma's fingers tightened beneath the shawl. It would only serve to remind her of the people who had lived there, especially Jerusha; but it would also remind her of him, of the man who had ruined her life: Carver Felton. Her lips tight as her fingers, Emma stared across the silent heath.

'...*now ask my brother to marry you!*'

The words, branded deep into her mind, came to mock her out of the past, torturing her as they had so often when she tried to sleep. She needed no help to remember Carver Felton or what he had done to her, but to see what once had been the home of a friend would serve to strengthen her vow: to make Carver Felton pay in his own coin.

'Can we, Emma, can we go and see?'

No smile breaking on her strained face, Emma nodded. 'Yes, Daisy,' she said softly, 'we will go and see.'

Seated on the cushiony heather, its gentle fragrance filling the air, Emma looked out over the rows of tents. Where the Croft had once stood was a vast hollow, the soil from its excavation built into a low bank where the houses had been. Here and there, among piles of blue bricks and heavy timbers, the smoke of camp fires curled lazily into the sky.

'I thought it were a canal you were digging?' Daisy's puzzled glance encompassed the scene below them.

'So it will be, eventually.' Liam twirled a sprig of purple ling between his fingers. 'This part here will be the basin where the narrow boats can bring in supplies and carry away products; the waterway will link to this.'

'Why don't the water just soak away like when you dig a furrow in the ground? We sometimes did that in the workhouse yard when the wardresses weren't looking, but it just soaked away.'

'That would be because you hadn't puddled it.'

'Hadn't what?'

Liam smiled. 'You had not lined it with a thick layer of clay, that is called "puddling". And then it is overlaid with the bricks you see stacked over there. Together they form the sides and bed of the canal and the water is held in.'

'Eh, who would have thought it?' Daisy said wonderingly. 'I wish I had more brains.'

'Oh, you have brains enough. To be sure the little people themselves have no more.'

'Mr Brogan.' Half turning, Daisy looked questioningly into his laughing blue eyes. 'Who are the "little people"?'

'Don't you know? Sure and they would be heart-rent should they hear you say that.' Dropping his voice to a whisper, he leaned towards her. 'They be the fairy folk.'

'Fairies?' Daisy tossed her head. 'Now I know you be teasing. There ain't no such thing.'

'Oh, and isn't that a dreadful thing you've done!' Laying the sprig of ling beside him on the ground, Liam shook his head sorrowfully.

'What? What have I done?'

Raising his eyes he looked at Daisy. 'Sure and

did no one ever tell you, whenever a mortal body says the little people don't exist, one of them dies?'

'Eh, but you had me going for a moment!' Daisy held a hand to her chest. 'I thought I'd done summat wrong and all the time you were making fun of me. Fairies? Get along with you!'

'I wasn't making fun of you, and one day you will believe as we in Ireland do. The little people are here to help us, all we have to do is ask.'

Opening her mouth, a flippant reply almost on her lips, Daisy hesitated as a carriage rolled to a stop on the road behind them.

'Oh!' She breathed as two women stepped from it and walked to the brow of the rise that looked down on the excavations. 'All I have to do is ask, you say? Then I asks for a gown like that!'

Following her gaze Emma studied the women. Dressed in pale honey-coloured silk ribbed velvet, delicately trimmed with chocolate, a matching feathered bonnet topping her raven hair, the taller of the two waved a hand towards the site, talking animatedly to her companion whose equally elegant fern green costume was a perfect foil for her pale skin and vivid chestnut hair.

'You see I was right, Melissa...'

Cara Holgate's bell-like voice carried towards them on the still air.

'...a part of this was the best wedding gift for which you could have asked, and it is one will give no joy to Carver Felton.'

A wedding gift, and one that would bring no joy to Carver Felton.

292

Emma's attention was caught as the women laughed together.

'It was my guess he hoped to secure that third for himself, to give him a firmer hold on the project.'

'Instead of which I have it.' Melissa's tone, softer than her cousin's, was nevertheless a needle stabbing at Emma's heart. This woman had been given a wedding gift, but it had not been given by Carver but by one over whom he wished to have a hold. Blood racing through her veins she felt it hard to breathe. There could be no one else, it could only mean Paul. Paul and this woman were to be married!

'Yes, my clever cousin, you have it.' Cara turned towards the waiting carriage. 'And before very much longer I shall have another third. I wonder what dear Carver will do then?'

Laughter floating behind them, the carriage rolled away. These women had as little love for Carver Felton as she herself did. Emma's heart beat painfully. But what of Paul? Was that woman marrying him for the love she could give him or for what she could take from him?

Rising to her feet, keeping her eyes lowered as she brushed dry leaves from her skirts, Emma hid the pain in her eyes.

Paul had forgotten her. The love he'd thought he felt for her had died. He was to marry the woman who had gloated over his gift. Was it that Paul had stopped loving her? Or was it his brother had forced his change of heart? But whichever way, who could blame Paul? The woman with chestnut hair was beautiful and obviously well-bred. So very different from a Doe Bank wench.

Tears blurring her vision Emma stumbled, throwing out both hands as she fell heavily to the ground.

'Emma!' Liam Brogan was beside her in an instant, and in that instant his world crashed about him. There, on the third finger of her left hand, gleaming in the late-afternoon sun, he saw a plain gold wedding band.

Chapter Twenty

'I am so disappointed Harriet could not come.'

'So was I.' Rafe Langton hid his satisfaction beneath a veneer of concern. 'She gets these sick headaches, last for days some of 'em. I wanted to stay home with her but she insisted one of us come after we'd accepted your invitation.'

'Dear Harriet.' Only her voice was sympathetic as Cara Holgate took hat and gloves from her visitor. 'So thoughtful for others. I really must send her some of my headache remedy, it was prescribed for me in London, it really is wonderful.'

Following up thickly carpeted stairs, gleaming woodwork attesting to the attention of housemaids, Rafe smiled into his whiskers. Harriet had no idea he was answering the invitation; after he'd told her there was a Guilds dinner he could not avoid attending she had made no objection, simply accepting the fact that he would be gone until the early hours. The Guilds story had come in useful many times over the years and once again it had stood him in good stead.

'That be right kind of you, Cara,' he answered, 'I know she will be grateful.'

Leading the way into her private salon Cara turned, flashing him a magnificent smile. Harriet would not be the only grateful one should this evening go as planned!

'There's no need for gratitude between friends, and we have been friends for such a long time, have we not?'

No need for gratitude? Rafe concealed a cynical smile. No, not so long as the price was right.

'We have that, Cara, but then we could be better friends, you and me.'

Her lids lowered demurely but beneath them her eyes gleamed with satisfaction. So Rafe Langton still lusted after her as much as ever? Tonight might just see him receive a taste of satisfaction. And what of Carver? Should he find out then any idea of marriage with him might go out of the window. But one man at a time. Cara filled two brandy goblets, smiling into their rich golden depths. Tonight she would take care of Langton and once that was done ... well, Carver always had found her irresistible.

Handing a glass to him, her eyes a green-gold dazzle, she baited the trap.

'How could you and I possibly be better friends?'

His glance rested for a long moment on the breasts peeping from the low décolletage of a tightly fitted gown of gold-flecked sea green silk georgette, an exact match for the eyes that taunted him as his gaze lifted to them.

'You bloody well know how, Cara,' he answered thickly, brandy spilling as he stepped quickly towards her. 'I've asked you often enough!'

'I had supper laid here, I thought it might be more cosy. I hope you have no objections?' She stepped away, careful that the gap between them was not too wide; it was meant to provoke rather than deter his ardour.

'It ain't supper I be interested in.' His eyes swept hotly back to her high breasts.

Keeping a smile hidden behind a pout, Cara touched one hand to the exquisitely laid table. 'Oh, Rafe! You have no interest in my supper, and I tried so hard to please you.'

'You can please me, Cara...'

She remained still as he stepped up to her. There would be no gain in rebuffing his advances too many times.

'...you can please me very much.'

'I had hoped to do just that.' Her husky voice was low and teasing. 'But here you are, saying you have no interest in the food I chose especially for you and Harriet. And then she couldn't come – too bad, isn't it?'

The pause was small but the meaning it carried was large enough to reach deep into the pit of Rafe Langton's stomach. His eyes seeming to fold away behind flabby cheeks he reached for Cara's hand, raising it to his moist lips. 'Forgive me, Cara,' he said, specks of spittle transferring themselves to her hand as it pressed against his mouth. 'The supper looks wonderful, it's just that when I'm with you...'

She withdrew her hand, resisting the urge to wipe it on her gown. 'Will you excuse me just a few moments?' She smiled. 'Help yourself to more brandy, or there's wine if you prefer.'

In the bedroom that adjoined the salon Cara slipped out of the lovely gown tossing it on to the bed. Her fingers swift and nimble she undid the laces of her whalebone corset sending it after the dress. Langton did not seem to need any extra persuasion; she had seen the look that lingered on her breasts, almost felt the heat in them as they played over her. But a little caution was better than a lot of regret and tonight she played for high stakes. Drawing off her silk chemise and drawers she stood naked.

Alone in the salon Rafe Langton gulped at his brandy. She had not refused outright as she had before. Perhaps Felton would be proved right?

Felton! The glass to his lips he paused. It was understood by those who knew them that he and Cara Holgate were as good as engaged, that they would marry, yet Felton had suggested ... had almost handed her over on a plate! What could be the reason?

In the bedroom, Cara touched perfume to the vee of her breasts. Parting the satin robe she had donned, she looked again at the naked body reflected in her long dressing mirror. Deep rose satin gleamed against skin the colour of finest ivory. Below taut breasts her waist curved inward before rounding out over slender thighs that tapered into shapely legs. Yes, she could please Rafe Langton – always supposing he met her price.

Returning the perfume to the dressing table, she smiled as she slowly buttoned the robe. Langton wanted her body and she wanted his share in the Wednesbury Canal. Green-gold eyes smiling back at her from the mirror, she touched one hand to her breast. Fair exchange, they said, was no robbery.

'Forgive me for keeping you waiting.' A brilliant

smile hiding the distaste that rose in her as she looked at the portly figure stood beside the fireplace, Cara moved towards the table. 'I wanted to be a little more comfortable. You don't mind, Rafe?'

'Mind!' His eyes devouring her, he came to stand beside her at the table lowering his glass unsteadily. 'A man would be out of his brain to mind seeing a woman dressed like this!'

Tilting her head back slightly, her carefully painted lips parting just enough, lashes lowering seductively, she murmured, 'Then we could begin.'

'Cara!' Catching her arm as she half turned toward her place at the table, Rafe's breathing was harsh and urgent. 'Forget the bloody supper!'

Her lashes lifting, Cara's eyes smouldered. 'Then what else can I give you?'

Fingers tightening on her arm, his voice almost a croak, he groaned, 'You know the answer to that.'

'Yes, I know the answer to that, Rafe.' Pulling her arm free she took a seat at the table. 'You want a mistress. Surely there are ladies a-plenty would be willing…'

'I ain't interested in others, I want you. And what's more, I be willing to pay.'

'Let's not become coarse, Rafe.'

'Coarse I may be, but that be what it comes down to in the end – payment. The only question be, what payment do you want? You've refused trinkets afore.'

'Trinkets are pleasant to receive but they can

only be sold once, their revenue is strictly limited, that reduces their worth to me.' Leaning forward she filled the crystal wine glasses, the movement carefully designed to reveal the mounds of her ivory breasts. Holding a glass out to Rafe who still stood beside the table she smiled up at him. 'I want something that will provide a more regular income.'

'...*Cara Holgate likes her independence*...' Carver Felton's words returned to Rafe's mind. '*Offer her that sort of money and she will warm your bed not to mention your blood...*' Felton had offered his own mistress on a plate. Rafe's hand went to the document in his pocket. It was a bloody expensive plate! But what else was money for other than to buy a man his pleasure?

Withdrawing the reassigned contract his solicitor had drawn up he laid it on the table, podgy hand resting on the cream vellum.

'That'll provide you with a regular income, but I sank a fair bit of money into it. How do I know I'll get what it's worth?'

Rising slowly to her feet, her eyes hazy, Cara pressed him into a chair. Keeping her glance fixed on his she released the buttons of her robe. 'Perhaps you should taste before you buy?'

Drawing the robe apart she heard the gasp as his eyes feasted on her breasts. Calmly picking up her own untouched brandy glass she dipped one nipple into the gleaming spirit then, bending over him, thrust it into his open mouth.

His hands closing over her hips Rafe pulled her body towards him, eyes closing as he sucked hard on her breast. But Cara's eyes did not close.

300

Cold and hard as glass they remained fixed on the contract lying on the table.

Leaning against the stall, Emma lifted one foot, taking the weight from her injured ankle. Daisy had protested strongly that morning, saying it would do no harm for her to stay in bed. Emma rubbed one hand across the bandaged foot. She had refused, saying it was not painful, but the passing hours had proved that a lie. Watching as Samuel struck a match, holding the flame to the candle stubs he had set inside jars strung over the stall, she found herself wishing the day was at an end.

'Sure and isn't that a pretty sight? Reminds me of the jack-o-lanterns that dance over the peat on a summer's evening.'

Turning quickly, her foot not yet on the ground, Emma had to grab the stall to prevent herself from falling.

'By all the saints, don't go falling again! You fair scared the life from me when you did so yesterday, and this is the only life I have.' Eyes bright as the candle flames, Liam Brogan smiled.

'I said for her to go home.' Samuel blew out the third match, flicking the burned out stick into the gutter. 'Ain't no need for her to be here, standing on that ankle. Ain't as if I can't manage on my own.'

'Good evening to yourself, sir.' Liam touched one hand to his ruffled hair. 'If she be at all like the women at my home in Ireland then you might well save your breath, for they go their own way in spite of what they be told.'

301

'Ireland, you say?' Samuel nodded. 'That be a distance, what brings you here to the Black Country?'

'The Black Country!' Liam laughed. 'Now why would you be calling it that?'

Pushing his boater to the back of his head then setting it straight again, Samuel regarded the tall young man with laughing eyes stood at his stall.

'Look around you, lad. There be more foundry stacks and colliery wheels than there be peas in broth here and the smoke of them sometimes has the sky dark as my black puddings.'

'I see what you mean, but still it holds great beauty.' As he said it Liam's glance rested on Emma.

Touching his whiskers, Samuel smiled. Always ready to chat he asked, 'Will you be staying long in Wednesbury, lad?'

Busying herself with the pile of paper held down by half a house brick, Emma avoided Liam's glance but she could not hold back the colour that flew to her cheeks.

'We're here to dig the new navigation,' he replied, eyes fixed on Emma's bent head. 'How long that will take I can't rightly say, nor yet what may happen once the job be done. It could be I will be returning to Ireland then.'

'Well, we none of us knows the future,' Samuel answered philosophically. 'That might be better all round or there would be some would put an end to life afore it was properly begun.'

'*None of us knows the future.*' Emma's fingers whitened about the rough paperweight. That was so true of Carrie and her mother, and once they did know it they had put an end to their lives. But her life … that had continued, she had not had the courage needed to end it even though she knew her future; it would be spent alone, caring for her bastard child.

Dim light spilling from the candle jars began their nightly battle with advancing shadows bringing with them a chill breeze, but it was the tension in Emma's slight figure, the droop that pulled at her head that Liam sensed was due to more than the pain in her ankle, pulled at his heart. He had sensed that same pain on the two occasions they had met before and it had mingled with his own as he had glimpsed the golden band that circled her finger. Now, much as he wanted to hold her and comfort her, he knew he could not. She was a married woman and he ought not to have given in to the urge to come and see her; it could do nothing but cause him more anguish.

'Well now.' He turned his glance away, switching it to Samuel. 'Much as I've enjoyed chewing on the wind 'tis time to be getting back or we'll be having supper for breakfast. I'll be after having six of your finest pork chops, supposing you have any?'

'I have, lad, and you'll taste no better. Though I say it as shouldn't, Hollington's be the finest meat in the Shambles.'

'Then I look forward to being a customer again.' Liam's eyes followed the glint of the ring as Emma first wrapped his purchase then counted his change into his hand. 'Good evening to yourself, Mr Hollington, and to you also, Mrs Price.'

He had addressed her as Mrs, he obviously thought she was married. Emma's hand went to her stomach. If only it were true. But it was not and never would be for what man would marry a woman who had borne another man's child!

As the shadows of the darkened street swallowed Liam's tall figure, the darker shadows of her future engulfed Emma's heart.

So Langton had parted with his share of the canal? Carver Felton smiled as he drew on pale grey chamois gloves.

Cara had said yes. He took the silver-topped cane from the manservant who at once opened the door for him. Had there ever been any doubt, given the price Langton had been prepared to pay? And did he still think the goods worth the cost?

Nodding to the manservant, Carver walked towards his waiting carriage.

Langton had given away a small fortune, given it to a woman in return for what? A few hours in bed! Carver smiled sardonically. And those hours would have given him no more than he could get in any bawdy house in Birmingham, for a lot less than he had paid Cara. True, her bed was probably more comfortable and her face more attractive than that of other doxies. But then it wasn't her *face* had Rafe Langton panting at her heels!

Heading the carriage towards Wednesbury he shook the reins, setting the horse to a steady trot. Cara had played her cards well. But she had not played with an expert. She had won that round, but then Rafe Langton was no great shakes as an opponent. Now she would play against a master … and this time she would learn how it felt to lose!

She had been so pleased with herself last night. She had greeted Carver with eyes so blinded with self-satisfaction they could see nothing else. Nothing that was until the pretty Melissa had walked in. Then her eyes had followed her cousin, watching the younger woman almost avidly.

Carver stared into the dark evening. Cara was jealous of her cousin, that much became evident to him with every meeting, but at the same time she seemed to take a pride in the girl. It was almost maternal. He smiled at the thought. He would never have described Cara as the maternal type.

Reaching the crossroads with Holyhead Road the horse faltered as a steam trolley lumbered towards it. Beneath his breath, Carver swore as he quieted the frightened horse. Guiding it to the left and into the quieter trolley-free Union Street, he gave himself back to his memories of the evening before.

Melissa had been barely able to eat for talking of her conquest of Arthur Payne. He smiled again, remembering the black look that had settled over the older woman's face. Surely she had not wanted Arthur for herself? No. He flicked the reins. Of one thing he was sure: Cara Holgate held no love for Arthur Payne!

'Arthur and I are to be married.' Melissa's boast had brought a frown to her cousin's brow but she had refused to be put off. 'He is such a darling, and so generous, I swear I shall be quite spoiled.'

'*Arthur is a fortunate man.*' Carver had spoken to Melissa, but his eyes had been fixed on Cara and as he watched the emotions chase over her face he had experienced a warm surge of confidence. He had planned the game he would play with her, planned it to the last detail!

' *...he cannot be blamed for wanting to spoil so pretty a wife.*'

'*You would not believe what he insisted upon giving me for my wedding gift.*' The boast became a crow and pale grey eyes glistened with the thrill of possession. '*He gave me the whole of his interest in the new canal. Imagine, Carver! I have a business in my own right, signed over to me as a gift.*'

'*You have a* part *share in the business of the canal.*' His reply had been cold, the emphasis heavy.

Melissa had smiled at him then but the smile had held daggers. She had taken the meaning contained in his words and it stung.

'*Melissa meant...*' Cara had tried to divert her cousin from saying more but the intervention came too late. Her animosity aroused, Melissa bristled and in doing so confirmed what he already knew.

'*I have one-third and Cara also owns one-third. That places the majority of the business in* our *hands, and also the majority vote as to how it should be run. As you said, I have only a part share but placed with Cara's...*' She hesitated, her smile thin. '*It puts you, my dear Carver, very much in the minority!*'

His hands tightened on the reins, but it was not

anger that firmed his mouth so much as determination.

'Smile while you can,' he breathed softly, 'smile while you can!'

Bringing the carriage to a halt and giving charge of it to an ostler, he climbed the steps that led into the Conservative Club, handing gloves and cane to a uniformed attendant. He often chose to dine here and now acknowledged the greeting of other businessmen who like himself frequented the establishment.

'There you be, Felton!' Brandy glass in hand, Rafe Langton called to him as he passed beyond the reading room and into the tastefully furnished lounge. Accepting the offer of brandy, Carver settled into one of the comfortable hide-covered armchairs.

'I trust Harriet is well? It has been some time since I had the pleasure of seeing her.'

'Been some time since I had the pleasure!' Brandy well on the way to achieving its end, Rafe roared at his own coarse wit. 'Then it never were much of a pleasure with Harriet. Fortunately a man can find that elsewhere.'

Lifting his glass, Carver breathed in the bouquet of the brandy but every ounce of his concentration centred on his companion. Langton was in talkative mood. A few more drinks...

'Yes, pleasures can be found.' Carver nodded. 'But travelling out of town...'

'Travelling?' Glass halfway to his mouth Langton laughed again, full scarlet cheeks wobbling with the effort. 'Who said anything about travelling?'

His glance innocent, Carver looked up. 'Then where?'

'You knows where, you sly dog. Ain't far to Cara's place.' Suddenly thoughtful, he stared across at Carver. 'Just why did you...? Well, I mean, a woman like that, why pass her on to another man? I thought you and her were thinking of being wed?'

'I may have thought of being wed, but not to Cara. Should a man marry his mistress, Langton, where would his pleasures come from then?'

'Where indeed?' Rafe laughed. 'I must thank you for your tip, Felton, but it were a bloody expensive one to follow.'

'Regretting it?'

Downing his drink and ordering another loudly Rafe shook his head, a lewd smile spreading into his whiskers. 'Not so far, and if she continues to perform in the same vein then I'll think it money well spent. It only be my bad luck she be entertaining tonight – summat to do wi' her cousin's property, so she said. Probably her solicitor.'

Watching brandy disappear down Langton's throat, Carver said evenly, 'I have no idea as to the others Cara has invited, I only know I have an invitation to call and bring a companion of my own choosing.' Meeting the other man's stare, he smiled. 'We might arrive together but we need not leave so.'

'Christ, Felton! Do you mean...?'

'I mean that after another brandy I shall be leaving for Cara Holgate's house. Unless, of course, you prefer to dine here at the club then I invite you to accompany me.'

An hour later, following Langton into the carriage, Carver's mood of confidence had deepened to satisfaction. He had just dealt the cards and given himself the winning hand.

Chapter Twenty-One

'I thought you were gonna stand chewin' the fat all night, Samuel Hollington! Don't you know a biddy has supper to get?'

The shrill tones turning her attention from the tall figure now merging with the shadows, Emma felt pain shoot through her ankle as she swung round to face a plump woman dressed in wide black skirts and shawl, a tiny black bonnet perched on top of hair that was scraped back into a bun.

'You might 'ave nothing better to do than gawp after a man, young woman, but there be some folk have more important things to tend to!'

The woman delved into her basket, taking out a black leather purse before sending a keen glance at Emma.

'Now then, Mother Timms, we all know your Ben and his lads will be in the tavern 'til chucking out time.' Samuel smiled genially. 'So what do you say to a nice piece of rump steak?'

'I says you can keep it!' The woman's button-bright eyes glinted as she looked at him. 'Since when can a biddy afford steak? You slice me up a pound of belly draught, and make sure it has plenty of fat on it. My lads like a bite of pork dripping for breakfast.'

Lifting down a large piece of meat from a billhook suspended over the stall, Samuel cut several thick slices, handing them to Emma to wrap.

Offering a coin the woman hesitated then looked once more at Samuel. 'Find me out a nice lean breast of lamb, that'll make tomorrow's dinner...'

'Eh up, Mother Timms!' Samuel's whiskers lifted as he grinned at the woman. 'Don't you go telling me your Ben likes a bit of breast?'

'Oh, he'd like it all right, but I ain't got much left in that department, and if he can't find a bit for free then he'd sooner do wi'out. My Ben won't go spending his coppers on anything but his ale.'

Both of them laughing together, Samuel reached for a small cleaver. 'You want this chopped, Mother Timms?'

'Arr Hollington, that will be a help to me.' She smiled at Emma. 'He be a good man be Hollington.'

'He might 'ave a chance to be a good man to a few more if you made your mind up quicker. There be folk 'ere wants to get on 'ome!'

Mother Timms turned slowly, wide skirts rustling, button eyes raking the small group of last-minute shoppers.

'You want to be served sooner?' Her voice rose, loud and asperic. 'Then you should come to market sooner instead of sittin' home on your arses drinking tea!'

'I *don't* spend my time sittin' on my arse drinking tea!'

Cleaver held in the air, Samuel winked at Emma who had turned a worried glance to him.

Beyond the stall the black-clad woman scanned the group with a sharp irritated glance before settling on the one who had dared interrupt her nightly banter with the butcher. Eyeing the other woman up and down with a slow deliberate motion she nodded, setting the bonnet waggling on her head. 'No, you don't look as if you've been sat on your arse. Looks more like you've been lying on your back all day!'

'Now then ladies, we don't need any argument.' Samuel brought down the cleaver as a burst of laughter filled the night air.

'Don't you go tellin' folk what they need!' The second woman directed her words at him. ''Tis time somebody told that old cow where to get off!'

'This old cow still be strong enough to wring your scrawny neck, you big-mouthed...'

A scream cutting her off in mid-sentence the older woman turned to see Emma, hands clenched into fists she had pressed against her mouth, staring at the block on which Samuel chopped his meat.

Screams rising in a chorus around her, Emma's stomach lurched as she lifted her agonised gaze to the butcher. The cleaver glistening in the candlelight was still raised above his head, but his face wore a look of disbelief.

'Lord! Oh, Lord!' a woman whimpered. Another sobbed, 'Oh, dear God!'

But no one moved, even the blood-stained cleaver remained suspended in midair. Then Samuel laughed, a short confused sound as he looked first at his bleeding wrist then his hand ...

lying severed on the chopping block.

'You must lie still, Emma, there's nothing you can do.' Face creased with concern, Daisy pressed her down on to the pillows.

'But Mr Hollington...'

'He be at Hallam Hospital,' Daisy answered, replacing the bed covers Emma had thrown aside.

'What about Mrs Hollington ... does she know what happened?'

'She knows. She be there with him now.'

'I don't remember.' Emma shook her head. 'I ... I saw ... but I don't remember.'

'Ain't surprising, seeing as you fainted.' Daisy bustled about with kettle and teapot. 'Went out like a candle in the wind so Liam Brogan said.'

Passing a hand over her forehead, Emma tried to soothe the pounding in her brain. 'Mr Brogan? But he had gone...'

Adding milk then sugar to the cups she reached from the rickety dresser, Daisy filled them to the brim with scalding hot tea.

'Arr, but not so far away he didn't hear the screams. He ran back to see what the commotion was and found you flat on the ground and poor old Mr Hollington staring at ... well, you know what he was staring at. Any road up, a few seconds later some men came to the stall. Liam sent one of them to bring a constable to see off the women still screaming and crying, then set another in a hansom along of Mr Hollington. Told him to stay by him at the hospital until he got there himself.'

Taking up both cups, she handed one to Emma with a curt instruction to drink it.

'After that he saw to bringing you home,' Daisy went on between sips of tea. 'Near gave me heart attack it did to see you laid across that handcart. He said you was all right, just fainted, then told me what had happened and said as he would go along with Mrs Hollington to the hospital. He looked wondrous pale when he carried you in, Emma, and he laid you down on the bed that careful like, you would think he was handling a china doll.'

Liam Brogan had brought her home. Emma frowned with the effort of trying to remember. She had watched him walk away, listened to those women bicker, and then ... but the rest was too painful to think of.

'We should be with her.' Emma laid her cup aside. 'Mrs Hollington should not be alone at the hospital, she needs someone with her.'

'Liam knew you would say that. He said to tell you he will stay as long as it takes, all night if need be; then he will see Mrs Hollington back to the house. He also said to tell you both that the cart be put away and the tin box that holds the takings be on the dresser in the kitchen. As for the knives and things, I washed them myself.'

'Thank you, Daisy.'

'Found me something to do while you was...' Daisy broke off, her eyes clouding with sudden tears. 'Eh, Emma! I was so scared when I saw you, I thought at first you was in labour with the child, and then when you didn't move or make a sound I thought you was dead. Lord, Emma! The shock near finished me.'

The child! Emma touched a hand to her stomach, remembering the sickening lurch it had made as she had looked at Samuel's severed hand. Had that terrible sight affected the child in her womb? Stories told by the pit bank women of children born with defects caused by experiences that had terrified the mother while she was carrying came crowding in on her.

'*...there is a child within you...*'

The words sounded clear in her head, clear as when Jerusha has spoken them.

'*...a child that will be born...*'

Emma closed her eyes against the memory. Her child would be born, but would it be whole?

'If you are sure you feel well enough to be left for a minute or so then I'll go and put some coals on the fire over at the house. Mrs Hollington will want it warm to come back to.'

Afraid the sight of tears she could not entirely restrain would add to Emma's grief, Daisy hastily carried the cups to the sink.

'She'll appreciate that.' Emma tried to smile but the fear inside her was too strong.

Climbing from the bed as the door closed behind her friend, Emma reached for her skirts.

Liam Brogan had run back to the butcher's stall. He had taken charge, seen the injured man off to hospital then brought her home. Had he asked about her husband? Emma's fingers paused on the buttons of her blouse. He had called her Mrs Price as he'd left the stall. He'd thought she was married, that her child had a father.

'...it will bear its father's name...'

Clear as before Jerusha's words echoed in her mind.

Paul bore the same name, Felton. But Paul was not the father of her child and because of that she could not marry him even had he still wanted her. The child had come of his brother's rape, and that man would never marry a pit bank wench. The last of Jerusha's words had been said merely to give her strength to bear her child.

Slowly, mouth set in a tight line, Emma resumed fastening her blouse.

Jerusha could have saved herself the lie, well-meant as it was. Emma Price needed nothing of Carver Felton, would take nothing from him ... except revenge!

Turning the carriage into the drive that led to Cara Holgate's house, Carver glanced at the man already half drunk and swaying at his side. Langton had jumped at the chance of spending a night in his mistress's arms. Poor Langton, that was the only jumping he would do tonight!

Cara had wanted to silence her pretty cousin when she had gloated over her bridal gift then blurted out Cara's own new acquisition. But the girl had gone on, sure that what she divulged was fresh news to Carver, that their holding of two-thirds of Wednesbury Canal would shock him speechless. It had not. He smiled into the darkness. Neither had the emotions that flitted across the older woman's face as her cousin spoke of her forthcoming marriage. They had been louder than any words. Jealous of the pretty

316

Melissa? Yes, Cara was all of that.

'Thought you said we was sh'pected?'

Rafe Langton slurred his words as Carver assisted him from the carriage.

'...house in darkness. Ain't the wrong evening, is it?'

'No, it is not the wrong evening.' Carver steadied the other man as he swayed. 'We are expected, never fear. Cara never has all the gasoliers lit when she wishes her entertaining to be a little more ... intimate.'

'Intimate?' Langton gave a drunken hiccup. 'I like the sound of that. It be a surprise, but a nice one. Yes, I like the sound of that!'

'Then what say we give her a nice surprise? We'll let ourselves in, not bother the maid. What say you?'

Leaning heavily on Carver's arm, the drunken hiccup belched again. 'I ... I say that'sh a good idea.'

Letting himself into the house, shushing the tipsy murmurings of the man clinging to him in the dim hall, Carver allowed a smile to return to his mouth.

The evening Cara was no doubt enjoying had not been intended to include him or Langton. There had been no invitation to them and there would be no welcome.

And if his theory proved wrong?

Helping the other man up the heavily carpeted staircase that led to Cara's private salon, Carver shrugged. If he was wrong, he was wrong! But somehow he did not think he was.

'I shall have such a beautiful wedding! I shall

choose the most expensive gown in London...'

Melissa's shrill tones reached the men standing outside the salon door.

'...I will be the most beautiful bride this town has ever seen. I will, won't I?'

'Yes, Melissa, you will be the most beautiful bride ever.'

Beyond the door Carver's inner eye watched the smile of a beautiful girl, her lovely hyacinth eyes radiant with happiness, a wisp of wedding veil caught beneath a garland of flowers set on pale hair. The Doe Bank girl had a soft beauty neither of the women inside that room possessed; she would be the most beautiful of brides and could still be Paul's. He had only to give his permission. But the very thought brought a double stab to Carver's heart. He had never before refused his brother anything nor had he ever lied to him, but keeping him from that girl in order to safeguard Paul's future in society ... that was a lie Carver had told himself.

'And you will arrange the most delicious reception afterwards? The guests must have the very best.'

Langton's tipsy giggle driving the picture from his mind, Carver caught the other man's arm, a warning finger touching his own lips. The surprise must not be spoiled.

'The very best.' The words reached them through the door.

'You do love me? I mean *really* love me.'

'Haven't I proved that already?' The deeper voice, thickened with emotion, came clearly to their ears.

318

'The gifts I have given you, do they not tell you how much I love you? How much I want you? You are everything to me, my darling, all I ever want is you. The taste of your lovely mouth, the feel of your body beneath my own...'

One hand silently turning the handle of the salon door, Carver flung it wide.

'Good evening. I trust we *are* intruding. Do come in, Langton, and wish our friends well!'

He half turned to the man who had staggered in after him and now stood with mouth open, liquor soaked breath coming in a long, loud wheeze. But Rafe Langton did not wish his friends well, Rafe Langton did not say anything, he simply stared at the figures sprawled on the bed.

'A pleasant sight, wouldn't you say, Rafe?'

Carver too looked at the two on the bed. Two bodies, each with skin the colour of alabaster, naked limbs twined together, chestnut hair mingling with raven black. They stared back at him, incomprehension in both pairs of eyes.

'I had hoped you expected no callers.' Carver's cold eyes glared contempt at them. 'That hope has been more than fulfilled.'

Her long hair swinging in a silken veil, Cara Holgate leaped from the bed. 'Get out!' she hissed. 'Get out, Felton.'

Leaving Langton to stand and stare alone, Carver waved an admonishing finger. 'Come, come now, Cara! Is that any way to treat a friend?'

Behind her a startled Melissa whimpered as she rolled herself in the silk bed cover, but Cara met

319

his contemptuous gaze with a fierce hatred.

'Friend!' she breathed. 'You have never been a friend to anyone other than yourself. Your only thought is how to benefit Carver Felton!'

'As I intend to continue. However I can be a friend of sorts to you and your pretty lover, or I can be an enemy: one with a loud tongue and the gift of eloquent description. Think of that, my dear Cara, while you are dressing, then we will discuss how best to benefit Carver Felton.'

Half an hour later, elegant once more in pale lavender taffeta, hair neatly arranged in dark coils on her head, Cara Holgate entered her downstairs sitting room.

'Forgive Langton's deciding to forgo the delights of your charming company, my dear, but under the circumstances...'

'What brought you here?' Cara's demand was as brusque as his shrug was nonchalant.

'The promise of what I might find. Of what I did find.'

'And him?' Cara glanced at the heavily sleeping Langton.

'Rafe? I wanted him to see you also. One man's word ... you know the form, Cara. I wanted it to be the word of two.'

Drawing in a long breath she crossed to where decanter and glasses were set on a long rosewood sideboard and poured herself some brandy, taking a long gulp.

'How?' She turned, eyes gleaming like deadly weapons. 'How long have you known ... when did you find out?'

'That you were more than it appeared on the

surface, you were your cousin's lover?' It was meant as a barb and as she flinched he knew it had found its mark. 'I guessed almost from the beginning. Your anger when I escorted Melissa to the Bilston enamel works; the way you reacted to my taking her to Beaufort House; the possessive way you touched her whenever a man made to approach her. It all spoke for itself. Jealousy of another woman is one thing, Cara, but what you felt for your pretty cousin was obviously more than that. It was obsession, and it was clear to any man who knew you as well as I do.'

'And now you intend to destroy me?'

Rising from his chair, Carver helped himself to a shot of brandy. Raising it, he looked at her over the rim of the faceted glass.

'Yes, Cara, I do. Unless, of course, you agree to my terms.'

'Those being?'

Returning to his chair, he swirled the amber liquid, watching it circle the glass.

'I think you know what they are.'

Cara knew. She had realised long before the last button was done up on her fashionable gown, the last pin stabbed into her hair, yet still she searched for a way out.

'Perhaps ... perhaps not. But what of Langton's terms, what are they?'

'I can see to it he makes none. Then again, I could see he made plenty, and all with my support.'

Venomous eyes stared into his. 'You would do that, wouldn't you? You would destroy not only me but Melissa too.'

'I don't know which of you destroyed the other.' He met her look evenly. 'I only know it happened long before your cousin came to Wednesbury. But let us not dwell on proven fact. My offer remains. Take it and no one will hear of your ... preferences. Refuse it and the whole town will know.'

Smashing her glass to the floor, Cara ground her foot on the shattered remnants as though stepping on a distasteful insect.

'You are a bastard, Felton,' she grated, 'a pure bastard!'

Cold and vicious, Carver's own smile spread. 'My birth certificate would have it otherwise, Cara. And, unlike yourself, I am no pervert. Remember, my dear, before you make your decision: no class, rich or poor, easily tolerates a homosexual, and a lesbian not at all! There will be nowhere you can go where word of your pretty lover will not follow.'

'If I agree, if I give you what you so obviously came for, what of him? How can I be sure of his silence?'

As if hearing the question Rafe Langton grunted and his eyes opened briefly before he settled once more to his rhythmic snores.

'The threat of my telling Harriet that he has spent so many of his "club nights" with you, and of telling his colleagues the woman who was his mistress was herself making love to another woman, will, I guarantee, seal his lips forever. On the other hand...'

'There need be no other hand!' Taking a key from a chain between her breasts, Cara crossed to a bureau set in a corner of the room. Unlocking it she withdrew a document. Holding it to her chest she stared at him for several moments before walking over to him.

'Your word, Carver?'

Taking the paper she held out to him, he unfolded it, scanning its wording and signature. Then, refolding it, he placed it in the inner pocket of his coat.

Light from the gasolier glinting on the silver swathes brushed back from his forehead, he looked into her eyes.

'No, Cara, you do not have my word. What you have handed to me was Langton's share in the new navigation. You will only have my word when you give me the share which Arthur Payne deeded to Melissa.'

It had all gone so smoothly, so exactly as he had planned. Carver stood up as Cara, her cousin and their solicitor left his study. Folding the newly signed documents he slipped them into the wall safe, locking the door with a smile.

Cara Holgate had become a threat to his complete ownership of that canal; she had thought to take a percentage of his business with threats and scheming. Now she was gone, he was rid of her as he had rid himself of that other threat. Paul had thought to marry a pit bank wench, but Carver had put a stop to that.

A man does not marry his mistress.

The words he had spoken to Rafe Langton returned to him now. Nor did a man marry his brother's mistress even though their one encounter had been unwilling on her part. The Doe Bank wench was gone and that was the way things would remain.

He turned from the safe, but as he did so the vision of vivid blue eyes staring at him pleadingly from a beautiful heart-shaped face danced in the air before him.

Chapter Twenty-Two

'Emma, do have a bit of sense. You can't run that stall by yourself, you don't know...'

'I know enough to get by.' Emma looped an elastic band over the button of her skirt to accommodate her expanding waistline. 'Samuel's customers usually ask for the same cuts of meat, they don't chop and change. At least not very often. And he taught me how to cut a joint.'

'Cutting and carrying be two different things,' Daisy added to her protest. 'You can't go hauling great chunks of meat about, think of the baby!'

One hand slipping into the pocket, Emma fingered the hard round disc sewn into its lining. She had touched that coin every day since it had been placed so contemptuously on her body; and every day and during the long night hours she'd remembered the man who put it there.

'You be seven months gone. Standing on the market from morning 'til night will be too much.'

Emma withdrew her hand but the feel of the coin seemed to linger on her fingers. 'I'm going to do it, Daisy, I have to. I can't see the Hollingtons go out of business without even trying to help. They have been kindness itself to us, where would we be without them?'

Daisy's last protest died. 'Like as not the workhouse.'

Emma reached for her shawl. 'They saved us

from that, now we must try to save Samuel's business. I know more than you think...' the confidence in her smile was far greater than that in her heart '...Samuel taught me a great deal about butchering. What to look for in a carcass, and what to avoid. I know his customers and they know me. I have to try. At least that way I shall feel I am doing something. Mrs Hollington trusts me enough to have given me money to buy supplies from the abbatoir. Won't you trust me too, Daisy?'

A cry breaking from her lips, Daisy threw herself across the room, her arms going about her friend. 'Oh, Emma, you know I trust you, ain't nobody on God's earth I trusts more, it ... it's just I worry about you.'

'Then don't.' But even as she returned the hug Emma realised their life here at the Hollingtons' was now under threat. Daisy could still earn her keep with her work in the house but without Samuel's meat stall there would be no job for Emma, and she would not stay without it. Emma Price had not been reared to impose upon anyone. To her parents, charity had been something to give, not to take. Work hard and honestly, had been her mother's maxim; obey God's law, that of her father. But the preacher man had applied that law only to others!

Watching Emma push the handcart out of the yard, Daisy waved after her but for the first time she did not smile.

The cart bucked and grumbled as it moved over the roughly cobbled road, jarring Emma's shoulder. She had been to the abattoir several

326

times and found none of those visits pleasant, but today the smell of blood and animal droppings caused her stomach to turn. Pausing, she leaned heavily on the handles of the cart, trying desperately not to breathe, not to take in any more of the odour that drifted over to her from the high windowless building.

'You Sam Hollington's wench?'

Sickness rising in her, Emma straightened to see a man in a long bloodstained apron that three parts covered trousers tied about his legs with string; a length of ragged cloth draped over one shoulder bore further stains of blood mixed with tiny pieces of flesh. Only his face was clean as he smiled at her.

'I am Mr Hollington's assistant.'

'How be Sam?' Pulling a rag from his pocket, the man wiped his hands. 'That were a nasty accident he had.'

Emma leaned against the cart as another wave of nausea swept her. All she wanted was to make her purchase and leave, but she could not snub the man. Swallowing the bile in her throat, she answered, 'Yes, it was terrible, but we hope he will soon be well enough to take up business again.'

'That won't be none too easy, not with one hand.' He stuffed the rag back inside his pocket. 'Meantime you be carrying on for him?'

Meeting his sympathetic smile, she recognised the honest friendliness behind his question and nodded. 'I'm going to try, though to be honest I don't know if I will be able to. I really know very little of this side of things; Mr Hollington was teaching me...'

'Arr well, Sam Hollington knowed his trade, you couldn't have no finer to teach you the meat. I've dealt with him here at the slaughter house since being a lad so I know the cuts he buys. If you like, I could deal the same way with you?'

Emma felt the weight that had rested on her all the way to the abattoir lift away and the fluttering fade from her insides. 'I would very much appreciate that, Mr...'

'Todd, my name be David Todd, but if you wants to find me then ask for Davey Porkchop.' He grinned. 'That be what I'm known as hereabouts, seeing as how every day I cut a chop from the choicest loin and takes it home for my supper.'

'I am Emma Price, Mr Porkchop.' Emma could not resist a smile. 'But folk hereabouts call me Emma.'

'Then, Emma me wench, let's get that cart of yours loaded up.'

The man had obviously not been boasting. He knew Samuel's requirements and had chosen her the very best. Now it remained for her to do the same for Sam's customers.

Laying the knives alongside the chopping board, she felt trepidation flicker again in her stomach. This was where it had happened. One minute Samuel Hollington had both hands and the next... Leaving the cleaver in the wicker basket, she covered it with the chequered cloth. That she could not face using!

Almost numb with cold, every part of her aching from weariness, Emma wrapped a steak fillet,

328

handing it to a woman who had spent an age prodding and sniffing at it before at last nodding her head.

'It was fresh from the abattoir this morning.' Emma took the ten-shilling note, sorting change from the tin box.

'Arr, so you said!' The woman grabbed the coins, meticulously counting each one. 'And if it be a lie I'll be back for my money afore you can blink, and wanting a free fillet in its place.'

'Sure and am I not broken-hearted?'

Emma looked up from closing the cash box to see Liam Brogan glance at the meat the woman was packing away. 'Hadn't I hoped to see you refuse to buy.'

'Why?' The woman's eyes snapped.

Raising one hand, Liam laid it over his heart. 'Wasn't it me own mother taught me always to be truthful? I hoped you would refuse it so I could have it for meself, for it's the freshest meat I've seen in all the place.'

The woman's hand closed over her purchase, her mouth tight. 'How would you know?' she demanded.

'How would I know?' Dropping his hand, he laughed lightly. 'Am I not the son of Patrick Brogan, and him the finest butcher in all of Ireland! Did not himself teach me the skills? He did so, and I tell you that fillet be the very best steak I've seen since leaving the old country, and so I wanted it for meself!'

The woman rammed the package deep into her basket at the same time glaring at Liam. 'Well, you ain't getting it. Bloody cheek!' Turning on her heel, she marched away.

About to thank him, Emma was diverted by yet another customer. 'I'm sorry,' she answered. 'But the sausages sold out this morning.'

'I suppose it was to be expected.' Lifting a corner of her shawl, the tired-looking young woman wiped the nose of the child she carried on her hip. 'You wouldn't have three pennorth of scrag would you?'

Emma glanced at the few pieces of meat left on the stall. There was no scrag end of mutton. That, she knew, had sold out shortly after she'd set out the stall. About to shake her head, she looked at Liam.

''Tis fortunate the last bit of scrag was taken an hour since.' He played his charming smile upon the young woman. 'For that leaves you as tasty a couple of pork kidneys as ever was.'

'Tasty they might be mister,' she hitched the child higher, 'but there ain't enough there to feed a man and four kids. What I'd pay for them would buy a dozen sausages. I'll just 'ave to try a bit further along, could be one of the other stalls will 'ave some.'

'To be sure they will, seeing as theirs be having nowhere near the taste of Hollington's, nor will they be cheaper. Now add to those kidneys these pieces of underbelly and you'll have a meal the little people themselves would cross the sea for, and all for no more than threepence.'

Reaching across the stall, he took a piece of paper, wrapping the meat in it and handing it to the woman who took it gratefully.

'Sure and Samuel Hollington don't be needing

your thanks.' Liam brushed aside her gratitude. 'But he will welcome your custom, and if you come tomorrow I guarantee there'll be sausages.'

'You shouldn't have told her there'd be sausages tomorrow,' Emma said as the woman turned away, trailed by her three small children. 'Samuel can't make them and I don't know how.'

'Since when was that a problem?' He gathered the knives, slipping them into the large wicker basket.

'Since now. You told that woman a lie.'

'Did I now, or was it yourself told the lie? I did not say the sausages sold out this morning.'

Emma turned to gather up the chopping board, feeling a flush rise to her face. 'Yes, I said that, and it seems tomorrow I'll have to say the same.'

'No, you won't.' He lifted the basket on to the hand cart then turned back to her. '*I* will make them.'

Chopping block in hand, Emma stared at him. 'You!'

'Me!' He grinned.

'But you're not the son of a butcher.'

'Ah, now *there* I lied.'

'You lied?' Despite her weariness, Emma responded to the infectious grin. 'And wasn't it your very own mother taught you always to be truthful?'

Running a hand through his hair, he looked at her with laughing eyes. 'Me mother now, God bless her, was a good teacher but her son didn't always learn the lessons he should. But the making of sausages and the butchering of animals I *did* learn. A lad learns many things living in a small village where every family does for itself.'

'So was your father a carpenter as you told Daisy and me?'

'Wouldn't I swear as much before the Holy Father himself! Now stop your blethering, woman, and blow out them candles and let's get you home. We have sausages to make!'

The moon was high and silver when at last Emma and Daisy climbed into bed.

'Liam Brogan's a good friend, Emma,' Daisy said softly. 'But he would be more than a friend if you let him.'

'That's ridiculous. He hardly knows me.' Emma turned down the paraffin lamp until it was barely a glow.

'Know you or not, he's in love with you.' Daisy turned on to her side, pulling the covers up to her chin. 'Given half a chance he'd marry you ... and you could do worse than accept him.'

'*You could do worse than accept him.*'

The words rang in Emma's mind long after Daisy's rhythmic breathing told she was asleep.

But how could she do that, even should he ask? How could she ask any man to take on the child of another?

'*...he's in love with you...*'

It seemed Daisy's words came back to her for answer. But that was not enough, surely? A man needed to be loved in return.

Beyond the narrow window the sky turned from black to grey.

But a child needed love too, the love of a father

as well as a mother. Liam was kind and thoughtful, and what was more he was honest. Once he knew the circumstances of the child's conception, that Emma was not married, he would tell her honestly whether or not he could become that father.

But would she come to love him?

In the shadows shrouding the room it seemed the face of Liam Brogan with its tiny Z-shaped scar smiled at her, but as she watched a darker, more brooding face appeared at his shoulder; one whose pitch dark eyes haunted her every night. The face of Carver Felton.

It had been more than a month since Samuel's accident. Emma packed away the last of the knives. A month in which she had looked after the business alone.

Though that was not altogether true. She glanced up as the clock of St Bartholomew's chimed a quarter to nine. She had not been entirely alone. Davey Porkchop had helped her choose her meat every morning, and Liam Brogan had taught her how to make sausages. He had come to the stall regularly for the first few nights and then...

She lifted the basket on to the cart, gasping as a pain streaked across her back.

Why did he not come any more? She glanced the length of the Shambles. Hers was the only stall with the candle jars still lit. Mrs Hollington had often said there was no need to stay at market so late, but Samuel had always stayed; not because he wanted to garner the last penny,

Emma had long realised that, but almost to give away the last of his meat to those so poor they came looking for scraps left at the end of the day. And to leave earlier would seem like breaking faith with the man to whom Emma owed so much.

The cart loaded and the stall brushed down with a screwed up sheet of paper, she glanced again along the narrow street. Why did she have this feeling, this wish almost, that Liam would come?

Blowing out the last of the candles, she collected the burned out stubs, putting them in the little wooden tray that Samuel had fixed to the side of the cart.

Weary from the day, her body clumsy with the burden it carried, she took up the handles of the cart, clamping her teeth as a fresh pain darted across her back. How much longer would she be able to keep this up? Half-bent, she shoved the reluctant cart over the uneven cobbles, the bitter wind that had blown the whole day tearing at her shawl.

Samuel had sickened, that was to be expected after such a terrible accident, but there had been virtually no recovery since and each morning Sarah Hollington's eyes grew a little bleaker.

Catching her breath against the sharp stabbing in her back Emma blinked against the strands of hair whipping across her face. What if he did not get well? And what of when her baby was born?

'One day at a time,' she whispered into the wind. 'One day at a time.'

'I guessed you'd be the last to leave...'

The words mingled with a sound like rushing wind and a thousand pin points of light dancing in the blackness as a blow to the back of her head sent Emma stumbling to the ground.

'Emma! Oh, thank God!' Daisy rushed into the yard. 'You're so late, I couldn't think what...'

Then, as Emma half fell into her arms, she gasped, 'Oh, Lord, what happened?'

Leaving cart and basket in the yard, she helped Emma into their little house. Sitting her close to the stove Daisy knelt down, taking cold hands into her own.

'Someone struck me.' The nagging throb in her head added its own pain to that which winced across her back. 'They took the cash box. Daisy, what will Samuel say?'

Pushing herself to her feet, the girl took down a dish from the dresser, filling it with broth from a pot on the stove.

'Don't think about that now. Drink that broth and then let me get a look at your head. We can talk about the cash box later.'

'No, Daisy.' Emma pushed the dish away. 'I must tell him now.'

'But somebody hit you, Emma, you can't go ignoring a bump on the head. Let me at least...'

'I'm all right, Daisy, really I am!' Emma stood up on legs still quivering from the effort of pushing the cart. 'I'm going to see Samuel, to tell him what's happened.'

'Won't do no good.' Daisy returned the broth to the pot. Holding the empty dish in her hands, she stared down at it. 'He won't be bothered about no cash box.'

'Of course he'll be bothered. It was robbery, it has to be reported to the police. Mrs Hollington must send for a constable.'

'Mrs Hollington ain't here.' Daisy's voice faltered. 'She's gone to her sister's house.'

Already at the door, Emma turned. 'But Samuel ... she wouldn't leave him alone!'

'There was no choice given her.' Daisy continued to stare at the dish. 'Samuel died early this morning.'

Samuel was dead! Emma clutched at the table for support. Samuel was dead!

'Happened soon after you left. I ran to get the doctor but it were too late. I heard him as he came out of the bedroom, I heard him tell Mrs Hollington he'd been expecting it. A poisoning of the blood so he said. Poor Mrs Hollington! She never said a word, not even after her sister come. A sharp one she was, a right bossy bitch! Sent me straight along to Webb's Funeral Parlour. Ordered that the body was to be moved straight away. I told her it weren't right, it weren't the way things is done round here, but she said it would be done the way she wanted it and so would a good many other things now she were in charge. But I still don't think it's right. A man should be in his own house and Mrs Hollington would have wanted that an' all.'

The pain settled to a dull ache but Emma remained leaning on the table. 'Didn't Mrs Hollington say anything?'

'Not a word. Like somebody dead herself she was, not that she had much chance against that woman. Eh, I wouldn't want *her* company for long!'

'Be you Emma Price?' The wind catching her skirts as the door was flung back on its hinges, Emma turned around to face a tall angular woman, hands crossed over her stomach. 'I asked, be you Emma Price?'

'Yes, I am Emma Price.'

'Then you be the one has Samuel Hollington's cash box. I'll take it.'

'This be Mrs Hollington's sister.' Daisy stepped forward.

'No need for explanations.' The woman's small eyes glittered. 'Just hand over the cash box and then you can leave.'

'Leave?'

'You heard me, girl, you ain't deaf!' the sharp voice snapped at Daisy. 'The both of you will leave this house tonight.'

'But we don't have no place else, and Emma is...'

'I can see what she is! But that be no concern of mine. 'Twould have been better to have thought of the consequences afore indulging in the act! But you be all the same, trollops the lot of you, follow your own evil ways and leave the paying for 'em to other folk. Oh, I know your game. You thought you had yourself well in here, thought you could go on living off the backs of my sister and that husband of hers; always was too soft was Hollington. Well, he ain't here no more, and your well-laid little plans be no more either.'

'Daisy and I lived off no one's back.' Emma

337

touched the other girl's arm, holding back the anger she saw in her face. 'We both worked hard from the moment of coming to this house.'

'Worked hard … worked *hard?* Her a bit of cleaning and you sitting in the market? I'd expect harder work from a five-year-old.'

'You would, and you'd get it too, you hard-faced old cow!'

Her mouth thinning with satisfaction, the woman looked at Daisy. 'How right I was. I told my sister you were nothing but guttersnipes, the lowest of the low, and your language proves it.'

'Arr missis, p'raps it does,' Daisy flashed. 'And while we be on the business of sayings, here's one for you. Low I might be but I reckon a worm with a top hat on couldn't crawl underneath you.'

'Like I told Sarah, guttersnipes! No more, no less.' The little eyes glittered venomously. 'Well, you can take your foul mouth somewhere else … if you can find a place that will take the likes of you. Not everybody is as soft as Hollington was.'

'Mr Hollington was very kind.'

'And you was very quick to take advantage, try to take over even. No sooner had he suffered that accident than you stepped in. Thought you'd have the lot, no doubt. But you reckoned without me!'

Beside her Emma felt Daisy bristle but still she answered quietly. 'I had no thought to take advantage, I thought only to help keep the business going until Mr Hollington recovered.'

Fingers clasping together, Sarah Hollington's sister pressed her hands more firmly across her stomach, her thin lips turning a little further

338

inward as she stared at Emma.

'Helped yourself more like.'

'What do you mean?'

'You knows well what I mean.' The words spat from the tight condemning mouth. 'Wouldn't be every penny that you took for meat would finish up in that box, there'd be more than a few went in your own pocket. You knew Hollington was too sick to reckon the takings and Sarah would have little time or thought for doing so while her was busy with looking after him. But I be neither daft nor too busy and I can count as well as the next, and believe me, I will. If there be a penny short...'

Indignation dulling the ache that nagged at her back, Emma held those glittering little eyes with her own steady stare. 'I am not a thief.'

'That has yet to be proved!' The woman snorted, her hands held out. 'Now, the cash box, if you please.'

'Emma don't 'ave it!'

Eyes widening, her voice almost a squeak, the woman demanded, 'What ... what did you say?'

'I do not have the cash box.' Emma's voice was firm as she looked into the furious face. 'I was robbed on my way home.'

'Robbed ... robbed!' The woman snorted. 'The only thief be you. If that money's gone then *you* have taken it!'

'That's not true!' Emma gasped at her accusation.

'No? Well, the constables can find that out.' The woman stepped away from the door. 'But one thing be certain. You'll not spend a moment longer in this place, you'll have no more chances to rob a poor dead man. Get out! Get out now!'

Snatching her own shawl from the chair back, Daisy glared at Sarah Hollington's sister. 'You get the constable, missis,' she grated, 'and while he be sorting out who really stole your brother-in-law's cash, get him to sort this out an' all!'

Lifting the dish above her head, she sent it crashing at the woman's feet.

'I can't … I can't go any further!' Pain, sharp and regular, had moved from Emma's back into her stomach, each pang snatching the breath from her lungs.

'Is it the crack on the head you took?'

Emma shook her head as another swift pain robbed her of speech.

'You mean, it's the baby! The child be coming?' Daisy looked wildly about the darkened streets as Emma gasped again. 'We 'ave to go on.' She grasped her friend about the waist urging her forward. 'I ain't never birthed no child, I don't know what to do!'

They had to go on. Emma forced one foot in front of the other. But where … where could they go?

'No more, Daisy, no more. I can't … I can't!'

Tears coursing down her cheeks, Daisy held the half-fainting figure in her arms. Ahead the black mass of both churches rose solid against a sky beginning to give way to dawn. The Vicarages would be close by, not that she had ever been there; surely they would help Emma? But if they refused, if they turned her away…

Feeling hands clutch her arm as a fresh spasm of pain shot through the girl slumped against her, Daisy clenched her teeth. The risk was too great, they had to go where help was assured.

'Not far,' she murmured, urging Emma on again. 'Not far now. You can rest soon.'

Turning left she led Emma slowly down a deserted Meeting Street towards the light by a single lantern. Reaching the low building with its pretentious pillars, she lowered Emma to the step. Glancing once at her friend's huddled figure she tugged the iron bell pull. Then, as its clang sounded beyond the heavy oak door, Daisy lifted her skirts and ran.

Chapter Twenty-Three

Braiding her hair into one long plait, Emma fastened it with a piece of narrow white ribbon.

It was more than a year since she had come to this place, more than a year since her son had been born. Crossing to the wooden cot, she stared down at the sleeping child.

Daisy had left her there on the steps of the workhouse. Memories of that dreadful night returned in full: the pain of her labour, the bitterness of that woman's accusation, the feeling of being utterly alone.

They had asked so many questions, the wardresses with their stony faces and grey uniforms. Over and over again they had asked who was she, who was her husband, who were her parents, where could they be found? But Emma had given no answer except to turn her head away. Her child had been born in the workhouse. She would not tell them that added to that stigma went the one of bastard.

She touched a finger to the tiny hand curled into a fist and resting against the dark hair curled close to his head.

She had laid three days in a bed shoved against a damp wall, one window high up towards the roof offering little light and no view on the outside world, her only companion an elderly woman who shuffled in twice a day with food, her eyes on the door the whole time lest she was caught talking.

Then they had brought Emma her clothes and she had dressed under the watchful eye of a wardress. She had received no answer to her queries about the baby, merely a snapped instruction, 'Follow me!'

Eyes closing she watched pictures form in her mind, smelled again the damp cloying air as they passed the laundry room, the strong smell of scouring soda that clung to corridors and stairs.

They had come to a halt before a door marked 'Governess' and waited until a voice gave permission to enter. This room had been lighter than the first, tall windows giving easier access to the pale March sunlight. Opposite them a fire had burned in the grate, its surround burnished to a silver sheen.

Black on silver! Emma had trembled as she looked at it. *He* had hair that was black marked with silver.

'Is this your wife?'

Her trembling stopped at the words of the woman sitting behind the heavy desk and Emma stood as if turned to stone. Over the fireplace an ornate clock ticked, marking the long seconds of silence.

'Emma! Oh, my dear!' Firm hands had taken her own. 'I only arrived back this morning. I found the house deserted, and you ... I've been half out of my mind with worry.'

The hands that pulled her close to his strong body.

'I thank you for taking such good care of my

wife and for the delivery of our child. It is, I trust, in good health?'

Afraid almost to breathe, Emma had stood with lowered eyes and listened to the voice she knew so well.

'Your son appears perfectly healthy.'

His son! She had trembled then but the arm that had circled her pressed down warningly upon her shoulders.

'Then once more my thanks, and allow me to reimburse the parish.'

She had caught the glint of a gold coin as it was placed on the desk, and the governess's murmur of thanks.

Then they had brought her child, swaddled in strips of blanket, but not until they were in the hansom that bore them away had she looked at the man who had come for her.

Emma opened her eyes. Liam had told her then. Told her how Daisy had run all the way to Plovers Croft, had sought him out and told him all that had happened. It had taken less than half a day for him to track down a man who was throwing money at tavern keepers like it was sawdust, one who was quick to confess to robbery when helped by a little persuasion. The constables found the box in his lodgings and that had put an end to the accusation against Emma.

It was Daisy who'd suggested leaving her a day or two where at least she would have a bed to rest in, then when he had insisted on bringing her from the workhouse had advised he call himself her husband.

Emma had wanted to protest. Much as her

344

child deserved a father, she could not go with him. Yet against his determination her strength had failed. And now she was here in his house, in the wooden hut Liam had built for himself.

In the months since her son's birth he had built on to the hut, adding bedrooms for herself and Daisy, while in return he'd asked nothing though his eyes, whenever he looked at her, begged for her love.

But how could she be sure what he felt for her now would be so in the future? What would he feel as he watched the child grow, knowing he was another man's son?

Emma loved Liam, loved his kind, gentle ways, but she could not risk hurting him more by marrying him.

Bending over the cot, she touched her lips to the tiny hand. 'You will never have a father, my darling,' she whispered against those tight-curled fingers, 'but I will love you, I will love you all my life.'

Climbing into her own narrow bed, she turned down the lamp. The name her child would bear would be that of the preacher man. One so innocent, the other so wicked. As wicked as the man she'd met in Felton woods!

Tiredness carrying her into the realms of sleep she moaned softly as black eyes regarded her, the silver streaks on his head glinting as he laughed. But the voice in her head was Jerusha's.

'...*he will bear his father's name...*'

Carrying her stool from the house, Jerusha set it beneath the branches of a tree heavy with

345

summer foliage. The months since the passing of winter had been hot and dry and the smell of earth closets hung thick on the evening air. Settling herself on the stool, she looked out over the parched heathland towards where Plovers Croft had once held a covey of houses, to where she had spent the years with Joseph. She fingered the empty third finger of her left hand. But now all of that was gone and soon she would be gone also. But where old life fades, a new one springs; and such a one had been born in the town where two churches watched over it from a hill top.

The silence had told her of it long months since, as it had told her many things; the heart-break of a woman, the ambitions of one man, the despair of another, and of a fear that would soon sweep the village, taking more than one into the arms of death.

Drawing a slow, deep breath she squinted into the setting sun.

The end was nigh.

There had been no word from the man he had made his head groom. Paul Felton stared out over the gardens of Beaufort House. There had been no word of a message to his brother from Doe Bank and in the week since his return he had failed to find any sign of Emma Price.

Carver had done a good job of keeping him away from home, always having some business or other that was of the utmost importance, always insisting it must be his brother who attended to it, and always wielding his authority as guardian.

But now he was of age. Carver could no longer

threaten him with an institution, nor send him anywhere against his will. He would have no more to do with the business until he had found Emma.

Turning on his heel, Paul strode out of the house and across the yard to the stables.

Carver, it seemed, was sole owner of all the shares in the new canal venture. Paul wiped one hand across a brow moist with perspiration. It was easy to guess how he had acquired Langton's portion, the man was an inveterate gambler, but Arthur Payne? That man was more of a fool than ever his father had been, but to relinquish such a prize ... he would not have done that easily. Carver must have had some hold on him, but what he would not say. In fact, his brother had said remarkably little about the entire affair, and had fallen into total silence whenever the subject of Emma had been raised.

But that reluctance to answer had not ended the matter. Paul wiped again at the moisture rapidly beading on his brow. Carver had listened to the ultimatum put to him, listened silent but stony-eyed; only when Paul had declared his intention of finding the girl and marrying her had he thrown the pen he was holding across the desk and strode out of the study.

Paul had hoped that in his absence his brother would come to accept that the feelings he had for Emma were deep-rooted and lasting, that his love was real and not the infatuation Carver always claimed. But he seemed, if anything, even more opposed to any marriage between them. Nevertheless Paul would find Emma, and he

347

would marry her.

Bringing the horse to a standstill as it crested a low rise he felt tiredness sweep over him, a weariness that had plagued him since leaving the port of Liverpool and one that sleep did not relieve. When he found Emma, he would rest.

Eyes stinging from the sweat trickling into them, he blinked. Across the heath in the far distance he could just make out the figure of a woman, her back toward him as she walked away. He blinked again then dashed away the perspiration. The rays of the sun were slanting red-gold across the scorched heather, slanting on hair the colour of moonkissed wheat.

'Emma!' His cry startling the placid horse it threw back its head, ears pricking.

It had to be her. No other girl he had ever seen had hair of such a wonderful colour. Touching his heels to the animal's sides, he sent it galloping across the heath.

She had watched her child walk towards her, his first baby steps faltering and unsure. Watched him as Daisy set him on the ground, watched him stand unmoving until the sound of the girl's voice caught his ear.

He had smiled then, showing the four tiny teeth that had given him so much distress in the cutting, smiled as he bumped into a chair pushed under the table.

That had been the final blow to her slowly breaking heart. Her child was blind!

Emma clutched the frail body tight against her own. She had known for a year, known her baby's sight was failing; she had prayed so hard that it would not happen, prayed he would not suffer for what she had done. But her prayers had gone unanswered. The child would pay for the sin of its father, and pay again for the sin of its mother.

It was *her* doing! Emma's dry sobs dropped into the silence. *She* had caused the child's terrible affliction. It had been a sin to ask for a potion, a sin to try to take the life of an unborn child; yet still she had drunk the mixture that woman had given her, a mixture that had inflicted blindness!

She had vowed never to return to Doe Bank, but Jerusha was there. Jerusha would help, she had herbs and medicines. But Jerusha could not help. She had shaken her head as Emma had sobbed out her story. Her herbs and skills were not enough, she had said, it would take a skill far greater than hers to bring sight to those eyes. Nor must Emma blame herself, she had added, touching her veined hand to the girl's. It was no potion had caused this blindness.

But it was ... it was! Her senses screamed their pain. It was her fault her child was blind!

'Emma!'

The sound of hooves drumming over the bone-hard ground seized at her brain but it did not drive away the thoughts that imprisoned it.

'Emma!'

It came again and this time she turned her head, looking behind her. Still half-lost in her misery, she glanced at the figure on horseback.

Paul? Instinctively she reached a hand forward then withdrew it sharply.

'Emma ... oh, Emma, I *knew* I would find you!'

349

Swinging from the saddle, he came forward then hesitated as she stepped away from him.

'I realise how long it has been. God, how I realise! But it is over now, we can be married. Oh, Emma...'

'No!' Her eyes showing the pain in her heart, she stepped further from him. 'It's too late, Paul, I can never marry you.'

'Emma?' He reached for her hand. 'You can't mean that? If it's because I've been gone so long...'

'No.' She shook her head, sending sunlight sparkling through its length. 'It's not your absence.'

'Then what? Tell me, my love.'

How could she? How could she tell him his elder brother had raped her? It had caused enough sorrow already, and she would not set brother against brother.

Hitching the child higher on her hip, she saw a look of understanding cross his face as he caught the gleam of gold on her left hand.

'I was gone too long,' he said softly.

Unable to answer, to voice her feelings, she watched him remount. 'I loved you, Emma.' He smiled wearily down. 'I think I always will.'

In her arms the child turned, its small hand dislodging the shawl she had wrapped about its head.

Glancing at it, Paul let out a swift breath. Smiling up at him were two coal black eyes and the evening light glistened on fine strands of silver set amidst the sable hair.

The child was Carver's.

Understanding giving way to anger, he whipped the horse around.

Emma Price was not his brother's wife, but the child she held in her arms could have been fathered by none other than Carver.

Why in hell had they not sent for him sooner?

Carver Felton sat in the study of Felton Hall.

Men on their way home from the Topaz mine had found his brother almost unconscious on the heath. They had carried him to Doe Bank where Jerusha Paget had cared for him. But the woman was a fraud, what did she know of medicine? Bloody herbs and plants! How could they cure Paul's illness?

They had at last sent to Felton Hall and Carver had gone at once, brought Paul home with him to be cared for. But the doctor he'd summoned had shaken his head. It was too late. As it had proved too late for many in Doe Bank.

Typhoid. Paul must have contracted the disease in Liverpool, from one of the boats. Even now, almost six months after his brother's death, Carver was not over the shock of it.

He twisted the paper held in his hands.

The doctor had carefully described the precautions that must be taken in the house. None but Carver himself had contracted the sickness, but he had lived while Paul...

The disease had raced through the village like wild fire, helped by the hot dry weather. The Paget woman had died too, but not until the worst was over. Age and overwork with the sick had proved her undoing.

He glanced at the paper twisting in his fingers, the paper the old woman had sent to him and which he had not yet brought himself to read.

Paul had asked her to write it. The man who'd delivered it had been awkward and afraid but refused to give it to any but Carver himself. Then he'd refused the shilling held out to him in exchange.

Carver had thought that strange, a man on the wages he must earn refusing a shilling. But the look the man gave him as he'd turned away had been stranger still for it was one of revulsion. Doe Bank men had no love for Carver Felton, that much he had long known, but the look he had been given that day was something new.

He would not have thought that old woman capable of writing though her eyes on the one occasion they'd met seemed to look into his soul. He opened the paper. Her hand had obviously been unused to such a task, but the writing was legible.

'Excuse my interrupting you, sir.'

Carver looked up as his butler entered the study.

'There's a lady asking to see you. I told her you were busy but she was most insistent.'

Emma! Carver's breathing quickened. She had come at last, come to see Paul. God, if only he had not been so selfish, so beset by pride... But it was more than pride had caused him to withhold permission for that girl and his brother to marry, it was jealousy. He too loved the woman his brother loved, that reason and no other had been the ultimate cause of his denying them marriage.

If only he could turn back the clock, given them what both had wanted. But chance of that was gone, it was too late, but now she was here, now at least he could offer some reparation for the harm he had done.

'Who is the lady, Morton, do you know?'

'Yes sir,' the butler answered. 'It is Miss Cara Holgate.'

The headiness of a moment ago fading swiftly, Carver opened a drawer of his desk, dropping the paper into it unread.

Cara Holgate! He had seen nothing of her since the evening he had caught her cavorting naked with her cousin. Now what did she want with him?

'Shall I tell the lady you will join her in the drawing room, sir?'

'No!' Carver shut the drawer. 'You may not tell the lady that, Morton. 'Tell her *she* may join *me* here in the study or she may leave.'

'Well, Cara.' Carver's eyes glittered darkly as she lowered herself into a chair. 'I don't think either of us could truthfully call this a pleasure, but whatever I owe it to please say directly ... I have little wish to prolong this meeting.'

'Nor I.' She folded her gloved hands against her amber velvet skirt.

'Then why come here?'

'Not for myself, Carver.' Green-gold eyes regarded him steadily. 'But on behalf of my cousin.'

'The pretty Melissa.' A flicker of satisfaction crossed Carver's face at the look his remark brought to Cara's. That jealousy was still present, if anything even more pronounced. 'What can she want from me?'

Cara's eyes were venomous. 'It seems she already has something from you – something you are going to have to acknowledge.'

'You interest me, Cara. Pray go on?'

'Melissa tells me she is three months with child.' Cara drew in a sharp, satisfied breath. 'She also tells me *you* are the father.'

A child! Carver's senses quickened for the second time in a few minutes. If only it had been the Doe Bank girl, that pit bank wench come to say she was carrying Paul's child. The news might well have riven him with jealousy but he would have hidden it, just as he had hidden his own feelings for her for so long; at least then he would have had some part of his brother left. But this was not Emma Price, and his brother had not fathered a child.

Forcing the pain that never truly left him into the background, Carver gave a thin smile but his dark eyes held no humour.

'Does she now? You are sure she does not mean Arthur Payne?'

'That fool?' Cara snapped. 'She would not let him get within a yard of her.'

'He did not get within a yard of her.' He leaned back in his chair, fingertips touching his chin. 'And you, my dear, try as you might, could not get within her! Therefore you think to place the burden upon me.'

'I place it where it should be. You seduced Melissa when unknown to me she called at

354

Felton Hall to explain what you saw that evening. Now she is carrying your child.'

'I see.' He lowered his hands. 'You know me better than that, Cara my dear. You know I would not touch a woman who had made love to another man, much less one who had made love to a woman. In short, your lover is not only unnatural, she is also a liar!'

In her lap, Cara's hands tightened. 'You deny you are the father?'

'Emphatically.'

'Melissa is more than willing to swear…'

'I have no doubt.' The smile remained fixed on his mouth but the ice in his eyes was unmistakable. 'But Melissa would do well to think carefully before making any such allegation, for pleasurable as I would find it to strip you of every last thing you own, I am willing to deny myself … just this one time!'

'You should have denied yourself three months ago! Now you must pay the piper.'

'Not for any tune you call, Cara. I will not go into detail here, we will save that for the courts. Let me say instead that if need be I can produce irrefutable evidence to prove what you claim is untrue. So, you see, if your delectable cousin is truly with child, which I very strongly doubt, then I advise you look elsewhere for a scapegoat!'

Watching the door slam behind her he slumped into his chair. It had all been for nothing, his planning and scheming to build a bigger, more profitable business, one he could pass on to his son. There would be no son. There would be no child to inherit, either his or his brother's. Why had it all gone so sour? Why had fate turned so viciously against him?

Why hadn't he agreed to Paul's marrying the Doe Bank girl? But he had not, and now it was too late. Why ... why had he refused?

Closing his eyes, he thumped one fist hard on the desk. He knew why not. God forgive him, he knew why!

Chapter Twenty-Four

The work would soon be finished and the men employed to dig the new waterway would move on. Emma looked across to the tents huddled together like a flock of forlorn sheep. Some had talked of moving on, looking for fresh navigation work; others had talked of going home to their families in Ireland.

When they were gone she too would have to leave. She should have done that as soon as her child was born. She watched him now, a sturdy two year old, walking between Daisy and the young man who had asked her to be his wife – Emma's son laughing up at them, as they tickled a buttercup beneath his chin. But he would never see the tiny flower that delighted him so, never see the colours of the sunset or the love in his mother's eyes.

Liam had taken them to the doctor in the town. Emma felt the same overwhelming grief rise in her now as she had felt then when the man had shaken his head. Like Jerusha before him he had not the skill to cure the blindness that held her baby's eyes, nor did he know of any who had.

They had journeyed back to Plovers Croft in silence, Liam carrying the child. Only when they were once more in the room he had built for her and Daisy had he spoken.

'Emma, you know I love you, and I love the boy

too. You don't have to bear this sorrow alone. Marry me, Emma, let me be a father to him. I will take care of the two of you, I swear by the saints I will.'

Swallowing a fresh surge of guilt and pain she remembered the look in his eyes when she had shaken her head, a look of hopelessness and despair. He had listened then while she told him all: told him of her father's betrayal of Carrie, the death of her family and of her rape; told him all except the name of the man who had ruined her.

''Twas a mortal sin your father committed.' Liam had taken her hand. 'And a great one that was done against you. But you must not blame yourself and you cannot go on paying for the sins of others. You have a life of your own, Emma, a life that should bring happiness as well as sorrow. I could bring you happiness, I know I could, if you would only say yes.'

But she had not said yes. She reached a pan from a nail hammered into the wooden wall. Liam would be a good father to her son and a loving husband to her, yet still she had refused him. There were no secrets left between them, no barrier to a life with him, so what was it held her back? Paul Felton would not look for her again. He had seen his brother's son. It was no longer the hope of marriage to Paul that held her back. But would marriage to him have brought her happiness or would the shadow of another man have destroyed it? She closed her eyes, picturing Paul's open boyish face, but saw only dark eyes topped by darker hair through which swept two streaks of silver.

In the silence of his study Carver rested one hand on the drawer that held that paper. He had placed it there the day Cara Holgate tried her little trick. Her deception had backfired. She had gambled and lost. He could have carried out his threat, gone to Court and taken their every last farthing, but he had not. Why? For old time's sake? No. He smiled cynically. It had been enough to see defeat on that once attractive face.

She had recognised that her tricks were over so far as Wednesbury was concerned. Carver remembered the venom spitting from green-gold eyes as Cara called down the vengeance of hell upon his head before she and Melissa had finally retired to Rugeley. But hell had already taken its vengeance on Carver Felton. Pride had driven him to commit rape, driven him to deny his brother marriage to a miner's daughter, then pride had turned to jealousy and lies as he came to realise his own love for Emma Price, and finally to misery when it became too late to tell Paul, too late to give them what they'd both desired.

Imagine Cara's triumph had she known. Known he had been vanquished by an enemy more dangerous and more lethal than she could ever be. He had recovered yet the disease had destroyed him as effectively as it had killed Paul.

'I am sorry...'

The words of the doctor making his final examination rang in Carver's mind as they rang nightly.

'...typhoid infected the testicles. It is regrettable but

virtually certain: you will never be able to father a child.'

Infertile. He almost laughed. Oh, Cara, how you would have enjoyed hearing that!

But he had let her go without learning of it, had turned his back on her as he had turned his back on the paper in that drawer. He had not read it, nor since Paul's death had he agreed to speak to his brother's solicitor or hear his will read.

It was his fault. If it had not been for that greed for power … his hand tightened on the gleaming brass handle of the drawer. It should have been he who died!

But all the self-recrimination, all the regrets in the world, would not bring Paul back. All that was left was for Carver to do what his brother might have asked, read the last words he had dictated. It was a duty that could bring him no pleasure but one he had put off for too long. The time had come to face it.

Pulling open the drawer, he drew out the paper. Slowly, the very act bringing a lump to his throat, he unfolded it. The writing scrawled uncertainly across the page relayed Paul's last words to him. Blinking against the tears suddenly clouding his vision, he began to read.

My dear Carver,
I realise that all you planned for me was well intended, though it was not what I wanted. You were wrong to forbid my marrying Emma Price. I loved her, Carver, in a way I fear you would find hard to understand. But that path to happiness is closed to me now, as I fear all paths are closing. I found her but she

is married to another.

I shall not see you again but I wish you the happiness I did not find and thank you for the years we shared. I leave you my love and my forgiveness.

Paul

His love and forgiveness. Tears he had held back for so long ran freely down Carver's face. After all the unhappiness he had caused his brother, Paul had left his love and forgiveness. Why could he not have condemned him, cursed him even? That would have been easier to read than the words of that letter

But another power had cursed him. A power that had shattered his plans and his life with one single blow; taken his brother and his own hope of an heir. There would be no other Felton after him, no child of Paul's to carry the name, no child of his to inherit! But that had not been all the curse settled upon him. He had learned his true reason for denying any marriage with the Doe Bank girl. He, Carver Felton, was in love with her.

Letting the paper fall to the desk he laughed softly, a dry humourless sound.

Even learning that had come too late. Emma Price was married. She was as forbidden to him as he had forbidden her to his brother.

Leaving the letter where it had fallen, Carver rose and left the room. There was still one duty he could perform for Paul. He would hear his brother's will and see that it was carried out.

'There are a few bequests...'

Carver sat uneasily in the solicitor's office. This

was something he did not want to do; it would finally mark Paul's passing.

'I do not need to hear them.' He spoke tersely. 'Whatever my brother wished is to be adhered to, to the very letter.'

'Of course, Mr Felton.' The man nodded, looking at him over heavy horn-rimmed spectacles. 'The smaller bequests, those to his household servants, can be dealt with immediately, but...'

'But?' Carver's eyes rested on the man who suddenly seemed less at ease.

'The final bequest.' The spectacles slipped forward on his nose as the solicitor bent over the papers on his desk. 'Perhaps it would be better for me to read it out to you?'

'Finally...' He cleared his throat. 'Finally, I leave the remainder of my estate in its entirety to my brother's son...'

Driving back to Felton Hall, Carver laughed long and loud. It was nothing more than he deserved. Paul had left everything to a child that could never be. He had thought his brother would marry and beget a child at some future date. The irony of it! He laughed again. Not only could Carver never beget a child, he could never marry the woman he loved. Had Paul's letter to him carried a curse it could have been no more bitter than this knowledge.

'I said for you to be away about your business!'

Emma reeled from the blow that caught her cheek and sent her sprawling to the ground.

'I'll have no woman interfering in mine, and you'll do no more of it with any man once I be through with you!'

Raising one fist above his head, the brawny Irishman reached the other to the neck of her blouse, using it to drag her to her feet.

'And I will have no man strike a woman!' Ice cold fury in every word, Liam caught the man by the shoulder, spinning him into the hard fist that waited.

'You have struck your last against a woman or against a lad!' Blow after blow followed his words as Liam's temper broke. 'Try a man for a change, Michael Flynn. See how you fare against one as big as yourself – and beg the little people to help you for I swear this day 'tis yourself will be beaten to a pulp!'

'No!' Emma scrambled to her feet as the man who had struck her measured his length beside her. 'No more fighting, please, Liam!'

'This man has asked to be taught a lesson long enough.' He breathed hard. 'Now he is to be given the teaching of it.'

'No, Liam.' Emma clutched at his arm. 'No more!'

'You hear that, Michael Flynn?' He stood over the fallen man who was wiping blood from his mouth. 'The woman you attacked asks you be given no more of the hiding you deserve. But you will be gone from here within the hour, for 'tis a brave man you'll be to stay.'

After watching the man slink away, he followed Emma into the wooden building he and the rest of the men had erected as a canteen where she could cook and serve the meals they were glad to buy.

'Be you badly hurt, lad?'

'I didn't play my mouth, Mr Brogan, though Michael Flynn said I did.'

Watching the lad, no more than twelve years old, wince as Emma held a wet cloth against his cut face, Liam felt his fury return. He should have ignored Emma's plea, should have dealt with Flynn as Flynn had dealt with the boy. As for striking Emma... He glanced at her, at the red weal that would become a bruise... He should have killed the swine!

'Get you back to my hut.' Liam smiled at the lad as Emma applied a soothing ointment to the boy's cuts. 'Rest you there for the day, none will disturb you. Go along now and don't fret over your work, you'll not lose by the leaving of it.'

'He's little more than a child,' Emma said as the boy left. 'He should be home with his mother, a boy needs a mother's love.'

As a man needs the love of a wife. His heart aching with the need to hold her, Liam watched her place a fresh towel against her cheek.

'That was the cause of his beating. The men tell me the lad was talking of his desire to be home, one he has spoken of many times since coming to England. That riled Flynn, who I think feels the same but is afraid to say so. That was the true cause of his hitting the lad.'

'Then why not let the boy return to Ireland?'

'It's not the easy thing you be thinking.' Liam shook his head. 'The boy came here to find work, work that would keep his mother from starvation.'

Emma's thoughts flashed to the child who had

been born to her. Was he not the most precious thing in her life? Would she not gladly starve rather than have him unhappy? Would not the boy's mother feel the same love for her son?

'I think she would rather have him home,' Emma said quietly.

'Even so, he could not travel alone, the docks be none too safe a place for a lad as young as him.' Liam shook his head. 'And there are none here ready to return, we all have families who need the money we send.' He could have added that he would gladly have taken the lad back to Ireland if only Emma would come too, as his wife. He could have said it but he let the words remain where only he could hear them.

Turning away, he returned to the digging. He loved her too much to cause her to feel guilt, or to have her marry him just to end a boy's home-sickness.

'There is a way he might get home.'

The last of the meals served and the dishes washed, Daisy sat listening to Emma's account of her day. Her own anger had flared as she heard about Flynn striking Emma, but now she spoke more calmly.

'Brady...' She blushed prettily. 'He was telling me only yesterday that the priest up at the church on the hill ... the one whose spire be green ... well, he's travelling to Ireland this coming Thursday. I bet he'd take the lad.'

A priest! Emma's thoughts moved quickly. No one would rob or harm a lad travelling with a priest.

Reaching for her shawl, she gathered her son into it.

'Well now, Daisy Tully.' She mimicked a soft Irish brogue. 'Why don't we be after asking?'

'And what church do you attend?'

Holding the sleeping child close against her, Emma heaved an inward sigh. They had sat for almost an hour answering one question after another.

'I attended Chapel until ... until two years ago, but not any longer.'

Seated opposite her, his clerical robe reaching his boots, four-cornered hat on a nearby table, the priest fingered the crucifix hung on a gold chain about his neck.

''Tis as well,' he snapped. 'Chapel's not after being a true church. Heathen, that's what it is, heathen!'

The child stirring in Emma's arms, Daisy inched forward on her chair, her voice sharp with impatience. 'Father James, we just want to know, will you allow the boy to travel with you to Ireland?'

'All in good time!' The priest crossed one booted foot over the other. 'All in good time. There be questions yet needing an answer. Tell me, young woman, what religion was it yourself was brought up in?'

Daisy's exasperation flared. 'I don't see what this has to do with letting a lad travel home with you!'

'Maybe you don't,' he answered blandly. 'But you'll answer all the same, supposing you wish me to take him.'

For several moments Daisy stared incredulously at the man regarding her. Then she was on her feet, eyes afire.

'I'll tell you the religion I was fetched up in!' she flashed. 'The religion of the workhouse. There was little time there given over to prayer, other than the one asking you survive near starvation and the punishments that were meted out, and no time at all spent bowing and scraping before an altar. Hard work was the Gospel they preached and obedience the Creed; but then, there was no priest either, desiring to know all the ins and outs of a person's life before offering a helping hand to a child. That is your religion, Father. It's one you're welcome to and one I can well do without!'

Treating him to a scalding glance, Daisy threw her shawl about her. 'I'll wait for you outside, Emma. The air there might be laden with the smoke of foundries but I find it more to my taste than the stink of hypocrisy!'

'I'm sorry,' Emma apologised as Daisy stormed out. 'My friend is a little overwrought...'

'No need to say more.' The priest held up one hand. 'Servants of Our Holy Mother Church have long been subjected to the abuse of the Godless.'

'Daisy has a faith as strong as any.' Emma rose to her friend's defence. 'She has love in her heart for the Lord, though she was not taught it in church, and what is as important to Him, she also feels a love for her fellow men. I believe you have given me your answer, sir.' Her own childhood teaching strong in her she did not give him the title 'Father'. 'I thank you for your time. Goodnight to you!'

'But I have not given you my answer, not at all.' He leaned forward, touching her arm as she made to stand.

'Then perhaps you will give it to me now?' Emma replied coldly.

'The bruise on your cheek? That comes of defending the lad?'

'I tried to stop a man beating him, yes.'

'I see.' He withdrew his hand but his eyes stayed on her face. 'The passage to Ireland, it will take money. Does the lad have it?'

She had not thought of that. It would be a pittance he earned at the digging, and the little left from his keep he had sent home regularly every month. She had often given him a hot meal, finding some insignificant chore he could do in return, but even that amount saved had gone home with the rest.

'I'll agree to his travelling with me, but the Church cannot bear the cost.'

'It will not be required to.' Emma stood up. 'The money will be paid.'

'Then have the lad meet me at the Turk's Head at six this Thursday morning.' The priest rang for his housekeeper. 'Goodnight to you, Mrs Price.'

'*The money will be paid.*' Emma walked beside Daisy who carried the child, the words echoing over and over in her mind. Would she have enough? Shoving one hand deep into the pocket of her skirts, she felt the hard round shape of the coin sewn into the lining. She had sworn not to

368

part with it except to fling it into the face of the man who had shamed her.

But what was pride against a boy's happiness? Slowly she withdrew her hand. If that shilling was what it took, then she would give it.

But she would not abandon the promise she had made herself then. The promise to take revenge on Carver Felton!

Chapter Twenty-Five

The bequests Paul had made to members of his household had been paid and the same amount added from Carver's own pocket in recompense for the delay he had caused.

Now he sat on his huge bay stallion, reining it in as he looked down at the excavation for the new waterway, gliding like a great black snake across the heath. The Irish navigators he had brought in had done well, the work was almost finished.

'The loading sheds were put up yesterday.' The site manager pointed to a group of timber buildings set on a small rise opposite. 'It only remains to lay the rails to run the bogies to the basin.'

Carver glanced over to the huge depression dug into the earth. Filled with water it would berth several narrow boats at a time, some offloading materials while others loaded coal for transportation. The project had gone exactly as predicted, but he could take no joy in it now.

'When can the joining be made?' He forced himself to show an interest.

'Depends on the brickworks,' the manager replied, his glance following the wide slash in the earth. 'We need to use only blue bricks, they be the best for lining canals, Mr Felton, the strongest brick for engineering works. But to make them takes a special kind of marl, a very dense clay. They brings it all the way from Stafford and the magnesium oxides it contains turns it blue in the firing. That's why the bricks be known as Stafford Blues. But it takes time to get that clay to the brickworks at Wednesbury and they be waiting on a load now. Consequently we be waiting for bricks.'

'Hmm!' Carver watched the men below, some feeding mounds of wet clay to others working along the bed of the canal. 'Any other troubles?'

'Them navvies work well enough. They have spats between themselves but they get sorted out, mostly by one called Brogan. He seems to keep the others in line without reference to me, though I did give a man his tin a while ago. On Brogan's advice.'

'And what's that building over there, the wooden one set apart from the tents?' Carver asked, not interested in whether or not a man had been dismissed.

Bringing his glance to follow where Carver indicated the manager shaded his eyes against the glare of the sun.

'Part of it be a canteen. The navvies built it in their own time, and the one called Brogan paid for the wood out of his own pocket. I made sure he used none of the company's materials.'

'A canteen.' Carver ran his eye over the low one-storey hut, another smaller one joined at right angles to it. 'And which of them is the chef?'

The manager smiled dutifully at what he saw as his employer's attempt at humour. 'I don't know about chef, but the cooking's done by a couple of women. One of them was the cause of my sacking the man I told you of a minute since.'

'You sacked him over a woman? A common prostitute?'

'No, Mr Felton, sir, she be no prostitute. Or not as I knows of anyway. I don't allow none of them sort on the site.'

'Why else would a man risk getting himself dismissed?' Carver turned his attention back to the excavation.

'For smacking a woman in the mouth!' the manager answered bluntly. 'I don't allow that neither. No matter what the woman's trade, I won't have no workman of mine knock her about.'

'And the woman?' He was not really interested. Carver's question merely served to prolong the conversation.

'Seems she was protecting a young lad that was being beaten, and for that she was knocked down. One of the men came running for me but by the time I got over there Brogan had already beaten the other fellow half senseless.'

'This Brogan seems to take a lot on himself.'

'The others respect him, sir, and he's fair in his dealings with them.'

'And why was the lad being beaten?'

'He was homesick, so the men said. Not surprising seeing he could be no more than twelve or thirteen at most. His talk of his mother and being back in Ireland irritated Flynn and so he set about the lad.'

'Then sacking the man was the right course of action.' Carver turned the horse about.

372

'The woman paid the lad's passage back to Ireland, wouldn't take no help from the navvies neither. Said they needed all they had to send to their families.'

'Indeed.' His reply indicating an end to the conversation, Carver set his horse to a walk.

'Arr sir.' The manager's voice floated after him. 'She be a good, kind woman that Emma Price.'

Jerking so hard on the reins that the horse whinnied in protest, Carver wheeled around to face his site manager. His mouth so tight the words would hardly come, he snapped: 'What name did you say?'

'Why, Price, sir. Emma Price.'

He had not misheard. The blood cold in his veins, Carver sat immobile. It could be coincidence, a maiden name and a married name the same, the name was common in the area, it need not be her...

He gripped the reins convulsively as thoughts rioted in his mind. But then again, it could be; Paul had found her, his letter had said so. It had also stated she was married.

The last word sounded like a bell in his brain.

Emma Price was married, it would do him no good to see her now. He should leave. Now.

Touching a heel to his mount he set it to a canter, his eyes fixed on the low canteen hut.

Having almost reached it, he heard a woman's laughter, the happy sound accompanied by the delighted squeals of a child.

Reining to a halt he watched as they tumbled together in a heap. The hair was long and beautiful but it was the wrong colour, it was not the colour he saw in his dreams, that delicate gold-brushed silver falling softly about a lovely face...

'I beg your pardon.' He spoke quietly, not wishing to alarm the girl whose eyes were already widening as she stared up at him. 'Can you tell me where I might find Emma Price?'

'Who is it?' The child struggled free of the skirts she had spread about it. 'Who is it, Aunt Daisy?'

His glance falling on the child as the woman grasped its shoulders, Carver sat stunned. Eyes dark as midnight, hair black as a raven's wing and marked with a narrow silver streak.

'*...the remainder of my estate, in its entirely, I leave to my brother's son...*'

Paul's words hammered in Carver's heart.

He was looking at his own child!

'Come along, you two, it's time...'

At the door of the hut Emma's face drained of colour. Suddenly she was back in Felton Wood, staring terrified into ice cold eyes as a tall man slid from his horse.

'*...you will know me every bit as well as you know my brother, maybe even a little better...*'

Words she heard in her every nightmare since rang deafeningly in her brain.

'No!' Emma's hand flew to her mouth and the dread in her eyes was echoed in Carver's heart as he glimpsed the golden ring on her finger. She was another man's wife, though her name remained the same. Another man's wife ... but the child was his.

Holding the boy's hand protectively, Daisy

went to Emma's side. 'Will I fetch Liam?'

Forcing his mind to function clearly, his eyes still on Emma, Carver said quietly, 'There will be no need for that, I mean you no harm. May I dismount?'

Voice locked in her throat, Emma nodded dumbly.

'I wish to speak with you, Mrs Price.'

Daisy's quick ears caught the title but not by a single flicker did her eyes tell him he was wrong. Still holding the boy's hand, she looked at the man who was his image.

'If you have anything to say, mister, then it be best said indoors, not out here where half the world can hear.'

'A sensible idea, Miss…?'

'Tully,' she snapped. 'Daisy Tully.'

'Perhaps you would lead the way, Miss Tully?'

'Can we go outside again, Aunt Daisy?'

'Later Paul,' Daisy answered as the child pulled his hand free.

Carver's glance flashed to the boy. Those eyes, the hair, the set of the features, they were a replica of his own, yet she had named him Paul. A sudden dart of pain shot through him as the silent questions formed. Had she and Paul been lovers? Could the child's looks be merely a prank of nature?

Ignoring the ritual of offering tea, Daisy turned to Emma who had dropped, trembling, into a chair.

'I'll take Paul into the bedroom then I'll be back.'

'No. He would be better outside in the air.

Would you go with him, please, Daisy?'

'If you be sure.' She glared at the dark man, his eyes still fixed on the boy. 'But I won't be far from the door.'

'I can do it myself. Watch, Aunt Daisy.'

Excited at the prospect of another game the child moved forward, one hand extended in front of him, feeling each object as he made for the door.

A look of disbelief on his face, Carver watched him go then, turning back to Emma, his eyes asked the question.

'Yes,' she answered. 'Paul is blind.'

'You named him Paul.' Carver spoke first. 'But he is not Paul's son, is he? He's mine!'

Breathless, she made no reply.

'He is my child, why was I not told?'

The tone of his voice chasing away the shock of seeing him, Emma drew in a sharp breath.

'Why? Why tell you … so you could laugh? The Doe Bank wench who dared to love a Felton.'

'It would not have been that way.'

Her courage returning, Emma stared at the man standing over her. He had stood over her in the same way in the woods as he'd prepared to take her virginity, but this time it was something infinitely more precious for which she must fight.

'Wouldn't it?' Her trembling over, Emma's voice was steady. 'If one Felton could not be seen to have anything to do with a pit bank girl, why should the other be keen to acknowledge her child?'

'Emma…'

'Mrs Price … my name is Mrs Price!'

It was like a slap to his face and he winced at its sting. 'I beg your pardon, but whatever *your* name, the boy's is Felton.'

'No!' Emma felt the tingle of returning fear.

'He is my son!'

'He is not your son!' She was on her feet. 'You have no right to him. You sold that right in Felton Wood – sold it for a shilling!'

Carver's face blanched and the light seemed to die from his eyes but his voice was firm.

'What was done that night cannot be undone, but the boy shall not be made to suffer for it.'

'Will he *suffer?* Does being with his mother cause a child to suffer?'

'Being without a father does.'

Her fear increasing, Emma recognised the determined tone of that voice, the tight set of the mouth. Not yet three years old, her son displayed the same characteristics when he wanted something denied him. Some of her fear reflected in her voice, she answered, 'Paul has a father.'

At his sides, Carver's hands clenched.

'He has a *stepfather.*'

'That is all he needs.'

'But it is not all *I* need...'

He said it softly but Emma sensed that beneath the softness an iron fist was prepared to strike.

'...I need my son and I intend to have him.'

'Why?' Emma's cry was bitter. 'Where is the logic, the purpose in that? You can have other children.'

'It is regrettable but virtually certain: you will never father a child.'

Sharp and clear the words returned to him.

377

There would be no other son for Carver Felton.

'So can you,' he answered. 'Why deny this one what is his by right? As for logic and purpose, it is logical for a man to want to pass his fortune to his son. That is my purpose for being here. I acknowledge my son and I will have him.'

'It was him, wasn't it?' asked Daisy, perched beside Emma where she sat watching the sleeping child. 'That was Paul's father.'

'Yes.' It was no more than a whisper.

'What did he want?'

'Paul.' Emma's voice shook. 'He wanted Paul.'

Daisy did not need to ask if Emma had agreed. The fact that she had not moved from the child's side since the man had ridden away was answer enough.

'He can't prove that Paul be his.'

'Look at him, Daisy. They're the image of each other. What other proof is necessary?'

'Looks ain't everything!'

'They leave little room for doubt and what they do leave could be made up for in money. Carver has that in plenty and equally as much influence. He would have no difficulty in claiming my child.'

'But you be his mother, surely that gives you the right to keep him?'

'No, it does not.' Emma shook her head. 'A child is like any other possession: the man has prior claim. The law would give Paul to him and there would be nothing I could do about it.'

'We could leave.' Catching Emma's hands, Daisy gave them a shake. 'We could leave now,

378

tonight. Liam and Brady have both asked us to go with them to Ireland. The boy would be safe there.'

Seeing the look in her friend's eyes, Emma tried to smile.

'We would never get that far. Think of it, Daisy. Liam and Brady suddenly give up a job they travelled so far to get, you and I disappear overnight. Anyone would be a fool not to see the connection, and that man is no fool.'

'Emma.' Daisy's hands tightened on hers. 'Do you really think he wants the baby?'

'Yes, I do.'

'But why?' Anger whitening her lips, Daisy stood up and went to stand beside the cot Liam had made. 'He ain't no old man, he can have other children, so why come for Paul? And why now? It's been almost three years. Why only now admit that he's the father?'

Looking down at her hand, Emma twisted the plain gold band. 'He didn't know before today.'

Across the cot, Daisy's eyes became soft with pity. 'What you told the Hollingtons and me ... about you being raped ... it was true?'

'Yes.' She nodded. 'It was true.'

'Then you hadn't never ... you know what ... you hadn't never done that before, not with any man?'

'Never before, not with any man, and never since.' Then, the quiet breathing of her son the only other sound in the room, Emma told the whole of her story.

'Jerusha said my child would bear his father's name,' she finished, 'that was the reason I chose to call him Paul Price. I had never known a prediction of Jerusha's not to come about but I thought that by giving him that name I'd avoided it, but it seems I was wrong.'

'We have to do something!' Daisy saw the tears that formed in Emma's eyes. 'We can't just let him take Paul.'

They had to do something. Still sleepless as dawn rolled back the tides of night, Emma turned her head to look at her son. But what? There was nowhere she could go that Carver Felton could not reach her, could not snatch back the child he had so ruthlessly planted within her.

He wanted to pass the business to his son, but why take hers for that? Why take a blind child? A pit bank girl was not good enough to bear the Felton name, so why should her child be? He could marry any woman in the county and produce himself an heir. Why raise a bastard?

Over and over the questions tumbled in her mind but always Carver Felton's departing words prevailed.

'I acknowledge my son and I will have him.'

'Why?' Closing her eyes, she sobbed quietly, 'Why?'

But the black eyes that stared back were cold and hard and the tight lips made no answer.

Chapter Twenty-Six

'The navigation will soon be finished, and work here will be over.'

'What will you do?' Emma looked at the man sitting beside her on the gentle slope that rose from the side of the cutting that would be the new canal.

Plucking a blade of coarse grass, Liam twisted it between his fingers. 'Some of the men are talking of being away back home, to Ireland.'

'Daisy told me that Brady's talked of the same thing.'

Liam nodded. 'He has that.'

Daisy had looked so unhappy. Emma remembered the night a week ago when she and the girl had talked of that very thing. That she was in love with the handsome Irish man was written plain in her eyes, as was something else. She had not needed to explain either emotion, Emma could read them for herself. Daisy loved them both. Not to go with Brady would break her heart, yet to leave Emma would do the same.

'Will he go back?' She asked it softly, almost hoping Liam would not answer.

The flimsy stalk twirling between his fingers, Liam stared out across the heath. 'Only the little people could be after saying. Brady Malone is caught among the rocks. He is in love with Daisy. To leave her behind will be a hard road to travel, but for him it will be no easier to leave the shores of Ireland for good. It is a hard choice he must be making.'

Was *he* trying to make the same choice? Glancing sideways at Liam's strong profile she felt a pang of guilt. Was he trying to decide which would be the hardest thing, to leave her or abandon his home forever?

He loved her. He had not only told her so, he'd made it plain in a thousand little ways; and he loved Paul, her son would have a father.

'He has a stepfather!'

The words leaped to her mind, throwing themselves into her consciousness with the same force Carver Felton had thrown them.

Carver Felton! Emma felt her blood quicken. He was the reason she'd refused to accept Liam's love, it was he who'd deterred her from telling this caring, gentle man she would marry him and go with him to Ireland. But was it truly fear of Carver's following after her, of trying to take her son that held her, or was it her own vow, was it her need for revenge?

'Hard the choice will be.' Liam flicked away the blade of grass, watching it twist and turn. 'But it will need the making of it before many weeks be past. Come the autumn the joining will be made and that great cut in the earth will be filled with water. When that day comes, the men of Ireland must move on.'

Will you go too, go with Brady and the others? she wanted to ask, felt the words on the tip of her tongue, but there they stayed. She was afraid of what his answer would be. She enjoyed this man's company, felt safe with him, and he had been so very good to her. But did she love him? The feelings Liam Brogan aroused in her were not the same as she had felt for Paul Felton. Those feelings had been ... but that had been a lifetime ago. Her world had been so different then, so full of joy and promise. But that joy had long died, as her family had died, leaving her with only the sad prospect of vengeance.

'Daisy must go with Brady.' She pushed the gloomy thoughts away. 'She loves him.'

'Would you go, Emma?' Liam did not look at her. 'Could you leave someone you loved? The girl loves you, Emma. You are the rocks barring her path.'

'That's unfair, Liam! I would never hold Daisy back.'

'Unfair it may sound, but it's true just the same. The girl will give Brady no answer for fear of losing you.' He turned to her, a quick, sharp movement, his eyes meeting hers. 'What is the fear that will not let you give an answer? What is it holds you so firmly you cannot say the words?'

Taking her hands in his, he gave a half smile, one that masked the pain in his eyes but could not hide that in his heart.

'I love you, Emma,' he said gently. 'Love you and want to marry you. Come with me to Ireland. You'll be happy there, I promise you, no cloud will touch your life.'

No cloud would touch her life. Lying in her bed that night, Emma remembered the pleading in Liam's eyes, the tenderness of his touch as he had taken her in his arms, the gentleness of his mouth as he had kissed her.

At the window shafts of silver moonlight streamed in among the shadows. Like his hair … hair that was black as midnight except for those streaks of silver.

She turned her head on the pillow but as she closed her eyes that arrogant face stared back at her from the darkness.

In Ireland no cloud would touch her life, but the shadow of Carver Felton would forever hang over it.

'You must go with Brady.' Emma hitched a wicker basket, heavy with meat, higher on her hip. 'You can't sacrifice your happiness and his, I won't let you.'

'I ain't going without you!' Daisy hitched her own basket. 'You can't manage on your own. It takes two of us to carry the meat from the abattoir, two of us to cook the number of meals we make in a day.'

Emma laughed, a clear ringing sound that echoed across the heath. 'I'm not completely useless, Daisy Tully.'

'No.' Daisy smiled. 'No, you ain't. But that don't mean you could manage alone neither, there be too much for one woman to do.'

'Now, maybe. But in a few weeks the work at Plovers Croft will be finished. There will be no more men to cook for. The navigators will leave and so must we.'

'What of the men it will take to work the canal? What of the boatmen?'

'You know they'll have their own wives to cook

for them, there'll be no call for our little canteen.'

Daisy set her mouth adamantly. 'So! We'll go some other place.'

'You will go wherever Brady goes,' Emma replied just as adamantly. 'You belong together, you know that as well as I do. Your marrying him will not break our friendship.'

'But you, Emma, what will you do? You'll be alone.'

'No, Daisy,' she answered. 'I will not be alone.'

'Emma! You mean, you'll be marrying Liam and coming with us to Ireland?'

Swapping the basket from one hip to the other, Emma smiled, but as her gaze travelled over the black scar of the canal excavation she made no answer.

'Eh, Emma, I'm that glad...'

The rest trailed away, drowned beneath the shout of a figure running over the heath towards them, skirts flapping against her legs.

'Mary?' Daisy shaded her eyes against the morning sun. 'That be Mary Foster.'

It was Mary. Emma felt her heart lift to her mouth. It was the woman paid to mind Paul while they were at the abattoir. But where was he? Where was her son? Lowering her basket to the ground, Emma began to run.

'I said for him to wait 'til you got back...'

Emma had searched the whole of the long hut, her bedroom and even Daisy's. Now, as the two women came in, she stared at Mary.

'I said he would have to ask you – I told him, Mrs Price – but he pushed me aside, said he had come for his son.' The woman sobbed noisily. 'I knew it were the lad's father ... well, it were easy to tell what with the hair, them same streaks an' all, but still I told him he couldn't take Paul without your say so.'

'Them same streaks an' all!' It could only be Carver. Her mouth quivering, limbs trembling with fear, Emma forced herself to speak.

'The man who came here, the one who took my son, did he give his name?'

'Arr Missis Price, he did.' The woman nodded. 'Said he was Carver Felton.'

Waiting to hear no more, Emma picked up her skirts and went running from the hut.

'Emma, why did you not send for me?'

His arm supporting her, Liam led her slowly back towards Plovers Croft.

'I ... I wanted my son, I had to get him back. I thought of nothing else.'

Of course, he would have expected no less of her than to go after the child, but alone ... who knew what might have happened?

His arm tightening at the thought, Liam said gently, 'You did what any mother would do.'

'But I did not find him.' Grief suddenly too much to bear, Emma sagged against the arm that supported her. 'I did not find Paul, they said he was not at Felton Hall, so where is he? Oh, God, Liam! Where is my son?'

Drawing her into the circle of his arms, he held her as wave after wave of sobs shuddered through her.

'We will find him, Emma,' he murmured, 'we

will get him back.'

They were words meant to soothe, but in his heart he knew they were empty. The father of Emma's child had taken what the law saw as his, and there was no way of getting Paul back.

Almost carrying her, every sob a pain that lanced through him, Liam helped her back to the hut.

'Where do you think Felton took the boy?'

Emma at last sleeping in her room, Daisy poured tea for herself and Liam.

'He could have gone anywhere.' Liam took the cup she offered. 'There's no telling.'

'But did them up at the Hall tell her nothing?'

'She was so upset when I caught up with her, I had a job to make sense of what she said. But it seems the butler told her the master had left that morning and was not expected to return for some time.'

'Oh, Lord!' Daisy set down her cup heavily. 'Poor Emma, it will drive her out of her mid. Did this … this butler not say where Felton had gone?'

'No, but then seeing the state Emma was in, the man would be weak in the head if he did not realise something unpleasant had taken place. For the sake of his position he no doubt decided least said, the safer he would be. On the other hand, he might have received specific instructions to say no more than he did.'

'But was Paul taken to Felton Hall?'

Liam shook his head. 'So far as I can gather, Felton left in the morning and did not return. If that is so then the boy was not taken to that house.'

'Then where *has* he been taken?'

'I don't know, Daisy.' Liam drew a long, slow breath. 'I just don't know.'

Dawn had clothed the sky in pink and grey when Emma woke. Her head ached and for several moments her mind refused to focus. But when the last filament of dreams were finally snatched away the nightmare remained.

Carver had taken her son!

Dressing slowly, every movement a chore for her leaden limbs, her eyes constantly on the empty cot, she sank heavily to the bed.

Carver Felton had taken her son!

Forcing her mind to work she went over the past hours. He had come while she was away buying meat. He had demanded Mary hand over the child to him, and when the woman hesitated had grabbed the boy and ridden away.

But he had not returned to Felton Hall. That was what the manservant had told her, and remembering the pity on his face she believed it to be true.

'He lifted the lad afore 'im in the saddle and rode off.'

Those were Mary's words as she'd pointed.

Emma turned, her glance going to the window now filled with the light of day.

But she had not pointed towards Felton Hall. Hands clenched together, Emma stared deep in thought. Mary had pointed in the opposite direction, pointed towards the town.

Carver had taken her son to Wednesbury. Would they still be there, in one of the hotels?

Throwing her shawl about her head, Emma ran out into the sunlight.

He had not come to the White Horse. The man at the door brushed Emma aside. The likes of her were not to be seen hanging about this establishment. But the anguish in her face had softened him and he had relented. No man with a child had come to this hotel, he said.

She had met with the same at the George and then at the Dartmouth. Neither hotel had received a man travelling alone with a small child.

But he had come this way. Emma stood outside the hotel. She had tried each place she knew of, except the smaller inns. Would Carver Felton choose one of them?

'I 'eard you asking questions, you lost something?' A woman of questionable age, rouge like ripe tomatoes stuck to her cheeks pulled a tasselled shawl around her shoulders.

Her mind in a turmoil, Emma looked vaguely into the painted face.

'Won't get nothing from him 'cept a kick in the arse!' The hennaed head nodded in the direction of the doorman watching them. 'But could be I can 'elp ... for a price.'

'I ... I don't have any money.'

'You 'aving me on?' The painted mouth tightened.

'No, really.' Emma felt the tears she could no longer hold spill on to her cheeks. 'I didn't think ... I just ran out to find...'

'Find!' Bloodshot eyes quickening with interest, the woman took a step closer. 'What was you expecting to find? The money some fancy city bloke left without paying?'

The inference behind the snort that followed those words was lost on Emma. She shook her head. 'My son,' she sobbed. 'I ran out to find my son, I … I did not think to bring any money.'

'Get along, you two!'

Ignoring the shout from the doorman, the woman took Emma's arm. 'You say you be looking for your son? He wouldn't bring a street woman 'ere, not to a place like this.' She glanced at Emma's patched skirts and threadbare shawl. 'This takes money.'

'You don't understand.' Emma dashed the tears from her cheeks. 'He's just a little boy.'

'A young 'un!' The woman's voice hardened. 'Some dirty bugger took off with a young 'un? Ain't the first I've 'eard of. Wenches or lads, makes no difference, they picks 'em off the street and that be the last anybody sees of 'em. I reckon it be men from Brummagem be taking 'em. Some men like it with kids, and the younger they be, the more they likes it. Filthy bloody perverts!' She spat on the pavement. 'Should be bloody casterated, the lot of 'em!'

Birmingham, the woman had said Birmingham. Perhaps Carver had taken her child there? For a moment Emma's heart lifted. But she had never been there herself. Where would she look, how would she find her way?

'How old be your lad?' The woman gestured with two fingers as the doorman shouted again.

'Almost three,' Emma said softly.

'Three!' The bloodshot eyes widened. 'Great God Almighty, the dirty bleeders! It be worse than I thought.'

'Please.' Emma touched the hand that held her arm. 'How do I get to Birmingham?'

'You don't. Least not without money you don't. 'Sides, if your lad be gone to that city you won't never find him. It has more dive holes than a rabbit warren. The bloke that took him could 'ave sold him along the line by this time.'

None of this making sense to Emma, she shook the woman's hand. 'He wouldn't leave my baby. The man was his father.'

'I've warned you two, now get along before I send for a constable.'

The woman glanced behind her. 'You can send for Father Christmas if you like, you sour-faced cow, but he won't give you what you'd like Nancy Clark to give you!'

Turning her back on the doorman the woman looked more closely at Emma. 'Say, does this babby 'ave black hair with a lighter streak across the top?' Then, as Emma nodded, she went on. 'And the man the same but with two streaks of silver going back from his forehead?'

Emma nodded.

Releasing her hold, the woman stepped back, the glance that ran over Emma's skirts and shawl blatantly disparaging. 'I seen 'em yesterday but that bloke weren't no half a dollar a day coal miner, he were dressed like a gent. But that's it, ain't it? He's buggered the kid off to get rid of the evidence!'

'I have tried all the hotels I know of. None of

the people I spoke to saw them.'

'Huh!' the woman snorted again. 'How many of them would tell you if they 'ad? Have you tried the Great Western alongside the railway station?'

Seeing from Emma's face that she had not, the woman continued, 'If they say he ain't there then ask at the station for Ernie Blount. Tell him Nancy sent you. He be a friend of mine, quite a good friend if you takes my meaning. If that man took a train from the station then Ernie will know.' Raising her arm the woman pointed. 'Turn right at the first corner, that be Chapel Street, it brings you on to the Portway. Follow the road straight 'till you gets to Great Western Street, the station be at the end.'

'I'm not telling you again...'

The woman turned the irate doorman as Emma ran the way she had pointed. 'Keep your arse in your trousers!' She spread both arms wide, pushing her breasts forward. 'Who knows? If you minds your manners I might pull your old dodger for you.' She grinned as she drew the shawl closed again. 'Then again, pigs don't fly, do they?'

Flourishing the tasselled shawl she walked a few yards along the street then flounced around to face him. 'On second thoughts,' she called, 'I'd rather pull the pig's tail!'

'Took a train yesterday, the midday for Birmingham.'

Emma walked slowly across the heath. Learning nothing from the hotel she had sought out Ernie Blount. He had been helpful but what he'd

392

said had killed any hope left in her.

'...but I reckon he had little intention of staying there, seeing as he enquired of the train for London.'

She had gasped at that. London! It might as well be the other end of the earth.

'Got no luggage with him,' Ernie had gone on, despite her cry. 'But there were boxes brought here to the station in time for the first train this morning.'

'Did they have an address?'

'Ar wench.' He had looked into eyes that pleaded to be told. 'Ar they did, but weren't no place I knows of. Had some fancy foreign name, one I couldn't read. Not proper like. But the last word I could make out. It said Switzerland.'

Switzerland? She knew from the atlas her father had sometimes allowed Carrie and herself to look at that it was a country of high mountains, and that to reach it meant crossing the breadth of France.

Even had she the money to get there she might never find them. But she had no money to speak of. What she had saved from cooking she had given to that young lad to pay his fare back to Ireland.

Now her son was gone. She might never see him again!

Blinded by tears, Emma stumbled on towards Plovers Croft.

Carver Felton had raped her and left her with child. A child he had now taken back.

Chapter Twenty-Seven

'You had me scared half to death, I couldn't think where you might have gone to. Eh, Emma, don't do that again. Don't get going off without telling me.'

'I had to look for him, Daisy.' Emma stared at the cup handed to her but did not touch it.

'I know you did, but I'd have come with you. Tomorrow we'll both...'

'It won't do any good.' Emma's voice trembled. 'Tomorrow or any other day, we'll not find Paul.'

Sobbing, she related all that had happened that morning. When she reached the end of her tale, Daisy sat silent for several minutes.

Outside the shouts of men going about the business of building the new waterway sounded louder than usual, their calls and laughter invading the silence that pressed in on the two women.

'Switzerland!' Daisy said at last, the word feeling strange on her tongue. 'I ain't never heard of no such place. Is it far away?'

'Yes, Daisy. It is. Too far for me to follow. I suppose that's why Carver chose to go there.'

'But he can't stop there forever, he has to come home to Felton Hall sometime; that business he thinks so much of will bring him back, supposing nothing else can.'

What Daisy said made sense. Emma stared at

her cup, seeing nothing. Carver would return eventually, but that did not mean he would bring her son with him.

'We can only wait, be here when he does come back. We will wait together.' Daisy rested a hand on her friend's shoulder. 'Like I told that priest, I was brought up without much religion but I reckon the Lord will listen when we pray.'

Had He listened to Carrie? Listened when another frightened child had called to Him? Emma could not stem the tide of bitterness within her. What use was prayer to a God who was deaf? He would no more help her than He had helped her sister.

Feeling the shuddering sobs, knowing it best to let Emma cry out her fear and sorrow, Daisy fetched bacon and sausages from the cool box. Work was one way of holding her friend together; beside which the navvies would be expecting their hot sandwich breakfast.

Setting the huge cast iron frying pan on the stove, she turned as Liam came through the door, shaking her head as she met his glance.

'I've set wood for the fire out along the back.' He gave a quick look at Emma, her face turned from him as she wiped away the tears, then back to Daisy. 'Is there anything else I can be after doing?'

'No, I don't think there is, not right now.'

'There's no word?'

Placing strips of bacon in the pan, Daisy gave another shake of her head.

'Then I will go into the town, might be he took the child that way. If so somebody must have seen them.'

'She's been there already.' Daisy poked the bacon with a fork. 'The swine was there all right and he was seen along of the child, but it seems he left almost afore he got there; it certainly wasn't his intention to stay in Wednesbury.'

'Emma.' Dropping to his haunches beside her chair, Liam took her hands in his. 'Emma, tell me, where was he seen?'

Sobs causing her voice to break, she told him of the street woman and the porter at the station.

'Switzerland!' He echoed her last word as Daisy had.

'Emma says that place be a fair way off, and be all mountains and such. Not that I've ever seen a mountain.'

'It is a fair way off, Daisy,' Liam answered, his eyes still on Emma. 'But 'tis not so far a man cannot be found. Where one has gone, another may follow.'

'That would take money.' Drawing her hands from his, Emma wiped her eyes. 'Far more than I have.'

Placing the strips of fried bacon on a plate, Daisy set to refilling the pan. 'Emma gave all her money away, kept only enough to buy what were needed for a day's cooking. And there ain't so much profit made from that as would pay her fare to Birmingham!'

'Gave her money away?' Liam stood up, his brown eyes filled with question. 'But why? And to whom?'

'Daisy!' Emma glanced up quickly.

'I know, I know!' Daisy shrugged. 'I said as I would keep it secret, but it be out now so you might as well tell him the all of it.'

Twisting a damp handkerchief between her fingers, Emma began falteringly. 'I ... we ... Daisy and I went to see the priest of St Mary's church, the one with the green spire...'

'You went to see the father?'

Nodding, Emma went on. 'We'd heard he was going to Ireland so we went to ask would he let the boy that was beaten travel with him.'

'And he agreed?'

'Ar!' Daisy snorted. 'After asking a thousand questions.'

'Sure and that sounds familiar, he would have made Grand Inquisitor so he would.'

'Well I don't know what that be neither, but if it be one poked his nose where it shouldn't be then that priest would take top prize! Anyway, he only agreed so long as the lad paid his own fare.'

Understanding spreading across his face, Liam looked at Emma. 'But the lad did not have the kind of money would take him home to Ireland, so you gave him the rest.'

Tending bacon, Daisy waited for Emma to reply, then when the silence seemed set to last she looked over at her friend, her voice gentle with affection.

'No, Emma did not give him the rest she gave him the lot, every penny. Said what the lad had earned should go to his mother.'

'But why, Emma?' Liam's voice was as tender as Daisy's had been. 'Why did you not tell me? I would have seen the lad had his money.'

'And deprive your mother of what would have been sent to her?' Emma smiled through tears.

'My own mother would have called that robbing Peter to pay Paul. I saw no reason for my needing the money, while that boy had every reason.'

'And now you have reason and no money!'

'You did it too, Daisy.' Emma met the gentle admonition. 'You gave him your money too.'

'Yes, well,' Daisy turned back to her cooking, 'I had no call for it either.'

'What's done can't be undone, but I have...'

'No, Liam,' Emma interrupted sharply. 'I have enough guilt in my heart at leaving Paul. I could not bear the extra of knowing I had taken money that was meant for your family. Please Liam.' She rose to her feet. 'Try to understand. I recognise your desire to help and I appreciate it, but I will not take your money or any other man's here when you have worked so hard for it.'

Taking her hands, he looked deep into her eyes, his voice no more than a whisper. 'My money is yours, Emma, just as my life is yours. Their only value lies in helping you.'

It had been the hardest month of her life. Every day had been given over to the hope she might be reunited with her son, every night to praying for a miracle that did not come. Only once before in her life, the night her family had died, had she felt so utterly heartsick.

Emma dried her hands and face on the scrap of snow white huckaback placed beside the jug and bowl in her bedroom.

Daisy had been a tower of strength, holding her together when grief threatened to pull her apart. And Liam ... how could she describe what he had been to her, his kindness, his gentleness and love? It was there in every look he gave her, in every touch of his hand, but it was a love he did not press upon her.

Pulling her calico nightgown over her head, she tied the narrow straps across her breasts. She should give Liam an answer, she would find no man more caring.

Looking down at her left hand, she twisted the ring Jerusha had given her. It had kept her free from unwanted attention, served the purpose it was meant to, but it should be exchanged for one of her own. She should give Liam an answer, but how could she? How could she hope for happiness without her child?

Crossing to the narrow wooden cot set opposite her own bed, she stroked her fingers across the pillow.

How had she lived? How had she survived this heartbreak? And how much longer could she go on?

'Oh, Lord,' she whispered into the silence. 'Give me back my baby ... give me back my son.'

'Eh, thank goodness that be over.' Daisy set the last dried plate in its place. 'I'll make us both a nice cup of tea afore I set that pork to roasting for the evening meals.'

Picking up the kettle, she carried it outside to the stand-pipe set up for the use of the camp. Holding it beneath the gush of water she glanced up at the sound of carriage wheels on the road behind the hut.

'Does a Mrs Price live hereabouts?'

Daisy stared at the man calling to her. Smart in dark livery, he held the reins of two satin black horses harnessed to a well-polished carriage.

'Does a Mrs Price live hereabouts?'

The repeat of the question driving away her initial surprise, Daisy straightened, one hand dripping water.

'Ar!' Her voice was hard and defensive. Dressed as he was he could only be from Felton Hall and that would bode no good. 'Mrs Price do live here.'

Alighting from the carriage, the young man looped the reins over a nearby gorse bush.

'Be you her?'

'No,' Daisy snapped, hostility cold and sharp in her answer.

Glancing towards the navvies, several of whom were looking in his direction, he reached into an inner pocket.

'Then would you give her this, please? And tell her I have instructions to wait for an answer.'

Drawing out an envelope, he placed it in Daisy's dry hand before stepping back to the carriage.

'Some chap in a carriage and a fancy suit...'

Deep in her own thoughts, lost in a maze of misery, Emma did not hear.

Putting the kettle on the stove, Daisy placed the envelope between her teeth while she dried her hands on her apron.

'He said to give you this.' She touched Emma's shoulder. 'Didn't say where he was from or who sent it, but he's to wait for a reply.'

Eyes empty of interest looked up.

'I can tell him to sod off if you don't want to be moithered. Tell him to take his envelope back to the one who sent it.'

'Envelope?' Still half a world away, Emma glanced at the pristine paper.

'I'll tell him you ain't to be bothered.' Daisy turned for the door.

'I ... I'm sorry, Daisy.' Emma's glance followed the other woman. 'I was not listening. What did you say?'

Daisy turned back. Time was having no effect on Emma, it was not having the healing folk were so fond of saying it would. In fact, she seemed more heartbroken with every passing day.

'I said, some chap in a fancy suit brought this for you.' She tried to keep the pity from her voice, tried to sound matter-of-fact. Emma needed no more added to her sorrow. Pity would only bring on the tears that dwelt just below the surface. 'He be waiting of an answer and I can give him that all right!'

Still uncomprehending, Emma looked again at the envelope flapping up and down in Daisy's hand.

'That is for me?'

'That's what he said, but if you won't want it...'

'I don't know anyone who would write to me.'

'Don't take no effort to find out who it be but judging by that man's get up and the carriage he be driving, I'd say this letter could only have come from Felton Hall.'

It wasn't such a long shot, but as light returned to her friend's eyes Daisy felt a pang of fear. What if it *were* from Felton Hall, from *him?* What if the letter was to tell Emma she had no claim to her child, that she would never see him again? She had wanted only to help Emma, to bring her up from the pit that was slowly swallowing her, but if her sudden fears had substance then she would have driven her further down in it, perhaps too far ever to surface again.

The thought frightening her, Daisy held the envelope behind her back. 'It be a mistake, the man must have brought it to the wrong place. I'll tell him to go.'

'No.' Emma reached out one hand, the gesture almost lifeless. 'I should at least look at it.'

'But it might not be for you, he didn't seem none too sure.' It was a lie but fear drove Daisy to say it.

'Then we will return it.'

Taking the letter from a reluctant Daisy, Emma looked at it. Her name was written boldly in a strong, elegant copperplate hand. Slowly tearing open the envelope, she withdrew a single sheet of folded paper. The same confident hand, black lettering flowing over white paper, stared up at her.

Glancing once at Daisy, who stood with hands clasped over her apron, worry as to what the letter might hold clear in her eyes, Emma began to read.

My dear Mrs Price,
I must first assure you that the child is well. I realise the past weeks have caused you great suffering, and for that I apologise. However, if you will do me the

kindness of coming to Beaufort House, I will give you the reason for my action in taking him away.
Carver Felton

The child! Emma stared at the words. Carver referred to him as the child. Not her son, not his, but *the child*. It was so cold, almost businesslike. He had dealt with her baby the way he had dealt with her. He had raped her then turned his back on her, one more hurdle to be cast from his path. Now the son of that rape was to be removed also; no hint of scandal must malign the name of Felton, no child born out of wedlock must become known to his associates. Emma Price and her bastard son must remain a shadow of the past.

'Emma, be you all right?' Daisy watched the pallor of weeks become even paler. 'Be ... be it bad news?'

'It ... it says...' She held out the letter to Daisy.

'I don't be no hand at reading, 'specially not fancy writing such as that.'

Hands shaking, voice breaking on a sob, Emma read the letter aloud.

'But that be good news.' Relief spreading a smile over her mouth, Daisy felt the tension drain from her. 'It says Paul is well and that he will explain the taking of him.'

Desolation in her eyes, Emma looked up from the letter. 'Yes, it says Paul is well and that Carver's taking him will be explained. But it does not say my baby will be returned to me.'

'You already be three parts along the way to meeting trouble!' Daisy took the letter, returning it to its envelope. 'Less you go to this Beaufort House you won't know what be the intention.'

Her face revealing the fear and pain that throbbed through her every vein, Emma looked at her friend.

'What if Carver should have Paul shut away somewhere? I could not live with that, Daisy, I could not live...'

'Why should he do that?' Stepping to her side, Daisy closed her arms about Emma's trembling shoulders. 'Didn't you tell me yourself the words he used, "I acknowledge my son." Does that sound as if he wants Paul locked away?'

A month ago. Just four weeks. But to her it had been a thousand lifetimes. Her shawl pulled tight against tremors of fear and apprehension, Emma stared unseeing through the window of the carriage. She had suffered the torment of hell and saw no way open for her to end it. How much more a child snatched from his mother? A little blind boy surrounded by voices he did not recognise, hands whose touch he did not know. How many times had he called for her, how many times had he cried himself to sleep?

Pressing her knuckles against her mouth, she stifled the sobs she could not stop.

And Carver Felton? The haughty impassive features rose before her inner vision as they did so often in the dark reaches of the night. He would not have cuddled the child, held him in his arms, talked to him softly until the fear was gone. Paul was his son but Carver did not love him, did not care that a little boy might be terrified. Had he any feeling at all for Paul, he would never have taken him from her.

'Beaufort House, Mrs Price.'

Bands of misery still tight about her mind, Emma looked blankly at the man who had delivered the letter and stood now beside the open carriage door.

'What?'

'Beaufort House.' He smiled sympathetically, handing her down from the carriage.

'Beaufort House?' She glanced at the mellow red brick house quoined with limestone weather and time had yellowed. 'But I thought ... were we not going to Felton Hall?'

'My instructions was to bring you here, after I had delivered the letter.'

'Of course. I ... I'm sorry. I was thinking of other things, forgive me.'

'Not to worry, Mrs Price, I sometimes gets lost in a daydream meself. Helps to make a hard time light.'

'Thank you.' Emma walked slowly up the steps that fronted the large house. Daydreams! She would need all of hers in the future.

'The job will be finished soon, a month at most, and I'll have to be moving on. It's a decision you have to be after making Daisy, do you come or do you stay?'

Daisy stared towards the shadowed tents. Already one or two had disappeared. Soon there would be none, and when the last was struck then Brady too would leave. Inside her chest her heart twisted painfully. She loved Brady and wanted to be his wife, to go with him wherever he went. But she loved Emma too. How could she choose? How could she give up either of the two people who mattered most in her world?

'How can I?' She returned to him, eyes moist with tears. 'I can't leave Emma, not now. It's enough for her to lose her son...'

'We all feel for Emma. Sure and wouldn't we be the heartless ones not to?' He caught her shoulders, turning her to him. 'But you have a right to happiness too, Daisy.'

Leaning into him, feeling the warmth of him, she knew that she would never be truly happy without him, but at the same time what happiness would there be in leaving Emma behind to face her heartbreak alone?

'Kilymoran is so pretty a place 'tis no wonder the little people themselves be after living there,' he went on softly. 'The valleys be like a mother's arms, spread wide and welcoming, and the hills like her skirts, ready to protect her children. But they cannot protect against the famine, nor provide the work whereby a man can feed his family. Life will be hard should you come with me, Daisy, but I would love you like no other husband.'

'Brady, I love you, I do, but...'

'No, mavouneen.' He touched her lips with his own. 'The decision is to be made soon, but soon is not yet. Keep your words 'til you be sure of their saying.'

Returning his kiss, Daisy leaned her head against him. Liam loved Emma, that was plain to see, and had asked her the same question as

Brady had just asked. But would her friend consent? Would she go to Ireland without her son?

Tears hot and quick squeezed beneath lids closed tight against the truth, tight against her own heartache.

Emma would never leave without her child, and she, Daisy, would never leave without Emma.

Chapter Twenty-Eight

Emma glanced about the room into which she had been shown. High windows streamed sunlight on to a soft, thick carpet, its blues and creams blending delicately with tapestried chairs and sofas. It looked and felt more beautiful than anything she had ever seen and exuded an air of gentleness, as if it were smiling.

'Mrs Price. How good of you to come.'

Surprised at hearing no one approach, she turned quickly. Carver Felton stood just inside the room.

Colour draining from her face, breath refusing to fill her lungs, she stared at the face that had so haunted her; dark sidewhiskers framed strong, well-cut features, black eyes gleamed in a face that was handsome but held a hint of cruelty. It was a face she knew well; one that was mirrored in the child he held by the hand.

'Paul!' Her voice broke on a sob as she looked at the small figure who made no move towards her. 'Paul ... oh, Paul!'

'Mama!' The high-pitched voice held a note of uncertainty, then he squealed: 'Mama.'

'Oh, my baby!' Emma fell to her knees as the boy hurled himself at her. Clutching him tightly to her breast, she sobbed, 'My little boy, my little boy.'

'I've been on a train, Mama.' The child

squirmed in her arms, anxious to share his excitement. 'It went so fast, and it made a noise like this...' he let out a snort '...and then it roared like a dragon. But I wasn't afraid.'

'I'm sure you were not, my darling.' Emma pushed herself to her feet, instantly drawing him to her side.

'No, I wasn't at all afraid. Dragons don't roar because they are angry, they roar when they are laughing. Father told me so.'

'Father!' The fear that had temporarily been forgotten flooded back.

'Yes.' Carver's glance swept from her to the child. 'It was a delight I could not deny myself, to hear my son call me Father. It was a word he might never use to me again, I had to hear it while I could.'

'Look, Mama.' A small hand tugged demandingly at her skirts. 'I can draw a horse, Father taught me.'

Unnoticed in her joy, she looked now at the paper held in her son's hand.

'I did this.' He held it out triumphantly. 'I drawed a horse, all by myself.'

Taking the paper, a tiny frown forming across her brow, she glanced at the pencilled outline of a horse.

'Do you like it, Mama? Do you like my horse?'

'It is a beautiful horse, darling,' Emma answered him but her eyes asked questions of the man.

How could Paul draw a horse? How could a child who was blind draw anything?

'Look at him, Emma,' Carver answered gently.

'Look at your son.'

Sinking into a chair, she took the boy's face between her hands. Tilting it slightly, she looked into eyes that gleamed brightly up at her. Gleamed with the brilliance of sight. Then, with a sob that tore her heart, she pressed her lips to each lid.

'How?' she asked when she could speak.

'Mama, I want to see the horses. Father said I could visit the stables.'

'And the rest?' Carver glanced at the child.

Watching the haughty face relax into a smile, Emma caught herself wondering how it would feel to have Carver Felton smile at her. But that was the one thing he was never likely to do.

'Tell all of it, Paul. Tell your mother exactly what I said.'

Clutching the drawing in his hand, the child looked at her, his smile catching at her heart. They were so alike in looks, her child and the man who had fathered him. She would never be able to think of one without remembering the other. In the lonely years that lay ahead the faces that peopled her dreams would be the faces of both of them.

'I could visit the stables, supposing Mama said so. So can I, Mama, can I?'

'Well?' Carver's eyes swept back to her.

'I ... yes.' Emma's glance fell before one she found unnerving. 'Yes, of course.'

Giving the maid who answered his summons instructions to hand Paul into the charge of the head groom, Carver nodded when Emma refused the offer of tea and took a chair opposite hers.

410

'My note said I would explain my reason for taking the child,' he began at once. 'I had not intended doing so without speaking to you first. But time, as they say, was of the essence. A day or two spent hesitating over the rights and wrongs would have made it too late.' Seeing the questions in her eyes, he raised one hand. 'Wait, hear me out before you ask me.'

Returning his hand to his knee, he went on, 'After being told my son ... Paul ... was blind, I spoke to a doctor in London. He is a good friend and one whose word I trust implicitly. He said there was only one man who might be able to help but that it was a long shot. If I wanted to take it I had to leave right away before that man left for America, and at the end of it all the child might be blind. But Paul was already blind, and seeing there was no threat to his physical well-being, I deemed the risk worth the taking.'

He had deemed the risk worth taking. *He* could not wait to ask what she thought. Emma felt rage harden within her. He had taken her son.

'I know what you must have felt, Mrs Price.' Carver seemed to swallow hard, as if a lump had settled in his throat. 'The same as I feel, knowing the time has come for me to give him back.'

'Give him back?' Her lips trembled.

There was no censure in Carver's voice and his eyes were curiously bright as he looked at her. 'Did you think I would not?'

'I did not know what to think. You took him without a word.'

'I have already given you my apologies for that, to do so again will avail us nothing. I have hurt

411

you twice, but that is something I will never repeat. I will never hurt you again. When you leave this house, Paul will go with you. But be kind enough to listen first to the rest of my explanation.

'I took the child to Switzerland. The ophthalmic surgeon recommended by my friend in London was optimistic, reiterating that there was nothing to be lost. He explained that the boy was suffering from something termed Glaucoma, a condition not yet widely understood in the medical world but one with which he had had some success. The operation meant creating a new channel that would drain the aqueous humour from the eyes, thus allowing them to return to normal. Thank God it was successful.'

'Paul will go with you.' The words sang in her mind. Her child had been given back his sight and she had been given back her son. The two miracles she had prayed so desperately for, the miracles she'd thought never to see, had both been granted.

Emma looked at the man who had made them possible. Tears blurring her vision, she murmured softly. 'Thank you.'

Again that same clearing of his throat as he rose to his feet and went to a window to stand with his back to her.

'Mrs Price.' He hesitated momentarily. 'Perhaps I should not ask this of you, and I will feel no surprise should your answer be no.' Again a thread of silence hung between them before he went on. 'Would you bring the child to visit me at Felton, or allow me to visit him at Plovers Croft?'

Slowly Emma stood up. Slowly her hand went into the pocket of her skirt, her fingers closing over the coin sewn into its lining.

This was the moment she had long promised herself. The chance to take her revenge.

'And did you tell him – tell him you wanted Paul to have no more to do with him?'

Daisy pulled the covers over the sleeping child.

Emma had meant to, but the look that had crossed Carver's face when the boy was brought back into the room... That could not have been pretence. And as Emma had argued with herself later, Carver Felton had no need to pretend, not to love Paul or to return him to her. Carver Felton need not do anything he did not wish to.

'No.'

Daisy's head jerked. 'You mean that after all that man has done to you, you have told him he can come see the boy?'

'What he has done to me does not matter, it is what he has done for Paul. It is due to him that my son can see.'

'But, Emma, you said he seems more than fond of Paul. What if that fondness deepens? What if he decides that Paul's place is at Felton Hall?'

'Ca– Mr Felton promised that he would not take him from me.'

'Promises!' Daisy answered scathingly. 'What be promises to his kind? Nothing more than a bad taste in the mouth. Spit it out and forget it!'

Would Carver forget? She seemed to feel the hardness of that coin between her fingers. She had meant to fling it in his face then pour out her detestation of him, to keep the promise she had made to herself so long ago. But seeing the look of love as he had caught the child in his arms had wiped it all away and she had nodded her permission for him to call.

'You saw his face when he said it. Do you really believe he meant it?'

'Yes,' Emma answered softly. 'Yes, Daisy. I think he does.'

'Well, let's hope you be right.' Her expression saying she did not for one moment believe it, Daisy led the way from the bedroom.

Adding coal to the stove, then brewing tea from the kettle quietly bubbling on the hob, Daisy watched a restless Emma move about the room that had to serve as dining room for the navvies, with a corner for their own use. Straightening dishes already neatly stacked, replacing benches that were perfectly in place. 'Fidgeting' was what the wardresses in the workhouse had called behaviour of that sort. Too little work their diagnosis. The cure was an extra scrubbing of the floors or a couple of hours spent pounding laundry with a heavy wooden maid and wash tub. That had cured many a case of the fidgets, women and children their arms almost too tired to lift the clothes from their backs, their legs almost refusing to carry them to their beds; but the hushed sobs that lasted far into the night had been clear testimony that the cure did not fit the malady.

And it was not curing Emma's. God knew she worked 'til she was ready to drop. Walking to the abbatoir for she would have Paul left with no one other than Daisy herself, making a daily journey for it was impossible to carry as much meat as two. Then she stood and cooked and baked, helping to serve the men's meals, it was more than any woman should be called upon to do, yet all of it was not the reason her friend was like a cat on hot bricks. There was something infinitely deeper and infinitely more painful troubling Emma Price.

'I've poured you a cup of tea, come drink it afore it gets cold.'

'What?' Emma turned, the movement sharp, almost guilty, as if she had been caught at something she should not be doing. 'Oh, yes, thank you, Daisy.'

She had lost weight. Daisy watched as her friend came to the table. But that was only to be expected after weeks of not knowing what had happened to her child. That too would account for her pallor. But where was the happiness that should accompany the child's return, the deep, abiding all-encompassing joy that should be in her face? True, she had been in heaven when she had brought the lad home, but now it seemed as if heaven had closed its doors. Watching Emma's fingers play along the rim of the saucer, Daisy set her lips determinedly.

'What's wrong, Emma?'

'Wrong...' She did not look up. 'There's nothing wrong.'

'Oh, yes, there is. You be going round and round like a fart in a colander, and I'm asking the reason why. Paul be home, fit and healthy, and you say you be sure Felton won't take him off again, so what be worrying you?'

Her last reserves of strength leaving her, Emma's shoulders sagged and her hands fell to the table.

'Oh, Daisy, I feel so badly!'

'Why! What is there to feel badly about?'

A sigh welling from the depths of her, Emma's words came hesitantly.

'Paul. I … I don't know if it is right for me to keep him.'

'Emma!' Daisy stared at her in disbelief. 'You can't meant that.'

'I've thought about it night after night, Daisy, and the more I think, the more convinced I become that I am wrong in keeping him. The work here will be finished in a few weeks and I will have to look for another way of supporting myself and Paul. You know how difficult that can be. Is it fair to the child to drag him from place to place, with the chance of going hungry at the end of it? Would it not be better for him to be with … with his father? He would have everything at Felton Hall, a secure home, warmth and comfort…'

'Everything except a mother,' Daisy cut in quickly. 'You can't give him up, Emma, don't even think about it. You love that child more than life!'

Eyes filled with sadness looked back at her. 'Yes I love him, but his father loves him too.'

A tiny frown of anger settled on Daisy's brow.

'So what if he does? He's got no right to the lad.'

'It's not Carver Felton's rights I am thinking

416

of.' Emma smiled wanly. 'It is my son's. He has a right to a better life than I can give him.'

'And he would have a better life!' Daisy was sharp. 'Liam Brogan has shown his love for both of you, he would care for you and be a good father to Paul.'

'*...your son has a stepfather...*'

Again the words Carver Felton had thrown at her rose in Emma's mind. Liam would be a good stepfather, but what would happen when Paul was of an age to understand, to choose for himself? Would he see being deprived of everything Carver Felton could have given him as being the best choice for him? Would he settle for a stepfather, or would he condemn his mother?

'Liam loves you, Emma.' Daisy's voice softened. 'He would marry you tomorrow if you said the word. And you have feeling for him. You could do worse than take him, you know that, so what be holding you back? You deserve a bit of happiness, why not take it with Liam?'

'And what of your happiness, Daisy Tully, what of taking your own? When are you going to become Mrs Brady Malone?' Emma forced her face to brighten, wanting suddenly to avoid the question of her own marriage. 'Have you given the man his answer yet?'

'No.' Daisy's glance fell. 'But I don't think I'll be marrying with Brady.'

Surprise sweeping her mind clear of her own troubled thoughts, Emma reached for her friend's hand. 'But you love Brady. What has happened to change that?'

'I ain't changed. I still feels the same.'

417

'Then Brady ... why have his feelings changed?'

'They ain't changed neither.'

'Then what?' Emma was perplexed. 'What has brought about this change of heart?'

'I can't marry him!' As if released from some prison the words tumbled out. 'I can't go to Ireland and leave you behind.'

'That is nonsense.' Emma's fingers tightened on the girl's hand.

'No! It ain't nonsense!' Daisy looked up, her brown eyes moist. 'I couldn't settle, not in Ireland, not anywhere, knowing you was on your own fending for that little 'un. There would be no peace in my mind, not for a minute.'

'But you can't give up your life with Brady, not for me!'

'And I can't take it without you, or at least without knowing you have the same.'

'But you love him,' Emma repeated.

Daisy squeezed the hand that held hers, her eyes bright behind the mist.

'I love you too, Emma,' she said gently. 'Too much to turn my back on you. Don't ask me to marry 'less you be going to do the same.'

'Then tell Brady you will marry him.'

'Oh, Emma! You mean...'

'Yes.' Emma nodded. 'I will marry Liam.'

Liam had been so happy! Emma walked slowly, her mind lost among the happenings of the previous evening. Liam and Brady had called at the long hut, Brady to take Daisy for a walk, and Liam to make this nightly check that all was well with Emma. Then, as if the whole thing had been

418

arranged by someone other than themselves, Paul had cried out in his sleep. She had gone to him and on emerging from the bedroom found Liam standing just the other side of the door.

'I love you, Emma.'

That was all he had said, and as he'd held out his arms she had moved into them.

Now she was promised.

She hitched the heavy basket of meat more comfortably on her hip.

She had given her answer to Liam. They were to be married.

In Ireland, he had said, where his mother could be present to see them joined.

If only her own mother could be at the wedding, with Carrie as bridesmaid ... would that have induced the emotion she knew she should be feeling? The marriages she had witnessed at Doe Bank had each girl breathless with excitement, every moment of preparation a joy. Was her own quiet acceptance because of her lack of family or...'

But there could be no 'or'. She hitched the basket, feeling it bite into her hip. There was nothing to detract from her happiness with Liam. She was tired, that was all. The waterway finished, they would move to Ireland and there her life could begin again.

Liam was happy. Her son would have a father. It all sounded perfect, so why could she not smile?

'Good morning, Mrs Price.'

Deep in thought, she had been oblivious of the carriage approaching from the opposite direction. Now as it drew to a halt she looked up at the driver.

Feeling the blood rise into her cheeks, she glanced quickly away from black eyes that instantly seemed to see deep inside her.

'Allow me to relieve you of that?'

He was already beside her taking the basket as he spoke, placing it in the back of the trap.

'There is no need … I can manage...'

'But I cannot.' He brushed aside her protests. 'I cannot talk to you while you have that thing stuck on your hip. Climb into the trap, please.'

He was the same imperious Carver Felton she had known before. Taking everything for granted, ordering things his own way. When she had watched him with Paul she'd thought he had changed, softened somehow, but now she saw she had been wrong. This man did not change his colours.

Resentment adding waspishness to her tone, Emma ignored the hand he offered. 'I prefer to walk, Mr Felton, and to walk alone. Please return my basket.'

'Not all preferences prove to be in our own best interests.' He dropped his hand to his side. 'If you insist on walking then we will walk, but carry that basket you will not do.'

'I carry it every day.'

'But I am not with you every day. When I am you will carry nothing. Except maybe our child.'

The colour already high in her cheeks flared wildly. Our child! He had not used those words before. He had referred to Paul as 'my son' or 'your child', but never as 'our child'. Why had he done so now? Was it to humiliate her?

Lifting her gaze to his she fought down the bitterness building in her, though her answer was icy.

'Paul is already a competent walker, Mr Felton, but should he need to be carried then his stepfather will be glad to do it.'

At his sides, Carver's hands curled into tight fists, but apart from the set of his lips he showed little of the blow she had just dealt him. In all the months since he had realised the depth of his love for Emma Price, in all those long lonely nights of seeing her face in the shadows of his mind, through it all he had felt a sort of hope. Now he watched those lovely eyes flash defiance at him. That hope had been a desolate one. Pride and arrogance had caused him to prevent a marriage between her and his brother, and stupidity had prevented him from seeking her out when his own love for her had forced its recognition. But he would pay, and for the rest of his life; pay with the pain of knowing she was another man's wife.

Taking the reins he turned the horse back in the direction he had come, walking towards Plovers Croft.

Why must he insist on helping her? Her silence stony, Emma fell into step beside him. She did not want his help or his company. Drawing her shawl tight she stared steadily along the road ahead.

She wanted no more of Carver Felton.

Chapter Twenty-Nine

'I still think you be making a mistake.'

Daisy's comment was forthright as she watched Emma button the boy's tunic.

'The break has to come so why not make it now? What purpose does it serve to take the boy to that house?'

Daisy made sense, of course. It served no other purpose than to strengthen the bond that had already sprung up between father and son.

Father and son! Emma's fingers trembled on the last button. Paul would grow up not knowing his true father, childhood memories soon faded. But would Carver Felton's memories ever fade? He would no doubt marry and have other children. Would that erase the memory of Paul?

'You should have told him when he asked,' Daisy pressed her point. 'Told him you didn't want him seeing the boy again, not ever.'

Emma pushed herself up from her haunches, her hand dropping from the boy's shoulder. He ran from the room. 'Would that be fair, either to Paul or to ... to...'

'And what of Liam?' Daisy took advantage of the hesitation. 'Are you being fair to him? How do you think he feels, seeing you going off to the Felton place?'

Frowning, Emma turned to her friend whose voice held a hint of accusation.

'What do you mean? Liam knows I go only so Paul may see the horses.'

'Does he, Emma? Does Liam really think that? Or does he feel the fear any man would? That the feelings which draws you to that house lies not with any horse, but with the owner of them!'

'Daisy!' Emma was aghast. 'Liam would never think that. He knows it is not true.'

Her eyes clouding with sudden sadness. Daisy regarded her closely.

'Does he, Emma? Does Liam know the truth? What's more important, do you?'

Daisy was putting entirely the wrong connotation on things. Emma watched her child explore every bush of gorse, run after butterflies that fluttered away as his eager hand reached out for them. But her happiness in his delight of a world that had lain hidden from him for so long was marred by memories of that conversation. Of course Liam knew the truth about her meetings with Carver Felton, and of course she knew it too. She saw allowing him these few meetings with Paul as only fitting after he had done so much for the child. But today would be the last time they would be together, the last time she would bring Paul here.

They were leaving at the weekend. Emma felt again the strange sharp pang she'd experienced when Liam had told her of his plans; the same emptiness that had followed.

The work was finished, it was time to leave. They would travel with Daisy and Brady and be married in Ireland. It all sounded so simple, yet inside she had felt a sort of turmoil and when that had drained away there'd been nothing left in its wake; none of the joy or excitement that radiated from Daisy's face, nothing but a cold empty void.

Why? The question had come to her a hundred times but now as then the answer would not follow.

'This is where we see the horses, isn't it, Mama?'

Emma pulled her shawl a little more firmly about her shoulders as she followed the small dancing figure through the high wrought-iron gates. The house was almost as beautiful outside as in. Red brick and cream stone gleaming in the sunlight of late afternoon seemed to smile a welcome, but today Emma felt none of its warmth.

'Father!' The delighted squeal breaking her reverie she stood still as the child ran towards the tall figure who waited with arms outstretched.

How could he give up the child? How could Carver Felton part from the son he loved so much? Emma's heart leaped as it always did on seeing the two of them together. Might he in the end renounce his promise and take the child from her? She watched as he scooped the laughing boy into his arms, whirling him round and round with a delight it was painful for her to witness.

This must be the reason for her feeling of emptiness, the lack of joy in her own forthcoming marriage. This was her fear. That one day Carver Felton would reclaim his son.

'I think we must let this young man go to the stables.'

The deep chuckle pulling at her nerves Emma remained unsmiling as Carver set the child down. Walking with them around the back of the house to where the stables and carriage house formed an elongated 'L' shape.

She would stay only a few minutes, just long enough for the groom to lead Paul on a pony once around the paddock. Accompanied by cries of delight, she watched Carver swing the child into the saddle. Just once around the paddock then she would leave. And before she went she would tell him that today was their final meeting.

'It is so good of you to bring him.' Carver turned to her, his dark eyes sweeping in every detail of her face. 'But I would much rather you'd accept my offer of a carriage.'

Emma turned her face to watch the boy and the groom disappearing around the far corner of the building. 'I prefer to walk, and Paul enjoys the freedom of the heath; he so rarely gets to run far, my work means he's mostly confined indoors.'

'It need not be that way.'

Carver's answer was surprisingly gentle but perversely it grated on nerves already worn raw and her answer came out with a sharpness she had not intended.

'It will not be from this weekend. I ... my husband is taking us to his home in Ireland. Paul will have plenty of open space to run in safety there.'

'Ireland!'

Carver could not stop the outburst and as

Emma turned her glance to him and saw the look of desolation sweep into his eyes, she felt an answering one sweep into her heart.

He turned towards the house, face averted from her, but when he spoke his voice held a thread of anger.

'I had not thought of your leaving this country. Please come into the house, there are matters we must discuss.'

Blood freezing in her veins, Emma followed dumbly. She had lived with this fear for so long. He had taken her son from her once, was he about to do it again?

Seated in the gracious room she had been shown into once before she sat staring at her hands, clasped together in her lap.

Beneath the high window, his back turned to her, Carver Felton's shoulders drooped as if carrying too heavy a load. When he eventually spoke it was with an anguish not completely concealed from her.

'Mrs Price.' He kept his back to her. 'There is something you must know. Perhaps it was dishonest of me not to have told you before. It concerns the child.'

Emma's fingers twisted convulsively, driving her nails deep into her flesh.

'When my brother died...'

'Died!' The cry that broke from her brought him round to face her.

'You did not know?'

Tears filling her throat, Emma could only shake her head.

'I'm sorry. Had I known I would have been less

abrupt. Paul returned ill from a business meeting two years ago...'

Emma's mind went back to the last time she had met Paul Felton. That was about two years ago. 'I ... I saw him. I did not know...'

'None of us did. He had contracted typhoid. He collapsed on the heath and was taken to Doe Bank. He was nursed there by a woman named Jerusha Paget. It seems she had some skill with herbal medicines, but by the time the fool of a woman sent word to me, my brother was beyond help.'

Feeling emotions war within her, Emma lifted her head. Carver Felton's pain was as real as it was raw, but that did not excuse his maligning a woman he did not know.

'I realise how you must have felt,' she said calmly, 'how you must still feel. But believe me, Mr Felton, Jerusha was no fool. She held no medical qualification but her skills were such that she had the trust and confidence of people from every village for miles around. She nursed many back to health when the parish doctor had written them off. If it had been possible to save your brother then she would have done so, but we all know typhoid to be deadly.'

'Deadly enough to take the old woman and half of that village with her.'

His words weighing on her like stones, Emma bit her lip. First her family, then Paul and Jerusha. The people she had loved most in the world all taken from her. There had been talk in the camp of illness at the Hall following Jerusha's death. But she had thought Paul to be abroad.

'But that is not what I have to discuss with you.' Carver walked from the window, taking a chair opposite hers. 'It is the matter of my brother's will.'

Confused, Emma looked at that strong face, marked now by something other than sorrow. Something she might have called guilt.

'Paul's will? I don't understand. That can have nothing to do with me.'

'Directly, no. But as the mother of his nephew...'

'His nephew? But Paul never knew, I...'

'You did not tell him.' Carver's tone softened. 'You did not tell me either. Paul saw the child in your arms and needed no one to name his father, just as I needed none. He did not need to guess what I had one, that I forced myself upon you to prevent your marrying him; deliberately kept you apart. I did my brother a great wrong, one I can never redress or forget, just as I will never forget the suffering I have caused you.'

'That is over and done with.' Emma glanced away, unable to watch the remorse that clouded those dark eyes.

'For me it can never be over.' He stood up, moving restlessly to stand staring into the empty fireplace. For long seconds he remained immobile, a gilt clock measuring the silence with a muted tick. At last, drawing himself up, he turned about. 'Mrs Price, I said earlier I had not been entirely honest with you on our previous meetings. Forgive me but I had my reasons. I did not tell you before because I had no wish for you to bring the child to visit out of a sense of moral obligation. I have no desire for you or the child to feel that. Nor, I feel sure, would my brother. The fact is that under the terms of Paul's will, this house, his share of the business and everything belonging to him, is now his nephew's.'

Beaufort House ... and everything Paul Felton had once owned now her son's! Emma sat in stunned silence. It wasn't true, it couldn't be true. It was a trick to keep her son here.

'You had to know, Mrs Price,' Carver said when she did not speak. 'You had to be told before you took your son away.'

'No!' Eyes suddenly flashing life, Emma rose to her feet. 'My son has no claim on your brother, he has no right to this house or to anything else. You can tear up any will that says otherwise, we want none of it!'

'That would not be legal,' Carver said firmly, though his eyes held a smile. 'Nothing can be altered except by Paul himself, and that not until he reaches his majority.'

'That does not mean he has to remain here.'

Only the merest twitch of his jaw betraying the blow dealt to him by her words, Carver answered.

'That is correct. If you have no wish to live here then the property will be looked after until our son is of an age to decide for himself what is to be done both with it, and with the other properties he will inherit from me. Until that time I have made financial arrangements for him and for you.'

If only he could say the words he wanted to say. To tell her he loved her, that it was love as well as pride and jealousy had caused him to keep Paul from marrying her ... that for the rest of his life he would live with the guilt of raping her and with the hopeless love that had arisen from it. But he could not say those words for she was another man's wife.

Watching her now, eyes brilliant with anger and accusation, Carver felt his soul reach the very depths of despair.

'I loved your brother.' Emotion catching her tongue Emma looked at the man who had destroyed her life. 'I loved him for his gentle ways, not for his position or his wealth. I did not want his money then and I do not want it now. As for you – I hated you when you raped me, hated you for knowing what you did was done coldly and deliberately, done to prevent my marrying Paul. As for your money ... you have already paid me, remember!'

Snatching the lining from the pocket of her skirt, she ripped the coin free.

'One shilling!' she went on through gritted teeth. 'One shilling was all you deemed my honour worth. But I set a higher store by it than that, and all the money you possess is not enough to repay me. Keep your conscience money, Mr Felton, I want nothing from you and neither does my son!'

Staring straight into those black eyes, Emma drew back her arm and flung the coin in his face.

'We could go and still have everything ready to leave on Saturday. Ain't neither of us got much to pack.'

Daisy glanced at her friend who had hardly smiled in several days. She had not said what had taken place over at that house, but something had, it was plain to see.

'The boy would enjoy it,' Daisy went on. 'His first party and probably the last for a long time. Let him enjoy it while he has the chance for we ain't likely to have money to spend on parties, not for years. Like Brady and Liam have said, life will be no bed of roses.'

'Daisy is right, Emma.' Liam Brogan too watched the pale face shadowed with unhappiness. 'The lad will enjoy the going and it will be a break for him before we set away for Ireland.'

'Brady will come and Liam, won't you Liam?'

Emma had turned away too quickly, turned away even before Daisy's question. Liam felt his heart quicken, but the worry that gnawed ever deeper with each passing day stayed hidden.

'I will if that's what Emma wants.'

'There you are, Emma,' Daisy smiled. 'You ain't got no more arguments.'

No, she had no more arguments. Emma felt a sinking in her heart. She would take her son to the celebration that would mark the opening of the new canal and come once more face to face with Carver Felton.

'You don't have to go if you would rather not.'

Outside the hut Liam turned to her, the fear in his eyes lost in the darkness.

'And have Daisy go on at me forever more?' Emma tried to laugh.

'That's not what I meant. I'm saying that

there's no need for you to come to Ireland. I would not hold you to a promise that would cause you grief. I love you and want to marry you, but not if your heart isn't in it. It's not too late for happiness, Emma, but you have to have the courage to reach out for it.'

'I am happy. I will be happy with you, Liam.'

Drawing her into his arms, holding her against his chest, Liam Brogan faced the truth, and it was not the one she would have him believe.

'Can we see the horses now, Mama?'

'Not today, darling.' Emma glanced at the boy trotting by her side.

'But we always see the horses.'

'I know we do, but they will not be here today.'

'Do horses not go to parties?'

Looking into the serious little face, Liam laughed then swept the boy up into his arms. 'Only people go to parties.'

'Why?'

'Why?' Liam threw him up into the air, catching him in strong arms. 'Why, why, why! Your mother will be sick of that word.'

'Let's go and get some lemonade.' Settling the delighted boy on his shoulders, Liam smiled at Emma. 'Go and settle yourself under that tree, we'll bring you a glass.'

'If you don't mind, Liam, I'd rather go back. I ... I'm a little tired.'

'We'll all go,' Daisy answered for them all.

'No.' Emma's smile was weary. 'I wouldn't want that, you and Brady stay for the dancing.'

'Yes, you two stay. Brady's quite a turn at the

432

jig, 'tis meself has the two left feet.'

'But...' Daisy looked at Emma.

'No buts.' Liam cut short her objection. 'Sure and can't a man be trusted to walk his fiancée back to her home?'

Going to stand beneath the tree, listening to its spreading branches protest against the breeze ruffling its leaves, Emma stared in the direction of Doe Bank. She had told herself today she would go back there, to say the goodbyes she had never said. But she had not gone to Doe Bank. What she had told herself had been merely an excuse, one invented to mask her true reason for coming to Felton Hall. Paul could not miss what he had never known, while she... She laughed, a soundless bitter laugh that tore at her soul. What had she gained but more heartbreak?

'Mama, can we go and find the horses?'

Emma sighed as the boy trotted back to her, his persistent question still ringing out.

'I know where there might be one.' Liam came up behind him, holding out a glass of lemonade. 'In the field beside the flour mill.'

'Felton Mill? That's not on our way home.'

'No.' Liam drained his own glass. 'But I don't mind the detour if you don't.'

Watching him return the glasses to a table set out a little way from the tree, Emma felt a pang of guilt. Liam was so good to her, so gentle and loving. He deserved every ounce of her love in return, but how was she free to give it?

They had all come, the people of Doe Bank who had survived the typhoid. They had talked to her of her parents, of Carrie and Jerusha. But all the time her eyes had sought a tall figure, his raven hair slashed with silver, all the time her heart had listened for that one voice. But it had not come. Carver Felton had not made an appearance.

'Let's sit for a while.' Liam broke the silence that had wrapped about them after leaving Daisy and Brady. 'Give the boy a moment to chase butterflies.'

Nodding agreement, Emma sank on to the soft heather. 'And give yourself time: time to listen to your heart as well as to your mind. Be sure of what you do, Emma. A lifetime is too long to pay for any mistake.'

'If you mean my marrying you, then I am making no mistake. I know what I am doing.'

But the laugh she forced had no heart in it, its hollowness echoing inside him. Perhaps it was as she said, perhaps his was the mistake, the mistake of thinking her love for him was not the love he yearned for. Yes, his was the mistake. Plucking a sprig of heather he lay back, closing his eyes against the lowering sun. The mistake of shutting out the truth.

It would be all right. On the edge of her thoughts Emma heard the soothing ripple of the mill stream. Once she was gone from Plovers Croft, once she was married and settled in Ireland, she would forget. Forget all that had happened and concentrate on loving her son, on loving Liam.

'There he is, Mama, there's the horse!'

The delighted squeal floating back to her, she looked across to where her son had been chasing

434

butterflies. But Paul was no longer there. Her eyes drawn by another squeal of excitement she saw his small figure. It was running straight toward the stream.

'Paul!'

It was a stricken whisper. Beside her Liam was on his feet. As if caught in some inextricable nightmare, Emma watched her son run with outstretched hands towards the horse on the opposite bank. Somewhere a thousand miles away a voice shouted his name but that would do no good, her son was only yards from the water. Then the horse was moving. One moment it was on the ground, the next it was in the air, its body rising in one great leap that carried it across the stream; and even before it landed its rider had thrown himself from the saddle, at the same time grabbing the child and flinging him in a sideways arc away from danger. Still caught in that world of nightmare, Emma watched the tall figure stumble then miss its footing on the damp moss and fall backwards into the tumbling waters.

Her own scream snapping the invisible bonds that bound her, she ran forward. Her son clinging fearfully to her skirts, she stared at the figure being dragged along by the millstream.

'Carver!' It was a cry every bit as stricken as that which had followed her child. Falling to her knees, Emma reached out across the churning water. 'Carver ...no!'

Then as the mill race caught him, dragging him beneath the great wooden blades of the wheel, she dropped into oblivion.

Chapter Thirty

'I hope it's the right thing.'

Moving a little closer to Liam, Daisy lowered her voice, not wanting it to reach Emma who was walking a little ahead beside Brady.

'I'm sure it is.' Liam glanced at the young woman he was to marry. Free of the shawl her hair glinted silver-gold in the late-summer sun, her patched skirts lending an air of dignity to her petite figure.

'She needs to be cared for, looked after,' Daisy continued.

'She will be cared for, Daisy, you need have no fear on that score.'

'That ain't enough.' Daisy's voice still held the concern it had showed when he had told her what had happened at that mill stream. Too much worry and too little rest had finally become too much and Emma had fainted under the strain of seeing her child running into danger. That was how Liam told the story to Emma the following day, but the evening of the occurrence, when Brady and she had returned to find him sitting alone in the long hut, the story had held a different twist.

He had insisted Emma put herself to bed at the same time as the child and then sat waiting for Daisy, to ask her to stay close to Emma for the night. 'It was quite a shock,' he had told them,

436

'seeing the lad so close to the edge of the water.'

It would be a shock for any woman. Daisy watched her friend, one hand protectively touching the child in Brady's arms. But she hadn't fainted then, nor when her son was safe beside her. That hadn't happened until she saw Carver Felton sucked under the mill wheel.

Glancing up at the man beside her Daisy remembered the look on his face as he had talked. The doubt and the pain had sat like a cloud over his fine features.

'Emma will be well cared for,' he repeated softly, as if in response to her thoughts.

'Being cared for is all well and good, but on its own it's not enough. People need to be loved, Liam. Emma needs love.'

'Can you doubt she will have that?'

There was a wealth of emotion in the answer, and it caught at Daisy's heart. This man had loved Emma from their first meeting, she would never be without love so long as Liam Brogan breathed.

'Emma will be loved like no other woman.'

'Do you think she knows that, though, Liam? I mean, really knows that?'

'I'm sure she does deep down, she's just afraid to admit it. Afraid to trust.'

'That be close to the truth.' Daisy nodded, her brown hair glinting bronze in the sun. 'Emma has had a hard few years. They would have killed many a lesser woman, what with her family dying the way they did and then the child born out of wedlock.'

'She will never forget the tragedies of her life,

437

no man would expect her to, but given the right kind of love and support, she will come to terms with them.'

'She will get that love, you be sure of that, Liam?'

He laughed softly, but it held more sadness than humour. 'You are quite a Doubting Thomas, Daisy Tully! But you have no need of being.'

'Perhaps not.' She glanced again at the woman in front of them. 'But I worries just the same. Worries in case we be doing the wrong thing. Maybe we should have stayed on at Plovers Croft a bit longer?'

'I don't think so.' Liam stepped to the side of the road allowing a cart to rumble past. 'We all knew there had to be an end to our life there, best to leave when we did.'

Daisy walked on in silence. Like Liam said, perhaps it was for the best. But Ireland was a long way from Wednesbury, and life there promised to be just as hard. She gripped the handle of the basket she had packed with food. Love was one thing, but it didn't feed a family!

Following the Lea Brook Road beneath the viaduct, the child cried out as a train rattled overhead. Seeing him stretch up his arms to his mother, Liam strode forward, but as Paul cried fretfully, Emma smiled.

'I will take him, Liam, it's not far now. The station is just at the end of the next street.'

But the street was a long one and the child weighing heavy in her arms, Emma was relieved when at last they turned into the station.

The platform was empty. She walked its length, boots echoing on the wooden staging. Towards the far end, sheltered by a wooden canopy supported on fluted iron pillars, was a solitary bench.

She was about to settle down on it when Liam touched her elbow. Smiling first at the child now sleeping in her arms, then at her, he said gently, 'Should you not take the lad into the waiting room? You could lay him on the seat in there. 'Twould be more restful for you both.'

'He could lie here.' Emma glanced towards the bench.

'Sure and he could,' Liam agreed. 'But should a train pass through before the one we will be taking the noise would wake him. 'Tis better for him to sleep as long as he is able.'

Her whole body weary beyond saying, Emma looked at Daisy.

Reading the question in her eyes, Daisy shook her head. 'You go along in, I'll stay here. Don't worry, I'll call you when our train arrives.'

Walking with her to a dingy brown-painted door, a metal plate marking it 'Waiting Room, Third Class', Liam opened it then stood aside for Emma to pass, closing it softly behind her.

Inside the same dull brown paint reached halfway up brick walls to be met by an uninviting green. Around them backless wooden benches were arranged around a cast iron fireplace, empty and lifeless without its flames.

Emma glanced fleetingly at it. It looked as desolate as she felt, and she should not feel this way. She had lain awake at nights telling herself

439

that very thing. She had good friends in Daisy and Brady, and a man who loved her and was willing to care for her and her child. But every one of those nights, as sleep had finally claimed her, vivid black eyes had stared at her, silver streaks had glinted among sable hair as two strong hands reached out to her; and every morning she had wakened, her very soul crying inside her, crying for the man she had seen sucked beneath those dark waters.

A sob breaking from her, she laid the child on a bench. Slipping the shawl from her shoulders, she folded it, placing it gently beneath the small dark head.

'I said the only thing I would see you carry would be our son...'

It was little more than a whisper but to Emma, her nerves raw, every syllable was like a blow. Breath catching in her throat, she whirled round, one hand pressed to her mouth as she caught sight of the tall figure standing in a shadowed corner.

'Carver!' The cry was more one of hope than recognition.

His voice still soft, he stepped forward. 'From now on I will not even allow you to do that.'

Eyes wide with disbelief, each word caught on a breathless sob, she stared. 'Carver ... I thought ... I saw...'

'I know what you saw, and I know what I saw in your face moments before I was drawn beneath that mill wheel. I saw a miracle, Emma. I saw the truth.'

'But I saw ... I saw you drown!'

'No, my love.' He smiled. 'You did not. How could I drown after what your eyes had told me?'

The tears she had fought so long spilling down her cheeks, confusion and shock trembling in her limbs, she stared at him, broad shoulders outlined against the window, light glancing from the streaks of silver running back from his wide brow. How could it be him? He had died saving her son.

'Liam told me ... he said...'

'Liam said what I asked him to say. I knew what I had seen mirrored in your eyes but still I could not be certain, it might just have been the last hope of a desperate man. Then, when I climbed from that stream and saw him holding you, saw the way he looked at you, I realised I could not come between you. That I had to live with my own mistakes, the ones my own selfishness had brought upon me. I asked him to let you believe I had died in that stream.'

'But why?' she murmured.

'Don't you know why?' he asked gently, eyes holding hers. 'Do you still not know? I love you, Emma Price, I have from the beginning but pride got in the way. My own stupid pride prevented me admitting that even to myself. It was that love drove me to send my brother away, to do all in my power to keep him from finding you: I could not stand the pain of seeing you married to someone else. It was that same love that told me I could not snatch away your happiness a second time. But I had to see you just once more, to prove to myself that what I saw in your eyes before going under that wheel was an illusion.

But it was not, it is there now. I love you, Emma, and whether you know it or not, you love me.'

His words produced no blinding flash in her mind, no breathtaking realisation. Just a quiet feeling of peace, a coming to terms with a truth she had long kept hidden. She did love Carver Felton.

'I can't let you go.' He reached for her then, drawing her into his arms, looking down into her tear-filled eyes. 'I won't let you go, not ever. I said I would never hurt you again, that never again would I take Paul from you, but I am too weak, Emma. I cannot live without you any longer. If taking Paul is the only way I can keep you then that is what I will do.'

'No...'

'Yes, Emma.' His grip tightened as she tried to twist away. 'I did not think to break my promise to you, to go back on my word, but I would break a promise to heaven itself if it meant keeping you. Marry me, Emma, marry me!'

Lowering his head, he pressed his mouth to hers and suddenly the feeling of quiet peace flared into vivid flame; senses that had been numb tingled and limbs trembled with a different shock: one that frightened yet at the same time filled her with a breathless, heady pleasure.

'I love you, Emma...'

He touched his lips to her eyes and temples then back to her mouth.

'Oh, God, how I love you! Marry me, my darling.'

How could she? The question pushed against the flood of exquisite feelings that held her captive, dragging her from the edge of acceptance.

She loved him. Her whole being had tried time and again to tell her that but she had refused to accept it, tried always to drive his face from her mind, wanting only to remember the harm he had done her. But all of that did not matter now. He loved her and she felt the same love, but to marry him was to turn her back on Liam, to part from Daisy. How could she do that? How could she turn from the two people who meant so much to her?

'Marry me, Emma.'

His whisper was soft against her hair, bringing a searing pain with its gentleness. She had to do it now or she would never have the strength. Using the last of her resolution she pushed him away. Stepping back from his arms, she whispered, 'No, I can't.'

The light dying in his eyes, Carver looked at her. 'But you love me, Emma, I know you do. Your whole body told me so.'

She could not deny it to herself but she would not admit it to him. She could not tell him her love for him would live with her forever.

Glancing at her fingers subconsciously twisting the gold band he smiled, and when he spoke there was no rancour in what he said, no reproof, only a quiet tenderness.

'That ring you wear on your left hand is a lie, Emma. It was given you by no husband and there is no title of Mrs before your name.'

Emotion shaking her every limb, she dropped her glance as he caught her hand.

Drawing the ring from her finger, he went on gently, 'I think Jerusha will forgive me for removing this and replacing it with my own.'

Fresh tears burning in her throat, her eyes misty as morning lakes, she lifted her head. 'Yes, it was a lie,' she whispered, 'but it is no lie when I tell you I cannot marry you.'

'Because of Liam Brogan?' He made no move to touch her, but love was visible in the depths of his dark eyes. 'He came to Felton Hall the evening before last. His words as I remember were, "I didn't come to chew on the wind." He told me everything, Emma. Of the deaths of your parents and your sister, of Eli Coombs and meeting Daisy at his farm. He told me of the Hollingtons and how our child came to be born in the workhouse, and how he brought you to Plovers Croft. Then he told me what he, and Daisy too, had suspected for some time. That although you may not know it yourself, you were in love with me.

'It seems they discussed it for a long time before he made his decision, and it was one it took a stronger will than mine to make. Liam said I must be told of your feelings, and should I feel the same then he would step aside. He would not hold you to your promise to marry him. He told me you would be here at the station today, that he would ensure you came into this room, but should I not be here then he would feel free to take you with him to Ireland.'

Reaching out, he took both her hands in his, drawing her slowly to him. 'But I am here, my darling.' He touched his lips to her hair. 'Here to tell you that I love you and ask you to forgive the wrongs I have done you. To ask you to be my wife.'

Liam had told him! Liam had been the means of bringing him here, was willing to forego his happiness for hers! A great surge of gratitude and love rose like the waters of a fountain inside her, washing away the last of her doubts. She loved Liam Brogan and always would, but it could never be the sort of love that filled her for the man who held her in his arms, the father of her child.

'Stay with me, my love.' Tilting her face to his, Carver searched it with a look of deep longing. 'Marry me and bring our son home.'

The love in those dark eyes almost too much for her to bear, Emma closed her eyes, a shiver of delight trembling through her.

Almost at once Carver dropped his hands, stepping quickly aside, his face closed and impassive.

'Forgive me.' He spoke curtly, his lips tight as though the effort of speaking was too much. 'It seems I have not yet mastered my own selfishness. I presumed too much, I'm sorry. Of course you could not marry me after all I have done to you, but you are free of me now, Emma. You have my most sacred vow, I will not bother you or seek to take our ... your son from you. Go with Liam. Whether he chooses Ireland or to stay and take the work I have offered him and Malone. I promise you you will not be troubled. The threat I made to take the child was made out of that same selfishness but it was an empty one, though the rest of my words were not.'

Turning to where the child lay sleeping, he crouched beside the bench, one hand tousling the mop of dark hair. 'I love you, Emma, and I love my son. That will be with you both forever, no matter where you go.'

Pushing himself to his feet, his back to her, he swallowed hard. 'I had hoped ... but when I felt you tremble I knew it was in vain. I realised you did not return my feelings, could not accept my love. But accept my blessing, go with Liam, go with him and be happy Emma. Love where you can.'

Love where you can. Now she could do that. The burden she had dragged for so long was lifted, and with its going came a joy that soared, a feeling so sweet it seemed all the music of the earth sang within her.

'But I do return those feelings,' she whispered shyly. 'I love you, Carver. I love you as you love me.'

With a cry that was almost a sob he turned to her. 'Emma! Oh, Emma, my love ... my love!'

'*...the child will be born ... it will bear its father's name...*'

The words Jerusha had spoken so long ago whispered from the shadows of memory.

Her eyes starry with tears of happiness, Emma lifted her mouth to his.

The publishers hope that this book has given you enjoyable reading. Large Print Books are especially designed to be as easy to see and hold as possible. If you wish a complete list of our books please ask at your local library or write directly to:

Magna Large Print Books
Magna House, Long Preston,
Skipton, North Yorkshire.
BD23 4ND

This Large Print Book for the partially sighted, who cannot read normal print, is published under the auspices of

THE ULVERSCROFT FOUNDATION

C